BEYOND SURVIVAL

They beat all the odds against them. Bitter cold and starvation couldn't stop them – disaster dogged them for a year in the wilderness of the north. They didn't have a hope and refused to accept defeat. This story is true to life and takes place in the mid '90s. It is however based on a true air accident that occurred in northern Canada in 1952.

G. Wm. GOTRO

Canadian Cataloguing in Publication Data

Gotro, G. Wm. (Gerald William), 1932-
  Beyond survival

  ISBN 1-55212-279-4

  I. Title.
  PS8563.O8384B49 1999   C813'.54   C99-911050-0
  PR9199.3.G648B49 1999

Book design - Desktop Publishing Ltd., Victoria, BC

ACKNOWLEDGEMENTS

Without a great deal of treasured help, I don't think this book would ever have gone to print. My sincere thanks to my old friend Buz Sawyer who inspired me to write when I was down. Buz gently helped in a thousand ways to forge my words into a story.

My wife who was so very patient, my daughter who encouraged me, and to my sister who applauded my efforts – I say thank you from the bottom of my heart. I was lucky enough to find Bruce Batchelor and the folks at Trafford Publishing, who guided me to Jim Bisakowski of Desktop Publishing Ltd. in Victoria who knocked down all the dragons in the printing jungle. Those dragons scared hell right out of me. Way to go Jim!

Gerry Gotro

BOOK ONE

1

The Beginning Of Life

The woman in the hospital bed held her newborn son, her finger tracing every detail of the eyes, mouth, and nose. Tears of anguish coursed down her face. In the bed directly opposite, an Ojibwa woman lay, her eyes closed, and she too cried softly. Her husband stroked her blue-black hair, and in the Ojibwa tongue, murmured endearments and consoling words to her. The two women, grief stricken, were internally incapable of trying to help one another. Leaving his wife's side, the Ojibwa man crossed the room and sat down beside the white woman's bed.

"Your heart is filled with sorrow," he said in a deep soft voice. "My woman's heart is also filled with sorrow. I do not know how to ease the pain that fills you. I would cut off my right hand if it would ease your grief." The white woman studied him through her tears, as he sat, forearms resting on his knees, his head lowered so his face was in shadow. "My wife has asked me to say this thing to you – she asks that you let her hold your son for only as many heartbeats as there are fingers on your hands?"

The white woman began to shake, racked with sobs. "My husband died five minutes before my baby was born," she said, "How can you ask me to part with my newborn son for as much as a heart beat?"

"I asked because I did not understand your sorrow, and because my woman has nothing to cling to," he said softly, rising to his feet, "forgive me – forgive me." He glanced back at the white woman and her child, "I am sorry I bothered you."

"What do you mean," she said, her anger dominating her words, "what do you mean your wife has nothing to cling to?"

The anguish in the man's eyes became even more evident, as he tried to speak the answer to her question. "My son died five minutes after taking his first breath," the man whispered. "You and I, we have both lost much this day."

The young Ojibwa man's words rattled and echoed in her head like a voice from a deep well. A nurse entered the hospital room with medication for her two patients.

"Mrs. McKenzie I have some medication for you," she said taking a small paper cup from the tray and pouring a glass of water.

"Wait," Elinore McKenzie answered, "This is more important." She held her baby up to the nurse. "She needs to hold him for a while," she said nodding in the direction of the Ojibwa woman.

The nurse, smiling in understanding, took the baby to the Ojibwa woman who also smiled in gratitude. She held the little boy in her arms for a long time, rocking back and forth, crooning to him in Ojibwa. And tiny infant, Carlin McKenzie, closed his eyes and slept. The Ojibwa man crossed the room again to stand by the white woman. Though her lovely face reflected the great suffering she was going through, she had stopped crying.

"I am Jonathan Peters," he said, "and I thank you for letting Tisha, my wife, hold your son. We have one boy – James – he was born last year, but you and I have suffered a great misfortune this year. Perhaps God wished it so for a reason." There was something much more profound on Jonathan Peters mind, but he was finding it difficult to express. "I am a father who has lost a son. Your boy has lost his father – the Great Spirit's wishes are seldom clear to mortals." He folded his arms across his chest, and stood looking out the window.

"Just what exactly does that mean, and what is on your mind Mr. Peters?" she asked wary of the answer and what it may imply.

"If you agree, I will be the boy's father. There is a name for this I do not know in your language. Not a stepfather or a godfather it is another word. It means a father to be there when he is needed."

"A surrogate father," Elinore McKenzie said, providing him with the word.

2

The nurse gently took the sleeping child from Tisha Peters, and returned him to his mother for feeding.

"Yes – yes that is a fine word," he said, a smile creasing his handsome face. "I offer myself as his surrogate father – when he needs me. Perhaps you will bring him to our home someday – then he could meet his surrogate brother James."

Elinore McKenzie was filled with gratitude at the desire of the Ojibwa family, to shield and protect her and her baby Carlin. What she would never know, was how close the bond would become as the years passed by.

Carlin McKenzie never really got to know his mother. The only time they were close was on the days she took him to the Peters home on the Ojibwa reservation. When their visits ended and they left, young Carlin couldn't stop talking about Jim Peters and his father.

Carlin was an excellent scholar, but disliked the conventions of schooling. He was deeply interested in people, but didn't make friends easily. Carlin never had a true friend until he began to understand and emulate Jim Peters. Through his adolescence and his teen age years he lived in the city, but longed for the wilderness and the freedom of the Ojibwa. When Carlin finished his first year of university he quit and worked as a guide off the reservation. He saved, and with a small inheritance after his mother's death, finally had a down payment on a used Cessna. Now, at thirty years of age, he owned little but the clothes he stood in, a three room log cabin, and a weary Cessna 172.

Carlin hadn't had a charter for more than a month and he was unsure about the pain in his gut. It could be attributed to the longing to fly again, but it was more likely hunger. It was his third day without a decent meal. The Cessna rocked gently at the dock, and a blue haze cloaked the low hills at the end of Little Spirit Lake. The wan autumn sun struggled to drive off the morning chill and the deep blue water was ruffled by a breeze. It promised a magnificent day for flying.

Carlin could only daydream about opening the throttle and coaxing the Cessna up on the step. He imagined her moving at better than fifty knots. He knew he could lift her from the lake now, but would let her gain a little more speed before easing back on the wheel. The fantasy was cruelly shattered when a dozen sparrows landed near him and ironically, bounced around, pecking breakfast from the ground. Carlin knew he wouldn't be flying today, because all he had was a full tank of stale fuel and he was broke flatter than piss on a plate. He had struggled now for seven lean weeks without a charter.

Jim Peters was six foot two, and a proud young Ojibwa. He was a shy, quiet man who balked at trusting anyone outside his clan. In particular, he didn't trust white men, with one exception, and that was Carlin McKenzie. They had been friends from early childhood. Now, Carlin intended to build a shelter and floating dock on Crown land adjacent to the reserve. Unknowingly, his foundations were infringing upon Ojibwa land. When Jim pointed out the error, Carlin's anger exploded and he told Jim to mind his own business. Unaccustomed to rudeness from Carlin, Jim advised the band chief of the encroachment, hoping to protect Carlin from future controversy.

Carlin, too angry to listen, threw down the gauntlet telling Peters to go to hell. Jim Peters knew a way to get this man's attention, and without saying a word, he picked Carlin up bodily and threw him into the lake to cool off. Before Carlin hit the water he knew exactly how to even the score. He remained under the water's surface and swam twenty yards farther out. Sputtering and coughing Carlin called out in feigned panic, "Help. Help me I can't swim!"

The big Ojibwa was instantly filled with fear. He plunged into the water and with powerful strokes, he swam out to Carlin, but Carlin pushed the big man's head under and held him there for several seconds. When he released Jim Peters, he swam frantically to the shallows. He reached shoulder deep water and standing on the bottom, looked back. There was no sign of the Ojibwa. Terrified now, Carlin submerged to look for the man. The moment his face entered the water he was pulled under and then released. They both came to the surface, coughing out water and laughing, and each had gained a new measure of respect for the other. Jim Peters asked Carlin about building a shanty by the lake.

"I need a place to live and a place to moor my plane," he said, "I figure it will be five years before the government knows I am on their land. It wasn't my intention to build on the Indian reserve."

"When the government finds your shack they will tear it down and charge you," Jim said, "You would do better on Indian land, but they wouldn't allow a shanty. We have struggled for a long time to change the Sloppy Indian image."

"I understand, your concern" Carlin answered, "but I have no money for decent materials – I only have the junk I collected."

"Perhaps you don't need money," Jim said, "you need help and manpower. I will talk with the elders, If they accept you, all the help you need is available, but you must always remember that land is never owned by anyone. It is only ours to use."

"Why are you offering to help me?" Carlin asked, dumping the water out of his boots.

"Because I think you are a man worthy of calling friend, and because it is our way to help those who have less than we do."

When he spoke with his father about Carlin, Jonathan Peters told Jim the story about Carlin's birth and his offer of surrogacy as Carlin's father. "This is the first time Carlin McKenzie has ever needed help," he said, "Now it is my duty to be a true father to your white brother. I will talk with the elders." Though he was unaware, Carlin McKenzie's life would be forever altered. In the weeks that followed, the Ojibwa helped Carlin build a fine log cabin with three rooms and a floating dock. Carlin McKenzie finally had a home of his own.

Now, Jim had just walked two miles through rough bush to bring a good news message to his best friend, but he checked himself before stepping into the clearing around Carlin's cabin. Jim saw Carlin sitting woebegone, on a log near the water. A pang of sorrow wrenched at Jim Peters' heart to see his friend alone, and miserable. Perhaps a square meal and the message he was about to deliver, would lift Carlin's spirits.

Jim wanted to clap him on the back and shout out the news, but his Ojibwa heritage, and shyness dictated a more dignified delivery. Stepping deeper into the woods he circled to a position where he could approach Carlin from behind. On silent feet he came undetected, to within two feet of his friend. His lean, strong arm shot out and encircled Carlin's neck, then pulled him backward in a neck hold.

"Are you my brother or my enemy?" he said, laughing softly.

"Let me go you damned Indian yahoo," Carlin protested, and he was laughing as well, for they were more like brothers than friends. Peters let him go and with his arm draped over Carlin's shoulder they walked out to the dock where the Cessna sparkled in the morning sun.

"There was a phone call for you at the band office this morning," Jim Peters said. "A woman called to ask questions about getting to an old Ojibwa village two hundred and fifty miles north of here. It was abandoned fifty years ago by people who had lived there for more than a century. The band council don't want her to go there because they think she may be an archaeologist who would desecrate the old burial grounds. She wants you to fly her in."

"So you're telling me you don't want me to take the job?"

"No, an Ojibwa never tells anyone to do anything. I am simply saying I wish to go along to protect our traditions if she decides to break the rules of our people," Peters said seriously. "I know you need the work – that's why I came here. Do you have enough fuel to get to Whitewater Lake?"

"Yeah, no problem," Carlin replied, "Is that where she wants to be picked up?"

"No," Jim answered quickly, "but Charlie Redwing has a cache of fresh fuel and oil there. He said you can use it and pay him back later. The poor bugger doesn't know you as well as I do."

"Hey, hey Geronimo, I always pay my debts when I'm flush," Carlin teased his friend. Deep inside Carlin felt a twinge of shame at having to borrow from Charlie Redwing, and he knew Charlie would rather take a swift boot in the ass than accept Carlin's payment. The Ojibwa people trusted him and he had never betrayed that trust. Carlin had spent many tense hours in the air during impossible flying weather, flying Indian women and children to hospitals, or out of bush fire paths. He had never asked for payment of any kind because he loved the Ojibwa people.

"Yeah but you've only been flush once in your life. That was when your mother sent you the money for your first year at university. Now come on – we are supposed to pick the woman up at the Vermillion River bridge at noon," Jim said putting some hand tools away in Carlin's cabin.

After securing the little log house, they taxied to the opposite end of the lake and turned into the wind. Carlin selected ten degrees of flap and pushed the throttle slowly to the stop. The acceleration on the water was slow, but soon the little Cessna grew light and bounced along the surface. Easing the wheel back, he lifted her into the air. His heart sang as he climbed above the trees behind the cabin he called 'OntAir Flying Service'. He raised the flaps and set the throttle for normal cruise. Carlin was happy. He was airborne again thanks to Jim Peters, and some old broad who wanted to find arrowheads and clay potsherds in the northern forest. He was aware that the fuel the Cessna was burning was stale and might be contaminated with water. The engine was sluggish. He didn't want to frighten Jim, and he tried to divert his attention.

"You never did tell me about your clan totem," Carlin said, glancing down at the map on his knee. "What is it – a sturgeon, or maybe a wolf – what?" The question was posed to cover up the occasional cough from the engine, but it didn't fool Jim Peters.

"No," Jim replied, listening for the sound again, "My totem is the hawk. He flies on energy from eating mice and rabbits. He doesn't get colds or coughs," Jim said pointedly. "I know the Cessna Sky Hawk doesn't get coughs or colds either – only when it has to burn stale fuel," Jim continued, "and maybe a bit of water eh?" He was looking out the window, estimating the distance to the nearest lake large enough for an emergency landing. The winding course of the Vermillion River was visible on the horizon. They were ten minutes from their pickup point.

Carlin's 'Old Broad' passenger, was Carol Danse, a thirty-one year old intellectual, whose mother wanted her to be a dignified librarian. Carol had other ideas that centred on archaeology. While she loved books, they were only tools for her, tools with which she could unearth the past. She loved history and was intrigued by the tenacity and common sense the early North Americans used, to survive against impossible odds.

Once, on holiday with her parents, they visited the restored Fort William in Northern Ontario. Outside the walls of the fort was an Indian village comprised of a few wigwams. The fort had been reconstructed with new materials made to look old. Conversely, the wigwams had been built from natural materials, in the same manner the Ojibwa used thousands of years before. They were truly authentic. Carol had entered one of the wigwams and sat for a half hour, talking with a very old Ojibwa woman. The elder was not completely fluent in English, and often reverted to her native language. Carol wished with all her heart she could speak the Ojibwa tongue.

Looking around the wigwam with its frail poles and birch bark covering, she thought about the contrast with modern housing in the white man's world. He spent months constructing a dwelling, while a wigwam could be built in a day or two. Carol thought about how cold the wigwam must be in the depths of a northern winter, and how these copper coloured people could survive for one season, let alone centuries. The myriad questions that floated through Carol's mind that day, and her profession, had led her to the present, and the Vermillion River bridge.

Standing on the bridge deck, a cold breeze ruffled her loose parka and then died away. She slowly turned through a full circle, drinking in the beauty of autumn. The big maples had turned to scarlet, and the poplars countered with bright yellow. Interspersed through the blazing colour, were tall pines and spruces, whose brooding dark green, enhanced the other colours even more. The air was filled with a sweet melancholy. Soon the leaves would fall and the land would become stark and foreboding as the long months of winter marched past.

The woman's short blonde hair was hidden under a toque, and she wore a shapeless blue parka and combat boots. A pack was slung over her shoulder, and on the ground at her feet were two bundles of gear. Carol surveyed the part of the river near the bridge, concluding it would be nearly impossible, for the pilot to pick her up at that point. He would, she reckoned, land on the part of the river above the falls. It would be necessary to haul her gear a half mile to the plane. She wished she had chosen another area for pick up, but it was too late now. There was nothing left to do but wait. Carol Danse removed her notebook from her pack and began to enter the events of the morning in the journal. She was engrossed in making the entry and didn't hear the Cessna until it was a scant mile from the bridge. The plane descended rapidly in a

G. WM. GOTRO

long dive, and passing over the road it frightened her enough to make her duck her head.

Carlin had seen the solitary figure on the highway, crossed it at fifty feet and opened the throttle wide. He climbed two hundred feet above the falls and executed a tight bank that pointed the plane's nose back at the highway. He sideslipped sharply, landed, and taxied almost to the bridge. It was a spectacular piece of flying. Jim opened the door and stood on the float, a nylon line coiled in his hand.

"Hey," he shouted, "take the line and make it fast to that tree – there's a current running here. Hurry up!" She scrambled down the steep bank from the highway, and was at the rocky water's edge quickly. She caught the thrown line like an expert, and gently pulled the plane close enough for Jim Peters to jump ashore.

"All my gear is on the roadside," she said, gesturing up at the bridge, "I will need some help."

"Me too," Jim replied, "You keep the floats from rubbing on the rocks while I get your gear," and without waiting for an answer, he began the climb to the road.

When he returned, Jim Peters helped her into the back seat, and piled her gear in with her before taking his place in the right hand seat. Carlin took a sharp breath when he saw her, and acknowledged her only with a nod of his head. Jim thought Carlin was worried about the short takeoff space. Carlin taxied to a spot under the bridge and held there watching the water for signs of wind. When the ripples began, he pushed the throttle to the panel. The Cessna, heavily loaded, struggled to get up on the step and the falls were dangerously close when it finally rose from the river. Carlin cleared the top of the falls by twenty feet. He nursed the Cessna to fifteen hundred before turning on a heading for Whitewater Lake and Charlie Redwing's cache of fresh fuel.

Carlin was a six foot, one hundred and seventy pound anachronism whose values were rooted in the past. Having grown to manhood without the hand of a father, he took nothing for granted, asked for nothing, and paid his way in the world. He welcomed the opportunity to earn a few dollars with this charter, and blessed Charlie Redwing when his dock and fuel cache appeared below the wing. As he rounded out for the landing, he pondered his reservations about the woman. Moored at the dock, he set to work draining his stale fuel and condensate into an empty drum.

Charlie was a meticulous man and a seasoned bush pilot. The four 45 gallon drums in his cache were dated and sealed, and the hand pump was wrapped in grease paper. Within half an hour they were refueled, and ready to leave. Carlin had still not spoken to the woman. Cavalier by nature, he was embarrassed at having to borrow fuel. He was sure the woman was aware of the unusual nature of the refueling stop.

She probably figured him for a gypsy pilot who would grub in the dirt for a fare and he hated the feeling. She was supposed to be an old girl from a museum. She was supposed to be wearing a long coat over her tweed jacket and her wool skirt. She was supposed to be wearing lisle stockings and brogues. She was supposed to wear her gray hair in a tight bun and her round silver rimmed glasses were supposed to glint in the sun. And finally she was supposed to have an irritating voice and a sour face. So much for his illusion of the modern day archetype of the female archaeologist.

Carol Danse didn't fit a single detail in Carlin's model, and for some reason it angered him. He didn't want to admit to himself that his judgment was off, or that she appeared to be everything he admired in a woman. He didn't want to admit that he was attracted to her, and he could never admit how dull his life had become. Carlin was internally confused and angry because he didn't know what was wrong, but Jim Peters knew exactly what was wrong.

"Let's get moving," Carlin snapped, after he finished the refueling operation, "I don't want to land this thing in the dark, so let's go," he said, settling himself into the left hand seat. His words were directed to her by implication, and Jim Peters saw the distress in her face. It was rude of Carlin and the woman was unaware of having done anything wrong – it was time to intervene.

"I would prefer to travel in the back seat Miss Danse," Jim said with a startling smile, "Can you push us away from the dock and take the right hand seat?" He asked in a charming manner.

"It's okay by me Mr. Peters, as long as I don't get bitten by the cobra," she replied softly, as she skillfully pushed the plane out from the dock and stepped onto the float.

"He is all noise," Jim said in a stage whisper, "but he is the best bush pilot in the country. It's just that he hasn't eaten for three days and that often makes him grumpy."

She swung up into the right hand seat as the engine caught. She fastened her seat belt without being told, and checked that her door was secure. Carlin turned and gave Jim Peters a withering look before opening the throttle to taxi, a look that said, "I didn't invite her to the right hand seat!"

Carol Danse didn't appreciate being slighted by some mean assed bush pilot with a chip on his shoulder, nor did she appreciate being ignored. "I don't know what your problem is Mr. Carlin," she said in a clear voice, "but I expect to be treated in a civil manner and YOUR manners fall far short of that." She adopted her righteous mode, and turned away, looking out the window. Had she glanced toward him, she would have seen Carlin blush to the roots of his hair.

Ten minutes passed as Carlin analyzed his feelings. The first moment he saw her he knew she was very special. He was certain that she was from society's upper class, certain that he wasn't in her league. He was angry because he believed she was unapproachable. But she was after all paying the bill, so he tried to apologize. He looked toward her but she was watching the panorama of Northern Ontario unfold beneath the Cessna's wing.

For some reason he still couldn't understand, she made him angry. Again he thought she should have been a wrinkled old prune dressed in a tweed jacket, a wool skirt, lisle stockings, and wearing brogues on her feet. But she was not. She should have spoken in a silly piping voice that spewed out inanities and laughed at the wrong times. But she did not.

She should have written notes that started with 'Dear Diary', notes that described everything she did, said, or thought, but she did not. Her name should have been Prunella Farnsworth, but it was not. She was Carol Danse, in her early thirties, sensibly dressed for the wilderness right down to the light weight boots she wore. Her voice was melodious and perfectly modulated, and when she spoke she was direct and succinct. Carol Danse didn't laugh at the wrong times either – she smiled in understanding instead, and she had no diary. She used a dollar fifty note pad, and a micro recorder, and she was right about him – he had been rude.

"I'm sorry Ms. Danse," he said, "I had no right to treat you badly." Her blue eyes searched his face and found total sincerity.

"No harm done Mr. Carlin," she said, "everyone has their bad days," and she turned away, looking out the window. When he looked at her, she thought he was scanning her soul and she trembled. There was a quickness and a strength about him that made her feel safe. She tried to get him out of her mind, concentrating on the wild country below. She was fascinated by the terrain, unable to decide if they were flying over a thousand small lakes, or if they were crossing an enormous lake filled with a thousand islands. "I don't know how anyone could find anything here. Everything looks the same," she said, studying the instruments. "How do you know where we are?"

"Oh there's nothing to it," he said laughing, "all you need is a compass, a map, a course called Bad Navigating 101, a hell of a lot of luck, and Jim Peters takes care of the rest." She looked at him and her eyes were the deep blue of the restless ocean, and Carlin was finding it hard to breathe.

Carlin was centred over Kerrigan Lake and turned onto a true north heading. As the plane banked, a moose raised its head from beneath the water, where it was feeding. Water cascaded from his antlers as he looked up. Carol was delighted at the sight of the big animal. Later they saw a family of black bears feeding on berries, the last gifts of summer, before going into hibernation. She thought about the bears surviving for months on the fat they stored through the summer. How, she wondered, did the moose manage in winter, and how could man survive here at all?

In the distance Carlin saw the exclamation mark shape of Crystal Lake. The lake began with a perfectly round pool, five hundred feet across, and emptied into the main body of water through a narrow opening, which broadened gradually for a mile to the rounded top end of Crystal Lake. From six thousand feet, it resembled a blue exclamation mark. Carlin started his final approach, reducing power and began a slow descent.

Jim Peters leaned forward to be heard. "My brother-in-law came in here with Charlie Redwing two months ago," he said, "They pulled out those two sunken logs from the narrows. He said it was safe now to do your touchdown on the pool." They had descended to four thousand feet, and Carlin powered the engine up briefly to clear it, then throttling back once more he continued his descent.

"Where is the village?" Carol asked, visually scanning the area around Crystal Lake, and finding only dense forest.

"Oh the village rotted away many years ago," Jim Peters answered, "There isn't much left now but rubble, and it is on a small river five miles northwest of here."

"Sorry Ms. Danse," Carlin said, "it's a five mile hike from here I'm afraid," and he turned onto his final approach.

2

DISASTER

In 1895 a narrow band of low land, separated the pool from the main body of Crystal Lake. Upon the low land, stood three huge trees known to the Ojibwa as the sentinels or guardians. They were put there by the Great Manitou, to keep the evil things from the centre of the earth from bursting forth from the pool, and entering the world. For many years the water levels had been rising, and the low strip of land was often submerged. The people were anxious and feared the Sentinels feet would soon let go of the earth, and they would fall. As they believed it, so did it happen; for the heavy autumnal rains had filled the lake and the pool and the feet of the giants were no longer rooted in the earth. Instead they were simply balanced on the spongy mud, and late the following night Great Manitou sent mighty wind to dry the land. The giants misunderstood the wishes of Manitou and toppled to the earth in submission.

The people were saddened, and took the event as a sign that the place had become unholy. They moved five miles to another place, where they built a fine village, and raised their children, teaching them to never go near the graves of the fallen guardians.

The strip of low land was now mostly submerged, and when the springtime winds blew from the northwest, the water and waves tore away the sodden land, and the pool became one with the lake. The sentinels broken and shattered, lay just below the surface of the water, and each year, growing heavier, sank lower in the ooze. There they rested in peace until two men descended from the heavens in a strange noisy bird, and with block and tackle, removed two of the broken logs from the water. The third, unbroken in its fall, lay directly across the narrows.

Freed of the weight of its companions, it rocked gently in the mud, six inches below the murky turbid water.

As he made his approach to Crystal Lake, Carlin noticed a large area of fallen trees at the south east end. From three hundred feet up, he could see areas where the water had encroached on the low land. It occurred to him that in a few years the pool would be much bigger. He rounded out and landed hard and a bit longer than intended. The result was a long bounce that carried him over the unseen sunken dead head. Carlin taxied up to the northwest end of the lake, and carefully ran the floats up on a small sandy beach. When the plane was unloaded, Carol Danse astounded the two men with a simple question.

"When will you pick me up?" She asked, shouldering her pack.

Carlin studied her face for a long time before answering. "When you fall down Ms. Danse," he said with a grin, "we stay here until you are ready to leave. That is how an OntAir charter works. I never leave anyone behind." He checked the survival equipment in the big nylon bag he had removed from behind the rear seat. It contained down filled sleeping bags, a nylon tent and fly sheet, and a ground sheet. In addition the locker behind the rear seat contained a .44 magnum revolver, a light hand axe and an over and under .410 and .22 cal. rifle. They took only the essentials and with Jim Peters leading the way they began the five mile hike to the village site.

The hike was over rough terrain and marsh. Two hours passed before they reached the site where the village once stood. There was almost nothing left to show it ever existed. A few rotten tree stumps and some overgrown mounds were all that remained.

Carlin was certain the woman would want to go back.

There was nothing here for her. Instead, she was delighted. It was just as she imagined it would be. The people had built their village beside what appeared to be a small lake, but was in fact, the wide part of a slow moving river. Carol could hardly wait to begin the exploration of the mounds. The sun dipped below the treetops and the gathering twilight heralded an early darkness. After sunset, the air grew very cold and frost began to form before the tent was pitched. Jim built a cheerful fire and within minutes, Carlin withdrew oatmeal, flour, and a rock hard slab of salt cured bacon from the shoulder pack he carried. Carol Danse heated a large can of beans while Carlin made a bannock and cooked thick strips of bacon.

The crisp cold air sharpened their appetites and in the frosty night, beneath a clear star filled sky, they ate until they wanted nothing more. Jim Peters saved the bacon rinds for bait, and he had become quiet and introverted, his mood driven by something internal. Carlin's hunger was sated, and he too became introspective. Carol Danse was blissfully happy, thinking about the historical treasures she would find in the morning. Each man was wondering what the other was thinking. Jim Peters was uncomfortable with the woman's purpose for being there. He didn't want to spoil her trip by stopping her from desecrating the graves of his ancestors, if that was her purpose. Carlin, on the other hand, was concerned about the weather. A freeze-up tonight meant smashing through thin ice in the morning, to get the Cessna to open water.

A loon, having lingered too long, called his mate with a long and wavering cry, but she slept in a nearby marsh, and did not answer. He called again, and more urgent. Her answer told him she wanted him. On whistling wings he flew low over their camp to join her, and together after sunrise they would fly to a warmer region, leaving the recent intruders to the lake and the coming winter.

The birds and animals knew that autumn was over and winter was upon them. The bears, big and little had already grown fat and too drowsy to roam any more. They snuggled down in a warm cave, where they would sleep until spring.

When Jim Peters banked the fire for the night, Carol asked him about the village. She was impatient to discover why the small band of Ojibwa separated from their southern brothers. Jim had of course, heard all the stories in the longhouse and he told them as he had learned them. The story enchanted the woman, and enlightened Carlin. It was almost midnight when they turned in and slept peacefully under a stark white moon. Carlin awakened at dawn, and for a long moment he studied the woman in the feeble light of early morning. She was beautiful. He slipped out of his sleeping bag and quietly left the tent. A heavy frost had settled in the open areas, and a low fog enfolded the lake. Carlin considered the possibility of being trapped here if Crystal Lake froze over. If that happened, they could be trapped by ice for two or three weeks. Then hopefully, someone might realize they were missing and come for them with a ski equipped plane.

He stoked the fire with dry wood, boiled water, and made coffee. Soon the aroma of it filled the air. In the tent Carol's nose twitched at the fragrance and she was instantly awake. She left the tent and seeing Carlin was in the woods, she went to the water's edge to wash. He returned with more wood, and seeing her there, observed as she brushed her hair. Carol sensed him watching, and turned toward him in mild anger. Then, seeing the look in his eyes, she smiled and came toward him.

"Did anyone ever tell you that you sometimes look like a little boy, with his hand caught in the cookie jar?" She asked, her rich voice bordering on laughter.

"Just how long have you been watching me Mr. McKenzie?" Feeling he had invaded her privacy he looked down at his feet, blushing.

"Not long," he said, "just since you boarded the plane yesterday." He looked up, making eye contact. "We had best get an early start," he said, pouring a cup of steaming coffee for her. "If the temperature drops much more, there is a good chance Crystal Lake will ice over. If that happens we are here for the winter unless someone comes looking for us."

"How much time do we have?" She asked, "I don't want you to take any risks on my account."

"Two days, maybe three if a wind comes up." he said, "the rougher the water, the less chance of freezing. How much time do you need?" He asked. He knew his estimation was very optimistic.

She proposed to map the village, and hoped to find one or two artifacts from each dwelling. She also wanted to explore the burial sites, to discover what items accompanied the dead, on the journey to the other world.

Carlin was uneasy with her plan. "The Ojibwa," he said,

looking away from her, "like all First Nations people, have strong beliefs about the remains of their ancestors and ..."

"No, I don't want to desecrate the remains of these people," she said, "I want to catalog the items they would have taken to their next life. It is a cataloguing, not a grave robbing exercise Mr. McKenzie!" Her face was flushed and she was angry.

"Researchers have been doing that for centuries," Carlin protested, "why repeat what has been done already?"

"Because these people died out much more recently," she answered testily, "if we can find out why, we can prevent it from happening again in the future. Why did they die out? Did they die from disease and ignorance or did they die from neglect. Don't you see Carlin – if we find out why, it need not happen again. Not ever!" She was passionate about it and she really did care about the Ojibwa. But she wasn't of the Anishinawbe and could not feel what they felt, though her intentions were noble and beyond reproach.

"Why not talk with Jim Peters," Carlin advised, "he can probably tell you what you want to know." She turned away from him. His last words carried the implication that her whole project was a waste of time, and her objective was so simple it didn't need research. She put her coffee down untouched, and walked to the water's edge, hurt and doubtful.

Carlin knew he had hurt her, and hated himself for doing so, but he also knew that Jim Peters wouldn't allow her to touch the graves of his people. He went to her side and put his arm around her shoulders. "Hey pretty researcher, I didn't mean to downplay the importance of your project. I just want to protect you from being hurt if Jim stops you from opening the graves. The Ojibwa are a very spiritual people Carol, and no one will ever know why this small group died out – It could be because they wanted to move on to the next world, and simply stopped living." Her eyes glistened with tears and she turned away, wiping at them with her sleeve.

"They couldn't just quit living," she said, sniffing, "a whole village couldn't just quit living – could it?"

"Ask Jim," Carlin said, "he knows his own people. Ask Jim."

Carol Danse was not easily dissuaded.

One or two of the old buildings were clearly marked by the

rotting timbers still showing above the forest debris. The remainder offered no clues other than a slight lump or depression on the forest floor. By noon they had marked twenty dwelling sites. Jim Peters helped in every way. He didn't mind her digging in the old building ruins because it kept her away from the grave sites.

"Do you know when the first people settled here?" She asked as she brushed the debris away from the corner of a house, collapsed some thirty years before.

"The stories say that these people lived on the north shore of Lake Huron. They had a dispute with the Midewiwin over their war with the Iroquois. Because of that, they chose to leave their homes and start a new band. They came here about a hundred and forty years ago," Jim Peters answered, "They lived in bark shelters – wigwams – on Crystal Lake. For some reason they abandoned that place after twenty years or so. Then they came here and built houses from logs chinked with clay. They trapped and sold furs, and they grew corn and beans. For a long time they were very prosperous. They discovered the great sturgeon in the river here and they never went hungry."

"What made them leave this village then?" She asked, scraping away more debris from the foot of what had once been a wall.

"The legends say that a messenger or angel from the Great Spirit came here one night. The elders could not understand his words, but the young men and women understood them. When the angel left, a bright shaft of light followed him into the sky, as he returned to Manitou. After a week passed most of the young people ran away from here and the young people that stayed began to die. Only the old people remained alive." Jim lit his pipe.

"Gradually the old ones weakened and could not tend the crops or trap for furs. They could no longer catch the mighty sturgeon and so one by one they died," he said sadly.

"Who told the other bands the story?" Carol asked.

"The last survivor was an old man. He buried all the others and then he built a birch bark canoe the old way. When it was finished he made the long journey to the north shore of Lake Superior where the Sleeping Giant rests. After he told the story to his people, he wanted to come back here to his home. Some young men accompanied him and stayed with him until he died. They buried him here with his people," he said with a catch in his voice. She turned and looked at him and saw the pain and sorrow in his face.

"I'm sorry Jim, I didn't mean to cause you grief by asking insensitive questions," she said sincerely, "Please forgive me."

"There is nothing to forgive," he answered gently, "You were just curious."

The little hand rake she was using struck something solid. Carefully she unearthed a small clay bowl. It was beautifully crafted from blue clay, and decorated around the rim with designs cut into the surface. Carol Danse, encouraged by her find, went back to work with renewed energy. By the end of the day she had acquired a large hook fashioned from iron, several flint arrow heads and a number of other stone, clay, and bone artifacts she couldn't identify. She laid them out before Jim Peters. "If it is okay by you, I would like to photograph these items, and I would like to take one of them for authenticating the dates."

"These were not items buried with the dead," he said.

"If you want to take them, it's okay by me. I speak for my people in this matter." He was delighted to see her face light up with a smile of pure happiness.

As twilight descended on the camp, the air was filled with delicious aromas as Carlin prepared their supper. He had caught two pickerel using Jim's bacon rind bait, and Jim had shot two plump partridge. The fish were baked in clay, and the partridge, were added to the stew pot along with vegetables and dumplings. A big bannock was cooked in a pan and the result was a hot nourishing meal – one they would remember in the future.

After dinner they sat by the fire and discussed the artifacts Carol had discovered. The men shared a pipe of tobacco, and as the three talked, a half dozen wild creatures watched from the darkness, attracted by the scent of the cooking. One was a fat, grumpy, old black bear who ambled away to his den, to sleep away the impending winter. The raccoons soon found the shallow pit containing the fish offal, and after washing the prize in the river water, dined as did the people. Late in the evening, the three retired to the tent and slept.

G. WM. GOTRO

Shortly after 4:00 A.M. they were awakened by a loud report that sounded like a pistol shot. Carol was terrified, but Jim Peters and Carlin knew what it was. The moisture in a nearby tree had frozen and expanded, causing the tree trunk to explode. Carlin said nothing, but lay awake wondering how thick the ice would be, on Crystal Lake in the morning, and if time had just run out for the them. Jim Peters knew the answer to that question but he lay silent the rest of the night considering their options.

Carlin, always an early riser, left the tent before daylight. Once again he coaxed the fire to life and made a pot of coffee.

The ice at the river's edge was almost thick enough to walk on. He broke a hole through it with the axe, and drew a bucket of water. The sky was overcast and Carlin expected snow within the hour. That was bad news – a dusting of snow would reflect sunlight better than dark ice, and there would be no chance of melting. He prayed for the cloud cover to dissipate and the temperature to rise. With a whole lot of luck and a good warm wind, the ice on Crystal Lake might just break enough to allow him to get the Cessna in the air by noon. Conversely, if it snowed, they were stuck there until someone found them – Carlin knew Charlie Redwing would bail them out, but he couldn't guess when. He went to the tent to arouse Jim Peters and Carol Danse. She was snuggled deep in the sleeping bag, and her breathing was slow and steady.

"Okay you two, we have a problem. Rise and shine," Carlin said, trying to keep the real urgency out of his voice. She wakened immediately, but Jim didn't respond.

"What's wrong?" She asked, sitting up, and letting the sleeping bag slide down from her shoulders. She shivered and reached for her sweater.

"There's ice on the river, and we are under heavy overcast. It is unusual to see temperatures this low under a cloud blanket, but if it snows and the weather worsens we're trapped here. I want to get moving as soon as possible. There is a very remote chance, that Crystal Lake is still open so let's go." He couldn't hide the concern in his eyes. "Wake Jim while I get us some breakfast."

Jim Peters struck the tent and packed their gear, while Carlin prepared a hot meal. They had marched less than three miles when the snow began. Heavy wet flakes fell and settled. A mile from the lake the wind came up, and the temperature dropped sharply.

The flakes became smaller and were wind driven, stinging the skin. When they reached the beach, the Cessna's wings were covered with four inches of snow. Worse, the ice extended out fifty feet from the shore, but the centre of the lake was open.

Now the problem became one of getting the plane to open water without falling through the ice themselves. They had to do it quickly or not at all. They brushed the snow from the wings.

"I want a vote on this," Carlin said, huddling deeper in his jacket, it has to be unanimous. If we stay, Charlie Redwing will probably come for us in a couple of days – if we go now we might get off the water, but one or all of us is going to get wet and that's dangerous. What do you want to do Carol?

"I vote we wait for rescue," she answered quickly, we know we can survive here for a few days."

"Let me have the deciding vote," Jim said bluntly, "What do YOU want to do Carlin?"

"I think it is best to stay. You know Charlie, he will be here in a day or so and we can fly out safely. We can get the skis at OntAir and fly back to do the change over. I can take the floats apart and fly them out one at a time in the Beaver." Charlie will ....."

"I vote we fly out right now," Jim Peters said interrupting Carlin.

"But ..." Carlin began to protest.

"No," Jim said cutting him off, "Charlie won't rescue us!"

Jim smiled sadly, "he doesn't know we're here. He left for South Carolina the day you got this charter. He won't be back until April." His words came as a shock, and Carlin wanted to berate him for not mentioning Charlie's trip south until now. Carlin put down his anger, remembering the stoic nature of the Ojibwa.

A light wind had risen, and the open water was rippled as they slowly pushed the Cessna across the ice. It wasn't a hard job – the floats' keels acted like ice skates and she slipped along without too much effort. Fifteen feet from open water, the ice gave way and the Cessna sat rocking in the water. They pulled her back to the unbroken edge and Carol was able to board with little more than wet feet. Carlin too managed to get safely aboard, but Jim Peters went through the ice and had to be dragged out soaked and shivering. The cabin heater would warm Jim once they were in the air.

Carlin primed the engine and rolled the starter. It was very sluggish, but the engine finally coughed and started. He taxied out to the centre of the open water and turned into the wind. A very thin layer of ice covered the wing, but there was nothing he could do about it. He guessed that it was not enough to be really serious. If he could just reach a larger lake, he could land and deal with the problem without fear of freezing in. Trying to stay without Charlie Redwing's backup was not an option. He taxied as far back as the ice would allow and turning into the wind again he opened the throttle.

At 60 knots he eased back on the wheel but the little Cessna was slow to respond and wouldn't leave the water. He pushed the throttle to the stop gaining a little more speed and she grew light, skipping across the surface. Almost at the narrows he knew he had only six or seven hundred feet left. He eased the wheel forward and then back causing a bounce.

She broke free of the water then, but couldn't sustain flight with ice on the wing. From three feet up she dropped again and the float tips dug in for only a second, before hitting the submerged sentinel log in the narrows. The floats ripped open and the Cessna flipped end over end, slamming into the centre of the pool upside down. The windshield shattered filling the cabin with broken plexiglass and ice water.

Carlin experienced the entire event in slow motion. He was aware of the end over end flip, and he saw the water hit the windshield. The impact of it hitting him in the face knocked him out for perhaps twenty seconds, and when he regained consciousness he realized the water in the cabin shouldn't be crimson. Someone was bleeding, and the thought that followed was worse – Carlin knew they were drowning. He managed to undo his seat belt and release Carol from her harness. He pushed her out the windshield hole and dragged her to the surface. She was badly cut and coughing water from her lungs, but she was alert enough to swim to the shore.

Carlin dived again, and finding the windshield hole once more he was about to enter, when Jim's face appeared before him. He grabbed at the shirt and pulled him to the surface and swimming hard in the cold water, Carlin dragged Jim to the beach. They were all injured, suffering multiple cuts and some breaks. Carlin's ankle and Carol's forearm were broken. Jim Peters' shoulder was dislocated and he was in agony. Fortunately during Carlin's football years he had helped reposition a dislocated shoulder. Now, with an immense effort he was able to do it again for Jim Peters. Carlin removed his jacket and shirt to get at his under shirt. Then dressing again, he used the undershirt to bandage a long cut on the back of Carol's head and slow the bleeding.

Within a few minutes, each of them had stripped and wrung the water from their clothing. Now what little body heat they had left was better conserved.

"We need a fire or we will freeze to death," Jim said, "wrap your arms around each other and share your body heat. I will start a fire." He headed deeper into the woods and returned five minutes later with dry tinder from the inside of an old log, a dozen strips of birch bark, and an arm full of twigs. He made a fire drill, using his bootlace and a sapling. With persistence, he managed to start the tinder smoldering, then feeding it with more tinder and tiny, thin strips of birch bark he started a fire. Soon the twigs were burning brightly and he was adding more dry fuel.

An hour and a half after the crash they were reasonably warm and recovering from the shock. "We have to salvage the stuff from the plane," Jim said softly, "If I hadn't voted to leave, this wouldn't have happened. I want to try right away."

"Don't even think about it," Carlin cautioned, "it wasn't your fault. It was me who risked a takeoff with ice on the wings."

Jim Peters smiled at his friend. "You can't even walk on a broken ankle Carlin, quit trying to be a hero." He removed his jacket, boots, and jeans and swam out to the plane. On the third attempt to free the big nylon bag Jim gave up and came to the surface. Diving again, he recovered the axe, some ammunition, and the rifle. Suffering now from hypothermia he struggled to the shore. Carol and Carlin had to drag the big Ojibwa from the water. They brought his clothes heated by the fire, and dressed him in them. It was two hours before they knew he wasn't going to die.

"I'll get the bag tomorrow," he said, and then fell asleep. They didn't recover the big bag the next day, because by morning Crystal Lake was an unbroken sheet of ice.

Carol took stock of their resources, and reported. "We have the clothes we are standing in, twelve .410 shotgun shells, twenty .22 cartridges, one over and under rifle, one hand axe, twenty five feet of nylon rope that floated to the surface, each of you have a belt knife, and I have a frozen ball point pen and a wet pocket notebook." She was shivering and moved closer to the fire. "That's the good news – the bad news is, we have nothing to heat water or to cook in, no shelter, no food and no medicine. We have five working legs and five working arms, thus crippling sixty-six percent of our crew. That adds up to zero hope unless we are found within maybe 72 hours." Her eyes glistened with tears.

"Ms. Danse," Jim Peters said, "My people came here with far less than we have. They survived for a hundred years. I will not give up to the wilderness – I will survive, and while I survive, you will survive." He turned and went into the forest to collect a stock of wood. When he returned he piled the wood near the fire for Carlin. "You stay here and look after the fire. Carol can come with me to help. We will be back in four hours. I need the gun and the axe – keep the fire hot," he said smiling at his friend, and then he turned back toward the abandoned village.

A mile from Crystal Lake, he shot a jack rabbit, and he knew that the .22 bullets hadn't been damaged by their brief immersion in the lake. When they were in sight of the village he spotted a four point buck. He sighted and squeezed the .410 trigger, but the shell didn't fire. When the buck heard the 'click' of the misfire he bolted, and Jim knew he couldn't rely on the shotgun. He reloaded both barrels despite the first misfire.

At the village he led Carol to the waters edge, and gave her a sharpened stick. "Dig here," he said, "the ground isn't frozen any more than a half inch yet."

"What am I digging for?" She asked, shrugging her shoulders.

"Blue clay," he said, we will be making pottery tonight. We need about ten pounds of clay. I am going for food. Don't wander away from here Ms. Danse – I will be back shortly." He left her picking away at the clay on the river bank, and headed into the woods. He followed deer tracks for ten minutes, then cut away from the trail. He picked it up again five minutes later. There were fresh droppings in the snow – the deer wasn't far ahead of him now. It was a doe and he closed on her fast – he was driven by hunger. He spotted her browsing fifty yards away. It was too far for a shotgun which may or may not fire.

He moved upwind before closing in on her. Now she was less than twenty yards from him. In his mind he looked into the inside of the shotgun shell and saw wet powder. He drew a bead on her rear leg joint and squeezed the .22 trigger. The little bullet slammed into her rear knee joint at 1300 feet per second. Her rear end collapsed into the snow, and she was struggling to regain her feet when the second bullet hit her in the head. She toppled over and again tried to regain her feet, but Jim was on her with his knife to her throat, and within a span of thirty seconds she was dead.

Jim Peters hefted the doe onto his shoulders and returned to the village, finding Carol in possession of twenty five pounds of blue river clay. "Let's get moving," he said, "Carlin will soon be out of firewood and we have food to prepare."

They arrived at the Crystal Lake site just before sundown. They were tired and hungry, their last meal being breakfast the previous day. Jim skinned and dressed the deer while Carol, using her good hand, piled dry wood on the rope, and dragged the load of fuel close to the fire. Carlin had made a crutch for himself, and hobbled around doing what he could to prepare hot food. He skewered bits of venison and placed them over the hot coals. They ate them as soon as the meat was cooked through, and it seemed it was the best food they had ever eaten. While Carlin skewered and cooked more venison, Jim cut some of the meat into thin strips and hung it to dry in the smoke from the fire. He knew jerky would keep for a long time. Carol made clay pots and plates, most of which would ultimately crack from drying too rapidly.

When the twilight descended upon them, Jim Peters had created a shelter of sorts. By stringing the rope between two trees, and draping the deer hide over it, he fashioned a roof. Carol cut fresh soft boughs from the copious evergreens to cover the floor of the shelter. The back wall was formed by two large stumps that were close together. The gap between them was closed by two foot wide strips of heavy birch bark, cut from a tree felled by a recent lightning bolt. Now, much of the heat from the fire was trapped in the shelter, and it became warm and cozy. Tired, but satisfied with their accomplishments, they fell asleep early and didn't awaken until the chill of dawn invaded their new lair.

Carlin was the first to awaken. It was the nightmare that shocked him into consciousness. Vivid in his mind, it was much too graphic to sleep through. He could see again, the crash of the Cessna, but more frightening. he could see Jim Peters and Carol Danse dying in the frigid water. Worse, in the dream he was the only one to survive. But his survival was ripped asunder by frequent visits from the dead, and they charged him with negligence, haunting him every day.

Carlin opened his eyes and shook his head. He scanned the shelter, happy to find Carol sleeping on the bough bed she had made for them, and Jim, was snoring lightly. Jim Peters was the man who could get them out of the tragedy that had befallen them.

Carlin crawled out of the shelter to stoke the fire again. Sitting at the edge of the original fire, were the clay items Carol had fashioned the night before. There were six of them, and four were cracked. The remaining pair had hardened without a crack, although they had warped slightly. One was a large bowl, almost fifteen inches across, the second was a deep pot capable of holding more than a quart of water. Carlin buried the latter two items in the hot coals and piled fresh fuel on the fire. Within minutes the flames were beginning to consume the small logs Carol had dragged to the fire the previous evening.

Carlin, with his crutch, hobbled into the woods. Remnants of his nightmare drifted through his mind like wisps of fog, and now a deep fear haunted him. How long would it be before a search was mounted for them? Who would initiate it? Could they survive on melted snow and deer meat? The answer to the question could be expressed in one small word – NO. More questions plagued him. If they found a source of food, how could they prepare it with no cooking utensils. If Carol's clay bowl wouldn't hold water, they couldn't even melt snow to drink. If only he had waited a little longer before trying to fly out – If only the sun had de-iced the wings of the Cessna – If only he had left the gear behind ....

"The Ojibwa believe that a hunter who comes home empty

handed, will be a better hunter the next day," Jim Peters said, "I know you are tearing yourself apart with guilt, but that cannot help us. You are a better hunter today Carlin, and so am I."

"I didn't hear you get up," Carlin said quietly, "I had a bad night. It was a series of nightmares!"

"Punishing yourself about an accident will not help our situation," Jim said, "we must prepare for a long stay, and we have to figure how to get out when the opportunity comes up."

"Cut the crap Jim," Carlin said, "we can't even boil water or cook without containers. How the hell are we supposed to get out?"

"It is possible we won't be found," Jim said, "and we must be ready to winter here if no one finds us. We can do it Carlin – we can do it. In the spring we will canoe out as soon as the rivers are open, but there are things we must do now to make it possible. Once the ground is frozen deep it's too late."

"Well it will be difficult for three of us to ride a one man inflatable kayak even if we can recover it from the plane," Carlin said sarcastically.

The sarcasm irritated Jim Peters. Jim understood the dangerous situation confronting them, and he had established a plan to deal with the dangers. He was an easy going mild mannered man, but now, for just a few moments he lost it. "Why don't you stop feeling sorry for yourself," Jim almost shouted, shaking with rage, "and stop being such a perfect asshole."

Carlin was shocked at the words from his friend – in all the years they had been companions, Jim had never spoken a word to him in anger. Carlin's face burned and Jim's words echoed in his head. He wanted to lash out and knock Peters to the ground. His feelings altered from a sense of shock, to a sense of outrage, and breathing deeply, he took control of his emotions.

For the first time in their long friendship, Carlin turned his back on his friend, and silently he hobbled toward the shelter.

Carol stood near the fire, examining the cracked clay items she had fashioned the previous evening. Her face reflected the deep disappointment she felt, and she could not stem the rush of hopelessness that overcame her. She heard Carlin approaching, and he intuitively read the message of fear and despair in her eyes.

G. WM. GOTRO

"They weren't all cracked," he said, trying to cheer her up. Carol counted the pieces.

"Oh yes," she said, "there were six. Where are the other two?"

"I buried them in the coals an hour ago," he said softly, "to finish baking, but we can rake them out now I suppose." Using a green sapling, he scraped away the hot yellow coals, and carefully withdrew the bowl and the jug. He placed them at the edge of the fire. "It would be best to let them cool slowly," he said, a sad smile crossing his face.

Carol was ecstatic at her accomplishment, but she sensed Carlin's distress. "What's wrong? What has happened, and where is Jim?"

"Oh, we had a disagreement earlier," he said, "I guess he told me my fortune, but I deserved it."

The alarm bells went off in her mind. "What was it all about?" She asked, concerned about the nature of the conflict between the two men.

"Survival," he said honestly, "a matter of survival."

"Do you doubt our chances Carlin?" She asked.

"If we don't see a search plane soon I do."

Jim Peters returned to the shelter twenty minutes after the incident with Carlin. He had time to think about the conflict and the ramifications of split opinions and objectives. Jim knew the situation was ugly, but he believed one of the band members would report them missing in the vicinity of the old village. He regretted the words he had said to Carlin, and now he wanted to make amends. He approached Carlin and placed a hand on his elbow. "I'm sorry for what I said back there Carlin. You are the best friend I ever had, and I was out of line talking to you that way."

"It's okay Jim," Carlin said beaming, "I was out of line too – what do you think we should do today?"

Jim felt a wave of relief. He loved Carlin like a brother and was despondent when they were at odds. "Why don't you two work at improving the shelter today while I go back to the village. There are some things I want from there, and I forgot them yesterday."

Carlin racked his brain for a clue to why Jim would hike five miles back to the village, but he respected the man's privacy.

"Okay you're on. Carol and I will turn this place into a palace of delight," he said laughing, and deep inside he was relieved and happy that his relationship with Jim Peters was restored to its former status.

Taking a few strips of jerky, and the rifle, Jim left them and trekked at a fast pace toward the village where his grandfather had died many years before.

Jim moved fast over the trail and though he saw a number of grouse he didn't shoot. Seventeen .22 bullets remained in his arsenal. As he neared the village he slowed his pace. Fresh deer tracks were everywhere, but his purpose was not hunting for deer but one of recovery. After a brief search, he found the big tin that had contained the beans Carol provided for their first meal. With it, they could boil water, make soups, and carry hot coals from one place to another.

Jim's next task was to locate one of the houses Carol had missed. It was located on the north side of the village, and was the most distant dwelling from the river. It was the home of his grandfather, but now all that remained were a few small spruce trees near the site of the original dwelling. Jim knew where to look for the treasures from the past, for he had seen them the day after he and his father had buried his grandfather. In what had been a root cellar of sorts he unearthed a pile of glass shards, and four glass jugs that had stored cider vinegar for the old people's use. These he took, along with three small sealing jars still in reasonable condition. Jim Peters covered the site with birch bark, leaves, and snow before returning to Crystal Lake.

Using his shirt as a carry all, Jim began the long trek back while his mind explored new ideas for survival. He would cut the bottom two inches from three of the jugs to make plates and cooking utensils. The tops could be plugged with whittled pegs and used as containers for either liquids or solids. The tin could be used directly over the fire for cooking – now all they needed was something to cook.

Jim moved off the established trail and deeper into the woods. He came to an area that had once been cultivated by his people to grow maize.

Now, the weeds stood tall above the snow in the centre of the field, and close to the tree line the ground was almost bare but covered with frost struck dandelions. He worked with his belt knife, loosening a square yard of soil, and pulling up the roots. He harvested a pound or more before continuing his journey. An hour later he could smell the smoke from the campfire at Crystal Lake and it encouraged him to increase his pace. He was astounded at what he found at the shelter.

Carlin and Carol had spent three hours harvesting bulrushes from the wet land around the pool. Some of the roots were cleaned and overfilled Carol's big bowl. The remainder were drying on the new rock fireplace. Those that had dried already had been pounded into flour in the small cups she had made. The entrails from the deer had been cleaned and hung in long strips on a rack made from small saplings. The rack was unique, as there were no fastenings used in its assembly – it was woven into a self supporting A-frame structure. The technique had also been employed in other ways.

The slender fronds or leaves combined with long thin willow shoots, had also been woven into large squares, which now formed a primitive roof over the lean-to. Using the same technique, side walls enclosed the shelter on all sides, except the front. It was now possible to stay comfortably warm with a much smaller fire. When Jim saw the new fireplace and shelter he was highly impressed and congratulated them.

"You have done very well my brother and sister," he said in a parody of Chief Dan George. "This is a fine longhouse, even though it is really short. In the next few days we may be able to build a real shorthouse – a one holer with a moon cut out in the door."

They all laughed at Jim's Indian joke, and then he opened his carryall revealing the four jugs, the sealing jars, the big tin can, and the pile of roots.

"Next summer we can pick grapes and fill the jugs with wine?" Carlin teased, "and can we smoke the roots perhaps."

"No my dumb white brother," Jim said in defense, "we will drink the powdered roots, for they are bush coffee."

"And the Jugs?" Carlin asked.

"Soon you will see the wonder of the red man's mind," Jim replied, continuing the parody, "for I your red brother, will create from these glass baubles, plates and containers beyond belief."

While he talked, he wrapped his bootlace around the jug to give him a line, and scored the glass with a sharp piece of granite from the beach. Jim then rubbed pine resin into a piece of fine root from a sapling. He tied it around one of the jugs, two inches from the bottom. Then filling the jug to the line with water, he ignited the root with a burning twig from the fire. As the flame died out, he tapped the glass with his belt knife, and with a 'zzzzzzzzzt', the top and bottom separated cleanly, leaving him a two inch deep plate and a jug without a bottom. He repeated the procedure on the second jug, but the third one shattered. They voted to keep the fourth intact for storing water from melted snow.

The tin can was filled with water, and set into the hot coals, and a piece of dandelion root was toasting over the fire. It began to smoke, and Jim removed it from the heat. He used his knife to scrape the roasted root, and it yielded a small mound of dark powder. When the water began to boil, the powder was added and the result was a hot bitter brew that might pass for coffee.

The bulrush roots were very dry and Carol powdered them, turning them into a nutritious flour. The tin can was filled with water and brought to a boil, fresh chunks of venison were added and allowed to simmer, and finally flour was added. The resulting stew was filling. After eating they experienced a sense of well being.

Jim Peters suddenly remembered he had put his pipe in the inner pocket of his jacket before they took off in the Cessna. He felt for it now and detected the lump that was the bowl. When he withdrew it, the stem was broken, rendering the pipe useless. He had seen kinnikinnick growing around the pond, and it could be used as a strong tobacco. Two good hours of daylight remained and while Carlin tended the campfire, Carol and Jim walked halfway around the frozen pond gathering anything that would be useful. The kinnikinnick was dry and they collected a large amount in a short time. Jim cut a number of maple saplings of differing diameters and lengths while Carol, at Jim's suggestion, collected milkweed pods, before returning to the campsite.

They sat round the fire through the evening, talking and working. Carol and Carlin were given the task of opening the milkweed pods, to recover the fine down surrounding the seeds within. Their efforts resulted in a large pile of clean, white hair-like material. It was useful as packing for pillows, clothing insulation, and being waterproof, suitable for a flotation device.

Jim carved the shape of a pipe from a piece of maple and when it was finished he split it in half along its length. Carlin thought Jim had gone mad.

"Why did you do that?" He asked shaking his head.

"Watch," Jim said, "how I drill a hole without a drill."

He hollowed out the bowl in each half, and then, using the sharp point of his knife he deftly stripped out the soft heart wood from the stem to the bowl. Next, he shaved thin slices of a deer hoof. In one of Carol's clay cups, Jim put the shavings and a little water. He set it in the hot coals to boil. While it heated, he cut very thin strips from the raw hide, and soaked them in water. When the mixture in the little cup had boiled he added a little gum from a nearby balsam tree trunk. After stirring the mixture to a smooth paste, he applied it to the two halves of the carved pipe and bound them with rawhide. Carol and Carlin had watched him with an intensity that bordered on reverence. The pipe was a masterpiece, and Jim knew Carlin would treasure it for the rest of his life.

Carlin, I know how much you like a pipe of tobacco. My pipe was broken in the crash, and decided to fix it. I thought you would like to have your pipe so I made one for you. Tomorrow the glue will be set and you can use it." Jim handed the pipe to Carlin, cradled in his big hands like a newborn child. It was an emotional moment as Carlin accepted the gift.

"Thank you Mr. Peters," he said sincerely, "but what about YOUR broken pipe?"

Jim took a little maple twig from his pocket and shaved the bark from it. "Oh mine will be fixed by morning." He grinned at Carol, "Should I make a pipe for you too Carol?"

"I don't smoke," she said laughing, "but an aspirin to dull the ache in my wrist, some soap, and a toothbrush would be nice"

"We will get the aspirin and toothbrush in the morning," Jim said, "but the bar of soap may take a little longer."

3

Farewell To Rescue

Seven days after the crash, they were planning a new and more comfortable home site when they heard the plane. Suddenly all thoughts of the home site vanished like eiderdown before a hurricane. The day was overcast and a fine powder snow was being blown about by a capricious wind. Jim feared going out on Crystal Lake, unsure of the thickness of the ice. From the lake edge he searched the sky, looking for the rescue plane.

Orren Flagg was Jim Peters cousin, and band chief. He asked Stuart Fraser, a local bush pilot, to keep a lookout for Carlin's Cessna around Crystal Lake. Chief Flagg told the pilot he was surprised that Jim Peters, Carlin and the woman had not returned. Orren Flagg and Fraser were unaware that the lakes to the north had frozen over, and Fraser's DeHavilland Beaver was still on floats.

On his next flight, Fraser noted that Chippewa Lake, fifty miles south of Crystal Lake was the last open water he had seen. He flew over Crystal Lake at five thousand feet, and could see little but blowing snow on its surface. Fraser turned for home, and for a moment he heard again the concern on the old chief's voice when he spoke about his cousin. Fraser eased the throttle back and sent the Beaver in a long shallow dive, leveling out at five hundred feet. He flew the length of the lake along the south shore, seeing nothing but a cow moose. Fraser opened the throttle again, climbing to two thousand feet, and with visibility diminishing, set a course for home. The following day, he would report back to Chief Flagg that he had searched the area at five hundred feet and Carlin's plane was definitely not at, or near Crystal Lake.

As the sound of the plane diminished, Jim Peters returned to the campsite, a deep sense of foreboding gnawing at his insides.

When he arrived, Carlin was hobbling around the fire, and Carol stood, her arms wrapped around her, as though hugging herself in consolation.

"Did he see us?" she asked, but the look in Jim Peters' eyes answered her question. Carlin remained quiet. He knew the pilot hadn't made visual contact. If he had seen Jim or the campsite he would have circled several times to show them that he too was on floats and unable to land this far north.

"No Carol," Carlin said softly, "the pilot didn't see us, but I think he will come back."

"Don't lie to me goddamit. I'm not some stupid twit," she said vehemently. "I know we're stuck here and it isn't likely we can survive the winter in this God forsaken place. If you hadn't ..."

"That's enough Ms. Danse. You have already said too much," Jim Peters growled, "You don't know what you're talking about." He turned his back on her and walked away a few yards, then facing her once more he said, "Most pilots wouldn't have had the guts to do what Carlin did. We almost made it into the air and safety. He didn't know the sunken log was there. Charlie Redwing told me they had removed the deadheads in the channel – but they missed one. I think you owe Carlin an apology."

"I don't owe Carlin a damned thing," she replied, "I want out of here, and soon." She tightened the drawstring on her parka and marched off to the lake. Her condemnation of Carlin's attempt to get them out was unfair and she knew it, but she was frightened now by the prospects of the impending winter.

Though Carol Danse was a strong and resourceful woman she found herself unable to face the deprivations and certain suffering of remaining at Crystal Lake for the winter. She began to cry silently, regretting the bitter words she had spoken to Carlin. She told herself that she was right in her assessment of his judgment regarding the flight out, and she knew she couldn't just go back and apologize. She heard a soft footfall in the snow behind her and turned quickly.

"You had better come back now Ms. Danse," Jim said gently, "It is too cold to be away from the fire for long. I want to remind you of something important."

"What?" she asked, wiping the tears away with her sleeve.

"Do you remember the question you asked Carlin the day we landed here? You asked him a question while you were still standing on the float."

"I don't remember," she said, "that seems like a year ago considering what happened."

"Then let me refresh your memory," Jim said, looking directly into her eyes. "You asked him when he would pick you up. He could have flown out to the comfort of his home but he didn't. You didn't expect him to stay, did you?"

"No," she admitted, studying her feet. "No I didn't expect him to stay."

"If he had left you, he would have returned to OntAir and safety. He couldn't have flown you out until the freeze up in the south. The plane that flew over this morning was on floats.

The lakes down there are not frozen yet or he would have been on skis. One way or another you would have been stuck here for two or three weeks. His decision to stay with you cost him his plane and a broken ankle that's a big price to pay for love!"

"For love," she repeated, astonished at the idea. "What makes you think Carlin could love anything but his plane?"

Jim looked deep into her eyes again, and turning away, he left her standing there, cold and alone. Carlin was sitting in the shelter braiding three thin strips of rawhide into a light rope. He was depressed and hurt, and once more he had taken the blame for their plight. Jim's kindness in defending him was, at the same time, appreciated and unwanted. If Carol Danse detested him for his ineptitude to get them to safety then to hell with her – he had done his best and failed. There was nothing more to say.

"Don't feel bad Carlin," Jim said, "she doesn't know what she is talking about." He took his pipe from his pocket and loaded it with tobacco, then taking a twig from the fire he lit it and inhaled deeply. "You want some tobacco?" He asked proffering the little doeskin pouch to Carlin.

"Nah," Carlin replied, "that kinnikinnick tastes like crap."

Jim knew Carlin didn't mean to hurt his feelings and laughed. "I know it isn't like Erinmore flake," he said, "but you will like it better by spring." Carlin thought about the long weeks before the sun climbed high in the sky again and laughed.

"You're probably right," Carlin agreed. "Gimme the goddam stuff before it's all gone and I have nothing to smoke." He drew his new maple pipe from his breast pocket.

He packed it with the dry kinnikinnick after moistening it with his breath, and lit it. The smoke was strong and sharp, and just for a second or two it made his head spin.

"Carlin, can we talk in private?" It was Carol Danse, and now, her once lovely face was streaked with tears. Her voice quavered, and Carlin, touched by the transformation, was filled with apprehension.

"Okay," Carlin said agreeably, and he struggled to get to his feet. He reached for his crutch, intending to walk a short distance from the shelter.

"No Carlin," Jim insisted, "stay here, I have to go anyhow, I saw fresh moose tracks at the lake, and we should get as much meat as we can before it gets away from us." He picked up the .410. "I opened the shells and dried them. I'm sure they will fire now. I will be back in a couple of hours – don't kill each other while I'm gone." He left the campsite, heading in the direction of the lake.

Carlin watched Jim disappear down the trail and then turned to Carol. "Look Ms. Danse if you want to flail me a little more about my decisions you are wasting your time and ..."

"No, no," she said, her eyes filling with tears again, "I will never raise that subject again – I was in the wrong and I apologize." She came to him then and with her arms around his waist, she laid her head on his shoulder. "I'm sorry I hurt you Carlin – so very sorry, can you forgive me?"

"There is nothing to forgive," he said, and he kissed her forehead lightly. "Let's work together at survival."

Through the afternoon Carlin taught her techniques for living off the land. He scraped the soft inner bark of a willow and gave it to her to chew. Within a few minutes the pain in her wrist receded. He explained the properties of the salicylic acid in the bark as natural aspirin. With a rock, he crushed the end of a little willow twig until it was soft and resilient. Then using charcoal from the fire, he cleaned his teeth until they sparkled as white as the new fallen snow, and she did likewise. Using fat from the venison and ash from the fire, he taught her how to make soap, and they laughed and enjoyed the remainder of the day.

It was three o'clock when they heard the shot – it wasn't the sharp crack of a .22, but the boom of a shotgun. The sun was almost down when Jim returned, staggering under the weight of a hind quarter of moose meat. He was covered in blood and looked like death itself. He had shot the moose at point blank range, and had cut its throat before the heart stopped beating. He dumped the fresh meat down in the snow. "Cut what you need from this for supper," he said, fatigue showing in his face, "I have to go back for the rest."

"Not tonight Jim," Carlin said, "we can all go tomorrow."

"No, it has to be now," Jim said, I must bring the hide back even if the wolves get the meat. We'll talk later – I must go."

"Then I'm going with you," Carol said, and Jim Peters knew it was no use arguing with her.

They returned three hours later, skidding the other hind quarter across the snow on the moose hide. They were exhausted and after a meal of roasted moose meat washed down with bush coffee, the three slept deeply until morning.

Shortly after daylight, Jim and Carol scraped the last remnants of flesh from the hide, and rubbed a paste made from ashes over both sides of the skin. Within three days or so they would scrape it again, thereby removing any remaining flesh and all the hair. Jim knew that three more hides cured in this manner, would give them enough to cover the poles of a tipi. Jim Peters was a man who respected life in all its forms, and he would not kill an animal wantonly. He also realized that there was no chance of surviving the bitter cold of winter without a decent shelter. Too many men in the past had been fooled by an early winter onset, believing that a three sided shelter would suffice. They died a few weeks later from exposure, unable to correct their mistakes. Today he would clean up the last remains of the moose, and move on to the village again. There was a chance for another deer or moose there and he would

G. WM. GOTRO

hang the meat, and bring back only the hide.

When Stuart Fraser told Chief Orren Flagg there was no sign of the Cessna at Crystal Lake, the old man was astounded. Fraser told him about making a high level and a low level pass over the region without spotting any sign of life.

"Are you sure the Cessna wasn't pulled up on the beach somewhere," Orren Flagg asked, "maybe they got frozen in. We have to find them Stuart, we have to find them or they will die."

Fraser felt sorry for the old man, but he had to tell him the truth. "Orren, the Cessna isn't there and it isn't at Lake Chippewa either. What do you want me to say?"

Orren Flagg bowed his head and stared at his boots. Finally after much thought, he raised his eyes and looked directly at Fraser. "I don't have much money Stuart, but I want to see for myself. Will you take me there?"

"I don't care about the money Orren, and of course I'll take you there, but remember we can't land until I convert to skis. This has to be a sightseeing trip – nothing more. I don't make the rules, Great Manitou does."

"I understand all those words Stuart but we can stop at OntAir and pick up Carlin's skis. We can air drop them when we find the Cessna. Okay?"

"Okay Orren," Fraser replied, but he knew they wouldn't need to drop the skis for the Cessna. He was certain it had gone down in the bush somewhere along the way to Crystal Lake. Maybe it was within ten miles of the Ojibwa reservation.

The following morning Fraser and Orren Flagg stopped at OntAir and collected the skis for the Cessna, and a few tools. Fraser was taxiing to the end of the lake when a new thought struck him. "Do you know where Carlin picked up his charter client?" he asked the old man.

"Yes," Orren answered, "they picked her up at the Vermillion River bridge. They had to go to Charlie Redwing's dock at Whitewater. The only fuel Carlin had was three months old."

"Well I hope to hell he made it to Whitewater," Fraser said, and now he was convinced that Carlin and his passengers were down within a few miles from his base. Fraser turned into the wind and opened the throttle. The Beaver was soon up on the step and then airborne. He climbed steeply and leveled off at 1200 feet. He reasoned that Carlin, knowing the stale fuel was dangerous, flew directly to Vermillion, and Fraser followed that course. As he passed over the Vermillion Bridge he turned on a heading for Charlie Redwing's float at Whitewater.

His eyes rarely looked at the instruments – he was too busy looking for a glint of aluminum that would lead him to what he believed would be the crash site.

Fraser landed at Whitewater and checked things out at Charlie Redwing's dock. He found a twenty gallon drum partially filled with fuel, and marked "contaminated". "So," Fraser thought, "Carlin had good fuel and he is somewhere between here and Crystal Lake."

In the days that passed, Jim Peters had taken two more moose, cured the hides, and smoked most of the meat that hadn't been made into pemmican. They had harvested a quantity of rosehips, leached the tannin from acorns, and salvaged a few pounds of shriveled frozen blueberries. Now, he wanted one more hide – then they could build a decent shelter. The bitter cold of winter had set in and life in the three sided windbreak was becoming unbearable. They were almost always cold, and in that state it was difficult to sleep. He had seen wild rice in a marsh near the river and suggested that some may still be salvaged. He and Carol returned to the village, while Carlin peeled the long poles for the tepee.

When Carol and Jim Peters returned, she had gathered several pounds of wild rice that hadn't yet fallen from the stalks, and Jim had the final hide needed for the tepee. Once more they had skidded the meat from the kill, to the camp, using the hide as a toboggan. With splints tightly bound to his ankle, Carlin was now able to limp from place to place without a crutch, and Carol's wrist was almost healed.

Three days later, the new tepee was finished. It was a fine looking structure, very spacious, and with a modest fire burning at its centre, it was warm and comfortable. They prepared a special meal to celebrate their first triumph over the elements.

First a thick venison stew was made using cattail flour, water, and wild mint. Next came thick slices of roasted moose meat and a generous portion of wild rice flavoured with a substance that tasted faintly of licorice. It was taken from the many ferns growing in the area. Finally each had a portion of rich nutty meal made from acorns. When the meal ended, they drank bush coffee and the men smoked kinnikinnick tobacco flavoured with maple. For the first time since the crash, a month ago, they were truly satisfied and happy. The fear had left them, and they knew that despite the many trials they must yet face, their survival was possible.

Rarely did they have brooding time on their hands – they were too busy stockpiling firewood and food, or improving their standard of living in other ways. They coexisted with the wild creatures of the region, they fished the lakes and rivers through the ice, and they fashioned new tools and weapons.

Jim had once found brush wolves raiding one of their meat caches and when he tried to chase them away they attacked him. He killed three of them before they retreated, two with .22 bullets and one with the butt of the rifle and his knife. The wolf pack made off with a substantial part of their cache, but left behind three wolf pelts to cover the trio when they slept. Jim was certain that he, Carol, and Carlin had the better part of the deal.

Oddly, amid their spartan possessions there was one incongruent anomaly – Carlin's watch. It was an electronic watch purchased for less than forty dollars, and had many functions, time, date, illumination and phases of the moon. It was true to the maker's claim and kept on ticking, having survived the crash and the water. Thus, Carlin knew, Christmas was fifteen days away. They had left civilization on October 28th and they survived for 43 days, seen one aeroplane, and heard others on three occasions.

Incredibly, when rescue came to Crystal Lake, the crash victims were not there. They were ice fishing on a river ten miles from their camp when a snow storm stopped them from returning for two days. The day after the snow storm a search and rescue plane landed on Crystal Lake. One of the crew searched the shores of the lake, failing to see the top three feet of the tepee, two hundred yards away, for it was snowcapped. No tracks could be seen on or near the lake and the inevitable conclusion was, that no one had been at this location for a long time. The search of the sector, having found no trace of the Cessna or its occupants, was complete, and the next part of the grid was ten miles to the east.

The following day when the survivors returned, they saw the tracks left by the Search and Rescue crewman, saw the tracks of the aeroplane's skis, and realized that it was unlikely they would return. Strangely, they accepted the hand that fate had dealt them without bitterness or anger. That night the temperature plummeted to forty-two degrees below zero, but in the tepee a hot fire kept the cold at bay and under their wolf skin blankets they lay warm and secure. All of them were assessing their feelings about the near impossible event that had occurred that day.

"We were not meant to get out of this place before spring," Carol said softly. There was no despair in the statement, nor was there much emotion, it was only a flat statement of opinion.

"We have been chosen to experience this event," Jim Peters announced in a low monotone. He stared at the flickering shadows on the tepee walls. "We were meant to remain here for a very good reason. It will be revealed to us in time," he said, closing his eyes.

Carlin lay on his side, watching the dancing flames of the fire. He wondered if Jim was right – wondered why they had been spared, and wondered what new event awaited them. Perhaps they had been brought to this time and place, just to analyze their own individual lives. In the normal world, two hundred and fifty miles to the south, they would be watching television, or discussing some news event, or tinkering with some piece of equipment. It was most unlikely that they would be examining their purpose for being. The smoke in the air irritated his eyes and he closed them.

"Carlin, why do you think we are here?" Carol asked. The inflection in her voice suggested she was afraid of the answer to come. Carlin opened his eyes and looked across at her. She had braided her hair into two short golden braids and she lay on her side, propped up on her elbow. Her eyes searched his face and she listened for his answer, almost holding her breath.

"I agree with Jim, but it goes beyond that. I think we are here to learn. We have already learned tolerance. I tolerate you, you tolerate me, and Jim tolerates both of us. But Jim knew tolerance before we came here. We have learned how to cope with disappointment, and we are to a large extent, masters of our own fate." She was contemplating his words and he smiled at her.

"Don't tell me you weren't disappointed when you saw the

aeroplane's ski tracks in the snow," Carlin said teasing her.

"Well of course I was," she said testily, and she lay back on her sleeping pad, her hands behind her head. She was thinking about the outside world and all the things she was missing. "What do you miss the most?" She asked seriously.

"Well, I guess it would be the peace and quiet," he said trying hard to appear wistful. Jim Peters roared with laughter, and Carol Danse made a vow she would not speak to either of them for a week. She turned over facing the tepee wall in mock anger, but she too was trying to stifle a laugh. They had come a long way – they were happy there.

The full moon spread a pale light over the snow, accentuating the black shadows cast by the conifers. The air was very cold and still, but there were moving shadows too. A wolf pack moved in closer to the tepee and the frozen deer and moose meat. The meat not needed immediately, was cached high in a tree at the edge of the clearing, but the piece they were using was bundled in a scrap of rawhide and buried in the snow five feet from the tepee. A big black and silver male detected the scent of the prize and began to dig down for it. The moment his paws touched the bundle he threw his head back and loosed a long, bone chilling cry of success to his brothers and sisters. Eager to share his prize, they bounded toward him yapping and whining to assert their needs. A fight ensued as a greedy male tried to rip more than his share from the haunch. The pack leader broke up the fight and put the renegade on his back with a bared throat. The renegade, beaten and subjugated loped away from the pack to lick his wounds

Within the tepee the sounds of the encounter were terrifying for Carol. In their frenzy the animals scrambled and tumbled against the walls of the tepee. Finally the pack followed the big male as he made off with the remaining meat. Later they heard the pack howling the news to the moon. The event had a devastating effect on Carol Danse – from that night she rarely strayed far from the tepee without one of the men. Jim tried to help her with the assurance that wolves scarcely bothered a human, but she did not accept his reassurance and her fears remained strong.

As the winter conditions deepened in January their situation became more serious. Jim suggested they ration the remaining wild rice and curtail the use of cattail flour to stretch it out as long as possible. Deer and moose meat were nutritious but it was not high in vitamins. They used a tea made from birch saplings, as a vitamin substitute, and boiled spruce bark and needles for the same purpose. On alternate days they consumed small portions of pemmican which contained fat and berries. Each of them had lost ten or more pounds, but they remained tough and resilient. They spent more time sleeping, but replenishing their firewood daily kept them reasonably active during the coldest weeks of winter.

Jim Peters made two pairs of snowshoes, and when the sun was high each day they trekked for miles through the forest. One morning as the sun warmed the air, Jim suggested ice fishing. Though it took more than an hour to cut through the thick ice on the lake, their efforts were rewarded with a string of fat perch. The return trip to the tepee was filled with the anticipation of a meal that didn't include moose meat and they were delighted. They were unaware of the disaster that lurked a hundred yards away as Jim cleaned the fish. The wolverine watched Jim bury the offal under the snow where they normally disposed of their ashes from the fire.

In the tepee Carol prepared green twig skewers while Carlin piled fresh wood on the fire. They made a soup from pemmican and a spoonful of flour, and roasted their fresh fish over the fire, while the wolverine uncovered the buried offal. He ate part of it then scattered the rest over a wide area, and in his brain he claimed the place as his own. Late in the afternoon, Jim left the tepee and discovered the tracks and other signs of the wolverine. When he returned to the fire, he was shaken. Carlin was concerned.

"There is something wrong Jim. What is it?" Carlin asked.

"We may be in trouble now," Jim said, "we are being visited by a wolverine."

"You told me not to be afraid of a timber wolf and you are frightened by an animal as small as a wolverine?" Carol teased.

"Timber wolves don't hunt humans Carol," Carlin said. "Wolverines are another matter."

"From now on, one of us must stay here at the tepee all the time," Jim said, ignoring Carol's earlier words. "If we leave this place unattended he will destroy everything we have. His ultimate purpose will be to drive us out."

She realized that Jim was serious "But how can a little ..."

"He will shred the tepee walls and ruin all our food stores by scattering them or urinating on them," Jim answered. "He will drag the wolf skins away and defecate on them, and chew through our ropes and snowshoes. Nothing will be safe until I kill him or he kills us – we cannot survive without our stores and shelter."

For two and a half weeks the war raged. At night the wolverine managed to destroy one of their major caches of deer meat, and through the day he remained hidden – finding him was a virtual impossibility. He was a forest ghost, and his weapon was urine. He contaminated every ice fishing hole they cut, and he was cunning, never doing what they thought he would. His campaign was going well, for he had destroyed fifty percent of their meat, and virtually stopped them from fishing. He had urinated against the tepee walls in the night and the place stank.

Had they been in a better position they would have ceded the territory to the beast from hell, but they could not survive anywhere else. They had to destroy him or succumb to the elements and starvation. Finally, Jim had a plan, and he executed it on the first clear night of a full moon. He laid out three pieces of bait, the first was a frozen perch. He placed it fifteen feet from the tepee door flap and urinated on it. The second was a small piece of urine tainted pemmican placed about eight feet from the door. The third was a choice morsel of thawed and untainted moose meat and it lay a hand span from the tepee flap. As darkness fell the survivors took turns watching from a hole in the flap. Three hours passed before the wolverine approached the bait. Carlin was on watch and signaled Jim by holding up three fingers, indicating the animal was at the third bait.

Jim sat patiently on the far side of the fire with the shotgun in his hands. The hammer was back and his finger caressed the trigger. The wily animal sniffed the perch and smelling the man's urine, passed it by disdainfully, and moved to the second bait. Now eight feet from the door, he sniffed the pemmican, uncertain about its origin. The wolverine showed his disdain a second time by urinating on the bait himself. Then he moved quickly to the moose meat, snapping it up and turning to make his getaway. Carlin gave the single finger sign and instantly Jim pulled the trigger. The .410 roared and the buckshot ripped through the deerskin door flap catching the predator squarely in the back of the head. Their ears were ringing and the air in the tepee was filled with the smell of gun powder. Carlin untied the flap and stepped out into the moonlight. The snow was spattered with blood and their enemy was doubled over as though protecting his prize to the end.

"You got him Jim boy, you got him," Carlin shouted in triumph.

"Yeah," Jim said softly, "but you should have signaled sooner. The sonofabitch got the moose meat." Then he dragged the animal back to the tepee where he skinned him. "This fur is valuable," he said, "frost doesn't form on it under any conditions. It is the only thing a wolverine is good for – parka trim."

Carol asked what they should do with the carcass, and Jim told her to let it freeze or let the wolves get it.

In the days that followed, Jim Peters dropped two more moose, and repaired the tepee, cutting away the parts contaminated by the urine of the wolverine.It became home again for them and they worked and whiled away the long winter days. They sometimes heard planes pass overhead but had long since given up trying to signal them. They joked about the day when one landed on Crystal Lake, delivering wealthy fishermen from Toronto or from the Europe. Carlin suggested that they offer them the tepee and early Canadian fishing gear for five hundred a week, guide included.

The days lengthened and Jim Peters began to spend more time hunting for special woods than for game. One morning he called Carlin to help and suggested Carol make breakfast for them all. Jim and Carlin tapped a maple and drew from it a gallon of sap. Carol boiled it down while the men went for more sap. By the end of the day most of their containers were filled with sap and Carol had a dish filled with maple syrup. Pouring a little syrup in the snow resulted in a sugar candy cane. It was the first real sweet they had tasted since their departure from civilization, and it gave the harsh bush coffee a superb flavour. Carlin and Carol worked for days, collecting sap and boiling it down to make maple sugar, but Jim's mind was on the canoe that would take them home.

Long cedar branches split lengthwise yielded the gunwales for a sixteen foot canoe. They were bound together at the ends, and four spreaders were inserted along the length to create the pointed ellipse that formed the general shape of the canoe. A set of stakes were driven into the ground, and the gunnels were suspended from them. In the weeks that followed, twenty five ribs were fashioned and fastened to the gunnels using sharpened maple pegs. An inner keel was constructed and pegged to the ribs in the same manner. Jim taught the others to split three foot long cedar logs into strips a quarter inch thick and three to four inches wide. By the middle of March, the frame was ready for the application of the cedar slats that had been steamed to the shape of the ribs. They were secured to the gunnels with wood pegs and lashings of thin black spruce root. Now the vessel was ready for the birch bark skin. They needed bark from trees that were nine to ten inches in diameter.

The birch trees near Crystal Lake, were too small to be useful. Jim searched five hours to the east, while Carlin searched five hours to the west, finding nothing suitable. The following day they searched to the north and south, but the result was the same, the trees were too small.

"To get back to civilization we need the canoe," Jim said simply, "we must find a good stand of birch, and find it soon." Neither Carlin nor Carol could understand Jim's anxiety.

Springtime was upon them, the snow melted a little more each day, and summer would soon follow – they had survived the winter. Jim Peters was worried, and Carlin was the first to understand. The moose meat was no longer frozen, and at the end of a warm day it began to turn rancid. Weevils had invaded the remaining flour, and the wild rice and pemmican were gone, yet Jim didn't go hunting – he spent every waking moment trying to finish the canoe.

One morning there was no breakfast and Carlin put the gun over his arm. "If you give me a few shells I will try to bag a deer while you finish the canoe," he said. The sarcasm wasn't wasted on Jim, but his answer hit Carlin like a slap in the face.

"The shotgun shells were gone three weeks ago," Jim answered.

Carlin didn't need a masters degree to know that they were in big trouble. "What about .22 cartridges," he asked, "how many do we have left?" With no ammunition they could not hunt big game.

"Eight," Jim answered, "we have eight .22 cartridges left."

He smiled at Carlin. It was a melancholy smile devoid of hope now. "We have to survive on fish," he said, "and at best, we have a two hundred and fifty mile journey ahead of us." Carlin thought about Jim's words – the berries wouldn't ripen until August nor would wild rice be ready until autumn. There was no way to store meat other than drying it in the smoke from the fire and fresh meat would only keep for a day or so. Indeed, summer might be much more onerous than the bitter winter they had just survived!

"Give me two or three bullets," he said holding his hand out, "you work on the canoe, and I'll search for birch bark." There was a strong commitment in his manner and Jim saw, for a moment, a side of Carlin he had never seen before. Carol recognized it too.

"I'm going with you," she said flatly.

"I can travel faster alone," Carlin said bluntly, but he knew she had no intention of changing her mind. He put a hand on Jim's shoulder. "I won't be back until late tomorrow, but I will bring you some bark." He turned to Carol. "Let's get moving," he said, "we have nine hours before dark."

They moved to the south east at a rapid pace, and though Carlin still walked with a slight limp, Carol found it difficult to keep up to him. Twice through the afternoon they encountered swamps and bogs which slowed their progress, but they found no groves of large birch trees. They stopped to rest, and glancing at his watch, Carlin noted the time at 4:30 P.M. They had left the campsite at 10:00 A.M. – six and a half hours elapsed and he estimated the straight line distance covered as less than nine miles.

"It's not good enough," he said, "we have to do better than this – let's try for another mile or two before dark." He flashed her a broad smile but she knew he wasn't very confident.

"I'm really hungry," she said, leaning against him, "meals seem to be a long way apart."She picked up the little buckskin pack Jim had made for her, and led the way. Two hundred yards later they came to the next swamp. Swinging westward they skirted it, keeping to the high ground, and it was deep twilight when they stopped for the night.

Carlin found some dry tinder in a rotten log and they opened the clay pot in which they carried some hot coals. He tried to blow them back to life, but there was little life left in them. He was about to give up when a tiny spark flared momentarily. He dusted it with a pinch of tinder and blew gently. A wisp of smoke rose from the cup and the spark brightened. He repeated the procedure and soon he was able to add a tiny curl of birch bark she handed him. Another gentle breath, and the bark burst into flame. He emptied the cup into the small pile of tinder, bark and twigs and nursed the little flame into a hot fire. They heated water in the jar she carried and added powdered dandelion root and a little maple sugar. Later they shared the sweet bush coffee and some jerky, and Carlin filled his pipe with kinnikinnick and smoked.

By the light of the fire she cut cedar and pine boughs with his knife and made a dry bed. The cold stars glittered above, an owl hooted the question 'WHO?' They crawled under the wolf skins and holding each other close, they slept. Several times through the night, Carlin got up to feed the fire and then returned gratefully to the bed and her warmth.

The morning dawned overcast and cool. Carlin made coffee again and as the day lightened he realized they were a mile from a high bluff – he also head the faint murmur of running water. While Carol finished her coffee he reconnoitred the area and found a fine little stream that fed a deep pool. He returned to the camp to tell Carol that he was going to take time out to shower! She laughed at him, and put more water on for coffee refills.

He stripped off his clothes and waded into the pool from a tiny sand beach. The water was ice cold and took his breath away. With a little fine sand he scrubbed himself from head to toe, and then immersed himself once more in the pool. Cleansed and glowing, Carlin spread his clothes on the sand and lay on them, to let the morning breeze dry his skin. He closed his eyes and thought about the winter they had just come through. He was hungry, and he salivated at the thought of the moose meat stews with wild rice. He was aware of another hunger too – he had fallen in love with Carol on that first day, but she always seemed to be behind a shield. He had convinced himself that she was in love with Jim and he couldn't interfere with their relationship. Carlin tried to get her out of his mind – to think of the canoe trip back to civilization, but she haunted him always. He drifted into a light sleep.

Drops of water pattered on his skin. He had hoped it wouldn't rain, and he opened his eyes. She was standing over him, naked, and laughing at his reaction.

"Carlin you're blushing," she said seductively, kneeling down in the sand, She leaned over, her wet breasts brushing his chest, and she kissed him. He drew her down on the sand and they consummated their love then, fiercely at first, then slowly with deep passion. Carlin at last, felt total peace and happiness.

"I always thought you were in love with Jim," Carlin said as he dressed. "I have loved you for months, but I didn't think I stood a chance. I guess I've been a loner for so long I don't know how to treat a woman.

"Carlin, the three of us have been together for months and I love Jim Peters as a good friend, but I never wanted him as my lover. I wanted you, but you never seemed to care." She shrugged her shoulders and made marks in the sand with her toe.

"Oh I always cared," Carlin replied, "I just thought I had no chance with you. It was easier to turn away than deal with rejection." He held his hand out to her and drew her close. Her arms encircled his waist, then she kissed him, and the promise in the kiss affirmed that she would never reject him. In that moment, Carlin was happier than he had ever been before.

They reached the top of the high bluff by 10:00 A.M. and from that vantage point, were able to scan the terrain in all directions for several miles. Though the forest in that part of northern Ontario was mainly coniferous, it was going through a change. Had it been full summer they wouldn't have seen the birch grove, but the leaf buds on the deciduous trees had not yet opened. The white birch bark showed clearly for miles. Carlin estimated the edge of the grove to be less than three miles away, and the surrounding terrain was well above any marsh or swamp land.

"Let's go and bring back a supply of bark for Jim," Carol said, her face flushed with the excitement of the find.

"No," Carlin answered gently. "Can you see the lake about four miles northwest of the grove?" He pointed it out for her. "Notice too, the water in that shallow valley to the west." She followed his out thrust arm, catching the glint of water in the morning sun. "I suspect that is a river emptying the lake." He pointed to the south where a big body of water sparkled. "The river must flow to that lake – it may be a major system, and it flows to the north."

She didn't have to be told, she understood immediately – they would bring Mohammed to the mountain. They would bring the tepee to the grove and build the canoe there, and when it was done they would use the river system to move south to civilization. Their trek back to Crystal Lake couldn't be done in a day. They had no more food and the hot coal they carried in the container had died, leaving them without fire. Carlin pushed hard toward Crystal Lake, but as the day ended and twilight deepened they cut cedar and spruce boughs to once again make a bed of sorts. They were cold and hungry but when she snuggled to him for warmth, he held her close and contentment filled him as their bodies melded together.

In the morning they moved out quickly and arrived at the tepee on Crystal Lake before noon. Jim Peters was not there to greet them. Carlin entered the tepee and found the fire pit to be almost cold. It had not been fed with fuel for what he estimated was a day and a half. He ran his hand through the ashes and digging there, he found a hot coal no bigger than a penny. Carol provided him with tinder and birch bark and he managed to nurse the coal to life. Soon they were able to feed themselves and sip hot bush coffee with maple sugar. Though their fare was spartan, they felt much better, and they speculated on where Jim Peters was, and why.

The frame of the canoe was virtually complete and appeared ready for covering, The signs of Jim's most recent activity suggested that he had been gone for more than a day. Carlin was sure that Jim would not let the fire die without a very good reason. He was also aware that he would not sleep away from the tepee unless he was forced by necessity. Carlin didn't voice his concern, keeping his dark thoughts to himself, but Carol sensed his anxiety.

"Maybe Jim is hunting for fresh food," she suggested, trying to ease Carlin's apprehension.

"Yeah, jerky is getting hard to take," he replied, turning away from her. "He is either hunting or searching for bark to begin covering the canoe." The lie was not very convincing and she knew it. The tension that lay between them was driving them apart like a wedge. An hour passed in near silence as they did the myriad chores around the tepee. Finally she came to him and with her head on his shoulder and her arms around his waist she began to cry softly. Carlin held her close and stroked her hair. "If he isn't back by dark, we will search for him in the morning," he said in an undertone, "He didn't go hunting," Carlin said. "we had the gun."

Throughout the day, they worked toward provisioning for their trip south. Carlin caught a string of fish, cleaned, and smoke cured them. Carol again, collected cattail roots. The heads of the cattails could be used to make a different sort of flour. While the new growth had not yet developed, she collected several pounds of old dry heads missed previously. The afternoon passed quickly as they processed their newfound treasures. After a meal of fresh baked pickerel and two small pieces of ersatz bannock they rested and talked of the planned return to civilization. They consciously avoided the subject of Jim, hoping he would arrive before dark.

The sun had dropped beneath the tree tops and the long shadows disappeared, leaving behind the gray twilight of evening. Carlin set water to boil and they discussed what they might find for an evening meal. Carol ambled to the lake, to wash the utensils they had used for their midday meal.

"Where is my birch bark?" She jumped at the unexpected sound of Jim Peters' voice.

"Dammit Jim you frightened me – in fact you frightened both of us. Carlin was very worried when we returned and you were gone," she said, scolding him as though he were a naughty child. He stood five feet from her, his hands behind his back, his head bowed slightly.

"I am sorry mother," he said, trying to suppress a laugh, "I brought you a gift." He handed her three pounds of unwrapped fresh pink meat. "Can we have supper now?" They both laughed at each other then, and returned to the tepee. Carlin was relieved and delighted to see Jim home.

"Where were you?" Carlin asked

"Hunting for fresh meat," Jim said seriously.

"Oh yeah," Carlin responded, "my red brother must have hunted locusts – for I, Carlin, have the thunder stick." They enjoyed the parody, both playing 'B' grade Hollywood Indians.

"I brought back fresh meat," Jim said nodding his head in Carol's direction, "I have given it to grandmother – what did you bring back?"

"Nothing but grandmother," Carlin said simply, and though she feigned anger they all enjoyed the joke – they were happy to be together again.

They ate their fill of the delicious fresh meat that tasted like pork or chicken, and after dinner the men smoked kinnikinnick.

"That meat was great Jim," Carol said. "What was it?"

"One of the few animals a man can take without a weapon," Jim answered, "it was porcupine. They are slow moving and even a light tap on the nose with a stick is fatal." He paused for a moment, and then, "Did you find any old, mature birches?"

"We found a big grove of old trees," Carlin said, "it's one and a half, maybe two days from here – nice country too. I suggest we move camp to that area – tomorrow."

Carol was enthusiastic about the move. "It is beautiful over there Jim, and Carlin didn't mention the river and lake system. It appears to lead directly south as far as the horizon."

The move to the birch grove was tough – they packed their meagre belongings into the skins from the tepee, and were surprised to find they had more to carry than could be moved easily. They worked late into the night making shoulder packs from one of the spare deer skins, and finally gave in to fatigue. Carlin was the last to fall asleep, concerned with the magnitude of the undertaking. It was one thing travelling lightly across the tangle of bush and outcroppings of granite, but it was quite another carrying sixty pounds of hide and clay containers. Crossing the swamps would take twice as long loaded down with the raw necessities of life, and of course there was the canoe skeleton.

4

DEATH IS ALWAYS EASY

The trek to what they called, Birch Grove was gruelling. Unable to find fresh clay near the swamps, they were bitten by black flies until their eyes were swollen shut, and when the flies receded they were replaced by mosquitoes. Even a small lump of clay would have helped – mixed with water, the clay paste applied to the exposed skin prevented many of the bites when it dried. The clay would not prevent the pests from swarming around them, but made it much more difficult for the insects to penetrate the skin. There was no way to avoid the swamps, and in them, the hydrogen sulphide gas stank and attracted more blackflies. Carrying the heavy hides, they stumbled and fell into the black muck, and when it happened they struggled to their feet and continued. Exhausted, they dumped their belongings at the waters' edge in the birch grove, late in the afternoon of the second day. They didn't bother with a fire, they didn't prepare an evening meal, they simply spread the hides on the ground and slept.

Carlin began his day an hour before the others were awake, by clearing a large area upon which the tepee would be built. While he worked he thought about Jim. Without him, he and Carol would have died. It was impossible to survive in this country without fire, and Jim was the one who provided it. If anything happened to Jim, he and Carol couldn't make it. He had to learn how to make a fire without a match. Carlin fashioned a fire drill similar to Jim's. He gathered a little tinder, and tried unsuccessfully to create a spark. On his third attempt, a tiny wisp of smoke began to rise from the point of the fire stick. Encouraged he doubled his efforts and two minutes later, he blew gently on the tinder powder. It began to glow and he added thin, slivers of dry birch bark.

Blowing gently on the tinder again, he coaxed it into a flame. He had done it – he had created fire without a match! Carlin knew that boy scouts were taught how to make fire, but he also knew that few of them ever succeeded. He was very proud of his accomplishment.

When Carol awakened it was to the scent of bush coffee. Jim Peters was snoring lightly and Carlin was sitting in front of a small hot fire. Whatever he was cooking smelled delicious. She slipped out from under the wolf skin blanket and unnoticed, made her way to the pond. She waded in and immersed her lithe body in the cold water. She soaped herself and scrubbed until she was clean, then she returned to the fire. Jim was still asleep but Carlin was nowhere to be seen. She sat by the fire and began to comb her hair. She was almost finished when Carlin silently moved behind her. He encircled her with his arms and pulled her close, whispering in her ear. She kissed him and they embraced for long moments before parting.

"What are you cooking – It smells wonderful," she said peering into the glass dish. It contained a thick pancake which he flipped over, and now the upper surface was golden brown.

"It is made from cattail flour, water, small cubes of meat and fat," he replied, dividing it into three equal pieces with his hunting knife. "I think I will call it Carlin's Super Survival Pizza." Carol accepted her portion and tasted it.

"Carlin, it's fantastic – you could make a fortune with this in civilization," she said laughing. "By the way, it just occurred to me that there was no fire last night. Jim must have brought a coal ...."

"No, no coal. I made a fire drill and it worked," he said trying to conceal his immense pride in the accomplishment. She studied him, trying to fathom the man. Each time she thought she knew him, he said something incredibly profound or did something impossibly difficult. Carlin was a survivor, she concluded, a survivor in everything he did,

Jim Peters also awakened to the smell of bush coffee, and as he approached them, Carlin noticed something he considered very serious. He poured coffee for Jim, added a lump of maple sugar, and pointed to Jim's left boot. "How far do you think you can get with that?" The leather of the upper had separated from the sole, and the boot gaped open. It would have been no problem in any city in Canada, but they were about to embark on a two hundred and fifty mile journey over some of the roughest country in the world. Jim grinned at them with the enigmatic smile of his people.

"These are good for a lot of miles yet. When they are no good any more I will make some new ones," he said, finishing his coffee and wolfing down his portion of Carlin's special bannock. "Hey this is good. You should give up flying and open a pizza place when we get back. You would make a lot more money and you're a better cook than pilot." The last was said in jest, but Carol was affronted by Jim's remark. Carlin suggested they get some work done.

By noon, the tepee had been erected by the men and Carol had collected everything for their beds. She prepared a small midday meal, and after eating they set out to the centre of the birch grove. Jim lost little time selecting the trees from which the canoe bark would be taken, and they worked at removing it in large pieces until the sun touched the tops of the trees on the horizon. They nested the pieces of curved bark inside the largest one, and returned to the campsite.

Carol stirred the ashes of the outdoor campfire and nursed the fire to life. After setting her tin of water to boil she laid a second fire within the tepee. It provided heat and light and the residual smoke kept the mosquitoes outside. She was moving toward the door to bring more wood for the night when she heard the roar.

It was loud enough to set the air to trembling. She had never heard anything like it, not even in her wildest dreams. The big black female bear, hungry from the long winter hibernation attacked the two men. She bounded into the clearing like a cannon ball, swinging a huge paw at Jim Peters, who, hearing her rush, turned toward her. The claws caught him on the side of the head, slashing through the scalp, and the cheek. The blow rendered him unconscious, and drove him to the ground. Turning, the bear roared her challenge again, and attacked Carlin.

He tried to sidestep her rush, and tumbled backward over the canoe frame. He was on his back on the ground when the bear smashed the light framework of the canoe with one mighty swipe of her paw and straddled Carlin. Leaving the tepee Carol jammed a shell into the shotgun and raced toward the bear, who was trying to bite into Carlin's face. Carol drove the butt of the gun into the back of the bear's head. The big animal turned and reared on her hind legs to deal with her attacker. She raised her front paws high, and throwing her head back she roared her rage. It was her first and last mistake. Carol jammed the muzzle of the shotgun into the underside of the bear's lower jaw and pulled the trigger. The gun bucked in her hands and the charge of shot blew the bear's brains out. The big animal toppled backward. She would have crushed Carlin, but he rolled out of her path before she hit the ground.

Carlin heard Carol's thin keening cry, and bleeding from numerous cuts and bites he drew himself painfully to his feet. He held her in his arms, trying to assuage her fears, and guided her to the tepee. "Hot water Carol, we need lots of hot water," he said softly. "I have to help Jim before he bleeds to death." Dragging the big man to the tepee took all the power Carlin had in reserve. They laid him on his bed, and though his eyes were open, he didn't speak, but just stared at them as if they were strangers, His lips were moving slightly but no sound accompanied the movement.

As if by magic, Carol produced four pieces of white cotton. She soaked one piece in warm water and began to clean the wounds made by the bear's claws. Carlin covered Jim Peters with the wolf skins to keep him warm and arrest the shock that was setting in, then he cut the nylon lining from his tattered parka and they used it to bandage Jim's head. Carol made spruce tea and gently urged him to sip it, and though he had not yet uttered a sound, his eyes showed his deep gratitude. After a few minutes had elapsed Jim relaxed visibly and closed his eyes. Carlin was terrified at the thought that his friend was dying, but shortly, Jim's breathing deepened and nature relieved his pain, with the anodyne of sleep.

Carol bathed and cleaned the cuts and bites on Carlin's face and they spent the rest of the evening whispering, afraid to waken Jim. Carlin was unusually introspective.

"Are you okay Carlin?" Carol asked, her eyes clouded with deep concern,

"Yes, a little bruised and battered, but a little older and wiser," he answered softly, staring at the fire. "If that rogue bear had killed Jim and me, what would you have done?" It wasn't set as a question, but as a point from which to view the future.

"I don't know," she replied, a sob catching in her voice. Then, after a long moment of silence, broken only by the popping and hissing of the fire, "I guess I would have buried you and Jim, and there would be no one to bury me. I couldn't survive alone." The tears that coursed silently down her cheeks were tears of gratitude for the lives that were spared. "I guess I would have starved or died of exposure – I don't know how to make a fire with a pair of sticks, I can't hunt, I have never butchered an animal. My life was in your hands from the time I climbed into the Cessna so long ago, and you and Jim have kept me alive for six months." She was crying openly now, fear and shock taking their toll.

Carlin moved close to her, his arm around her shoulder. "No, my love, we survived TOGETHER – as a team, and today YOU saved us all by doing the right thing with the shotgun." He hugged her close and she relaxed, secure in his presence. "By the way," Carlin said, "Where the hell did the white cotton bandages come from?"

She wiped her tears away with her sleeve. "A couple of months back," she said softly, "I was thinking about accidents and I decided I could live without my T-shirt, so I washed and dried it and cut it into strips for bandage." She smiled at him then, and leaving him she went to Jim and touched his forehead. "I don't think there is any fever yet," she whispered.

"I have another question for you," Carlin said, a perplexed look on his battered face. "Where did the shotgun shell come from?"

"The first time the gun misfired after the crash, Jim ejected it in the snow. I picked it up and have had it ever since. I thought that it would dry out sooner or later and I just kept it for an emergency."

The sunrise was still an hour away when Carlin slipped out of the tepee and revived the outdoor fire. In its light, he examined the wreckage of the canoe frame. Three of the main ribs were broken, as was one gunnel. The keel had separated from the stern piece and the small stern ribs lay akimbo. It was a hard judgment call – repair it or start again? He decided to continue with Jim's craftsmanship, and began with the toughest part first. He repaired the stern piece and the small ribs associated with it. The sun had topped the trees before hunger and thirst halted his efforts. Carlin entered the tepee quietly. Carol was asleep, but Jim's eyes were open and unmoving. Carlin was smashed by a fist of fear – the fear that Jim Peters was dead. "Jim," he whispered, "how are you?" To his immense relief, the eyes moved, focusing on his face.

"You look terrible," Jim said in a half whisper.

Carlin was overwhelmed. Jim was okay. "I was really afraid," he said, "I thought you were a goner." He knelt down beside his friend and his hand rested momentarily on Jim's forehead. He didn't comment, but was very much aware that a fever was raging in the big Ojibwa. His concern showed on his face.

"How bad is it?" Jim asked, referring to the damaged canoe frame.

"You have three claw marks that run from the top of your head to just below the lower jaw. The cuts are very deep and you have lost a great deal of blood. The bear missed your jugular though, and Carol has bandaged you very well. You need about thirty stitches and I don't know what to do about that," Carlin said, his eyes glistening with tears barely in check. "Somehow we have to close that wound, and very soon." He was still deeply concerned for Jim's chances of survival.

"We are talking at crossed purposes Carlin," Jim answered in a weak voice, "I meant the canoe frame."

Carlin felt Jim's pain, and saw him wilting visibly. There was a tone of resignation in his voice. "The canoe frame is damaged," Carlin answered, "I started to repair it before daylight. If I get stuck I will come to you for help, but for now you must rest."

Carol had awakened when Carlin entered the tepee, but she lay under the wolf skin in silence trying to analyze their new position. Now she sat up and rubbed her eyes with the back of her hands. "What – no coffee yet," she chided, "you're literally falling down on the job Carlin."

"Coffee would be good," Jim said, and he turned on his bed to make himself more comfortable. Carlin heard the sharp intake of breath as pain engulfed his friend.

He made coffee and maple sugar for Carol and Jim and he

brought a dozen small pieces of tender willow bark. While Jim sipped his coffee, Carlin scraped the salicin from the inner surface of the bark and fed it to Jim to ease his pain. Once ingested it would turn to salicylic acid, the key ingredient in aspirin. Then turning to Carol he said, "You're on your own, boil some water for me, and keep it hot. I will be back within two hours," and then he was gone.

The sky clouded over and the day had grown humid. Mosquitoes and blackflies swarmed in the thousands, attacking anything warm blooded. Carlin was a prime target. With a number of open cuts and wounds, blood was easy to acquire for the insects.

Carlin's long association with the Ojibwa had taught him a great deal about natural healing substances, and now he searched the small lakes and slow moving streams in quest of white water lilies. The roots and leaves could be used to make a healing antiseptic substance for Jim's wounds. Infection had already occurred at two sites and if it could not be stopped he was a candidate for gangrene. Within an hour Carlin found a large pond with a profusion of the white lilies on its surface. He collected only what he could use, leaving the rest to prosper and multiply. Before returning to the tepee Carlin also acquired the last item he needed to treat Jim Peters. He took two lumps of spruce gum from one of the old trees that grew in profusion in that area, and returned to the campsite.

Carol bathed Jim's head wounds again, while Carlin prepared an antiseptic jell made from the water lilies. He coated the freshly cleaned wounds with the substance, and prepared six strips of nylon from his parka liner. These were fashioned into oversized bandaids by coating the ends of the strips with spruce gum. The ragged sides of the wounds were drawn together and held in place by the home made bandaid strips. Jim felt better by the following morning – the antiseptic was working and his temperature was down, but he would not resume work on the canoe for another five days.

Carlin skinned the bear, and smoked the meat. He was not sure about its fitness for human consumption but they dared not waste anything now that their ammunition was almost gone. They had to keep their meat from being contaminated by flies, and after smoking it, Carol suggested they sew it into its own skin. The idea worked well and kept the meat fresh for a longer period of time. While she worked at her task, Carlin repaired the canoe frames. The broken gunnel was repaired, and all the frames and ribs were sound by the time Jim Peters was ready to have his bandages removed.

They were up before daylight on that memorable day, and anxiety charged the air. They were delighted to find the wounds healing well, but Jim Peters would carry the scars of his encounter with the bear for the rest of his life. A small pocket of infection remained on his jaw, just below the ear, and Carol treated it with the pond lily extract daily, until it too healed. Jim often thought about the attention she gave him. She was a good woman, sensitive and thoughtful. Carlin was a lucky guy – it was obvious she was in love with him.

Studying Carlin's repairs to the canoe frame, Jim was impressed with the craftsmanship. The time had come to put the skin on the bones of the canoe, and they began to apply the bark covering. It was a tedious slow process. The bark was sewn to the ribs and gunnels with black spruce roots Jim had saved for months, and the joints were sealed with a compound the Ojibwa had used for centuries. It was made from spruce gum, charcoal powder, and fat. Twice, sections of the bark cracked and split open and they were forced to remove them and start again. All of their time was spent on the craft – there was no hunting or gathering, and their food supplies dwindled. During the evenings in the tepee they fashioned paddles and packed the items to be used on the trek.

Then one morning, Carlin awoke early and realized Jim was gone. It was unusual because Jim was normally the last person to awaken. Carlin opened the tepee door and found the canoe was missing, and the fire was freshly stoked. Perplexed, he made his way to the lake. The sun had just topped the trees and an early morning mist hung low over the water. Carlin could make out a moving shadow in the fog. It was moving toward him and he could hear the soft swish of a paddle. Jim Peters was singing softly, a prayer to the Great Spirit. His was a prayer of thanksgiving, and elation. The grin on his face was cherubic as he beached the canoe. "I finished the canoe this morning and we are on our way home Carlin, we are on our way home!" Carlin had always looked upon

Jim Peters as the great, all wise, strong man, capable of doing impossible feats as routine. Now, Carlin saw the dancing black eyes verging on shedding tears. "For a while, I didn't think we would make it, but we survived and we prospered," Jim said. "We should be able to leave here in a day or two – we need some provisions, but other than that there is no reason to remain here any longer. It's time to go home."

A rare emotion rippled through Carlin. It could best be described as envy. Jim would soon be back with his people, Carol would return to her job, and become a celebrity, and he could go back to the OntAir cabin alone, broke, and without his plane. He felt guilty about the jealousy and tried to hide his true feelings.

"Yes Jim, it is time to go home," he said, but he was just mouthing a platitude. Home meant a new and great loneliness. It meant trying to find work at something other than flying. It meant losing Carol. The guilt struck him again, and he was ashamed that he was thinking only of himself.

Carol, finding the men gone, came down to the lake looking for them. She was delighted to see the canoe in the water, but she was instantly aware of a change in Carlin. "What's wrong," she asked, "you don't look happy, is there something wrong with the canoe?" Her question was directed to Carlin, but before he spoke, Jim answered her question.

"No, the canoe doesn't leak, and it seems to be very stable, but we must check the freeboard." Seeing the puzzled look on her face, Carlin explained.

"He wants to know if it will sink or float with three people and our gear aboard," He jogged to the tepee for another paddle, then they boarded and floated just off shore. The little craft had ample freeboard, did not sit too low in the water. Carlin and Jim began to paddle and the canoe shot forward, skimming over the calm water faster than a man could jog. Gradually the thrill of movement overcame Carlin's concern about his future, and he began to thoroughly enjoy himself. They skirted the shore of the lake for more than a mile before they realized they were hungry. A gentle breeze had arisen to chase the mist away and now they drifted, letting it carry them back to the campsite.

During their breakfast, Jim talked about the journey that lay before them. "Now that we have the means to travel quickly we will have to travel light. That means, the axe, the gun, our sleeping skins and a minimum of utensils. The big bean can, a plate and a cup each and a small cache of food. Any more than that and our freeboard will be compromised in rough weather. Moreover," he said, We are high up in Ontario and most rivers will be flowing north. We will be working against the current most of the time."

"What about shelter Jim? How DO we deal with the rough weather?" Carol asked, concern clouding her eyes.

"I gave that a lot of thought over the last few weeks," Jim answered, "but other more important things pushed comfort aside. We have no shotgun shells left and a few .22 bullets. If we are very lucky they MAY provide enough meat to get us out, but I doubt it. Berries will be ripening through the summer and they can supplement our other rations. We will fish at every opportunity because we will be on the water anyway."

Carlin was quietly scratching images in the dirt with a stick. They made no sense and had no definite form, they were just lines and squiggly closed shapes. Carol was becoming annoyed at his reticence. "Do you think you could join us and perhaps add something to the conversation Carlin," she said sarcastically. He stood up and stretched, then turned to face them. With the stick, he drew a straight line above and below the squiggles he had drawn.

"Yeah, I can add something," he said, pointing to the top line with the stick, "we are here." He moved the stick, pointing to the bottom line, "We want to be here, because this is where we started. The distance between the lines is two hundred and fifty miles or more." Carlin began to connect the closed shapes and squiggles with a torturous twisting set of lines. "This line represents the way out and it is, at a best estimate, three hundred and fifty miles or more."

Carol's face flushed and she went very quiet. Every time she took a cheap shot at Carlin she came out the loser, and she made a mental note to find another way to deal with her negative feelings about him.

Jim stood up and looked carefully at Carlin's rough map. He mentally overlaid it with a grid and realized Carlin had drawn it to scale. Studying the map he saw that fifty percent of the distance was overland. Jim never dreamed that Carlin had known all along that the canoe wouldn't solve all their problems. "Okay," Jim said, "your point is well taken. What mistakes have I made?"

"None," Carlin said, "unless you thought you could canoe all the way to the Vermillion River bridge. We are going to walk two hundred miles through some damned rough country.

Crossing some of the swamps and muskeg we will average two hours per mile carrying a canoe. Through the bush we might make one mile per hour, on the lakes five miles per hour and on the rivers ten miles per hour WITH the current and maybe two miles per hour against it." He sat down again cross legged. "I have drawn the rough map from memories as a bush pilot not a cartographer."

"How could you remember any of the lakes?" Carol asked in awe of the man. "There are thousands of lakes all connected somehow."

"Right," Carlin said, "they often are connected and we have to take the maze effect into consideration. There will be dozens of times when we come to a dead end and it will be necessary to backtrack to get out. It all adds to the distance we will be travelling."

"You're right," Jim said, "but we have no other choice. We are out of ammunition and could never survive another winter."

"How did your people survive without a rifle or ammunition?" Carlin asked, teasing his friend.

"They were good with a bow," Jim said, but they were born to it. I am sure it would take a hell of a lot of learning before we got good enough to bag a deer with an arrow."

"I think we had better learn," Carlin replied, "otherwise its going to be six months between meals."

They planned and talked late into the night, about the dangers of the journey. They developed strategies to deal with the most obvious problems, and they decided that within two or three days each of them would be practicing with a bow.

The following morning Carol discovered they had used the last of the jerky. They had a small quantity of dried fish, some cattail flour and a handful of wild rice. She opened one of the packages of bear meat that had been wrapped and sewn into its own skin. The meat inside was crawling with maggots and stank. It took her half an hour to get over the repulsion. Finally she managed to make a very bad bannock and boiled a few pieces of fish. The time for hunting was long past.

They located a dry old cedar log and split it in six foot lengths. Through the day they worked at tapering the cedar from the centre outwards, checking its flexure as they progressed. In late afternoon they strung the new bow with finely braided strips of hide. Carlin had made a very respectable arrow, and now all that was needed was the feather flights. it came down to a catch 22 – no feathers, no arrows. No arrows, no birds, and no birds, no feathers.

"Birch bark," Carlin said, "let's try birch bark flights." And so it was that they arrived at the new original arrow. It didn't work very well, but it was better than throwing rocks. Carol made the first improvement to the arrow by shaving the arrow shaft down to a smaller diameter where the flights were attached. The improvement allowed only the soft flexible part of the flight to touch the bow, and not the bulky glue joint. Their accuracy improved immediately. Four days elapsed before they were ready to hunt.

In the early morning light Jim moved toward the northwest and along the lake shore, while Carlin and Carol, fifty feet apart, traveled eastward through the open birch forest. He was approaching a very small creek, not more than a foot or two wide, when he saw the partridges.

They were drinking and pecking at gravel for their crops. Carlin drew the arrow and loosed it. His shot missed the bird he targeted, but hit another, killing it. Carol also shot at the covey but her arrow went wide, disappearing in the brush. They hunted until mid-morning when Carol also got a partridge with her third and last arrow. Happy with their success, they returned to the campsite.

"It's too bad the arrows fly so far," Carol said as they prepared a partridge stew, "we should have short range arrows."

"Mmmm," Carlin mumbled as he saved the best of the tail feathers for his next arrows. He had read about bow hunting for birds several years ago. He recalled the use of short range arrows. Suddenly it all came back to him. They were called flu-flu arrows, and they were tipped with a small flat weight. The flights on the flu-flu were wrapped around the arrow shaft in a spiral. The flu-flu would spin rapidly in flight, and fly straight, but lose all its energy in a short distance. They were used for hunting roosting birds or birds in flight.

It soon became apparent that arrows were precious – they were hard to make because the shafts had to be dead straight for accuracy. Once again, Carol discovered a first class solution to the problem. She was collecting bulrushes for flour, breaking off the heads when she realized the stalks were perfectly round and very straight. She cut about twenty of them, and brought them back to Carlin. "Okay fly-boy," she said, dumping her treasure in front of him, "you figure out how to point them."

Carlin picked up one of the old bulrush stalks and cut the head from it. He sighted along the stalk and found it perfectly tapered and straight. It was also perfectly round.

"Carol," he said throwing his arms around her and laughing, "that was pure genius. Now all we need for arrow heads, is a source of good flint and a talented flint napper."

"Or a big gob of blue clay," she answered, "what's wrong with ceramic arrow heads complete with a blind hole for the shaft?" She saw the surprise on his face and she too began to laugh.

Together they returned to the lake and trekked for more than a mile before the discovered a good clay deposit. They took twenty pounds each and returned to the campsite. Jim had also returned and was dressing a small deer. He had shot the animal with one of their first made arrows. They concentrated on preserving the meat as quickly as possible. Drying the jerky in the smoke of the campfire prevented flies from laying eggs on the meat. They worked with infinite care, and by nightfall almost all of the fresh killed meat was preserved reasonably well. Carlin had been working at two tasks throughout the evening. He had helped with preserving their meat supply, and had also fashioned six arrow heads from clay. By late evening they were leather hard and showed no signs of cracking. Before he bedded down for the night he placed them, not in, but near the hot coals of the fire. Neither Carlin nor Carol told Jim about the new arrow system, but he knew they were up to something.

Carlin was up before daylight and stoked the fire after burying the arrow heads in the coals. At seven A.M. he raked them from the fire. Within the next thirty minutes he had assembled three complete hunting arrows.

Jim emerged from the tepee and stretched. "How long have you been up Carlin – don't you ever sleep?" He poured himself some bush coffee from the big bean tin, and sweetened it with a lump of maple sugar.

Jim found himself a long thin sliver of red cedar, and began to shape it with his knife. "You know, we spend more time making arrows than we do hunting. I guess my ancestors were a hell of a lot better hunters than I am. I lost two arrows yesterday and ...."

Carlin sat down beside him. "That's okay Jim," he said, handing him the beautiful hunting arrow he had just finished. "I made a bunch of these just to pass the time. Carol taught me how to do it," he said laughing. Jim took the proffered arrow and examined it with great care. He ran his thumb down the edge of the broadhead, drawing blood.

"Carlin this is fantastic – its a real hunting arrow," Jim said in astonishment. "Ceramic arrowheads. I don't remember the Ojibwa teaching you that," he said with a broad grin, "Have you tested the points?"

"No," Carlin replied, "I was just about to do that when you got up." He nocked one of the arrows on his bow string, aimed at the drying deer hide from Jim's recent kill, and loosed the arrow. It hit with an explosive force after flying true, the tip fractured on impact, breaking into three pieces and ripping the hide to shreds at the impact site. The arrow shaft continued through the hole and landed on the ground ten feet away. Carlin considered the performance of the ceramic arrowhead. "Well," he mused, "it is a one shot arrowhead, but it DID make a mess of the penetration site."

"It's perfect," Jim replied, "How long does it take to put a new arrowhead on the shaft?"

"Oh, only a minute or two," Carlin said, "providing we had a stock of arrowheads, but we could make a hundred in an evening."

In the warm spring days that followed, they made their final preparations to begin the journey southward to civilization and safety. There were mixed emotions as they pushed the canoe away from the shore. They were happy to be under way – they were sorry to leave behind those items so hard won, the items they couldn't carry in the small craft. The tepee was left intact along with the utensils they could not accommodate. Their course would take them south east to the end of the lake, a distance of some six or seven miles. As the campsite grew smaller with distance, their elation dwindled and their normal chatter waned.

Carol looked back, but the campsite was now little more than a smudge on the distant shore. The connection severed, anxiety began to fill her. The plan was to paddle until early evening before making camp, but she wondered how she could sit still in the canoe for the long hours ahead. She tried to concentrate on the future and what she wanted from it. She knew she would likely become a celebrity by virtue of having survived the ordeal. Carol considered Jim Peters future. He would certainly be a different man, a man who really knew what hardships his ancestors had faced. He would likely be honoured by his peers. Would it change him?" She wondered.

The rhythmic swish of the paddles was hypnotic. And what about the ubiquitous Carlin – Carlin, ever the enigma. What about him? He would return to his small OntAir cabin, would see all the little things that reminded him of his previous life. The skis for the Cessna, all the accoutrements that related to flying, but there would be no comfort or peace, for he had no Cessna now. Carol knew that he had no reserve of capital – he hadn't eaten for three days before she came into his life, he had nothing then and even less now. She suddenly realized that this trip didn't matter to Carlin – there was no reason for him to return.

Carlin matched the rhythm of Jim's paddle strokes. Once or twice fatigue robbed him of energy, and his stroke matched Jim's in timing but not in strength. When it happened the canoe swung slightly in the opposite direction, and Jim, sensing it, followed with a lighter stroke. Carlin's shoulders ached, and hunger gnawed at his innards, but he continued matching his Ojibwa friend. Jim began to sing an Ojibwa song and they paddled to the cadence. Carlin had been playing a little game in which he never looked up at the destination point. He kept his focus on the water just ahead of the canoe. Now it was time for his reward and he looked up, and was delighted to see the end of the lake not more than a quarter of a

G. Wm. Gotro

mile away. Within minutes they beached the canoe, then stiff and shaky they stepped ashore.

The sun had dropped below the forest canopy at the far end of the lake. Carol, glad to be able to move freely, scrambled to get tinder for the fire, and water for some bush coffee. Jim chose a sleeping place for them, and began to cut soft boughs to lay beneath the hide they would use as a ground sheet. Carlin collected wood for the fire and soon they would be comfortable for the impending night. They prepared a scant meal and when it was finished, the men smoked a pipe of kinnikinnick. There was little talk between them for fatigue was claiming them early.

It was three in the morning when Carlin awoke. Jim was snoring very lightly, and Carol was not there. A pang of fear burned in the pit of his stomach. She never left the shelter until after daylight. He sat up, and rubbed the sleep from his eyes. She was nowhere to be seen. He threw fresh wood on the fire to brighten the blaze, and taking a brand for light, he made his way quietly toward the water. He found her beneath a small spruce, whose branches almost touched the ground, and she was sleeping deeply as one who has collapsed from exhaustion.

In the flickering light from the torch, he saw the tear stained face. He didn't know what had driven her away from the comfort of the camp to this place, but he did know she had cried herself to sleep. His heart overflowed with his deep love for her, and he realized that he rarely ever told her how much she meant to him.

Sticking the firebrand in the earth nearby, Carlin knelt down beside her, and lifted her gently from the ground. Still sleeping, she nestled her face into his shoulder as he carried her back to her bed, and covered her with her wolf skin. He went back to the fire and sat in deep thought for more than an hour. What made her get up in the middle of the night, and why did she cry herself to sleep, he wondered. He found it difficult to believe her when she said she loved him. If it was true, she must love him only because there was no one else around.

At daylight, he walked to the lake and looked at himself in the mirror smooth water. The reflection was a shock. He had always been clean shaven and well groomed. Now, the reflection that stared back at him was dreadful. His hair was long and dishevelled, and his face was hidden by a disarrayed and ugly beard. He slipped his knife from the sheath and honed it on a smooth stone from the beach. When he had restored the edge, he stropped it first on the leather of his boot, and then on the palm of his hand. He tested the edge with his thumb. It was sharp – very sharp. Carlin hacked at the lank facial hair with the knife, cutting it close to the skin, and when he had finished, he attacked the long lank hair of his head. It was a painful operation but now he looked much better.

Carol was awake before Jim, and she lay there thinking about how she got there. She faintly remembered being carried in the night, and knew Carlin must have brought her back to her bed.

Carol knew he was a very special individual, and he cared for her deeply. She got up and went to the fire. Water was boiling, and she spooned some of the roasted and powdered dandelion root into it for coffee. She sweetened it with maple sugar, and sipped some of the hot brew. Carlin returned from the beach.

"How about a hot coffee for an old friend," he said. She had not seen him coming and was momentarily frightened by the sound of his voice. She turned and stared at him. He looked totally different. Though his self administered hair cut and beard trim were ragged, he looked much younger and better groomed.

"I don't fix coffee for total strangers," she said laughing. "What have you done to yourself?"

"My barbering skills are better with scissors than they are with a hunting knife," he said. "I had to get cleaned up somehow." He poured coffee for himself. "Why did you cry yourself to sleep down by the water?" He asked directly.

"I don't know," she answered, "I guess I was just lonely – don't you ever get lonely Carlin?" He didn't answer for a long time.

"The number of people you know and care about, sets the depth of a person's loneliness," he suggested logically. "If you didn't know or care about anyone you would never be lonely I suppose," Carlin said, throwing another stick on the fire. "I don't have many friends so I don't get lonely very often."

"Are you ever lonely for me?" She asked, looking at him.

"Yes," he said softly.

"What will you do when we get back," She asked.

"Try to find a job," he said with a cynical little laugh. "OntAir

G. Wm. Gotro

is history now – the plane wasn't insured." Her heart was filled with compassion for him.

They breakfasted on jerky and talked about their plan for the day. They had gone as far south as the lake would take them, and it was time for the first portage. But portage to where?

"Any progress southward is an asset," Jim said. "I will carry the canoe for the first mile. You and Carol can bring the rest of our gear." He judged his direction by the sun and started in a generally southward line through the bush.

Carol finished packing their gear and she followed Carlin. In less than a quarter mile they caught up with Jim. He was resting on a big rock, his face and shirt drenched with sweat.

"This isn't going to be easy," Jim said, "I'm tired out already and I've only covered a quarter mile."

"We all carry the canoe from here on," Carlin said, "You and I positioned just ahead of centre, and Carol at the stern. When Jim was rested they began again. It was a much better way and they covered a half mile before stopping to rest once more. Their stop was shorter this time, and they pressed on for another quarter mile. Ahead of them was a high hill.

"You rest," Carlin said, "I'm going to climb that hill to see if there is another lake in the vicinity."

Without further discussion he left to assault the upthrust rock of the pre-cambrian shield. When he reached the crest, to the south he could see the swath of a wide creek. It emptied into a lake reaching five miles or so to the south west. Returning, he gave Jim and Carol the good news. The creek would let them tow the canoe where the water was shallow, and ride where it was deep enough. They set out immediately for their objective. Sweating and cursing they fought their way through the dense underbrush, arriving at the creek as the setting sun touched the treetops. Their total progress for the day was less than two miles, but they were confident that they would do much better the next day. Sitting around the fire after eating, Carol and Jim chatted animatedly, while Carlin was quiet and introspective.

He considered the pitiful progress of the day and wondered how bad things would get in the days to come. The water in the creek was brown in colour, which meant it was laden with tannin and decaying vegetation. It was draining a large swamp to the north. The creek was also very slow moving, suggesting to Carlin that it may run only a mile or so. His greatest concern was that it drained into an even larger swamp. Carlin had flown low over areas like this on many occasions. At its maximum, the water was seven or eight feet deep, falling to two or three feet in the shallows. The swamps were flooded forests cluttered with the tangled branches of fallen trees, and were all but impassable. He also knew there were two other repulsive elements to the swamps. The first was the presence of leeches. He had often seen small animals that tried to swim across such places. Their corpses were covered with leeches that didn't leave their hosts until the animal was devoid of blood. The second was the presence of large numbers of water snakes. They frequently grew to six or seven feet in length and they were very curious. Though they were harmless enough they often came by the dozen to investigate anything unusual in the swamps.

Carlin hoped that this swamp was not infested with snakes and leeches. They broke camp just after daylight. It had been a bad night for mosquitoes and blackflies and they were swollen from bites. For the first twenty minutes, the water was too shallow to paddle, and they kept moving by digging the paddle blades into the muck of the creek bottom. Gradually more and more tributaries emptied into the creek, broadening it and speeding its flow. The water deepened and they were running with a lethargic current. Just before midday they rounded a bend in the creek and entered a totally different world.

The swamp was five miles across and eleven miles long. Humps of black soil knitted together by roots were everywhere. Ten foot patches of saw grass grew between the hummocks, and all around were dead, gaunt trees from fifteen to sixty feet high. Many had toppled over to become sixty foot barricades to anyone or anything attempting to cross the swamp. Carlin wondered if this was the lake he had seen from the hill top the previous day. The canoe shot into the disarray of the swamp, and they bounced from one hummock to the other trying to halt their progress. The bow of the canoe was punctured just above the water line by a broken root sticking out of a hummock, Thirty minutes passed as they tried to find a way to dry ground at the edge of the swamp.

They beached the canoe and while Carol prepared a meal of jerky, the men repaired the hole in the bow of the canoe. Jim covered the hole with a paper thin patch on the outside. It was applied using hot spruce gum. This was followed by a thick bark patch on the inside, applied the same way.

They debated for an hour before continuing the journey. If they ventured into the centre of the swamp and got trapped it could take days to get out.

Conversely, if they tried to follow the shoreline it could add miles to the journey, and still deny them access to the lake. Carlin was uncomfortable with all of the choices available to them except going back the way they had come, but he didn't voice his concern. He would later regret his decision to keep his apprehensions to himself.

Driven by their aspirations to move southward to freedom, they elected to cross the swamp. At 3:00 P.M. they launched the canoe once more and embarked on a torturous path that led toward the centre of the swamp. They failed to notice the build-up of cloud over the region and by four thirty, were in the midst of a dull gray afternoon. Soon, everything looked the same and they were unsure of their direction, They were, in fact, almost in the centre of the swamp, having made hundreds of twists and turns around hummocks and deadfalls. Now without the sun for reference, they were lost under a sky turned gray-green with storm clouds.

The rain began with a few large drops, and then a long pause, before it became a steady fine sheet. Carlin, paddling in the bow, turned to look at Jim. His taciturn Ojibwa manner was badly shaken – Jim knew they were in serious trouble, but didn't want to frighten Carol more than necessary. "What do you say Carlin, should we try for high ground?" He asked in a voice filled with concern.

"I think we have to ride it out now," Carlin answered, "we have to get out of this damned swamp."

A cold wind now accompanied the rain that blew in sheets across the huge tangled chaos that was the swamp. The wan light was fading fast and they knew they were trapped. It wasn't possible to move in the darkness without running the canoe into an obstacle, that could damage it beyond repair.

The only action left open to them was to ride it out, drifting wherever the wind and current took them. Rain water was collecting in the bottom of the canoe, and Carol was bailing steadily to keep ahead of the torrents of rain. It was fully dark now, and they had no idea where they were. A lightning flash illuminated the swamp for a second. The scene registered in Carlin's mind, and he knew there was a clear space of about a hundred yards directly in front of them. He dared to hope that they may have unwittingly come to the exit from the swamp. They paddled gently to reach the centre of the open space.

Another lightning bolt struck, hitting the top of a tall dead tree. It burst into flame and the top ten feet crashed into the water beside the canoe. Blinded by the flash they failed to see what happened. The tree top shot to the surface beneath them and overturned the canoe. Carlin surfaced and fumbled in the darkness for anything solid. He could make out the faint outline of the canoe's bottom and leaning across it he righted the craft. "Carol – Jim, where are you?" He called. He heard someone coughing, and called again. Jim answered him but there was no reply from Carol. A big air bubble burst to the surface beside Carlin and he knew she was underwater. He dived, grappling in the muck and silt. Fear coursed through him like fire and he was terrified that he would lose her, then his groping hand touched her arm and he dragged her to the surface. Coughing up inhaled water, she gradually began to take air and her breathing regulated itself.

"Carlin, what happened?" She sputtered. "Where is Jim?"

"Jim – where are you?" Carlin called again.

"Over here," Jim replied, "keep talking so I can find you."

The lightning flickered again and they could see each other for one brief moment. They converged on the canoe, joyful to be together once more. The rain had passed and they bailed the canoe using Carlin's socks as sponges. When most of the water was gone from the canoe, they helped each other into the frail craft, and huddled together for warmth for the remainder of the night.

In the half light of dawn, a mild jolt rippled through the canoe, waking Carlin from an uneasy sleep. Looking about him he realized the current had drifted them to within a mile of the swamp's exit. In the strengthening light of early morning Carlin looked over the side of the canoe at his reflection in the still water. What his reflection showed him turned his stomach. Three fat leeches were attached to his face and neck. With some difficulty he managed to pull them off and throw them back into the water. He awakened Carol and removed one from the back of her hand, one from her cheek, and a third from her neck. She was horrified and screamed at the sight of them, waking Jim. He too had been a victim, and Carlin had the unenviable task of plucking the leeches from his friend. When he threw the last of them into the swamp a new death dance began as the water snakes swarmed in, to take the blood engorged leeches.

"Carlin, please, please get us out of this hideous place," Carol sobbed. He placed his hand on her cheek to reassure her that the worst was over.

"Shhh – shhhh," he whispered, "there is nothing to be afraid of now. We will be out of here very soon." She was soothed by his assurance and she began to relax.

"What have we got left?" Jim asked, still unsure of what had happened. He was taking inventory.

"Your bow, and the axe are all that's left – the food is gone, my bow is gone, and most important, the shotgun is gone. I think we are in big trouble now," he said in an undertone. For the first time since they met Carlin saw true fear in the big man's face. He had come to the end of his will to fight, and that spelled disaster for them. He was the rock. He was the quiet wise one who always knew how to defuse trouble, and now he was losing the will to survive. Carlin had to set Jim Peters back on the path. He tried the red man white man parody again.

"Three leeches have taught my red brother to speak with the tongue of a woman," he said, trying to goad Jim out of the depressed state.

"Cut the red man bull shit Carlin. Things won't be so funny when we start to starve. You know goddam well we can't hunt big game with a toy bow. We are in trouble – don't you understand?"

Carlin's face flared with hot blood. "No. You cut the bull shit Jim. Your forefathers didn't know what a shotgun was until the white man came. They survived with a bow and they didn't even have ceramic arrow heads. Get back into the real world. We have

an axe and two sheath knives – we don't need anything else."
Carlin was surprised at his own words, but he was amazed to find
he really believed them.

They beached the canoe at the mouth of the river that drained
the swamp. They had to begin all over again. Carlin took his bow
and his sheath knife, leaving the axe. "I'm going to get us
something to eat. Will you build a fire Jim?" He asked.

"Yeah, of course. We might as well stay here tonight," he said
scuffing the earth with the toe of his split boot.

"Go ahead, I'll look after things here, and good hunting." Jim
turned away and entered the forest.

"Can I come with you Carlin?" Carol asked in a small voice.
She had never seen the two men argue about anything through the
worst months of winter and now she was uncomfortable with the
invisible barrier that had arisen between them.

"Sure," he said, "but we have to be quiet."

They made their way along the east bank of the river until they
found bulrushes. He collected the dead dry ones for arrow shafts
while she collected the growing ones for their roots. She also found
wild watercress and harvested a small pile. Carlin asked her to find
birch bark, and he pointed out a low growing plant with dark green
smooth waxy leaves and small red berries.

"It is wintergreen," he said, "We can make a tea from the leaves
and the berries can also be eaten." He had a cattail arrow nocked on
the bow string. It had no arrow head, nor was it fletched, and all he
could hope for was a blessing from Manitou. "Stay close to the
river bank," he said, "I'll be back soon."

He walked for ten minutes and stopped where he found fresh
rabbit droppings. After five minutes or so, he heard the little
animal move in the underbrush. Carlin had the gift of infinite
patience and waited the rabbit out. When it hopped down to the
water, he loosed the arrow. It wobbled badly but he had a good eye
and the makeshift arrow killed the rabbit instantly. Picking up his
prize, he returned to where he had left Carol but she was nowhere
to be seen. He moved into the woods and stopped to listen, but
wherever she was, she wasn't making any noise.

His heart began to race as he imagined a thousand things that
might have happened. He called to her but there was no answer. He

tried again – still no answer. He returned to the creek, and there, he heard something splash in the water. Around the next bend in the creek he found her. Carol had learned the art of hunting crayfish and had managed to catch a dozen of the largest he had ever seen.

Jim's depression deepened when Carlin and Carol went hunting. He wandered into the woods looking for tinder and dry wood. It had rained most of the night and good tinder would be hard to find. His eyes scanned the immediate area. This forest had been burned over in bygone years. The tall spruces and tamaracks were still fire blackened spikes reaching into the sky. The new growth was mainly deciduous – poplars predominated and were interspersed with maples and birches. He took a thin layer of birch bark from one of the young trees and twisted it into a conical cup. Then searching, he found an old cedar dead fall. He drove the axe blade into the log and gave it a twist. The log split cleanly, for the centre was rotten. Jim scooped out a cupfull of dry tinder. Five more minutes with the axe yielded an armful of dry cedar sticks three feet long. Returning to the campsite Jim came across an old birch deadfall and collected a pile of heavy bark.

He thought about his ancestors as he split the cedar sticks. The grain was straight and without knots and yielded six strong stakes, the lightest of which became the material for his fire drill bow. His grandfather had made fire this way and Jim accepted his ability to do so. The knowledge was born in him and he knew he was responsible to pass it on to his sons. Jim strung the little bow with his bootlace and twisted it round the fire stick, then for three minutes, he whipsawed the bow back and forth, spinning the stick back and forth. The point of the fire drill began to smoulder and a wisp of smoke rose from the tinder board.

With a soft breath Jim blew the spark to life, and soon he had a blazing fire. Unlike Carlin, Jim had no great feelings of pride in the making of fire – his people had done it for ten thousand years. He had hurt his own Ojibwa pride by even suggesting they couldn't survive without the gun. Carlin had lashed out, reminding him that he had an Ojibwa heritage to live up to. His anger subsided and gradually he saw a funny side to the whole affair. He intended to tease Carlin about being the great white hunter when he came back empty handed. And Jim was sure Carlin would come back empty handed – his friend had left with a poor imitation of a bow, and a cattail stalk. It wasn't even a semblance of an arrow – no fletchings, and no arrowhead – it was just a damn cattail stock.

The fire was well established and Jim built a lean-to shelter from saplings, and went to the swamp exit for bulrushes. He would roof the shelter with woven bulrushes. He cut and piled a good supply and was cutting the roots away for food when he heard the sound. The big bean tin, half full of water, had drifted to the exit of the swamp, where it beached itself. It was rocking to and fro in the shallows and bumping on a rock. The Great Spirit had not abandoned him after all, and Jim thanked Him in humility, with a prayer. He finished the shelter and covered the floor with a deep bed of soft boughs, then stoked the fire once more. Early twilight had begun to settle, yet Carlin and the woman were not back. He was about to set out to find them when he heard their voices.

They prepared their first and only meal of the day, in the dusk of evening. The rabbit was dressed and on a spit over the coals of the fire. They had watercress and crayfish but the crayfish had to be boiled.

"How did your people boil things Jim?" Carol asked.

"They boiled most things in water," he said, trying to keep a straight face.

"Yes, I know that," she said impatiently, "but what did they use to hold the water?"

"Oh," Jim said with a big grin, "I will show you." He got up and walked behind the shelter. "they boiled most of their water in these," he said, holding up the big bean can.

"Where the hell did you get that?" Carlin said laughing.

"The Great Manitou sent it to us half full of swamp water. It arrived this afternoon. Other than us and the canoe, it's the only thing that survived the storm." Then, laughing they feasted on roasted rabbit, watercress and crayfish soup, and wintergreen tea. When they had eaten Carlin carved green poplar arrowhead patterns, while Jim fletched arrow shafts. In the morning, just after dawn, Jim would take Carlin's bow, and a half dozen arrows to go hunting for deer.

The day dawned cool and overcast. Jim Peters was leaving the campsite when Carol awakened. They talked in undertones for a few minutes before he left.

"It is unusual for me to be the first up," Jim said softly. "Carlin is always the early bird. He must be very tired."

"Yes, he didn't have much energy left yesterday," she answered, "he said he was tired."

"It is best that he gets extra sleep then," Jim said thoughtfully, "I have a long way to go. Will you stoke the fire?" "Of course," she said. "Good hunting Jim." She watched the big man until he was out of sight. He was limping slightly, and she remembered the torn and broken boot. He was very thin and the threadbare jeans he wore hung loosely from his hips. There was no spring left in his step, and the once bright black eyes had become dull and listless. Carol recalled the bickering between the two men after the capsize. Through the plane crash and the bitter cold of the long winter they had rarely spoken a harsh word to each other, and now that had changed. She stoked the fire, and sensed an unwelcome transformation in their lives.

Making her way to the water, Carol filled the bean can, then scooping water in her hands she splashed it over her face and hair. Kneeling there, looking into the water, her reflection would not form, as the drops of water from her hair, kept shattering the mirrored surface. Finally the water settled and the image that looked back at her was frightening. The once golden hair framing the face was lank and unkempt. The eyes had lost their lustre, and the cheeks were gaunt and hollow. For months she had thought of herself as she had looked that morning so long ago on the Vermillion River bridge. The degradation had been slow but certain and the pathetic image in the water, filled her with fear and melancholy. Unable to cope with what she saw, Carol hurried back to the fire.

Carol set the water tin to boil, and quietly looked in at Carlin. His breathing was deep and regular, but his face twitched as she watched him. Perhaps he was dreaming. She remembered the stern handsome face of the super confident bush pilot at the Vermillion River bridge, but the image now was much different. His once strong hands were thin and gaunt. A dark bruise was prominent on the back of the left hand. In the centre of the bruise was a circular pattern. She knew what it was.

It was where a leech had attached itself to suck fresh blood. Carlin had torn the thing away without breaking the suction. She shuddered at the thought. Her heart was filled with pain when she remembered that it was Carlin who took the leeches from Jim, from her, and finally from himself. For them, he had eased the blade of his knife between the skin and the mouths of the leeches causing them to let go, But for himself, he simply ripped the things from his skin.

A new fear pervaded her being. Not an immediate and consuming fear, but a lingering indefinable thing that reached into the future. The thinking she had done since Jim left, had led her to some conclusions. They were suffering from malnutrition. They were living off their reserves, and Carlin was right. The journey back to life as they once knew it could be much worse than the impossible winter they had survived. For the first time since the snow left, she wondered if they would die here. and the doubts brought tears to her eyes. They were not accompanied by sobs, they were the slow tears of understanding that they may lose one another to the northern wilderness.

When Carlin opened his eyes, it was to full daylight. For a few minutes he simply lay there thinking about their situation. If Jim was unlucky today, he would come back empty handed, and they would not eat tonight. They had to tip and fletch arrows today or there would be no hunting tomorrow. He sat up and watched Carol working at the fire. For the first time he saw the woman she had become. She was unhappy and listless. Her clothes were tattered, and she looked resigned to whatever fate had in store for her. Gone was the feisty manner, and gone was the self confident poise.

He pulled his boots on and laced them, and joined her at the fire. "What time did Jim leave?" He asked scratching his beard.

"As soon as it was light," she answered. "He won't get very far either." Her words startled Carlin. "The side of his boot was broken – remember? This morning he didn't mention it, but it was much worse, and he was limping," she muttered, stirring the fire. "There is tea in the big bean can, but we lost all the cups."

"Did you see any clay along the river bank yesterday?" Carlin asked. She didn't reply, just shook her head in the negative. "Well we had better find some today," he suggested, "otherwise it's three hundred miles to the next drink."

For three hours, they scouted the river bank in search of clay. Just before noon, they came across a huge deposit of fine blue clay, and carried back a generous supply. Moreover the material they had collected was almost the exact texture they required, and they were able to use it without adding water. Carol had learned by her mistakes in the past and now, they knew how to cure the green ware with almost no cracking. Carol made bowls, jugs, and cups, while Carlin fashioned dozens of arrowheads of different sizes and shapes. The items were placed in a warm environment and left to dry very slowly.

They spent the late afternoon gathering wood, and anything that could supplement the meat Jim would bring back. They found fiddle head ferns and dandelion greens, and they picked a quantity of wintergreen berries. They collected and washed pounds of dandelion root for coffee, and the south end of the swamp held an inexhaustible supply of bulrushes. When they returned to the camp, Jim was waiting for them. He was on the edge of total exhaustion and sat slumped by the fire. Carlin knew by the big man's expression that he failed at the hunt, and for an Ojibwa that was the most crushing blow of all.

"Jim you look about done in," Carlin said, trying to steer away from the subject of hunting. "We should all get some rest and tomorrow we should canoe a couple of miles down river to see if we can escape the mosquitoes."

"Yeah it might be good," Jim said softly, the grief of his failure reflecting in his tone. "paddling will be better than walking." Only Carlin understood Jim's oblique reference to his useless boots.

Carol wasn't sure what was going on between the two men, but she knew the conversation was about failure. Was it the failure of Jim's boot – the failure of the hunt, or failure to survive?

5

THE SPARK BEGINS TO GLOW

When he opened his eyes it was still dark, and he was cold. Carol lay huddled in a little ball beneath the boughs. It was difficult to sleep when the cold nagged throughout the night. Jim lay still, his shallow breathing barely discernable in the darkness. Carlin slipped from under his blanket of boughs, and covered Jim with them. It seemed an odd gesture, the woman was cold too, but he knew Jim needed the help more than Carol.

Outside the shelter, he raked the coals of the fire back and set the clay pieces in the bed of ashes, covering them lightly with the coals. He piled fresh fuel on the fire, and then set about preparing the canoe for the day's journey. He partly filled the bean can with water and set it to boil, after dropping wintergreen leaves into the tin. He kept feeding the fire and at 8:00 A.M. he began to uncover the clay pieces – they had baked for four hours. They would cool slowly over the next four hours.

Carol and Jim went to the river to wash away the vestiges of the night. Carlin's tea had boiled and was cool enough to drink. They shared it, drinking from the big tin. When it was gone, Jim uttered a cynical little laugh.

"Isn't it strange how much we appreciate four wintergreen leaves in some hot water when there is nothing else." They were very hungry, having had little sustenance the previous day.

"We will eat tonight Jim," Carlin said, "somehow we will find game today." He rummaged in a small patch of coals with a stick, and withdrew four arrowheads.

When they were cool enough to handle he gave them to Jim. "The other clay ware will be cool by noon," he said, "once we recover it we can move out in the canoe. There is no need for you to walk anywhere until your feet are healed." Carol glanced at Jim's feet. There were large blisters on heels, toes, and soles, most of which had burst and started to bleed. Jim Peters wouldn't be walking anywhere for a week or two at best. "For now, you fletch and point arrows, and I will go out and lose them."

Carol stayed with Jim to care for him, while Carlin moved at a fast pace along the river bank. He was constantly watching for tracks in the ooze at the water's edge. After an hour, his gaze fixed on some tall grass on the opposite bank, and he studied it more carefully. A few of the tall shoots were bent or broken. It wasn't much, but it gave him a vital clue. He threw a little stick on the water's surface, and watched it carefully. The stick drifted very slowly down river, yet it was drawn to the opposite bank, telling Carlin exactly what currents to expect in the water. He removed his boots and socks, and waded into the river. In the centre where the water was deepest it reached his chest and he was able to keep his footwear dry.

Reaching the opposite bank, he removed his clothes and after wringing the water from them, dressed again. The deer tracks were fresh and Carlin was able to follow them to the edge of the long grass where they appeared to end. He had never been an avid hunter and knew very little about tracking. It was time to become an Ojibwa from the past. Carlin sat on the ground, his legs crossed and his open hands turned palm upward. It was, he imagined, a gesture of reception of the gifts of Manitou. His face turned to the sun, he prayed. "Oh Mighty Manitou – Great Spirit we are suffering. We need your wisdom – your help – your guidance. Teach me to hunt this day, that I might feed my companions. Bless me with an Ojibwa mind and skills." He sat still, listening, waiting, waiting for the Great Spirit to answer. Then suddenly he realized that the Great Spirit HAD answered even as he asked. Lesson number one was – Listen and Wait. Lesson number two – Manitou made him cross the river, and then gave him the good sense to wring out his clothes, washing away the man smell that would surely alert his quarry.

He remembered that the tracks at the water were leading to the river. Perhaps the deer had crossed the river and were long gone on the opposite side. Carlin returned to the river bank where the tracks were clear, and found some leading to the river and others leading back to the grass.

He retraced his steps toward the forest, this time scanning the tall grass on each side of the trail. Fifty feet from the forest edge He noticed some broken grass about six feet from the trail. The deer had stopped here and made a six foot jump to the left side of the trail. Six or seven feet from the first landing point was a second sign of broken grass. The animal had made several long jumps through the grass, almost eradicating its tracks. Carlin dropped to his hands and knees and crawled toward the second jump spot in the tall grass. Reaching the spot, he waited and listened. The only thing he could hear was the buzzing of a fly – a deer fly. He raised his head cautiously, and kneeling, he nocked an arrow tipped with a ceramic point. As he stood for a better view of the area, a doe rose quickly to her feet. Carlin loosed the arrow and it hit her in the neck, penetrating deeply. She staggered for a moment and then made three long jumps before collapsing to her knees, He moved in on her and quickly put her out of her misery with his knife.

He shouldered his prize and returned to the campsite just before noon. Jim Peters looked at his friend with new eyes, and the three began to butcher the animal and preserve it. A large roast was placed on a spit over the fire. Carol brought Carlin a cup of hot tea. When she handed it to him he examined the cup carefully. It was perfect, and it was wonderful to drink again from a cup instead of the communal big bean tin.

"Not one of the pieces cracked," she said proudly, "we have a set of cups bowls and jugs, and three plates are hardening." She walked over to the canoe and brought back a birch bark cup, handing it to Jim. "Found this for you and Carlin this morning," she said. The cup was filled with kinnikinnick all ready hand rubbed into a useable tobacco. The men filled their pipes and smoked.

Jim studied Carlin for a long time before he spoke. "You have done what I failed to do Carlin – I congratulate you!" He turned his face away from them to better conceal the pain of his failure.

"It is not correct to congratulate me," Carlin said, "If you find it

G. WM. GOTRO

necessary to say these words, direct them to the Great Spirit. It was Manitou that gave me the doe while teaching me how to be more like you. By teaching me to be more patient – to listen and to wait." Jim's face broke into the first smile in days.

"I have listened," he said, and now I shall wait.

There were many things to do, and they stayed at the river mouth for two more days. The deer hide was curing and late on the second day, Jim took his useless high top boots and studied them carefully, then took his knife to them. His action shocked Carlin.

"What the hell are you doing Jim?" he asked.

"The hide of a small doe is very thin," Jim answered, "it would not make good moccasins. The leather from the uppers of my boots is better for soles and I will make the tops from the deer hide." The following day, Jim did an expert job at making himself new footwear. Part of the hide was used to make a good supply of thin thongs that could be used as lacing or braided into leather ropes. The remainder of the hide was allowed to cure fully, and each night it served to cover them as they slept.

On the third day after Carlin's successful hunt, at six o'clock in the morning they packed the canoe and set off on the next part of their journey. This time loose items were tied into the canoe. Fortunately the nylon rope that survived the crash, had been tied to the bow of the canoe, and wasn't lost in the capsize. Now it was looped around the lead paddler. The canoe and its contents could no longer drift away after a capsize unless the lead paddler was forced to relinquish it, They were comfortable, paddling slowly down the river draining the swamp.

Throughout the day the trip was idyllic and peaceful as the canoe moved steadily southward. When the afternoon shadows lengthened, they beached at a wide part in the river. Carlin had been in the stern, and Jim in the bow, and while Carlin steered the little craft, Jim carved a half dozen fish hooks from bone. He had unbraided his boot laces and fashioned the individual strands into a respectable fishing line.

Now, in the early evening, as Carlin and Carol prepared the campsite for the night. Jim fished from the canoe, allowing his line to lay upon the surface of the water. The hook had been hidden by a few feathers taken from a dead robin. For more than an hour, nothing happened, and as dusk settled, Jim decided that his efforts had been wasted. In disgust, he yanked the line in.

It moved a few feet or so across the water. Suddenly the water exploded as a five pound bass leaped clear of the surface taking the bait. Minutes later, the unfortunate bass was in the bottom of the canoe, and Jim Peters limped into the campsite on tender feet, holding up his prize. They grilled bass fillets and ate them with Carlin's Survival Pizza, they drank bush coffee, and after the repast the men smoked.

"For the first time since the storm, I feel like we are going to make it," Carol said. "Oh what I would give for a hot bath with real soap."

"Yeah," Jim said, "there are not many frills when you are living off the land – my people know all about hardship."

"In the city a bath is in water laced with chlorine," Carlin said with a chuckle, commenting on Carol's wish.

"Better that, than water swarming with leeches," she responded acidly. Her response irritated Carlin, and he grew moody. He stood and stretched, then walked into the bush to relieve his bladder.

"There are times when I think Carlin actually enjoys facing the hardships of survival," Jim said, "He certainly is very good at it. Without him we would both be dead."

In the days that followed, they fell into a routine – they paddled and portaged for three days, then stopped to hunt and fish for two days. Carlin's boots finally gave out, and he too walked many miles in moccasins. They were unaware that they had strayed from their true southerly course and traveled west south west for ten days. On a number of occasions they were forced to backtrack five or ten miles. At other times, when there were no high hills to climb they made almost no southward progress and knowingly traveled in a circle to find another waterway. The days slipped by, May gave way to June and with that transition nature became more bountiful. They often found themselves in a sea of blueberries. They picked and ate copious quantities and used more berries to make pemmican which could be stored indefinitely.

Though they were unaware of the straight line distance traveled, it amounted to ninety miles. In actual miles traveled, they had accumulated one hundred and eighty seven miles. Such were the vagaries of the wandering streams and lakes they had selected as their highway. With fresh food, they had become whipcord tough and often joked about staying in the bush another winter just for the hell of it.

Carol and Jim were gathering foodstuff and it was Carlin's turn to reconnoitre the area to find the next useful waterway. Taking his bow and six arrows Carlin followed the river bank for three miles or so before he saw the big hill. Its base was but a quarter mile from the river, and he sighted three land marks that would take him to its crest. He trekked toward the hill and at its base he found his way blocked by a long narrow lake. To climb the hill, it would be necessary to walk to the end of the lake, and backtrack on the opposite side. Carlin estimated the distance at two miles. It was too far. He turned back toward the river, and then for some unaccountable reason he changed his mind.

The hike around the lake was tough, and hard on his moccassined feet, but he had made a choice and was determined to climb to the hill top. He rounded the end of the lake and at the base of the hill he tried to sight his land marks. To align them he was obliged to hike to the midpoint of the lake's shoreline. Skirting the lake and the base of the hill was easy walking.

From the hill's base to the water's edge was mostly gravel. Carlin kept sighting back on his three land marks until he reached his destination. The place was clean and beautiful. Large stands of pine mixed with maple and oaks made up the lower slopes of the hill. He drove a long stick into the gravel bed to mark his place and continued walking the shoreline.

The sound of water running drew him, and he found a picturesque stream and waterfall cascading down the hill side into the lake. He knelt at the stream bed where it crossed the beach and splashed the cold water on his face. Filling his hands, he drank deeply, and then wet his face again. Carlin was about to leave the stream when he saw the glitter in the water. He bent closer. It had to be iron pyrite – he reached into the stream bed and scooped out a handful of gravel. The water drained through his fingers, and left in his hand twenty small pieces of gravel and stone, and in the middle lay three gold nuggets. His first thought was to go back for Jim and Carol, but dropping the nuggets in his pocket, he sat down on the gravel to think this through.

Would they go crazy over the lure of gold? No, he thought, they would want to stay long enough to take a substantial treasure home. And what about him? What did Carlin want most of all? He would of course, acquire another aeroplane. After ten minutes of soul searching, Carlin reached the inner truth. He wanted to finish his charter – he wanted to take Jim and Carol back to the point from which they left. Would the gold change Jim's relationship with him? No that would never happen – avarice wasn't strong in Ojibwa culture. What about Carol. Would the gold change her? Maybe – maybe not. He wasn't sure. The Great Spirit had blessed him this day – He had given Carlin a gold bonanza and suddenly, an answer to all the foregoing questions. With a new energy Carlin began the climb.

From the peak he could see the general course of the river and a huge lake to the south east. Moreover Carlin was almost certain of his location. He made his way down the hill to the beach, and without looking back at the bonanza, he pulled the stick from the beach and began the long walk to the far side of the lake. Using the landmarks he was back at the river within an hour. He had to hurry for it would soon be dark, and jogging along the river bank he arrived back at the campsite just before twilight turned to darkness. The campfire was welcoming and supper was ready. They ate venison steaks, dandelion greens sautéed in fat, and a thin bannock made from cattail flour, blueberries, and fat. Jim had a surprise for them – their coffee was sweetened with wild honey, and they now added beeswax to their stores.

When supper was over, and they sat smoking and drinking coffee, Jim asked Carlin what he had discovered.

"I know where we are," Carlin said, "from a high hill, I could see what I believe is Lake Missinaibe. We should reach it in four or five days. It is much too treacherous to cross in a canoe, but there is a river to the east of it that will take us to a village on the CNR railway line. From there we are home free." Jim said nothing at first, but Carol exploded with happiness.

"Oh Carlin you are just too good to be true. We are on our way out of this hell hole at last. How long will it take us to get to a city?" Her eyes were bright and she had instantly become highly animated. "How long Carlin, how long?"

Jim watched Carlin's reaction to her drastic change. Carlin tilted his head back, looking upward as he made his estimate .

"About an hour and a half from the hell hole where I picked you up," he replied, and turning his back on her, he settled himself on the sleeping pad. "Have you ever thought about getting free meals, free clothing and tranquillity in Toronto or New York? For some folks they are the real hell holes."

She jumped to her feet and stood over him, feet apart and hands on hips. "You don't care if we ever get out do you Carlin? This whole ordeal has just been a big game for you hasn't it." She ranted at him for a full five minutes before she realized he was snoring. "That ignorant son of a bitch. He didn't hear a single word I said. Can you believe it?" She said, turning to Jim who sat smiling passively.

"Sit down Carol," he said, "we move toward our objective one day at a time. We are here – we are clothed – we are healthy, and we are together. You are not one inch closer to your civilized paradise for all your anger at Carlin. Perhaps his hell hole is civilization now, and yet he moves you toward it day by day."

She sat down in resignation, thinking about Jim's words. They were true. She wasn't hungry, and she was not suffering from any malady. She now wore doeskin pants and shirt that they made when her clothing began to fall apart. She was safe with Jim and Carlin, she could not deny that. Carol stared into the flickering flames of the campfire, trying to visualize her return to the normal world, where she would undoubtedly be a celebrity with a story to tell. She imagined the conversation with the press and her peers – heard them asking her how she stayed alive during a winter with -40 degree temperatures. When she listened to her own answers, she heard 'we' far more often than 'I'. Examining her feelings now, Carol found more humiliation than anger. Looking up, she realized Jim was watching her, his dark eyes boring into her very soul.

Once again he had led her to assess her feelings properly, and she wondered at his depth of understanding. "Goodnight Jim," she said, and settled herself down to sleep for the night.

Jim's thoughts formed slowly and they were very clear.

Carlin's comment to Carol was based on something unusual. Jim was certain Carlin knew something that he hadn't spoken about. It was true that he didn't have the same reasons to go back to OntAir now the plane was gone, but he wasn't a quitter. He couldn't make a fresh start up here in the wilderness, and yet, when he returned today he was confident and, Jim thought, happier in some odd way. He knew Carlin would tell him everything at the proper time.

When Carol and Jim awakened the following morning, their breakfast was ready, the canoe was packed and Carlin was sitting on a log enjoying a pipe of tobacco. There was a serene look about him that said he was totally relaxed. Jim and Carol ate breakfast and Carlin drank coffee with honey, and nothing was said about last night's tirade. Carol thought she should apologize to him, but Carlin showed no resentment for her outburst and treated her in an open and normal manner. As she and Jim were finishing their breakfast, Carlin surprised them with a question.

"Do you think we should stay here for a few more days, or should we push for Missinaibe today?" Carlin asked.

Jim diverted the question to Carol. She didn't want to give the impression that she wanted out this very minute. "Why don't you guys make the decision – you're the survival experts." She effectively placed the burden of decision on Jim's shoulders. He was annoyed with her manipulation, and startled, when Carlin nodded toward him.

"Jim," he said, leaving the question unfinished.

"One place is much the same as another," Jim replied philosophically, "there is nothing left to do here – we might as well break camp and move southward."

"Most of the loose gear is already packed, and in the canoe," Carlin said, "the shelter items and your breakfast dishes are all that is left to stow."

They were on the river once more, and during the mid-morning it was idyllic. They let the current do the work and Carlin steered from the stern. Jim fished from the bow and tried to teach Carol an Indian song. They stopped in two places through the morning. At the first, they collected wild mint, and at the second they harvested watercress for the midday meal. The random light clouds that had dotted the blue morning sky built steadily, and by noon the sky was

G. WM. GOTRO

completely overcast. The gentle early morning breeze died away, leaving the air still and heavy, and thunder rumbled in the distance. Carlin turned the canoe toward the left bank, and Jim stepped ashore before the bow touched. He knew what Carlin was thinking, and after setting Carol on the bank they lifted the canoe from the water. They carried it fifty yards across a small grassy area and set it down at the edge of the forest and began to make camp for the night.

Jim looked about and scanned his surroundings and the sky. Nodding at Carol and walking across the grassy area, they came to a small frog pond and motioning her to be still, they listened to the chorus of the frogs. He made hand signs to her that told her to watch his hand and listen to where he pointed. She nodded rapidly in understanding and wondered at the complexity of this man. Jim was listening, and he slowly pointed to the north side of the pond. Her eyes followed the pointing finger and suddenly she saw a big bullfrog on a lily pad.

"Guruk, guruk," it said, and then it paused for ten seconds, "Guruk – guruk," it said again. Then Jim waved her back to the campsite, and they walked across the grass in silence.

Though the air was sticky and warm, Jim started a small cooking fire. Carlin was nowhere in sight. Jim piled a few green branches on the fire and smoke began to billow around them. The smoke brought tears to her eyes, and she moved back from the fire.

"What was that all about at the frog pond?" She asked.

"I cannot tell you," he said, "you must ask Carlin," Jim replied, "it is very important." She knew he was playing her, but she didn't know why.

"I wonder where he is," she said, concern clear on her face.

"He has gone again to the big hill," Jim answered, an enigmatic smile creasing his face, "he will return before dark."

"How can you possibly know where he is and when he will be back?" She asked, annoyance and frustration evident in her manner.

"We have lived as brothers for many years," he said, throwing more small green branches on the fire. "Carlin has gone to the big hill to speak with the Great Spirit. He will come back when Manitou has answered his questions."

"But Carlin is not an Indian. You are talking as though HE was the Ojibwa," she said, losing patience.

"Carlin is white," Jim said, "that is his outside colour. His heart is Ojibwa. Carlin might have been born my brother, for his heart is Indian. When he returns ask him about the frog pond."

The heavy still air before a rain, drives mosquitoes and black flies to a frenzy. Their thirst for blood becomes relentless and they are aided in their quest by the smell of perspiration from their quarry. Carol was being tormented by the voracious insects, and the only refuge was in the smoke of the little fire being fed with green plant materials. That is where Carlin found her when he returned in mid afternoon, and he too, moved close to the fire.

"You disappeared – where did you go?" She asked.

"No need to worry," he said, "I went back to the top of the hill to confirm that the lake I saw yesterday was really Missinaibe." He stirred the fire with a stick. "Now I am not sure if it is Missinaibe. It looks different today."

"I will go tomorrow," Jim said, "perhaps I can identify it."

He stood up and collected his fishing gear. "The fish always bite best before a rain," he said, "I'll go and catch our supper."

After he left, Carol moved close to Carlin. She told him about her incident at the frog pond with Jim. "When I asked Jim about it, he said to ask you." Carlin smiled, and he thought for a long time before he answered her.

"It has to do with human relationships," Carlin said, feeding the smudge fire. "And it has to do with rain." Her brow was furrowed and she was more confused than ever.

"I don't understand," she said, "want to fill in the blanks?"

Carlin put his arm around her shoulder and pulled her closer to him. "At the frog pond, he tried to teach you three things," Carlin said, "The first, is the value of silence. When you are silent you hear much more – hearing the bullfrog and pointing it out to you was proof. The second, is the value of listening. When you listen you begin to learn. His proof was your mimicking of the frog a moment ago." Carlin placed the bean can full of water on the coals of the fire.

"What was the third lesson he was trying to teach me?" She asked, unsure of her understanding.

G. WM. GOTRO

The first drops of gentle rain hissed as they hit the fire. "The third lesson was about interpreting what you hear. The bullfrog's song was always the same wasn't it? Guruk – guruk, then he paused and repeated it. Guruk – guruk. It has to do with rain." He glanced at his watch. "when did you go to the frog pond?"

"Oh a couple of hours ago," she replied. "Why?"

"The bullfrog was telling you it would soon rain – within two hours," Carlin said, and holding his hands out, palms upward he shrugged. This is your proof." She smiled.

"What a wonderful lesson," she said, "but I have two more questions." Carlin nodded to her. "The first is, what does all this have to do with human relationships. The second is why didn't Jim tell me these things?

"When we are silent we hear, when we hear we begin to see, and what we have heard is very important if we take the time to interpret it correctly," Carlin said, "Those are good lessons for a human relationship."

"Yes, the rules would build a strong relationship," she admitted. "Why would Jim not explain that to me?"

"Because your relationship with him was fine. Our relationship was not." Carol blushed, and she knew her reference to their odyssey being a hell hole had been in very bad taste.

The following morning a cool fresh breeze bathed the northern forest, and bright sunshine dried up the excess water from the previous night's rain. Jim left for the high hill at dawn. When Carlin arose, Carol was sitting near the water and softly, she sang the Ojibwa song Jim taught her. He padded to the bank of the river, and kneeling, washed himself in the cool water. He was stripped to the waist and sat in the sun letting the rays dry his skin. He sat cross legged, his forearms resting on his thighs, head back and his palms open and upward. His eyes were closed and he had not yet spoken to her. As she watched, she realized he was praying.

Carol had never contemplated the spiritual side of Carlin, and now she reflected on things she said in the past that may have offended him. She resumed humming the Ojibwa song. It was a strange tableau and did not change for more than five minutes. Finally she turned to look at him, and he was standing and smiling at her.

"You were praying," she said, "Do you pray to Great Manitou?"

"I pray to God," he said, "Jim and his people think of Him as the Great Spirit. I think of him as God. We are praying to the same Supreme Being. Do you not pray to God?" He asked.

"I didn't have a spiritual upbringing," she said, and she turned toward the campsite. "I will make some breakfast for us."

Jim Peters found the path Carlin had taken around the lake at the base of the hill. The signs were obscure, but Carlin had left enough clues to follow. On the beach Jim discovered the hole left by the stake Carlin had driven in the sand. He heard the running water of the little stream and explored it briefly, then dismissed it as unimportant. Walking back to the hole made by the stake, he discovered a twig in the shape of a 'Y'. It was three inches long and weathered white with time. It was lodged in the gravel by the short arm of the Y. and pointed toward the stream. He picked it up. It wasn't anchored to anything. Twenty feet away he saw the second one, almost the same, but pointing to the stream. He tapped it with his finger and it fell over. The twigs looked natural, but could never have assumed that position without the help of a human hand. Carlin had left directions, and he returned to the stream.

Standing at the stream bed, he carefully surveyed the scene. The only possible clue was an old wet stick trapped in the flowing water. Jim looked at it for several minutes before its message became clear. If the stick had been washed down from above, and driven into the stream bed by the force of the water, it would have been pointing in the opposite direction to the flow. As it was, it pointed to the lake and had been driven into the stream bed against the current. Jim wriggled the stick with his finger and it shot away toward the lake carried by the force of the water. it was a brilliant trick on Carlin's behalf. He wanted Jim to explore the stream! He ruffled the bottom of the stream bed with his fingers. When the turbid water flowed away Jim saw one tiny flake of gold. Taking a handful of small stones and sand from the dry bank, he covered his find.

Jim climbed the hill and studied the big lake in the distance. It didn't look like Missinaibe, but like Carlin, he wasn't sure.

He returned to the beach and walked to the campsite an hour

G. WM. GOTRO

away.

They had managed to acquire a substantial supply of food, hide leather, and hunting arrows. There would be no need to hunt or gather for several days. Only one question remained. Were they going in the right direction? The general direction was south west, but using the river systems without a map, could lead them a hundred miles off course before the error was discovered.

Carlin and Jim considered the options; they could portage straight south as best they could determine it, until they found another river. They could continue by canoe on the present river, trying to determine an average heading by keeping track of the twists and turns. They opted for the latter. While they discussed the options and the possible ramifications, Carol, bored by the talk, went alone to the river bank. She did her best at washing her hair.

While she was away Jim talked to Carlin about the signs left on the beach. "They were very good Carlin, I almost missed them."

"If I had made them better and you had missed them they would have been useless," Carlin said laughing. "What did you find?"

"Exactly what you found. A stream rich with gold." Jim said with a subtle smile playing at the corners of his mouth. "I take it that you don't want to enlighten the archaeologist."

"Oh I have every intention of telling her, but not yet. I think we should do a river cruise first thing tomorrow. Jim, within three days we should be certain of our true location. Once that is established, we will be out in four or five days at the most."

"What will you do with your gold mine Carlin?" Jim asked.

"When I was fifteen years younger and struggling to stay alive, I looked at you and the Ojibwa and envied you. Six months later you talked with the band chief and the council and offered to adopt me as an Ojibwa. My stupid pride made me reject your offer and I regretted it all these years. You will always be my brother Jim – it is not MY gold mine – it is ours. When we get back, I will go to the band and ask them to make me an Ojibwa."

"The council will say yes Carlin, they have always thought of you as one of the band. You didn't need a gold mine to become a member," Jim said seriously.

"We can change their lives," Carlin said, "build schools and a hospital, and restore the spirituality that has weakened through the years, but Jim they must never know who their benefactor is."

Carol was on her way back from the river and the two men changed the subject and filled their pipes with tobacco. Jim prepared their supper. He made a stew from venison, cattail flour, watercress and the edible roots of Queen Anne's Lace. After they had eaten, they cleaned their utensils and fished the river for catfish or barbet until the light was gone.

Once more they were on the river shortly after sunrise. There was little work to do. They had passed the point at which the rivers flowed north, and the current carried them now almost due south. Aware that the current was moving faster now, and the river wider, they joked about being unable to consume their supplies before reaching help.

At mid morning the canoe was being drawn along swiftly by the ever increasing current. They swept around a long bend into the confluence of a second and larger river.

Ahead of them the water boiled and rolled, and from bank to bank, eddies and whirlpools spanned the river. Both men were paddling hard to keep control of the canoe. The river banks, deeply undercut, rose ten to fifteen feet above the water, and should a capsize occur there was no way to get out. Jim wished he had taken the stern seat. He was much better with a canoe than Carlin. White with fear now, Carol sat silently, holding tightly to the gunnels. Jim coached Carlin from the bow, and a mile farther on, the river widened again, and the turbulence subsided. The river banks were lower here and they beached the canoe when the sun reached its zenith.

"Well, it looks like we beat 'Ol Man River' this time," Carlin said, rummaging through their supplies for pemmican.

"It could get worse," Jim cautioned, "we aren't out yet."

After a rest and a meal, they prepared for the afternoon run. Carol had been quiet since the wild ride through the turbulent water. Now, the fear of the unknown ate into her like an acid. She was pale and frightened as she settled herself in the canoe. Carol had often envied Carlin and Jim their almost mystical foresight. Now she experienced precognition, and felt her lungs filling with water. The experience was so strange to her, she hesitated to talk about it, and frightened, she embarked on the final part of their

G. WM. GOTRO

journey. As they pushed the canoe into the water, she wondered if they knew the dangers ahead.

For three hours the canoe hurtled on the swift flowing water. Carlin guessed they were making close to fifteen miles an hour, and he and Jim were exhilarated by the rapid movement of the canoe. Jim was in control in the stern, while Carlin paddled at the bow. They entered a wide languid part of the river and let the canoe drift.

Slowly the canoe began to pick up speed. It was negligible at first and they didn't notice it, and kept to the centre of the river. All three had become mesmerized by the thoughts of freedom from the grip of the wilderness. Carol found difficulty resisting thoughts of a hot bath with scented soap, fashionable clothes, and a real bed to sleep in. Jim Peters' mind was on his friends and family. He would go to the sweat lodge and align himself spiritually as he was physically cleansed. Then he would dress in fine clean clothes, and he would also sleep in a comfortable bed. Carlin thought about OntAir. His cabin would certainly be a sorry mess and most of his equipment that was left outdoors would need a great deal of attention. The dock would look forlorn with no aeroplane moored to it, and he knew it would be a lonely life without Carol or Jim at every meal, and having someone to talk with. Of course searching for a new plane would be fun, but it was still an activity that left him very much alone.

Jim was aware of it first. The river slalomed once or twice, and it had become hard to keep the canoe under control. The banks were closing in and the water was moving much faster, and then they heard the first noise of the falls and the rapids below. He knew it was going to be a close one – they had to reach the river bank and soon. He began to swing the stern to the left, but now the current carried them forward at an angle. They were running out of luck.

Carlin realized what had to be done – knew what Jim wanted and he began to paddle furiously at the left bow. The falls were but a hundred yards away now. Gradually the canoe began to turn her side to the river's flow and that was fatal. Though the two men paddled furiously the canoe now presented a much larger area to the current and it was moving very rapidly toward the falls. Ten yards from the edge a great chunk of granite lay, inches below the rushing water.

The canoe struck the granite sideways and flipped over, dumping them into the river and they were swept over the brink. The men tried to avoid being drawn over the edge by swimming furiously, but they failed. Carol, taken totally by surprise was the first over the edge.

Fortunately, the falls were fairly small, being only twenty feet high, but the toll taken on each survivor was critical. Ten feet from the top of the falls, the water cascaded into a pool, whose base was a milieu of large and small granite chunks. The pool at its centre was seven feet deep. It emptied into a much larger basin at the foot of the falls, which in turn emptied into the narrow, fast flowing river. For half a mile the lower river was relatively shallow and festooned with standing waves, whirlpools, and white water. In several places along the turbulent half mile stretch, large trees had fallen, and with roots still anchored in the banks, their tops thrashed and bobbed in the chaotic water.

Carol was taken completely by surprise when the canoe hit the submerged rock that flipped it over. She was terrified by the prospect of going over in the canoe and couldn't comprehend going over without it. One moment she was clinging to the gunnels, and quaking in fear – in the next she was underwater and swept over the edge of the falls. She dropped ten feet into the small pool, and struck her head on the bottom rendering her unconscious. Then, washed over the edge of the pool, she dropped an additional ten feet into the raging water at the foot of the falls. Carol's limp body was tumbled about, then swept away from the falls into calmer water. Her slack body snagged under a toppled tree that had fallen in the river. As the tree rose and fell in the current, her face cleared the water long enough for another life giving breath.

Jim, feeling the canoe swing, presenting its side to the current, expected the immanent capsize. As the canoe rolled pitching them out, he tried to hold on to the gunnel. For a single second he was successful – enough time for him to align with the current before his grip was broken. He went over the falls feet first, and landed flat on his back in the first pool. A deluge of water hit him in the face, tumbling him before he was swept out of the pool, and

G. Wm. Gotro

dropped at the base of the falls. Stunned after his head hit the rocks, he paddled weakly, managing to gain enough control to avoid hitting anything else. The tree that snagged Carol, also snagged Jim. He hung on to its topmost branches, his weight stopping the bobbing motion that was giving Carol vital air. Unaware of her presence, Jim was drowning Carol Danse. Thirty seconds passed while he regained his senses. He had to get out of the water. Downstream he saw a second fallen tree just beyond the rapids. He let go of the branch and was swept through the turbulence, then, swimming hard he managed to grasp the second tree, and hand over hand he pulled himself toward the river bank and out of the maelstrom. He lay on the ground, trying to assess the physical damage he had sustained. Where was Carlin, and what happened to Carol? Was he the sole survivor?

Carlin felt himself being swept over the falls head first. There was a momentary glimpse of the first pool, and he mentally thanked God that the drop wasn't two hundred feet. Then he hit the water landing on his belly. Stunned, he was immediately dumped over the edge, dropping into the pool at the base in a fetal position. Beneath the surface, the small of his back slammed into a slab of granite. The pain was blinding and he was helpless as the current hurtled him downstream. His eyes filled with water, and his mind was clouded by pain. Carlin saw only enough to dodge the fallen trees. He lifted his face clear of the water to breathe as he plunged down the river into calm water half a mile from the falls. In agonizing pain he dragged himself ashore. A prodigious fear filled him as he realized he was alone. He rested in the sand and wriggled his toes. Seeing them move confirmed that his back wasn't broken. Carlin got to his knees, and finally to his feet. Slowly, carefully, he staggered back toward the falls. It took him thirty minutes to cover the short distance.

The thundering of the falls and rapids beat against his eardrums, and in his weakened state he thought he could hear their voices crying out in terror as they plunged to oblivion. He was dizzy with the noise and sat down to keep from falling. The pain in his back was so intense, he rocked gently back and forth, moaning out loud as he did so. Slowly, like the spreading of a stain, anger filled Carlin. They had been through so much, fought so hard, and come so far. Now the Great Spirit had spared him alone. What the hell for? The pain, the noise, and the voices were all conspiring against him and Carlin cried out in anguish.

"Why have you taken my best friend from me oh Great Spirit – why have you taken my innocent woman?" Carlin shouted the words, and as if in answer, he thought he heard her voice, faintly calling for his help. Tears of remorse welled up in his eyes and he sat, his arms hugging his knees to his chest, watching the top of a fallen tree bobbing in the rushing current. Then he heard the voice again. He made his way down the bank and listened. At first there was nothing but the roar of the falls, and then he heard it again. It was weak but not far away, and he waited for the cry to come again. He remembered Jim's lesson for Carol; he heard the sound once more, and sighting along his arm and pointing finger he saw the wet buckskin of her shirt. The tree rose upward a few inches, and her face was clear of the water. She took a deep breath, and tried to call out, but the tree lowered in a trough, submerging her head, and cutting off the sound.

Trying to ignore the pain, Carlin plunged into the fury of the rapids. He knew if tried to edge himself out along the tree, his weight would drown her. He waded and swam, trying to lift the tree trunk to give her air. Ten minutes passed before he reached her. He lashed her arm to his with his belt, and then cut away the leather of her shirt. The splintered end of the branch that held her had punctured her shirt and driven itself under the muscle around the shoulder blade. She was impaled. Her screams tore him apart as he forced her against the current to free her body from the spear that held her. The agony of the movement was too much for her and she lost consciousness. Her body went limp and he freed her. Dragging her, he inched his way along the tree trunk until he could carry her ashore. His back burned with pain as he carried her up the bank to a soft patch of moss, and gently set her down. Then Carlin lost consciousness and he collapsed beside her.

Jim Peters considered the situation. Dead or alive, his companions had to be downstream from him. Reasonably dry now, Jim began to search the lower levels of the river. Within half a mile the river widened into a lake that was tranquil and calm. They would not have gone beyond this point, he concluded, and now with the sun lowering in the west, he made a bed for himself and slept until sunrise. When he awoke, he washed the sleep from his eyes, and began the search from the lake back to the falls. He had to know what fate had befallen his friends and he knew he could never rest until he possessed that knowledge.

Jim scouted the river and its banks, searching for any sign of his friends. Then, almost at the falls he saw the patch of buckskin still impaled on the broken branch of the fallen tree. It had to be from Carol's shirt – Carlin was wearing the shell of his parka minus the sleeves and lining. Looking high above him, Jim was stunned to find the canoe had not taken the plunge.

He would later discover that its bow rope had become tangled in a mass of roots projecting from the water at the head of the falls. Now, three feet of the stern protruded beyond the edge. He was relieved to know the canoe had not been dashed to pieces. Jim had no idea how long it could resist the turbulent waters – he had to climb to the top of the falls and secure the canoe. He found a reasonable access and after climbing to the crest, he was able to snag the bow rope and bring the canoe ashore. It still contained all of their food and belongings which had been fastened to the craft with leather thongs. Jim drew the canoe high up on dry ground, and turned its bottom up to shed any rain that might fall.

He stood at the head of the falls studying the surrounding terrain. In retrospect he realized there was no way the accident could have been prevented without walking the river's course before canoeing it. He shook his head in despair and looked back into the ravine that claimed his companions. Jim was about to descend to the foot of the falls once more, carrying a load of supplies from the canoe. At the edge of the precipice, a movement below caught his attention. He watched for several minutes but saw nothing more. Perhaps, he thought, it was a deer browsing. He continued the descent to the foot of the falls, and deposited the heavy load on a big rock near the river. Jim intended to go back to the canoe for the rest of the food and gear, then find a way to bring the canoe down to the lower level. Tired after recovering the second load, he sat resting on the big rock.

The thunder of the falls became an anodyne, and sitting with his knees drawn up and arms around them, he dozed for a few moments, lulled by the heartbeat of the river. He was almost asleep when he heard the cough. It was faint, too faint to be certain, but now, his senses fully alert, he stood listening for confirmation. A full five minutes passed before he heard it again, and this time it was accompanied by a whimper. On silent feet he moved toward the sound, and a hundred feet from where he had rested he found them. Carlin lay on his back breathing deeply in sleep. Beside him Carol lay on her stomach in the moss, not yet fully awake. The gaping hole in her shirt revealed the ripped and ugly wound in her back.

Jim removed his cotton shirt, cut away the sleeves and gently covered her wound. He disappeared into the woods and returned with a handful of large oval leaves, smooth on one face, and covered with fine hair on the obverse. He crushed the leaves in his hands and then soaked them in water for a few minutes before applying them to Carol's wound. She awakened as he pressed the leaves to her skin, and she was frightened until she heard his voice.

"Jim," she cried out trying to get to her knees, "we thought you were dead." Carlin opened his eyes at the sound of her voice, and tried to sit up. The agony of pain from his back forced him down again.

"Where the hell have you been?" Carlin asked in mock anger.

"In a rest home compared to you two," Jim answered. "what happened to you – did you beak any bones?"

"I don't know what I broke – all I know is excruciating back pain."

"Rest on your stomach," Jim said, helping Carlin to turn and exposing his lower back. From the bottom of the rib cage to the buttocks a massive bruise extended out for several inches on both sides of the spine. "It looks pretty bad," Jim said.

"I don't know what to do or say – except try not to move – just rest for now." He returned his attention to Carol, Packing the wound with the root flesh of the pond lily he then covered it with common plantain leaves. Within an hour Carol's pain had subsided, and Jim concentrated his efforts on reducing the swelling and the bruise in Carlin's back.

After an hour of searching, he located a patch of stinging nettles and carefully collected the leaves. He steeped the leaves in water

G. WM. GOTRO

for ten minutes and applied the infusion to Carlin's lower back. Pressing a little juice from the nettle stem, he mixed it with an equal amount of water and gave it to Carlin to drink. Unable to do much more, Jim made a small cooking fire and boiled water for a venison broth. Within the hour he had fed them and they began to respond to his administrations. They rested through the day and by nightfall Jim had set up a temporary shelter and soft sleeping pads for them.

In the days that followed, with Jim Peters tending to their needs, Carlin healed remarkably well, but he would later learn the extent of the damage, and experience intermittent back pain for the rest of his life. The wound in Carol's shoulder healed very slowly, and she lost part of her range of motion. Fortunately for her, both Carlin and Jim insisted that she exercise the arm and shoulder lightly, three times a day. Though she found it most painful she was dedicated and persistent about the exercise and made an almost full recovery.

In one area however, Carol could not recuperate. She had an inordinate fear of the canoe, and travelling on the water left her frightened and living in a private hell. She tried to hide her fear and apprehension, but both men knew what she was going through, and tried to help her at every opportunity by taking no risks.

They towed the canoe through the rapids and after walking the banks of the river once more, paddled to the lake Jim had seen on the day following the accident. They estimated the lake to be about five miles long and two miles wide. It was calm as a millpond in the early morning, and they were tempted to traverse it from end to end. For Carol's peace of mind, they skirted the shoreline rather than cross through the middle. Shortly after ten o'clock, the gentle breeze that had arisen, strengthened into a strong wind. The waves on the water were crested with foam, and they guessed the troughs depth to be two or three feet. By ten thirty they were obliged to draw the canoe high on the beach until the winds subsided. The lake was shallow and the waves' crests grew to five feet or more. Spume from the beach blew through the air, and by 2:00 P.M. they had to withdraw from the beach to stay dry.

"It's a damned good thing we skirted the shoreline," Jim said, "there is a lesson in that – we should have learned it long ago."

The high winds died as quickly as they were born, and at 4:30 they put the canoe back in the water and paddled slowly along the shoreline, until the sun settled on the treetops. The shore was no longer comprised of pebbles and beach sand, but now its character had altered to large rocks and eroded banks. Once or twice they felt rocks just below the surface, lightly scrape the canoe bottom. When they landed for the night, they poled the canoe sideways to the shore, allowing Carol to step out without getting wet. Once she and Carlin were on dry ground, Jim paddled a hundred feet farther to a small sandy spit. He drew the canoe halfway out of the water, unloaded their provisions, and tied the bow rope to a small tree.

In scouting the woods, they found a huge patch of blue berries and soon picked several pounds. On returning to the campsite, they were crossing through a little meadow, when Carlin suddenly veered off and jogged to the edge of the woods. He called to them and they followed. Carlin was standing under a massive apple tree.

"Look," he called out, "I found the gift of some traveller or bird from fifty years in the past."

The tree was laden with green apples, and they filled their arms. The apples would stay fresh for weeks and would provide them with vitamins. Later, at their campfire on the beach, Carol baked a half dozen and topped each one with a dollop of honey. While they ate their fill of the delicious fresh fruit each of them mentally thanked God – The Great Spirit, for the bounty He had given them in their hour of need.

They were contented with their day and talked until almost midnight before falling asleep to dream about their impending return to a normal happy life.

6

WIND, WAVES AND FIRE

Carlin awoke to the sound of the wind moaning in the trees just after daylight. At first he didn't want to get up, but the call of nature was insistent. He walked to the edge of the meadow and relieved himself, then returned to the campsite. A shower had passed through during the night and the fire was dead. He walked along the shoreline to check on the canoe. From a hundred feet away, he knew something was wrong. The line to the tree was drum tight and the bow was high off the sand. His heart began to hammer in his chest as he jogged to the little spit of sand. It was far worse than he thought. The canoe's bottom was in shreds and four ribs had broken from the pounding on submerged rocks. Their little watercraft was useless. Carlin drew the wreckage high on the beach, untied the lashings and carried the remainder of their gear to the campsite. The lake was very rough again, but it didn't matter. Their travel by water was at an end unless they could find a miraculous stand of white birch.

"Jim, wake up." Carlin shook him by the shoulder. Jim opened his eyes and for a few seconds he wasn't sure where he was. "We have more trouble," Carlin said, "We must do some serious planning."

"What happened?" Jim asked, coming to full awareness.

"This wind," Carlin answered, rubbing his hands through his hair, "it came up during the night and the canoe beat itself to death on the rocks."

Jim was on his feet and moving toward the sandspit. "C'mon," he called back, "we can't let this happen now." Carlin didn't hurry, but when he joined Jim, the big Ojibwa just stood there assessing the disaster, his head bowed and his shoulders slumped in defeat. He tried valiantly to recover. "We can fix it," he said, "we can have it back in the water in a few days," but he knew he was whistling in the dark.

"We must walk out now," Carlin said, "we haven't seen a white birch in three weeks. The trek out will be very slow and torturous, so we had best get going as soon as possible." They returned to the campsite where Carlin awakened Carol. "Time to go Sleeping Beauty," he said, stroking her hair.

She opened her eyes, and realizing she was the last to wake up, she tried to push herself into a sitting position. Her weak right shoulder sent a stab of pain through her and her breath caught in her throat. "What's the big hurry?" She asked. They told her about the canoe, expecting her to go to pieces. Slowly a smile came to her face.

"Well that's the first good news I've had in weeks," she said, "I never did trust that goddam boat after almost drowning in that stinking swamp." She got to her feet and stretched languorously. "So what do we do now?"

"We walk from here," Carlin said, "We are likely fifty miles from the main railway line but we will probably have to travel twice that far to get to it. If we are blocked by water we could be stuck here for another month."

They packed their possessions and began the trek at dawn the following morning.

Foot travel was difficult in the rugged terrain and they made poor time. Again and again they stopped to rest, and each time the rest period grew longer. They refused to acknowledge that they were in poor condition, with important vitamins and minerals missing from their sparse diet. After three days of hard hiking, they concluded that the only way out was the way they came. They were surrounded by water on three sides. To the west lay a wide, fast flowing river, they were unable to cross. To the south the river emptied into a huge lake that lay in an east northeast line, and they were trapped in the vee made by the two bodies of water. The forest was also changing. The coniferous trees were larger and

G. Wm. Gotro

grew in distinct groves. Where the conifer groves ended, the broad leaf trees were interspersed by dense brush and walking was slow and difficult. Seven days after leaving the canoe's remains on the sand spit, they arrived back where they started.

The sun was setting as they reached the sandspit and they dropped their packs and collapsed on the sand. They lay there exhausted for ten minutes, listening to the hum of the mosquitoes and the peeping of the frogs. Suddenly they heard an aeroplane engine cough and burst into life, and moments later Carlin determined that the pilot had started his takeoff run. Stunned, they watched as the plane appeared from behind a point of land, and they were looking at the tail, as it rose on the pontoon steppes and lifted off. They jumped and shouted and waved, but Carlin knew that the pilot and passengers would be watching the trees on the far side of the lake and would not likely circle back.

As the plane continued in a straight line, growing smaller in the distance, Jim stopped waving and his arms hung loosely at his sides in defeat. Carlin imagined being in the cockpit and easing back on the stick. As he mentally flew the plane, he circled back to see the three people standing dejected on the tiny sandspit.

For a moment his breath caught in his throat. He felt dogged by disaster, and knew the pilot would not be coming back.

Carol kept waving until the plane disappeared and then she fell to the sand. "Come back," she cried, "Come back you miserable evil bastard – you can't just leave us here," and she kept shouting long after the engine noise had been absorbed by the silence. She called out after him until her voice was hoarse, and then she sobbed until there were no more tears. Carlin cradled her in his arms and tried to give her hope – tried to allay her fears. Finally she grew quiet and a strange calm came over her. Without eating her evening meal Carol fell asleep just after dark.

Jim made a fire and he sat with Carlin, smoking his pipe and drinking wintergreen tea. The sight of the plane on the water, so near and yet so far, had changed Jim Peters too. He was quiet by nature, but now there was introversion as well. For the rest of their wilderness ordeal he never mentioned the plane again. In another side of his character, there developed a deep sense of purpose – a resolve that only death could destroy. He was going to put them on the Vermillion River bridge if it killed him.

Carlin had the advantage over the others because he didn't expect the pilot to turn back once he was in the air. He knew what had to happen in the cockpit once the throttle was opened. the pilot would never look back, he was too absorbed with the takeoff routine, and had no reason to think three survivors may be trying to signal him. Carlin knew the outside world had written them off as dead months ago. He had seen the sudden defeat when Jim's shoulders slumped and he quit waving to the vanishing plane – Jim was losing hope. Carol was moving into a state of advanced depression and that could be fatal for all of them.

He lay awake trying to develop a strategy to bring them back to life, hope, and determination. And finally he slept.

As usual Carlin was the first to awaken. He had dreamed of something exciting. He could almost focus it, but it fell apart. Now he sat in the early morning mist, nursing the feeble coals of last night's fire back to life, and thinking about the dream. A heavy dew had fallen through the night, and the kindling was damp. The new fire was smoky and brought tears to his eyes. They had to cross the lake or the river if they were to reach the railway line and rescue. The question was how. A whimsical puff of air swirled the smoke into Carlin's eyes again and he leaned away from the fire. Something scratched at the outer edge of his memory but he threw it away, concentrating on the problem of crossing the water. An idea began to form. A quarter mile from the sandspit, the lake emptied into the river, and Carlin remembered one place where the river water flowed very fast. Suddenly he wanted to go there – for some obscure reason he had to go there.

Carlin made good time getting to the spot on the river and it was better than he thought. The water flowed very fast through the narrow channel, and he estimated it to be waist deep. It would certainly sweep a one hundred sixty pound man away, but he wondered if a three hundred pound man would suffer the same fate. From the bank, he probed the bottom with a pole, and his guess at the depth proved accurate. Carlin threw a small stick upstream and watched as it swept past. He threw a much larger piece of wood in and noted that it did not sweep past at the same speed. It moved slightly slower. The odds were not good, but they

G. Wm. Gotro

were better than being trapped. He hurried back to the sandspit.

"Where did you go night walker?" Jim asked, pouring fresh coffee for him.

"To the river headwaters," Carlin replied, "I have an idea for getting to the other side." He sipped the hot coffee, and told Jim his theory. "If a big boulder sat on the bottom of the river at that point it wouldn't be swept away because of its weight. Maybe if we were heavy enough, we wouldn't be swept downstream either."

Jim didn't speak for a minute or so – he was thinking hard about Carlin's suggestion. Finally he reached a conclusion. "If you are right," Jim said thoughtfully, "we could have walked across the head of the falls rather than being swept over."

"But we were out of control. We were not starting out on our feet, but horizontal in the water," Carlin countered, "I am certain that we could walk across the head of the falls if we were carrying something heavy for ballast."

"How long will it take us to walk to the top end of this lake and then follow the river to the falls where we started?" Jim asked.

"Four days at the most," Carlin said, "I say we start right now. Where is Carol?"

"She said she was going to get washed," Jim replied, "I don't know what's taking her so long." The two men looked at each other, and then in unspoken mutual understanding, Jim started walking the lake shore to the north while Carlin went south to the sandspit. Jim found her – she ran into his arms.

"We have to get out of here," she said, "while I was getting washed I smelled smoke and it wasn't from our campfire. I went to investigate. The people who left in the plane must have been careless because there is a small bush fire back in there!"

She pointed to the northwest. Jim could see the smoke now.

"Stay here," he ordered, "don't move – I have to find Carlin."

When Carlin saw the fire he blanched. The wind was out of the northwest. If the fire expanded, as he knew it would, they would be trapped in the vee. The smoke was starting to billow now. They had to move fast. "Our only chance is to follow the lake shore back to the falls. If we can get across there we will be safe until the fire jumps the river. Let's go." They stuffed their meagre belongings into the packs, and followed the lake shore northward as fast as they could move.

They kept up the pace until noon, then stopped to rest. Looking back they could see the ugly smoke from the fire, and Carlin remembered the anxiety he felt in the early morning, when his eyes burned with smoke. He laughed, but the sound was cynical.

"What's so funny," Jim asked.

"We have spent the best part of a year trying to keep a fire going, and now we have to run like hell to get away from one. What is even more ironic is the fact that this fire will either kill us, or bring us a rescue team."

By late afternoon, exhausted, they reached the falls that almost killed them. The tree that impaled Carol was now their salvation. Jim led the way. With his arm around Carol's waist he waded into the fast water of the river. Carlin followed, his arm also around her waist, ensuring she wouldn't be swept away. They edged their way along the fallen tree and within ten minutes they were safe on the opposite bank. Looking back they could see the first tongues of flame reaching into the high trees a mile away. They trekked their way down river as fast as they could move, reaching the headwaters of the lake before dark. They cut boughs and made a sleeping pad, and they watched the progression of the orange glow in the sky as the fire devastated prime forest. Fortunately for them, the fire was moving toward the northwest.

Early the following morning, they were awakened by the roar of a water bomber as it doused the leading edge of the conflagration. Two helicopters also collected water from the lake and dumped it in strategic locations to contain the fire. At 10:00 A.M. a DeHavilland twin Otter landed with the first fire fighters. Carlin attracted the pilot's attention as he taxied near them. Minutes later a Zodiac skimmed across the water and a Forest Ranger began to question them about the fire. Carlin told him of the fishing party and their negligence with the campfire.

The ranger couldn't understand why they were partly dressed in buckskins, nor could he comprehend the woman's tears. "How long have you folks been here?" He asked, studying their clothes and generally poor condition.

"I crashed my Cessna at Crystal Lake last November," Carlin said casually, "we managed to survive the winter and we have been trying to get out ever since."

"Well you're on your way out now," the ranger said smiling, "You were given up for dead by the end of November as I recall," and he switched on his radio and told the Otter pilot to hold for transport. They boarded the Zodiac and within minutes they were seated in the aeroplane and turning into the wind for takeoff. After they were airborne the pilot contacted the Ontario Department of Lands and Forests and was directed to fly them to Sudbury Ontario.

When they sighted the smoke stacks at International Nickel's Copper Cliff operation they became very quiet and introverted. Minutes later the plane landed and they stepped out on the dock. Jim Peters took Carlin's hand and Carol's and they formed a circle.

"This circle is unbroken and eternal," Jim said with bowed head, "There is no beginning and no end and we will be together always. Time and distance have no meaning, for we have been made One by Manitou – The Great Spirit." Then he released their hands and hugged them in a bear hug while flash bulbs popped, and Forestry officials and reporters converged on them. The police stopped them from being mobbed by the small crowd of press, television and radio personnel. Carlin spoke for them.

"We are tired, hungry, dirty, and confused," he said, holding up his hands in supplication, "We want a hot bath, a hot meal, a real bed, and some comfortable clothes, so how about a press conference tomorrow at 10:00 A.M." The police cordoned them off from the media, and then hurried them into the Forestry building. Within an hour they were showered, and provided with fresh clothes and footwear. After a light meal and some real coffee, they were debriefed by the Forestry Department officials and allowed to contact their families.

Carol was the first to leave, and after arranging to meet them at the press conference the next day, she kissed Jim and Carlin goodbye, and left for the home of one of her colleagues. Jim's family arrived to take him back to the reserve and Carlin stood alone, looking out the window at the lake and the aeroplanes moored there. After spending nine and a half months with Jim and Carol he knew the bitter loneliness he would live with from here on. He turned at the touch of a hand on his shoulder.

"Come my brother," Jim said in a voice choked with emotion, "It is time for us to go home." He put his arm around Carlin's shoulder and pressed him forward.

"You have your family Jim, you should be with them, not with me. But I would be grateful for a ride to the reserve. OntAir is only a short walk from there."

"You will not stay at Ontair tonight. You will stay with your people. They have adopted you Carlin, and you cannot, you MUST not turn your back on them."

Though they had been given little or no notice, they had prepared a great feast in honour of the return of their sons from the dead. The celebration went on until midnight. It was then that the Grand Chief called for attention and a gradual silence filled the long house. A drum beat began and an old woman sang a song in the Ojibwa tongue. Her voice, cracked with age, uttered strange sounds, and finally her song ended. The cadence of the drumbeat changed.

"This woman is the sister of my deceased mother," Jim said nodding in her direction, "she has taken us as her sons, and now she is our mother, and you are my brother." The Grand Chief began to speak and the drumbeat altered again. When he stopped speaking, the drum beat also stopped and for a moment the long house was quiet. "He welcomes you to the Ojibwa family," Jim said with a smile. "Now you are one of us, and now you have all the privileges and responsibilities of the tribe. There will be a sunrise ceremony tomorrow morning at OntAir – I think he is going to bestow some sort of rights on you." The celebration went on long after midnight, and a very tired and happy Carlin retired in the house of his brother, to sleep until an hour before dawn.

Jim woke Carlin at first light, and they made their way to OntAir. The place was a mess. Inside the cabin, the rooms were festooned with spider webs and dust. Outside, weeds and grass were a foot high, the dock needed repair, and the windows in the cabin were caked with grime. Carlin looked around the room, touching this and that, remembering.

"Well Jim," he began, shrugging his shoulders, "it will give me something to do for a month or so," indicating the state of disrepair with a broad sweep of his hand. Jim laughed, shaking his head in

G. WM. GOTRO

the negative.

"We have much more important things to take care of – come with me," Jim replied, leading Carlin outside again. "Look."

Chief Orren Flagg and thirty people had assembled at the edge of the woods, and now, men, women, and children gathered near the dock. Jim pointed to the water. Two hundred yards away, four young men, straddling the floats of Charlie Redwing's Beaver, were paddling it toward the dock and singing an Ojibwa song as they moved in unison. Orren Flagg put his hand on Carlin's shoulder.

"Charlie Redwing went south for the winter," he said in a voice filled with emotion. "but he never came home. Before he died, he asked that you should have his plane, and Stuart Fraser went down the coast to fly Charlie's body home in the Beaver. It was a fitting thing to do. Stuart Fraser is a good man – he looked for you every time he flew over the north country but he could never find you. Now, Charlie's family want you to have his plane." The old man's eyes filled with tears – tears of sorrow for the loss of Charlie Redwing – tears of joy for having a new son amongst his people. "Now you and Jim must go to the city to tell your story. When you return, your place will be as you left it a year ago."

And so it was that Carlin and Jim Peters became true brothers, and Carlin became an Ojibwa.

Carlin was choked with emotion. The old man opened his arms to his new son and Carlin embraced him, his eyes filled with tears of joy. "Thank you Orren – this is the proudest day of my life. Please thank my people – in Ojibwa." The old man nodded his assent.

At 10:00 A.M. Jim, Carol, and Carlin told their incredible story to the media. The questions were legion, and some of them opened old wounds.

"Was the crash carelessness or was it caused by a malfunction of the aeroplane?"

"No,"

"No what? – Was it carelessness or was it a malfunction of..."

"No it was not carelessness and no it was not a malfunction of the aeroplane."

"Did you start the forest fire now raging near Crystal Lake?"

"No. It was started by careless fishermen."

"Can you prove the fire was not your doing as a means to get out?"

"No. The question is not worth answering. We are survivors not arsonists."

"What will you do now that you have been rescued?"

"We plan to do it all over again but under much better conditions."

"Will you write a book now?"

"No. I am not an author."

"Is it true that you are a white man living with the Ojibwa?"

"I think it is obvious that I am a white man. What is not obvious is that I am an Ojibwa.

"Are you an Ojibwa by birth?"

"No. I was born to be an Ojibwa – ask my brother."

The media questioned Jim and Carol in more depth, having given up on Carlin.

"Ms. Danse the ordeal you survived must have been terrible for you – what will you do now that it is over?"

"I intend to go back to my job, and frankly, I can't wait," She looked toward Carlin and Jim. Carlin's face held the faintest trace of a smile, while Jim studied his own feet. Carol blushed. "Of course it wasn't all bad," Carol said, "There were some happy times too."

"Will you be writing a book about your survival since Mr. McKenzie doesn't seem interested?"

"That is a distinct possibility," Carol said, "presuming I have the time of course."

"When will you be returning to work?" The reporter asked, his pencil poised over the note pad.

"Perhaps as early as tomorrow," she replied, "I want to get back to my project. There is a great deal of new information to add to the files about the Ojibwa culture."

The questions continued for several minutes while Carlin watched and listened. Carol Danse was running out of glib answers, and the press turned to Jim Peters.

"Mr. Peters it seems quite apparent that your native skills saved the lives of Mr. McKenzie and Ms. Danse. How difficult was ..."

"We cared for each other," Jim said, cutting the reporter off in mid sentence. "Ms. Danse and I would have drowned had Carlin not rescued us from the submerged plane. Ms. Danse also saved my life by shooting a bear that attacked me. Carlin and Carol Danse developed a system for making arrows that would take down big game. By doing that they ensured our food supply. We didn't survive singly, we survived as a team."

"Would you tell us about the special arrow?"

"No, not at this time."

"Okay, would you tell us about Carlin the Ojibwa? Does he have Indian blood?

"Carlin's blood is the same colour as mine, and he has the same status as any Ojibwa male – there is no difference."

"How did you survive the -40 temperatures?"

"In a tepee," Jim said, trying to look very serious.

"How did you ward off starvation?" The reporter asked.

"By eating a lot," Jim answered.

"What did your diet consist of?"

"Bulrush bannock, moose meat roasts, water cress, wild rice, wild honey and bush coffee." Jim looked across at Carlin who was smiling broadly. "Of course breakfasts were not as elaborate. They were simple – rice sprinkled with maple sugar, bannock, and coffee." Finally the reporters left them alone, hurrying off to write their stories.

Carlin asked Jim and Carol to join him for lunch. He had twelve dollars that he found in a coffee can back at OntAir. Over a sparse lunch, they talked about everything but the inevitable parting of the ways.

"What will you do now Jim?" Carol asked.

"Oh I have a great deal to do for my people," he said, smiling at her. "There are families in distress, houses to build, a school to be repaired, and calls to be made to the Department of Indian Affairs."

"And you Carlin – what will you do now – will I ever see you again?" She asked, and her heart pounded awaiting his answer.

"If you want me for any reason Carol, you need only to call," he said softly. "I will be doing a lot of flying for my people I suspect."

"Where will you get a new plane?" She asked, puzzled by his reply.

"Charlie Redwing died in North Carolina last winter," Carlin explained, "His family wanted me to have his plane. The Beaver is moored at the OntAir dock. The Great Spirit was very generous toward me," he concluded. Carlin didn't want her to go, but he knew she wouldn't be happy at anything but her archaeology.

Carol was happy for Carlin – now, at last, he wouldn't be alone. He had more than a friend, he had a nation to cherish. She wondered if she would be completely happy ever again. Oh she had a generous lump of back-pay coming to her, and her job seemed to be secure, but did anyone love her as Carlin and Jim had through the ordeal? She suspected not.

When the meal ended and they stood outside the cafe. They stood for a moment in a triangle, facing each other. Carlin reached into his pocket and then he held out his closed hands to them. "Take these," he said, flashing them a mysterious smile, "I found them in a little creek." He opened his clenched fists and in each hand there lay a sizeable gold nugget. Carol and Jim accepted the proffered gifts. Then Carlin took the third nugget from his pocket and they each held out a hand containing a golden nugget.

"The circle is still unbroken," he said repeating Jim's words, "It has no beginning and no end. It is eternal, and we will be together always."

Carol's heart was full, as she turned and left them, and in His heaven, the Great Spirit smiled at his children and He knew they were good.

The following day Carol Danse reported in for work at the Northern Archaeological Institute where she was welcomed back by the director, and her immediate supervisor. After the formalities were concluded, Carol's supervisor walked with her to the workplace.

"Carol, there have been a few minor changes in the staff. When the air search failed to find you, a replacement was brought in to finish your project." The supervisor, Mrs. Stapp, was being very guarded. "Of course there is no need for you to be concerned. You are more valuable to the Institute as a celebrity than as a field worker at the moment. Your incredible story will draw a great deal of interest to the Institute's work. In turn, that will attract financial benefits which would be most appreciated."

G. WM. GOTRO

"I am certain you are right," Carol countered, "and while I am delighted to help the Institute with its funding, my first love is my job as an archaeologist – that is what I really want to do." Carol was trembling inside. Was Mrs. Stapp saying Carol's days were numbered?

The older woman smiled at Carol and for a split second Carol saw the grin of a great white shark. "Come and meet Stella Bronte," Mrs. Stapp said, opening the door to the reconstruction centre. Carol's heart sank – there was only one person in the room, and she had to be Stella Bronte. The woman was about twenty five years of age, and she worked with the easy confidence of a true professional. She was tall and exquisite, with dark hair and flashing green eyes, and all her curves were generous and in the right places. Stella left her project when they entered the room, and approached them with a smile more radiant than sunshine.

"Oh Mrs. Stapp," she said effusively, "this has to be Carol Danse." Her delicate hand shot out in a welcoming gesture, "she is even more lovely than you described her." Mrs. Stapp was glowing – everything was going very well indeed. "It is a privilege and an honour to meet you Ms. Danse."

"Well I am certainly honoured that Mrs. Stapp has chosen such a bright and beautiful successor to fill the position," Carol said pointedly. "Congratulations Mrs. Stapp."

"Oh I am not your successor Ms. Danse," Stella said sincerely, "it would take me years to acquire your depth of knowledge of the Ojibwa people." She blushed. "I am just here to help in any small way that will assist you in your work." Stella Bronte was a master tactician.

"Come Carol," Mrs. Stapp said, "we should go over to Accounting – I'm quite sure they will have your back pay ready. You should take a few days off to become accustomed to a normal life once again." Was this the bum's rush Carol asked herself, as Mrs. Stapp chattered away about what Carol found at Crystal Lake, and how she would have to report the findings at the dig.

For the next three weeks, Carol's time was filled with reporters, television producers, radio talk show hosts and magazine editors – all asking the same questions. Each developed their own slant on the answers she gave. She attended an endless number of dinners and evening meetings as a guest speaker. What Carol did NOT do however, was any work as an archaeologist. Frustrated and hurt, she made an appointment to see the director of the institute.

"Ah Ms. Danse, it is very good to see you are recovering from your terrible ordeal. How are you feeling now?" He asked with a shallow level of mock concern. He sat behind a huge desk that was devoid of the smallest scrap of paper. He leaned forward, his elbows on the desktop, and his finger tips touching, not unlike the spire of a church. It was, she supposed, his classic pose when dealing with an underling, and it irritated her immensely.

"Well Mr. Borland," she began, trying to restrain herself from blurting out something that would get her fired, "I don't seem to be suffering any serious physical after-effects from my time in the wilderness. I am, however, deeply disturbed by something else."

"Oh I am sorry to hear that," Borland said, smiling incongruously. "Is there something I can do to help?"

"Yes sir," Carol answered, "You can let me return to my job."

"But you have been back at your job for a month now, have you not?"

"No sir, I have not. I have been running around telling and re-telling the story of our survival, and that has nothing to do with my job. I am an archaeologist, not a celebrity with a great story."

"Well Ms. Danse I am very sorry to hear that you are unhappy. I will have a word with Mrs. Stapp and perhaps we can settle this matter. Will that suit you?"

"Yes sir," Carol said with a smile, "that will suit me just fine."

The following week Mrs. Stapp gave Carol a field assignment at Clara Belle Lake in the Sudbury District. The lake was extremely high in acid, being within a mile or two of the Copper Cliff smelter. Only a few stunted and misshapen trees dotted an otherwise barren landscape, and local residents referred to it as a moonscape with water. When Carol arrived there she knew she was being given the fast shuffle. Mrs. Stapp and/or the Institute were intent on getting rid of her by forcing her to quit of her own volition. But Carol Danse did not respond well to that type of pressure and she remained, unhappy and unfulfilled in her job for three long years.

When Carlin and Jim returned from the press conference,

       G. Wm. Gotro

Carlin's OntAir cabin was freshly painted. The windows sparkled and the place was immaculate. The grass had been cut and two new flower beds had been set out with plants. The dock had been stained and the railings were painted, and best of all the DeHavilland Beaver rocked gently at the dock. Carlin was deeply grateful for what they had done, and he finally realized that the Ojibwa had truly adopted him as one of their own. He experienced a deep warmth in that, and his love for his adopted people grew stronger day by day.

He awoke late one morning, after working most of the night. Someone was tapping on his door. Wiping sleep from his eyes, he responded to the insistent tapping. Mary Whitebird stood on the step, her eyes filled with tears. In her arms she held a three year old boy. The child had been bitten by a Mississauga rattler an hour before. He was clinging stubbornly to life. His little leg was swollen and discoloured with poison, and Carlin guessed the child would die before he could get him to a hospital. He laid the baby on the table and filled a milk bottle with hot water. Then, after sterilizing his knife, he cut into the bite area, and emptying the bottle he placed the mouth of it over the incised bite area. As the bottle cooled it drew much of the poison and a little blood from the wound. Carlin bandaged the child's leg and hurried mother and child into the Beaver.

Within minutes he was in the air, and by radio, he called for an ambulance to meet him at Ramsey Lake in Sudbury. He set the Beaver down gently, and taxied to the Austin Airways dock where the ambulance and a doctor were waiting. Carlin lifted the little boy in his arms and carried him to the waiting gurney. The doctor administered antivenin before the baby was loaded into the ambulance. One of the other bush pilots gave Carlin his car and he drove Mary Whitebird to the Sudbury General Hospital. It was two hours before the doctor advised them that the baby was stabilized and sleeping, and they could see him in the morning.

Mary Whitebird was relieved, knowing now, her little boy would live. Relaxed, she made a request of Carlin.

"Could you drive me to the Salvation Army Hostel," she said, embarrassed, "I only have ten dollars with me, but they will let me stay there tonight." The truth was, Mary Whitebird was married to an alcoholic who spent every cent they had, and the ten dollars was all she had in the world.

Carlin took her to the finest hotel in the city and he booked separate rooms for himself and the woman. When they were settled in, he tapped at her door as she had done at OntAir earlier in the day. She opened it cautiously, and was relieved to see the visitor was Carlin.

"Come Mary Whitebird," he said gently, "you haven't eaten, we will go for a late lunch." She demurred, feeling insignificant and poverty stricken, but Carlin knew what she was feeling and insisted on her acceptance. They had a light lunch at her request, and afterward he took her to see some of the sights in the city. They stopped at the hospital on the way back to the hotel, but were told the boy was sleeping peacefully and should not be disturbed.

They would be allowed to see him in the morning. Later in the evening Carlin took Mary Whitebird to dinner, and cared for her until bedtime.

The baby was released two days later, and Carlin flew them back to the reservation. Mary's husband had sobered up only to find his wife and child gone. Jim Peters told him about the snake bite and Carlin's action. Sam Whitebird was ashamed that he had failed to care for his family, and called Alcoholics Anonymous.

When Mary and Carlin returned with the little boy there was a celebration. Sam Whitebird continued going through the twelve step program and never touched a drink again. The word about Carlin's kindness toward Mary Whitebird spread throughout the village and true bonding took place between Carlin and his adopted people.

Jim Peters approached the Minister Of Education and the Minister of Aboriginal Affairs. After six months of lobbying a sum of money was transferred to the band council. It was to be used for education, and within the following six months Jim, Carlin, and four young men built a school complete with a small daycare centre. Teachers were hired and by the end of the following year, Ojibwa children came from miles around to be educated. They were taught more than the three 'R's, were taught their own history, and spirituality, and they would, become leaders of the Ojibwa nation.

G. WM. GOTRO

Carlin recognized the need for a hospital in the Ojibwa community, one that would merge surgical, homeopathic, and pharmaceutical skills, with the medicinal knowledge and spiritual practices of the Ojibwa healers. It became his dream.

For Jim, the dream became a decent sanitation system. In the villages on the reserve there were still many outhouses. In more affluent areas septic systems were in place but most of them were old and many were failing. When Jim solicited estimates for sewers and a plant to process the waste, the cost was in the millions. It appeared there was no way to turn his dream into reality.

When Carlin was not flying charters, he was working in the villages on the reserve. He and Jim Peters set up three locations where the young people could gather, listen to music, and dance. On alternate nights, there were acting classes and plays. Gradually the use of alcohol and drugs diminished, and the kids stayed out of trouble. The success of the three centres gave Jim and Carlin deep satisfaction and the teen age suicide rate fell.

They estimated the cost of the hospital and it was far beyond what Indian Affairs, or any other government agency would consider. As for the sanitation system, it would cost three times as much as the entire hospital project – the future for both projects seemed very bleak.

Almost three years had elapsed since they returned from the crash. Jim was visiting Carlin at OntAir which had been renamed Air Ojibwa. He was depressed. A recent letter from the Department of Indian Affairs advised them that the Department's budget was unable to provide funds for any projects on the reservation for at least twenty-four months.

"The projects do not have to be scrapped," Carlin said, honing his knife. "It is time for us to return to Camp Good Fortune." It was Carlin's name for the Dawson Lake gold find. Jim laughed at his term.

"That sounds like a Boy Scout Camp," Jim said, watching Carlin hone the knife.

"That is precisely why I use the silly name. The last thing we need is to have someone get wise to our gold discovery." He began to strop the knife on a piece of leather. He tested the edge, and it was sharp as a razor blade. "I have been collecting small pieces of mining equipment for well over a year," Carlin said, "a little here and a little there. No one will ever connect us to a gold mine operation." Carlin slipped the knife into its sheath. When he looked at Jim, each man saw a new light in the other's eyes.

"Have you ever heard from Carol?" Jim asked. It was a question completely out of character for him.

"No, have you?" Carlin answered with a question. Jim shook his head in the negative, and picking up Carlin's honing stone, he began to sharpen his own knife.

"No," Jim said, "but she was in love with you."

"Nah, I don't believe that," Carlin replied, "Her first love was her work and the publicity when we got back. I doubt I will ever hear from her again." He began to draw file the blade of the light axe they used throughout their survival days.

"I think that is an unfair comment," Jim said. "Neither of us has tried to contact her. We don't know what has happened in her life since our return."

Carlin had learned much about the Ojibwa spirituality and realized that his opinion did not fit with the ethics of his new found nation.

"When do you intend to leave for Camp Good Fortune," Jim asked, "and how long do you intend to stay?"

"I hope to leave on June 23, and we will stay through July, August, and September. If necessary we can stay until mid October to finish up, but I will never risk another freeze-up," Carlin answered.

They made preparations for the project, and on June 19th Carlin disappeared. Jim couldn't find him anywhere. His cabin at Air Ojibwa was locked, but Jim knew where the spare key was hidden. Inside he found nothing that gave him a clue to Carlin's whereabouts. Jim checked the Beaver and found the doors locked. Carlin had gone out on foot. Jim trudged his way home and returned the following morning. Carlin was busy around the cabin and had made coffee for both of them.

"Where the hell have you been?" Jim asked in mock anger.

"Oh, I had some business to attend to," Carlin said with a smile. "Let's go get your gear and load the plane."

G. Wm. Gotro

"My gear is already in the plane," Jim answered, "we should load yours." They worked most of the day at final preparations, and by late afternoon the plane was loaded with the finest gear money could buy. The last item stowed was a brand new sixteen foot fibreglass canoe.

Late in the evening of the twenty second, they finished tidying the cabin, and disposed of any perishables. After a final cup of tea and a pipe of tobacco, Carlin stood and stretched. "It's time to turn in," he said. "takeoff time is 07:30 tomorrow morning."

BOOK TWO

7

THE FULL CIRCLE

For three years Carol Danse had struggled at her job. The Institute had been most unfair in their treatment of her. Within the upper echelon were several people who detested her, simply because for a brief moment she had been a celebrity. Throughout the three years since her return to civilization she had been given only the most boring, mundane jobs. Carol felt insignificant and though she had often thought of Carlin and Jim, she shunned them, rejecting any urge to contact them out of shame of her position.

When she decided to leave the Institute, she planned her own future for the first time since her return from the wilderness. She would go to Toronto and make a fresh start, and she would give her resignation to the director at the end of June. The decision made, she returned to her lab stopping at the Institute's bulletin board.

A piece of birch bark with a message written on it riveted her attention. The message was the ultimate in simplicity.

"Vermillion River bridge, 8.00 A.M. June 23 rd. The circle is not complete."

Carol's heart soared when she read the note. It had to be from Carlin! He wanted her to meet him at the same spot they had first met. She prepared her resignation and submitted it to the office of the director. He had long been a party to the ostracizing of Carol Danse. His was the guilt of omission, for though he was aware of the bad treatment, he did nothing to correct it. After such a long time, Carol's resignation came as a total surprise.

"Are you certain that you want to do this?" he asked, raising his eyebrows.

"It's done," Carol said, looking him square in the eyes. "You can accept it or not – I won't be here tomorrow."

"May I ask what prompted you to take this drastic action?" He asked trying to evade his self imposed guilt.

"I will answer your question Mr. Director," she said, her manner cool and detached, "you already know the answer but you can't face your own failure to confront the real problem – Mrs. Stapp. My capability as an archaeologist has been untapped for three years and you know it. Hunting for fossils at Clara Belle Lake is the work of a high school student – not the work of a professional archaeologist. You just didn't have the guts to fire me because you didn't have a just cause. I denied you that comfort by doing exactly what was asked of me. Now it's my turn. I am going back to Crystal Lake to finish my research into the most fascinating archaeological story in this century."

She turned her back on him and walked to the door of his ornate office. Before leaving she paused for a moment, studying his face. His shame was evident by the deep blush he couldn't prevent. "You see Mr. Borland, I think I know why the Ojibwa culture died out there after a hundred years, and I have proof. Moreover I have the draft of a book on the subject and I intend to give it to one of the prominent universities. They will enjoy the honour of publishing the work – they deserve it, and you, and Stapp do not."

"BUT," he was fuming, "But ..."

"Go to hell Borland, you just lost the game – and take Stapp with you." She slammed his office door, and a picture of a young Borland receiving his degree, fell to the floor, a long shard of glass penetrating his heart in the photo.

The following morning, a much happier Carol Danse sang in the shower, had a long luxurious breakfast, and looking great, went shopping.

At 7:15 A.M. on June 23rd Carlin started the P&W Wasp engine on Ojibwa Air's De Havilland Beaver. It roared to life filling the air with the intoxicating smell of 100 octane aviation fuel and Castrol Aero oil. He taxied the Beaver to the end of the lake and turned into the gentle early morning breeze. Carlin set the flaps and began to nudge the throttle forward. He looked across at

Jim Peters and grinned.

"We haven't got a full load," Jim said, "otherwise everything is the same as it was three years ago when we left for Crystal Lake,"

"I intend to fly the exact same pattern as I did then Jim, I would like to remember it all over again." He eased the wheel back gently and the Beaver leaped into the air, trailing a stream of silver water from the floats. Carlin glanced at the compass and swung the Beaver onto a heading for the Vermillion River bridge.

It was precisely 8:00 A.M. when Carlin spotted the solitary figure on the bridge. He knew she would be there, and at the sight of the plane she scrambled down the embankment. Once again, Jim loaded her gear into the plane, and she took the right hand seat. Carol leaned across and kissed Carlin.

"I haven't kissed a cobra in three years," she said laughing, "come to think of it, I haven't kissed anyone in three years."

"We can make up for that when we get to the lake," Carlin said ruffling her hair. He opened the throttle, and the Beaver surged ahead. He circled the bridge once before turning north to Crystal Lake. The flight northward was to visit the past, and as the miles slipped away beneath them, Carol recognized some of the places they had been, when Carlin pointed them out to her. At several places along the way Carlin descended to three or four hundred feet above the terrain. Jim guessed that Carlin was looking for something special, but Carol didn't understand why he risked flying so low.

Carlin landed the plane at noon, on a long narrow lake at the base of a high hill. He turned the Beaver toward the hill and ran the floats up on the sandy beach. Jim knew where they were, but to Carol it was just another lake.

"This is a pretty place," Carol said, her head tilted back to see the hill top. "I thought we were going to Crystal Lake. What made you stop here?"

Carlin was the last out of the plane and as he stepped off the float, he bowed to her with a sweeping gesture of his hand. "Welcome to Camp Good Fortune," he said, taking her hand, and though she didn't notice he winked at Jim. "Come with me for a minute," he said. They walked a hundred yards down the beach and stopped. "Listen," he said, "what do you hear?"

"Nothing," she replied, and paused, "I don't hear anything."

"Ahhh you have been too long in civilization – you have forgotten Mr. Peters lesson about the frog."

He listened and slowly he turned, pointing his finger. Then he stopped. Carol listened carefully.

"Yes, yes," she said you're right – I hear it now. It is a little waterfall." Pulling Carlin by the hand she ran to the miniature cascade of clear water. "It is beautiful Carlin – you knew it was here didn't you?" She hugged him. "I'm happy to be with you again." He walked to the edge of the brook and knelt down.

"Come and see what I found Carol." She knelt down beside him and looked into the miniature pool. The flashes of silver light reflected from the sunlit water were almost blinding and she shielded her eyes with her hand.

"Carlin, it is like something from a fairy tale," she said happily.

"You don't know the half of it," he said with a deep laugh, and he plunged his hands into the pool. Jim was standing silently behind her, his face radiated a cherubic smile.

"Stop teasing her Carlin," he said, "show her what Camp Good Fortune is all about."

Carlin lifted a flat rock from the water and looked carefully at the bottom as the murky water was flushed away. He plunged his hands into the stream again, and withdrew them from the sparkling silver water. He opened them to her. Each hand held small mound of stones and gravel. Buried within the gravel were seven small nuggets. Jim picked them out of Carlin's outstretched hands and rinsed them in the water. Now free of any detritus and sand, the seven tiny nuggets sparkled in the sun.

Jim emptied the nuggets into Carol's hand. "Here," he said, "don't drop these, I haven't any idea what they are worth now, but at the end of the war they would have been worth about thirty dollars. He went back to the plane and returned within minutes carrying a gold pan. Carlin grubbed around the hole left by the rock, filling the pan with gravel and mud. He held the pan in a manner that allowed the flowing water to wash out the mud and the light sand, then he rocked it gently until only the heaviest material remained. In the bottom of the pan now lay a number of small gold flakes. a little gravel, some black sand, and three small nuggets. At

G. Wm. Gotro

2:00 P.M. they stopped work at the stream and prepared a midday meal.

"What is the value of the gold we collected since noon," Carol asked excitedly.

"Oh about two hundred, maybe two hundred fifty dollars," Carlin answered, "It depends on the market prices day by day."

When Carlin looked up, she was studying him intently. "Is something wrong?" He asked.

"No," she answered, "there is nothing wrong – I am just curious. How long have you known about this gold mine? This is where you got the nuggets you gave Jim and me, isn't it."

"Yes," he said casually.

"You have known about this place for three years and this is the first time you have taken anything from it." She spoke it as a question, but he didn't answer her. Instead he threw a few more sticks in the rock fireplace they had built.

Jim answered her instead, and he answered with a question. "Were you pressed for money after we were rescued Carol?"

"No," she replied, I went back to my job and I collected back pay for all the time we were stuck here. I was in very good shape financially, but they never gave me a decent assignment or even an interesting project. I lived in an occupational hell. What did you and Carlin do for money?"

"We worked for our people – they took care of us and gave us the money we needed for projects that made the reserve a better place to live," Jim said, patting Carlin on the back.

"And what about you Carlin – how did you acquire an aeroplane?" She asked.

"It was given to me by my people, remember?" he said softly.

"Oh I didn't know your parents were still alive," Carol said.

"I never knew my father," Carlin answered, "He died when I was born. My mother died when I was twenty. The plane was given to me by my people – the Ojibwa. When we returned from the north, the Ojibwa granted me full Indian status – I am Ojibwa – they are my people." She was astounded. Carlin wasn't kidding, he really believed he was an Ojibwa, she thought.

"Why did you wait three years before coming back for the gold. Wouldn't it have been easier to make the reserve a better place with money," Carol asked, directing her question to Carlin.

"No," he said, closing his eyes for a moment of reflection. "We exhausted all the other resources first. We used junk that would have been thrown away prematurely."

"We worked hard for every dollar, and that builds character and dignity. We are known for our hard work and accomplishments – not for our money. That is important is it not?"

"Yes I suppose it IS important to you, but..."

"It isn't just important to me," Carlin answered in a slightly sharper tone. "To be judged by what one does is valuable – to be judged by what one has, is of no value." He saw a change come over her. It was confusion, it was anger, it was the fear of not understanding him and of not being understood by him. Carlin wanted her to understand and he got to his feet. He put his hand out to her and she took it. He pulled her to her feet and put his arm around her waist. Jim also stood and stretched his arms above his head.

"Why don't you two get re-acquainted while I set up the tent and make camp?" he said, waving them away.

"Under the trees?" Carlin asked with a grin.

"They will need heat sensors to find us," Jim said smiling.

Pilot and archaeologist walked along the beach in silence, each wondering how best to explain their feelings to the other. Following the stream they climbed high above the beach. They found the source of the stream. It was a miniature lake perhaps two hundred feet across and it was rimmed by large rocks. Within the confines of the boulders lay a fifty foot sand beach, from which three large trees grew. The outer two were massive pines, the centre one a huge old maple. The air was filled with the scent of pine, and Carlin sat in the shade of the maple, his arm around Carol's shoulder. She leaned against him, her head on his chest.

"Carlin this little lake, this place, is a glimpse of paradise. This is what it must be like," she said with a sigh. "Why didn't you tell me about it before?"

"Didn't care about it until ten minutes ago," he answered, then, "Why did you not contact me for three long years?"

Carol didn't answer for a few moments. "I couldn't," she said, her voice timorous. "The Institute took every shred of dignity away from me. At one point I discovered my name wasn't even on the directory of archaeologists. When I found it, I was classed as a field research worker." I was afraid to call you – afraid you would think I had lied to you about my qualifications. I was ashamed Carlin, ashamed that I put up with such treatment."

"If I had known, things would have been different," Carlin said.

"What could you have done – I was fool enough to stay there, hoping the situation would change – the next day, next month, or next year, but it never did. What could you have done?"

"I would have taken you out of there – you could have stayed at Air Ojibwa with me."

For a long time she just listened to his heartbeat and she was quiet. "Isn't it strange," she said at last, "Three times you saved my life. The first time was when you dragged me out of the Cessna as it sank to the bottom of the lake; and you pulled me from under the water in the swamp when the canoe capsized. Then when I was impaled in the river, you risked your life again to save mine. And still my foolish pride stopped me from calling you when I was undergoing the ultimate mental abuse at the Institute."

He held her close, explaining why they had come here at this time. "I was not sure you were still at the Institute," he said, "but I knew the note would be meaningless to anyone else, and I knew that if you wanted to be with us you would come to the bridge." He kissed her tenderly. "I was very happy when I saw you there."

They talked for another half hour, and returned to the lower lake. The Beaver was still on the beach, but Jim was nowhere to be seen. Not until they reached the plane could they make out the campsite. It was almost perfectly camouflaged and could not be seen from the air or the water. Jim appeared in the canoe a few minutes later. He had landed four perfect speckled trout and Carlin and Carol looked forward to supper. The only major problem left was to find a method of hiding the plane from the eyes of other bush pilots.

They found the answer in a narrow arm of shallow water at the end of the lake. It was ringed by trees that almost met overhead. After some consideration Carlin was sure an overhead flight would not detect the Beaver moored there. They were secure and free to mine Camp Good Fortune. The work would be hard, but each day the creek yielded a little more than the day previous.

As July turned to August, they estimated the value of the recovered gold to be close to $12,300. In one record day, Carlin began working a high water bank of moss. He pulled up several clumps and washed them into a gold pan. After some very careful panning, he discovered colour and black sand in the pan. Carlin called Carol to help him. They collected all the moss and set it out to dry. After drying they burned the moss and very carefully panned the ash and detritus. By nightfall they had recovered almost two ounces of fine gold.

One morning Jim got up early and went to the lake to bathe. He lathered himself with soap, and plunged into the cool water to rinse the soap away. It was a wonderful feeling and invigorated, he swam to the place where the creek emptied into the lake. Though he was only ten feet from the shore, when he tried to stand, he discovered he couldn't touch bottom. He turned and swam back the way he had come. After only four or five strokes he tried to stand and found the water to be less than waist deep. He waded onto the shore and hiked back to the Beaver, then with a pair of fins, a snorkel and a face mask Jim returned to the Creek's exit point.

He snorkelled the area around the exit point and made three or four dives. When he surfaced from the last one, he left the gear on the shore, walked back to the camp and dressed. Carlin had brewed fresh coffee and poured some for Jim.

"Is the water cold?" He asked, lighting his pipe.

"No it is really pleasant, but you will find it colder around the creek exit."

"I'll remember that when I go for a swim tonight before supper," Carlin replied.

"No good," Jim said, "the light will be wrong. I think you should go right now. The fins, mask, and snorkel are on the beach."

Carlin looked at him, a question in his eyes. Jim nodded in the affirmative. Carlin knew there was a special reason behind Jim's suggestion. "How about bacon and eggs today," he said.

"I was thinking the same thing," Jim answered, "it will be ready when you get back."

Carol was awakened by the conversation and came out of the

tent. She saw Carlin hurrying along the beach toward the creek. "Is he starting work without breakfast?" She asked Jim.

"No, he is going for a swim."

"Anyone who gets out of bed to go for an early morning swim is in serious need of a shrink," she said stretching.

"If you think he is a nut case now, wait until he comes out of the water," Jim said with a big grin.

From a distance Carol watched Carlin don the snorkel gear and enter the water. He snorkelled for a few minutes and then dived. He was down for a little over a minute. When he surfaced, he regulated his breathing and then charged his lungs with air and dived again. This time Carlin stayed down much longer. Finally, when she thought he was in trouble, his head broke the surface of the water and he let out a shattering war whoop.

"What the hell is wrong with him," she said, shielding her eyes from the reflections on the water.

"There is a sizeable pocket of black sand where the creek empties into the lake," Jim said. "It is almost certain that it bears fine gold."

"Do you mean 'fine' as in very good or 'fine' as in dust or flour?" She asked, baffled at what it all meant.

"The latter," Jim said, "the gold borne in magnetite is often so fine it cannot be panned – sometimes it is not even visible and it gets thrown away."

Carlin approached them. "Carol can you find an empty tin for me – I want to sample the sand on the lake bed."

"Sure," she said, and hurried to the supply box. She returned quickly with a small square tin that had held tea bags and it was complete with a lid. "Is this okay?"

"Perfect," Carlin answered, There is only one problem. The food smells so good I can't go back."

Jim handed each of them a plate with two eggs and slices of bacon. The whole thing arranged upon slices of golden toast. "Wrap yourselves around that, while I go and sample the black sand," he said, I have already had breakfast." He took the tin from Carlin and started toward the creek.

Jim was back within a few minutes with the can of black sand. He emptied the contents out on a sheet of plastic to let it dry in the sun. Carol looked at the magnetite and shook her head.

"I don't believe there is gold in that sand," she said, "Isn't there a saying – 'there is always black sand where there is gold, but there isn't always gold where there is black sand'."

"Perhaps the saying is true – I don't know, but I am sure there is gold in THIS black sand," Jim said beaming. "we will know before the day is out. We have mercury and nitric acid and we can test for gold."

Carlin had finished his breakfast, and sat smoking his pipe. He heard the conversation between Jim and Carol but paid no attention to its content. His mind was far away, and he was concentrating on more complex matters.

The panning for gold was not very efficient. He had saved all the concentrate from which they had panned the small nuggets and flake gold, insisting on dumping it at a specific site where it could be recovered easily. He planned on doing two tests during the afternoon. The first would be to test the magnetite from the lake bottom, the second would be a test of the discarded concentrate. Carlin had a mild suspicion that one of the two would reveal a small amount of gold that would normally be lost or thrown out.

Jim was aware of Carlin's withdrawn state. He knew something was brewing in Carlin and wanted him to resolve it. It would be better if he were alone to seek new visions. Jim nodded to Carol.

"Carol and I will take the canoe down the lake to the Beaver. We will bring back the stuff to do the amalgamation test. Do you want anything else?" Jim asked.

"Yeah," Carlin answered, "bring the scuba gear will you?" He got to his feet and stretched. "I want to explore the top of the hill again – I have a couple of ideas."

"Can I go with you Carlin?" Carol asked, "You both know I don't like the canoe and ..." Jim interrupted her.

"I need you with me Carol," he said, "I don't want to risk losing the mercury trying to transfer it from the plane by myself."

"She thought about the effect her words must have had on Jim Peters, and realized they were tactless."I'm sorry Jim, of course you're right, I will help you. I will probably never be comfortable in a canoe again, after what happened to us in the past."

G. WM. GOTRO

"After we unload the canoe, and if you will give me your trust, I will change your feelings about the canoe. Deal?"

"It's a deal," she said with a radiant smile.

"Now you're talking," Carlin said, and he put his arms around her and lifted her off her feet. She was trapped in his arms and he kissed her – tenderly at first, then with passion. She responded to his kisses, and the quickness and heat of her response was a promise of good things to come. Carlin set her back on her feet. "I should get moving, and I have some deep thinking to do."

Carol and Jim waved goodbye from the canoe, and he watched them grow smaller in the distance. Then Carlin's eyes traveled up the high hillside. He scanned the peak and picking up his small shoulder pack and a tool bundle, he began to climb, following the creek bed. Carlin stopped once more at each of the many small pools he encountered in the climb, and mentally mapped them. From some he took a few samples, marking and coding them for future reference. Climbing higher a pattern began to form, and he knew he would learn the ultimate secret of Camp Good Fortune's promise.

When Carlin reached the hill's highest elevation, he could see for miles. He knew the inner feelings that drove him to make the climb had a purpose, but what it was escaped him. It had to do with the treasure they had discovered, and the answer hovered just beyond his consciousness. Visually, the panorama was just about what he expected – thousands of acres of densely forested land rising and falling as far as the horizon.

Immediately below him was the lake, and beyond it a mile or so he could see silver flickering through the trees. That would be the river they had traveled so long ago; the river that brought him here for the first time. Far off to the southwest Carlin could see the dark smudge left by the forest fire that drove them to their ultimate rescue.

Beyond the river and the lake in the distance, the land leveled out to low rolling hills covered with old growth timber. He wondered at the change in the topography, and concluded that the Great Spirit, the God, the Manitou who created it all was very whimsical.

He turned, to look northward again. There, the landscape was different. The word that came to Carlin's mind was 'chaos'. It was as if great hills of rock and debris, had been dropped from the heavens by a celestial dump-truck travelling at high speed. There was no order, and thinking about it he realized he was standing almost at the end of chaos. To the east, perhaps ten miles, the topography rose and was more placid and uniform. Something tickled Carlin's consciousness but it would not coalesce. It aggravated him, because whatever it was that whispered in his mind, was very important, and just out of reach. The words to express it were on the tip of his tongue, but he was unable to speak them.

Frustrated, he turned to descend the hill. He wanted to stop at the upper pool that he and Carol had found, for it WAS paradise. For no particular reason he wanted to stop there. Perhaps he would simply rest and smoke a pipe of tobacco. Perhaps his purpose was just to be where he had been so happy with her. She had been on his mind a great deal lately. Fifteen minutes later, Carlin settled himself on the little beach where he and Carol spent a most pleasant hour in the past. Was it a week ago, a month, or ten years – he couldn't place the time. They were all tired. He filled his pipe and leaning against one of the big trees, he drew in the satisfying smoke, and tried to think about everything. But 'everything' was far too much so he settled down to thinking about Carol.

She had changed a great deal in the three year interval they had been apart. Now she was more mature and no longer had the headstrong tendencies of the past. She was quiet now, but not in a sullen way. All things considered, Carlin found her more appealing than before. He remembered the first time they were intimate – there was an urgency to it then, as if they would never have another chance. It had little to do with love, it was plain sexual satisfaction – Biff-Bam-Thank You Ma'am, and, You're Welcome Stranger – It Was Fun – We Should Do It Again Sometime.

He remembered the last time he was at this place and she had sat with her head on his chest, reminiscing. He had thought about intimacy then, but she gave no indication that she wanted anything more than to be held and comforted. Yes, she was much more mature now. He had no doubt she had plans for her own future, and he wondered if they included him. Carlin decided he would ask her.

Rested, he tapped the ash from his pipe and slipped it into his shirt pocket. He treasured the pipe – it was the one Jim had made for him after the crash, and it had comforted him and given him much enjoyment through the years. He shouldered the pack and picked up the tool bundle, then paused, studying the lake. Breezes had always rippled the surface of the water in the past, but now for a few moments the surface was flat and calm with a single incongruity. Near the opposite side there was a turbulence that suggested the water was being pushed up from below. The rock formations were such that he couldn't reach the place on foot – he would have to swim across the pool.

On impulse Carlin stripped off his clothes and cautiously slipped into the water. It was quite cold and with strong strokes he swam to the turbulence. As he entered it the water temperature changed from cold to frigid.

Ice cold water, perhaps from deep below the surface entered at this point, and the force was strong enough to buoy him up. The water was so cold Carlin's strength was failing. Quickly he returned to the tiny beach, and dressed, then Carlin went down the hill side and directly to the campsite.

It was just 3:00 P.M. and Jim had brewed a pot of tea. The tea was made in the manner used by Canadian forest rangers and fire fighters from bygone days. The water was brought to a fast boil in a bucket. A handful of black tea was thrown into the water. It was followed by two or three spruce twigs and a clutch of needles from the tree. It was then allowed to boil for fifteen minutes, and taken off the fire. It stayed hot for an hour or so, but cold or hot it was consumed throughout the day. Carlin filled his cup and took a long swallow.

"Where is Carol?" He asked Jim.

"She went to pick some blueberries," Jim said, "She should be back shortly.

"Which way did she go?"

"Down the beach – toward the creek," Jim answered. "Why – what are you concerned about?"

"I don't know," Carlin said, "I just have a strong feeling of danger." He grabbed the rifle from the tent and started down the beach. "Stay here Jim – guard our resources." Following her tracks became easier once he crossed the creek. She had walked along the water's edge for a while, then cut toward the bush. Half a mile from the creek she appeared to have entered the woods. The tracking was much more difficult now.

Carlin prayed to the Great Spirit to infuse him with the skills of the Ojibwa hunters, and it became so. He noticed a piece of bent fern here, or a freshly broken twig there, and occasionally a scuff mark from her boot in the softer soil of the forest floor.

Ahead, Carlin could see an open area, and her tracks led there. It was logical enough, blueberries don't grow well in the shade of the forest canopy. He entered the clearing and stopped to listen. He could hear a snuffling sound directly in front of him, and he cocked the Winchester as he moved slowly toward the sound. Then he heard the humming, and he could see the top of her head as she knelt, collecting the lush berries.

The big black bear made its attack, running toward the human that was in his berry patch. Carlin couldn't shoot – the bear was directly in front of Carol. The answer was to shoot high. Carlin dropped to his knees and aiming upwards fired one shot as the bear reared up on its hind legs. The bullet hit the bear at the base of the skull and destroyed the animal's brain before exiting between the eyes. The bear remained towering over her for an instant. Then the massive head wobbled from side to side twice and with a rumble from its throat it fell to the earth. Carol couldn't stop screaming, and she was covered in blood. Carlin was horrified when he saw her – he was certain the bullet had hit her too.

He dropped the gun and wrapped his arms around her, holding her tightly as she struggled to be free of him. "Hush – hush," he kept saying, "Hush, hush my darling. Easy, easy, it is all over now." Gradually she stopped screaming and struggling, and going limp in his arms, she was racked with deep sobs. He wiped the blood from her face with his shirt but could find no bullet hole.

"Are you okay now?" he asked as she began to settle down.

"Yes I think so," she sobbed, "where did he come from? Where did you come from?"

"I was afraid for your safety – the Great Spirit sent me to find you. I knew you were in danger." He slung the rifle over his shoulder and taking her hand he led her from the scene. When they reached the beach he sat her down on the sand. "Take your shirt off Carol, it is soaked in blood." She was still shaking as she undid the buttons and slipped out of the shirt. Carol knelt at the water's edge and rinsed the blood from her clothes and from her skin. Carlin couldn't turn his eyes away from her – he had forgotten how incredibly beautiful she was. He too washed out his shirt and washed the blood from his hands. When he stood up at the water's edge she was watching him.

"It has happened again," she said, her voice barely above a whisper, "I was in a lethal situation and once again you were there for me – you saved my life."

"Carol I was thinking about you earlier today – thinking a lot. There are many things going on inside me that I don't understand. I was never very good with words, and often when a conversation ends, I wish I had said a thousand things. It is always like that when I am with you."

"What was left unsaid last time Carlin, and what are you trying to say now?"

"That I love you," he blurted, and he blushed to the roots of his hair, "and when you are not around, it is like part of me is missing." She saw that he was shaking visibly, and her first reaction was to tease him but she knew how difficult it was for him to talk of tenderness.

"Carlin, that was the finest thing anyone ever said to me." Carol knew that she loved him – she had loved him from the moment she saw him, and her love grew each and every day.

"Do you ever feel like that?" He asked, his eyes downcast and looking at his feet. At first she thought he wasn't serious, and perhaps he was just playing with her. She moved closer to him, lifting his chin with her finger until his eyes met hers.

"Please don't tease me." she said. "Did I hear you right?"

He looked deep into her eyes and in a voice so low she could barely hear him, he said, "Do you love me Carol?"

Her eyes filled with tears and she clung to him, her head on his chest. "Yes I love you Carlin." She felt him relax, and looking up she saw his eyes were closed and he was smiling. This complex individual who could reduce everything to its simplest form, really did love her. And now, he had just told her he wanted to be with her forever.

They returned to the campsite where Jim was busy making supper. As they walked into the camp he heaved a sigh of relief.

"I heard the shot," he said, I didn't know whether to get dinner for two or three, but there's enough to go around."

The following morning, Carlin panned the black sand from the lake bed. The best he could show for the effort was a minuscule amount of colour in the sand. It was enough, Carlin said, to do an amalgamation. Before they ate dinner, Carlin and Jim brought up more black sand from the lake bottom and loaded the small amalgamation barrel.

Carlin added a detergent mixture and flipped the switch. The barrel was rotated slowly by a geared 12 volt motor running off a car battery. They let it run for 20 minutes while they ate supper. They drained the detergent from the barrel and replaced it with water and baking soda as a rinse. After a short time they poured the rinse away, added mercury to the black sand, and threw in a few links of chain to help disperse the mercury into the concentrate.

"Do you think the battery will hold out for another twenty minutes?" Jim asked.

"I hope so," Carlin answered, "We can't recharge it until the sun comes up tomorrow."

"What does the sun have to do with it?" Carol asked.

"Oh – we have a solar panel charger," Carlin said, "we didn't want the noise of a small gas engine to give away our position."

The battery drove the amalgam barrel for the required time and by 8:00 P.M. they started panning the concentrate to separate the amalgam from the black and gray sand. Jim worked for an hour at panning and poured the amalgam into the retort. He used a magnet to remove much of the magnetite from the pan, but could not manage to separate the dark gray spheres from the amalgam.

"What is this stuff Carlin?" he asked, rolling the BB sized particles in his hand. "There is always some left in the pan when I empty the amalgam into the retort."

"I don't know," Carlin answered, "but we should save it in a separate container until we find out what it is."

"Yeah, I saved most of it," Jim replied, emptying the stuff into a small plastic bag. The bag already contained enough to fill a teaspoon. "I weighed it earlier," he said, "it is heavy – almost as heavy as gold. It is hard to estimate. It could be heavier than the gold."

They heated the retort in the fireplace. As the temperature rose, the mercury became a vapour that tried to escape through the spout. But the spout was cooled by a small flow of cold water through a coil of tubing wrapped around it. As the vapour cooled it condensed back into its liquid form and the mercury dripped into a beaker. Through the night, they took shifts tending the retort, and by morning the flow of mercury had stopped. When the retort was opened, an ounce and a half of gold lay in the bottom!

They celebrated by taking a day off. After lingering over a substantial breakfast, they basked in the late summer sun, and listened to the breeze whispering to them. During the late morning they swam and played in the crystal clear water of the lake at Camp Good Fortune. The three, climbed the hill to the upper lake, where they swam again, and then dried off in the sun. They lay on the miniature beach, and tried to imagine what they would do with the very large amount of money they were accumulating. They agreed it should be invested wisely, they agreed they would travel to some exotic place for a month or two, and then ...

Carol studied her companions. Jim Peters, she concluded, was a very handsome man. The facial scars from his encounter with the rogue bear in the past, did not spoil his appearance, but enhanced it. His hair was not long, but he wore a blue sweat band around his forehead. Jim's black eyes sparkled and danced with life, and yet he was suffused with an easy tranquillity that touched those near him.

Carlin was lean and well muscled. The summer sun had turned his colour to a pale copper, and he too wore a sweat band around his forehead. It was made from a soft black leather and richly beaded with Ojibwa designs. His surrogate mother had given it to him when she adopted him into her family. Only his eyes belied his racial origin, for he had the high cheek bones, the colouring, and the mannerisms of a full blood Ojibwa. Carlin's eyes however were a startling shade of blue. Jim was squatting on his haunches, drawing a diagram in the sand. Carlin, kneeling there, questioned Jim about every new aspect of the diagram. Carol was always amazed how these two men from different cultures could be so completely in tune with each other.

"What time is it?" Carol asked. Carlin glanced at his watch.

"12:30," he answered.

"Why don't I go down to the camp and get some lunch for us," she suggested, "Our supplies are running low and it is getting harder to fix anything but the simplest meal. I'll see how creative I can be." She collected her things and descended to the lower lake.

At the tent, Carol was rummaging through the supplies box when she heard the voices. At first she paid little attention, thinking Jim and Carlin had followed her immediately. She left the tent and started toward the beach. Carol almost stepped out from the cover of the woods, but stopped when she saw the canoe. She dropped to her knees, and hidden from view she watched as the two men cruised ten feet out from the shoreline. They were rough looking characters and she was frightened. They were silent now, and she was certain they had seen her, but they paddled to the creek. Carol wondered if Carlin or Jim had left equipment on the beach.

When the men passed and their backs were toward her, she risked a look and found that Carlin's discipline about security had paid off. On the beach there were no signs that anyone had ever been there. Fortunately, Carlin and Jim followed her minutes later.

The impatient strangers fished off the mouth of the creek with no success until fifty yards ahead of their canoe, in deeper water, a fish jumped. They turned the canoe toward the circle left in the water. Five minutes later they heard another splash still farther away, and paddled to the spot where it occurred.

Safe now, Carol cautiously stood up, hidden from their view by a patch of gorse. Suddenly a hand was over her mouth and a voice whispered, "Don't make a sound." She nodded, recognizing the voice as Jim's.

"What about Carlin," she whispered. "If he steps out, or hollers, he could give us away."

"Carlin is busy 'jumping fish'. He is leading them to the end of the lake by throwing stones where they are not looking, and

G. Wm. Gotro

leading them to where he wants them to be."

"Hmmm – an old Ojibwa trick," she said in a whisper.

"No," Jim answered in an undertone, "new Carlin trick," and he laughed softly. "I don't know how he will get them off the lake and back to the river though." They watched the strangers in the distance and finally saw them begin to paddle hard for the opposite shore. Ten minutes later Carlin came in drenched in sweat. He had been running through the woods along the shore.

"It worked," he said flopping down on the ground, "It worked."

Through Jim's binoculars they watched the two men lift the canoe onto their shoulders and begin the portage back to the river.

"That was too close for comfort," Jim said, "they almost found the mine, got the gold, and the woman."

Over the lunch Carol had fixed, they talked about their immediate plans. Carlin wanted to scuba dive the upper pond to explore the spring. The gold, he reasoned, had to come from somewhere, and the powerful flow of the spring could be its source. He also wanted to spend some time on the lower lake bottom, and in particular around the mouth of the creek. Jim suggested it would be wise to move the recovered gold to safety and then return. It was only September third, and they knew they had at least six weeks before there was any risk of freeze-up. By late afternoon their decision was made. They would break camp in the morning and fly out. Two days in the south would allow them to re-provision, acquire fresh scuba tanks, and deposit the gold into a safety deposit box. Carlin also had another problem to be addressed, but it had to be handled by a trustworthy professional.

At 7:15 A.M. the tent was struck leaving no sign they had been there. Carlin taxied the Beaver up to the beach and they loaded it with the equipment. At 8:00 A.M. the plane lifted off and turning south, it disappeared in the distance.

The lake was quiet after the plane climbed away into the distance, with only the haunting cry of the loons breaking the stillness. Two miles down the river, the strangers were startled at the sound of the Beaver's radial engine, and speculated where it might have been based. After a considerable amount of conjecture they concluded correctly that it had come from the lake they fished on the previous day.

The two men could not recall seeing the plane moored on the lake, nor did they hear it land after they returned to the river. The question tantalized them, and they decided to go back to the lake and fish it one more time before moving on up the river.

They were an odd, unsavoury pair, drawn together by a mutual history of minor encounters with the law, and a bilateral need for permanent shelter. Harold Cone was a thirty-seven year old, ex-pulp mill worker, fired for petty theft from the mill. His grade eight education did little to enhance his chances for employment, and he had become a long term vagrant. Cone had been arrested five times, on charges ranging from car theft, through living off the avails of prostitution, to break, enter and theft.

George Wassermann on the other hand, was a twenty-eight year old truck driver. George completed grade eleven before venturing out into the world. The summer months always provided work as a forest fire fighter, and through the winters he struggled to feed and shelter himself by working as a backyard auto mechanic. For two years George was unemployed and toward the end of that part of his life he was arrested and served 28 days for welfare fraud.

It was while milling around the courthouse that he met Harold Cone. The pair hit it off right from the beginning, and shared their woes and joys. In the 'joys' category, they shared an enthusiasm for fishing, and a need for shelter. Thus it was, that they found a tattered old abandoned cabin belonging to an elderly lady unable to attend it. They made a verbal agreement with the poor soul, to maintain building and grounds in return for use of the premises as a domicile.

Two months after moving into the pathetic cabin, Cone found an old canoe adrift on a nearby lake. He immediately claimed it.

He took measures to insure the rightful owner would never recover his loss – Cone painted the canoe.

When George Wassermann was laid off by the trucking company Cone suggested they take a fishing holiday. They convinced a small air carrier to fly them to Krane Lake in exchange for labour at repairing the company's dock. The small plane transported them and their canoe to Krane Lake which fed into the major river system. Two and a half weeks later they arrived at

Dawson Lake, and Camp Good Fortune, where fish were jumping but were very difficult to catch. Now, a day after leaving Dawson Lake they decided to return and explore it more closely. Again they made the long portage. They plied the canoe around the lake, fishing the likely looking spots. Their reward was four good sized speckled trout. They made a fire on the sand, and cooked the trout. Both men were nauseated by the smell of rotting meat as the breeze passed over the carcass of the bear that had attacked Carol. Carlin had hurriedly buried the remains, but other carnivores had unearthed them. After eating, Cone washed the fry pan in the creek. He scooped a handful of sand from the creek bed to scour the pan. Had he looked into the water again after the dirt settled he would have seen a magnificent nugget missed by Carlin.

"Let's get the hell out of here," Cone said, "I know what that stink is."

"Yeah – what is it?" Wassermann asked, his nose wrinkled in disgust.

"It's a corpse," Cone replied, his eyes wide with fear. "me and my brother found a dead guy once – he smelled just like that, and you know what – that ain't the worst of it."

"What d'ya mean?" George Wassermann asked, in fear.

"I mean the cops – they was all over us for six months. They tried to pin it on us," Cone said, putting the gear in the canoe. "couple of things bother me about this place. How come we didn't see that plane yesterday, and second, is this." He pointed to the the creek bank where Carlin and Carol stripped away all the moss.

"Maybe it was a bear done that," George said, "They look for grubs or somethin' don't they?"

"Yeah, but this wasn't no bear. Look, somebody burned that moss. It looks like they cleaned up the ash. It don't make sense."

"I think maybe they was going to burn the corpse but it stank so bad they changed their minds. Like you said – let's get the hell out of here," George said, pushing the canoe off the shore.

Cone took his seat and they paddled for the opposite shore. "There is somethin' weird about that place," Cone said, "I ain't finished with it yet." Deep within him, Cone sensed there was something of immense value at Dawson Lake. It didn't matter to him whether or not it was his to take. He knew better, he simply didn't care – he would take anything on which he could lay his hands.

George Wassermann was cursed with an overactive imagination. Often while driving on a long haul, especially at night, he created incredibly complex scenarios in his imagination. George peopled his dreams with colourful characters, introverts and extroverts, idiots and geniuses. Now as they paddled in silence, remembering Cone's words, he created a murder scene horrific enough to frighten himself. George didn't like the idea that Cone wasn't finished with the place, but he knew Cone would manipulate him into returning.

8

DON'T DISCARD THE
TREASURE

Carlin made a low pass over the reservation to let his people know they had returned, and Carol watched as dozens of Ojibwa waved at their roving sons. He climbed back to one thousand feet and lined up for a landing at Ojibwa Air. Side-slipping, the Beaver touched the water in a gentle caress and Carlin taxied to the dock. Jim stepped down and made the Beaver fast to her mooring. Carlin followed Jim out and reaching up, he lifted Carol from the plane. He didn't put her down, but carried her to the pretty little cabin that was his home. The kids from the village had cut the grass, and the flowers in the window boxes had been watered and tended. The whole scene was like something from a holiday magazine.

Jim unlocked the door for them and Carlin carried her inside.

"Welcome home," he said, setting her down in the middle of the room. Carol was entranced by the place and she didn't answer but scanned the room carefully.

"I will see you two in the morning," Jim said from the doorway, "I really want to get home." When he had gone, she came over to Carlin, who watched his friend jogging into the woods.

"Carlin, is this place really yours or do you rent it from the Ojibwa?" She asked, slipping her hand into his.

"Oh it is mine alright," he said softly, "remember I AM Ojibwa. None of us owns the land. The people are only Manitou's tenants. Do you like it?"

"I LOVE it," she said, looking out the miniature bay window. "it looks too perfect to be real."

"Good – then you WILL be staying?" He asked, hoping she would confirm the arrangement.

"What will your people think?" She asked teasing him.

"They will accept you or reject you," he said, holding her close, "it all depends on us and if we were meant for each other."

It was 1:00 P.M. and after a good meal he showed her his collection of wood carvings. There were twenty in all, each one a veritable masterpiece. Most of them were carved from maple, and each was fashioned in miniature. There were bears, eagles, beaver and wolves. A set of four Ojibwa figures told the story of a boy who was chosen by Manitou to become a great warrior and chief.

The first carving depicted the boy in adolescence, standing on a rock jutting out into a lake. He was bent at the waist, looking downward. His arm was drawn back, and in his hand, he held a spear, poised to spear a fish. The expression on the boy's face was one of intense concentration, and the detail was exquisite.

"Carlin these are incredible – who carved them?" Carol asked, running her fingers over the boy's head.

"The four miniature Ojibwa figures are my own. I carved them the first winter after the rescue," he said softly. "The idea came to me in a dream. The boy is being taught to hunt and fish by the Great Spirit. This is his first serious responsibility," Carlin handed her the second figure. It was a young warrior. A bow was in his right hand, held high over his head.

His left hand held a clutch of arrows, and the arm was also held high in victory. The warrior's mouth was open as though he were shouting. Examining it carefully, Carol's fingers traced out the details. When she looked up at Carlin there was a new respect in her eyes.

"Tell me about this one," she said, "it looks like the same person but older."

"Yes. Now he is eighteen and has just won his first battle," Carlin said. There was a trace of sadness about him as he told her the story. "He is shouting the praises of mighty Manitou or God, and he asks for more enemies to slay for his nation." After a minute or two Carol put the carving down beside that of the boy. She picked up the third figure, and as she studied it, her expression changed from wonderment to intense inner sorrow.

The third figure was infused with fatigue and sadness. It portrayed a warrior in his mid thirties astride a horse at the top of a cliff. The warrior's head was bowed in a posture suggestive of fatigue. His shoulders were slumped forward, and his right hand loosely held his lance with its point resting on the ground. The horse's head was lowered as though he was grazing. The warrior's facial features expressed the very essence of remorse as he thought about the carnage of the battle that lay below on the plain.

"How terribly sad and moving," Carol said, finding herself experiencing the warrior's pain and sorrow. "He is grieving for the comrades he lost in battle isn't he?"

"Yes, and much more," Carlin replied, "he is trying to make sense of the deaths on both sides. They were men filled with vitality and passion – now they are still and cold – dead."

"Nothing has been accomplished by it all, and he recognizes the futility of living that way." He took the piece from her and handed her the fourth and final carving. Aware that these were masterpieces she cradled the work in her hands, frightened at the responsibility she was taking on. To have dropped it would have been as devastating as ruining the smile of the Mona Lisa.

The figure she held was that of a very old Indian chief in a war bonnet. He sat, cross legged on a rock, his wrinkled hands turned palms upward on his knees. The old man's head was thrown back and his closed eyes were turned to the sun. One hand cradled a long carved pipe. There could be no question about his origin or purpose. He was the boy in his final year of life, and he was communing with Gitchee Manitou about what he had learned through the years.

Carol looked up into Carlin's eyes through the tears in her own. "You were born white," she said, "but you are truly Ojibwa – I believe it now, though I never did before."

"Yes," Carlin answered, looking out across the water, "I was Ojibwa before I was born. I fished, and hunted, and fought for my people in another life and another time. I am the third warrior – righting the wrongs of the past. Now they have welcomed me home."

Though they intended to return to the wilderness as soon as the gold was secure, a week passed before they did so. They had panned fifty ounces of flake gold, and recovered sixty-five ounces by amalgamation. The nuggets weighed 14.7 troy ounces and were valued at $7,000. The total value of their work amounted to $41,500 for three months. Dividing the number by three people, they each earned roughly $4,600 a month. They decided to draw down a total of $3,000 for operating expenses, and hold the rest in reserve.

They bought provisions for another month, acquired two large air cylinders for recharging the scuba tanks, and other items to make their work easier and more productive. The day before their departure, Jim contacted Carlin to tell him that the assay lab wanted him to call. Carlin and Carol went to the band council office and made the phone call. Carlin listened carefully, then, with a few final words, he ended the call. Carol had never seen him change so rapidly. She knew something BIG was happening to Carlin. Chief Orren Flagg read Carlin's face as surely as he could read the tracks of wild animals.

"I'm happy that you received good news Carlin. Your eyes say it was very good news," the Chief said in a voice just above a whisper. Carlin put his arm around the old man's shoulder.

"Yes, Chief," he said, "It was very good news. Now I am certain our people will have their hospital, AND a proper sanitation system. Will you send someone to tell Jim that we must leave immediately?"

The Chief uttered a few words in the Ojibwa tongue to a young man working in the office. He nodded to Orren Flagg and left in haste. "It is done Carlin ... Jim will meet you at Air Ojibwa as soon as he can get there. Be careful; our Cloud Walker is very precious to the people."

As they loaded the plane, Carol asked Carlin a question. "What did the chief mean when he talked about the Cloud Walker?"

"He was talking about the Beaver and its pilot," he replied. "The first time he broke the bonds of earth was with me in the Cessna. It was on a beautiful morning and the sky was dotted with hundreds of small puffs of cloud at about three thousand feet. We climbed just above them and as we flew over them he said it

G. Wm. Gotro

was the first time he had ever walked on clouds. He called me Cloud Walker, and he has never forgotten it."

"Hey ... wait for me." It was Jim Peters and he was running toward them. "What happened?"

"Come inside," Carlin said, taking Carol's hand and walking toward the cabin. "It is better if you are sitting down when you hear what I have to say." Carol and Jim sat at the table watching him, waiting for his words. Carlin's face broke into a beaming smile. "Remember when you asked me about the little gray BBs, and I said we should save the stuff until we discovered what it was."

"Yes," Jim replied impatiently, "what is it? What the hell is it?" Then he answered his own question. "Oh – I know – I know, it is uranium and we are all radio active," he said with a mischievous grin.

"It's platinum and it seems to be concentrated at about three to one with the gold," Carlin said softly.

"You mean for every three ounces of gold we are getting an ounce of platinum?" Jim asked incredulous.

"NO," Carlin shouted in laughter, "for each ounce of gold we are getting three ounces of platinum!" For the next ten minutes the cabin was in an uproar. They were all talking at once and dancing around each other. Their assets had just tripled! The wave of emotion gradually subsided, they finished loading the plane, and secured the cabin.

By noon they were one hundred and ten miles from the reservation and Air Ojibwa. Five miles out from Dawson Lake the Beaver was at nine thousand feet and throttled back to a point that just maintained altitude. Carlin flicked on the carb heat and made a long gliding descent. The engine was just ticking over and they crossed the lake at two thousand feet. There was no sign of anyone on Dawson, but Jim spotted the two strangers a couple of miles up the river. Carlin saw them too and made a low pass over them. He circled around again and flew up the river toward the swamp. Jim watched the two as they put the canoe in the water and began to paddle upstream following their lead. When the paddlers reached the falls, the roar of the water drowned out the sound of the plane. Carlin executed a very low pass over the swamp to the north, dropping a newspaper in the water. After a ten mile diversionary circle, that took him back to Dawson Lake, Carlin landed, undetected. The Beaver was unloaded on the beach and then hidden in its tree hanger at the end of the lake.

On the river, Cone and Wassermann neither heard nor saw the plane as it passed over Dawson Lake. They only heard the engine when Carlin cruised low over them, leading them up the river toward the swamp. The two men, at Cone's suggestion tried to follow the plane's course, because Cone believed he was on to something big. They made the difficult portage around the falls, and continued up river for two days before reaching the swamp. On the second day in the swamp, Wassermann spotted something in the water near the north end. They found the newspaper dated five days before. The deception was complete. They believed the pilot had landed at the north end of the swamp and they were closing in on him.

"We got him now Georgie boy," Cone said excitedly, "he's here somewhere or we would have heard him taking off. He's here in this swamp and we're goin' to find him."

"Then what -" George Wassermann said, "What are we going to do then? We're almost out of supplies, and the Cessna is supposed to pick us up tomorrow fifty miles south of here. What's the big deal Cone?" It was the first time in their relationship that George Wassermann ever questioned one of Cone's suggestions.

"They're hiding something from us, and they killed somebody – that's the big deal you dumb ass." He glared at Wassermann.

"Yeah – how do you know they killed somebody – we never seen no corpse. How do you know the plane is even connected to the stink at Dawson Lake?" George said, risking Cone's anger.

Cone was furious. His partner was right – they had only sighted two planes since they arrived, and maybe they weren't the same plane. They didn't see a plane at Dawson Lake and they had circumnavigated the whole lake. Cone was hungry and their supplies were down to a bit of flour, some salt, and some bacon that was furred with green mould.

He baited a hook with some grubs he had collected from under a rock, and cast his line out. Cone lay the rod across the gunnel of the canoe and reached for the paddle. The water exploded as a five pound large mouth bass took the hook and headed for the swamp

G. WM. GOTRO

bottom. Cone dropped the paddle and tried to catch the fishing rod as it too headed for the bottom. The paddle was drifting away from them and Cone tried to grab it. He lost his balance and turned the canoe over dumping everything into the swamp.

The water was less than ten feet deep, but the bottom was a cloying black muck. Splashing around and cursing each other they righted the canoe. George managed to pull himself out of the water and back into the canoe.

Cone dived twice, trying to get the fishing rod back, but the bottom sediment had been stirred up and the visibility in the water was virtually zero. A small current in the swamp was drifting them away from the capsize site and any chance to recover their gear. Cone dived again, surfaced empty handed, and swam for the canoe. Wassermann stared at him in horror. Cone's face was covered with leeches, one of which had attached itself to his eyelid. He brushed at it with the back of his hand, but its mouth was firmly fixed to his skin and the thing was sucking blood. Cone panicked and went under again. Wassermann was terrified and simply sat transfixed as Cone's head shot out of the water screaming.

"Oh Sweet Jesus," he shouted in terror in a thin keening voice, "get them off me George – PLEASE get them off me." Another leech had attached itself to his upper lip and the body flapped as Cone's mouth moved. Cone's hands tore at the things on his face and he submerged again, wailing in anguish. A great bubble of air burst to the surface and for a second or two the water was calm. Then Cone's hand and arm broke the surface and sank once more. A few smaller bubbles rose and then the swamp was still except for the moaning coming from Wassermann. He wanted to dive and bring Cone to the surface before it was too late, but the thought of being covered in leeches terrified him. George just sat in the canoe rocking back and forth, and the moan became a dirge.

"Where are you Cone – come back Cone – don't leave me by myself – I don't want to be alone . Come back Cone." George Wassermann's mind snapped and he repeated the words like a song, over and over. Though the dirge would never bring Cone back, it did bring George some company. Eight or ten large water snakes gathered around the canoe, attracted by the sound. When

Wassermann finally became aware of them he went wild. He shouted and ranted and raved, driving his paddle deep into the water.

He didn't stop until he was exhausted, and hopelessly lost in the great swamp. Finally, curling up in the fetal position in the old canoe, George slept.

Four days later, the bacteria in Cone's gut multiplied, rapidly filling the body cavity with a vile gas. Soon, the body became more buoyant and began to rise. It broke the surface and rolled over. What was left of Harold Cone was hideous beyond belief. The leeches had feasted for days and the body was bloodless and white. The gasses that filled the body cavity distended it until it was no longer recognizable as having been human. Unfortunately for him, George Wassermann found his deceased friend, and was devastated by the shock. Wassermann's broken mind would never recover from the sight.

Carlin, Jim, and Carol took bets on how long it would be before the strangers returned to Dawson Lake. Carol concluded that they wouldn't be fooled by Carlin's ploy for very long, and would find their way back very quickly – probably three or four days. Jim gave them four days up the river and four more to return. Carlin said he didn't think they would be back at all.

The day following their return Carlin donned the scuba gear and dived at the creek's entrance to the lake. This time he used a suction dredge and cleaned a ten foot square area. Jim and Carol collected the concentrate and began processing the material. It was very rich in flake gold and contained many small nuggets. They found that it saved time to pull the magnetite out of the concentrate with a large electro magnet. When the last of the visible gold was recovered from each pan, a generous portion of heavy material was still left, and now they knew it was mostly platinum.

The last week in September, Carlin lugged the scuba gear up the hill side to the upper pond. This time he was prepared, and setting tank, mask, and fins on the sand, he donned the new wet suit to complete his diving equipment. As before, the water in the pond was very cold, but the wet suit would allow him to explore the vent feeding the pond in relative comfort. After checking the equipment for the third time, Carlin entered the clear water, and slowly, two feet from the bottom, he swam over a mental grid that left nothing unexplored. At random points he brushed away silt and dug his hands into the lake bottom. Here and there he encountered bed rock, but for the most part, the bottom was comprised of basket ball sized rocks and gravel. The discovery was very much what he expected, and after thirty minutes, Carlin finned his way to the feeder vent.

The visibility was good and he could see the vent clearly. It was eighteen inches in diameter and the flow from it was fast and powerful. "Where did the water originate?" he asked himself, and he knew that it had to come from a large body of water that was at a considerably higher elevation. The force of the vent mesmerized him and he was content to just watch the jet pouring water into the miniature lake. After a few minutes, Carlin glanced at his watch. Soon he would be running out of air – it was time to go.

Suddenly a flash of light caught his attention. It came from the column of water rising from the vent. His eyes followed the course of the flashing object for ten feet or so, and then he lost it. He wanted to follow it but his air began to fail. Carlin pulled the reserve ring that allowed him a little more time, and slowly he rose to the surface. He snorkelled to the beach and divested himself of his gear.

Carlin rested in the sun for fifteen minutes, then went back in the water without the scuba gear. With mask, fins, and snorkel, he swam to the Lake's outlet, then working hard against the current he finned his way almost to the vent. He dived to the bottom twice, the dives being about fifty feet apart. His heart was hammering in his chest and his mind ran rampant as he swam back to the beach. Thirty minutes after coming out of the water he was on the lower beach, and walking toward the campsite. Carol ran out to meet him, and to help him with the scuba gear.

As they walked along she became aware of a marked change in him. Something had happened up there, but she couldn't imagine what it might be.

"Are you alright Carlin?" She asked, concerned with the quiet introversion that now possessed him.

"Yes," he said, lost in thought, "yes I'm fine." He smiled at her and put his arm around her waist. Carol glanced up at him as they walked and noticed that the smile had broadened perceptibly. Carlin was very happy about something.

Jim Peters met them and took the heavy tank from Carlin

"Good dive?" Jim asked Carlin, pouring him a cup of fresh coffee.

"Mm Hmmm," Carlin answered, lost in thought, "a lot of interesting things up there. I want to go back early tomorrow morning." The enigmatic smile had flickered across his face again, telling Jim that he was holding something back – something very portentous. Jim knew him – knew that Carlin would tell him everything in time.

A few days after Carlin's dive, he was awakened not by the light of early morning, but by cold. Getting out of his sleeping bag he made a fresh fire and put water on for coffee. Picking up twigs for the fire, he realized they were touched with a faint film of frost. There was a new feeling in the air now, a feeling almost impossible to define. The leaves on the maples and poplars had subtly turned to red and gold, and the indefinable scent of autumn permeated the air. It was a feeling of urgency to finish things undone before the winter set in – it was a feeling of melancholy for something that had slipped away from him, like the departure of a good friend after a visit too short. It was the loss of summer.

He knew the scenario well. Unnoticed, many of the leaves had fallen and the scent of them was in the air. It was unforgettable. In a week or so, the landscape would be a riot of colour, as the leaves put on their final glorious display. Then with the coming of the first cold autumn wind, they would fall, gently, as if to protect the earth, from the bitter cold that would soon follow.

The scent of brewing coffee was suddenly alien, and like a seductive woman, it was momentarily more alluring than seemed possible. Carol tapped him on the shoulder, frightening him, for he thought he was alone. He turned toward her, his eyes wide. "Oh – you frightened me," he said, relaxing, "Coffee?"

"Please," she answered, handing him her cup. "You must have been lost in thought. What were you thinking about Carlin?"

"Nothing much," he said, filling her cup, "the change of seasons I guess. Autumn is upon us – Animikii will speak to us today," he said, looking at the dark clouds in the northwest.

G. Wm. Gotro

"Animikii?"

"Yes – thunder – it is an Ojibwa term for thunder," Carlin said, as he drew his pipe from an inner pocket and began to fill it with Erinmore Flake. Carol smiled – she loved the smell of fresh brewed coffee and found it enhanced by the smoke from a pipe.

"Does Animikii have an earthly sign?" She asked after sipping her coffee.

"Yes. Think of a huge pair of silver eagle wings with the tips raised to the sky. That is Animikii – Flies With Thunder." The air was chill and a wind had risen. Carlin fed the fire with a log and he shivered. "Today I will make my last trip to the hill top," he said, "and tomorrow we will fly out."

Carol had been dreading those words. She had no idea what she would do on her own. She didn't want to leave Carlin but there had never been a firm commitment between them. Now the situation had to be resolved and she was frightened about the outcome. Carol decided to face the problem head on. "What about us Carlin?" She asked, "What about us?"

"My decision was made a long time ago," Carlin said, turning away from her so she could not see the colour rise in his face, "when we shared a sleeping place almost four years ago we talked of the love we had for each other." She saw how difficult it was for him to talk of love, and she knew that he loved her but couldn't express it in fancy words.

"You know Carlin, you are a great bush pilot and a very talented man," she said looking into his eyes, "but the Great Spirit shorted you on the ability to tell a woman what you want."

"I know," he said simply.

Jim Peters had come out of the tent and overheard the latter part of the conversation. He was softly laughing to himself because his white brother seemed more Ojibwa than he himself. Jim knew this conversation was going to end in disaster if he didn't intervene.

"Carol, have you seen my coffee cup?" he called out. "I can't find it."

She was furious. 'Damn you Jim,' she thought, 'I am trying to get this flying white Ojibwa to propose to me, and you can't find your damned coffee cup'. "No Jim," she hollered at him in anger, "I haven't seen your coffee cup." Carlin softly heaved a great sigh of relief – his red brother had saved him from disaster.

"I might be able to find it with your help," Jim said in a tone that made it imperative.

Carlin understood what Jim was doing and he was relieved. He knew that Ojibwa rules prevented anyone telling another what to do. Jim wasn't telling her to help him look for the missing cup, he was suggesting that her assistance was valuable. Carlin also knew why Jim had interceded and he was grateful.

"Jim, I don't know where ..." Carol began, but he cut her off in mid sentence.

"Carol, there is something you should know about Carlin," Jim said in an undertone. "It has to do with the concept of time and importance."

"Dammit Jim, I don't want a lecture about time," she said haughtily, "Carlin was about to propose to me when your damned coffee cup interfered."

"Do you want to drive him away from you?" Jim asked bluntly, stopping her in her tracks.

"No," she replied, "of course not."

"Carlin is more Ojibwa than I am in many ways. Time is different for us. When an Anishanawbe is doing something, he has devoted his time to it, and other matters are less important until he finishes that which he was doing. Carlin will propose to you in time. He has not finished this part of his journey through life yet. Be patient Carol – he loves you – he will ask you to share his wigwam – in time." Jim Peters took a few steps away from her and bending down he picked up his coffee cup from a rock. "Oh look," he said in mock amazement, "HERE is my coffee cup!"

"You have to be kidding Jim, you have to be kidding. I want to make a life with him and I am prepared to give up almost anything. Now you tell me he is too busy to make a decision. If that is the case, and other things are more important to him, we can never have a life together," Carol said, her eyes glistening, very close to tears.

"I know this is hard for you to understand because you are not of the Anishanawbe," Jim replied, "It has little or nothing to do with what EVENT is most important. It has more to do with what is right and wrong for him. He feels that leaving an event unfinished is not the way of his people."

Though she didn't understand the principle completely she had begun to comprehend the complexity of the culture. "But Carlin is NOT of the Anishanawbe – he is white," she said in anger and frustration.

"Hmmm – now, I must admit, it is I who doesn't understand. I don't know how Carlin became Anishanawbe, but the only elements missing are the pigment of his skin and the colour of his eyes. In every other way Carlin is of the people. The best plan to solve this is for one of us to ask him WHEN he will tell you about his intentions," Jim said wisely.

Carlin had finished his breakfast and was gathering the items he would take with him on the climb to the hilltop.

Carol went to him directly. "Carlin," she asked, "when you come back from the hill will you tell me your decision about us?"

"Yes of course," he said, "as soon as I return."

"How long will you be gone?" Jim asked him.

"Three hours," Carlin answered, slipping the pack over his shoulder.

"Carol and I will take the canoe across the lake and hike out to the river," Jim said, "I need something from the river bank. We should be back just in time to meet you."

Carlin climbed the hill to the upper lake, and after a ten minute rest he continued to the hill's summit. From there he could see for miles. He opened the pack and withdrew Jim's binoculars. Scanning the panorama before him, he discovered a fairly large lake almost on a level with the hill top. It lay about two miles away and Carlin was certain it was the feeder for the pond's vent. He took out a note book and sketched the relevant details of the area's topography. When he finished, he packed his gear and began the descent to the upper pond.

Jim and Carol searched the river bank until they found a large blue clay deposit. They filled two plastic bags, each containing ten pounds, and began their return journey. After walking for a time, they rested. The river was slow moving at that point, and from around a bend an old and battered canoe appeared. At first Jim thought it was empty but it rode too low in the water to be so.

As the canoe came closer they could see a man curled up in the bottom. He appeared to be unconscious, and Jim waded into the water to secure the canoe. He dragged it up on the low bank. The man sat up and looked about, confused and frightened.

"Cone," he said staring at Jim, "Is that you Cone – where have you been? I came all this way alone. Do you have anything to eat?"

Jim held his hand out to the man. "Come," he said, "we will find something for you to eat." He knew the man's mind was gone, and he recognized the canoe. Jim connected the bits of information and rightly concluded that the second man had left his friend, and for some reason he hadn't returned.

George Wassermann was too weak to walk without help.

Supported between Carol and Jim, Wassermann made it to the shore of Dawson Lake. They helped him into their canoe and paddled across to the campsite, where they helped him up the beach. Carol fixed some soft, easily digestible food for him. Wassermann was too weak to eat quickly and they fed him slowly. After eating he fell into a deep sleep. They covered him and watched over him while he rested.

"What did you want with all that clay?" Carol asked.

"Oh it is not for me," Jim said, "it is for you. When Carlin is carving this winter, perhaps you can model things in clay."

"What makes you think we will be together through the winter," she said. "I don't think he made any plans that include me." Her words were spoken as though the situation had ended, words that were cloaked in finality.

"It will be interesting to learn what Carlin has planned for this winter," Jim answered as he checked on the sleeping stranger.

Within the half hour, Carlin returned and exchanged a few words with Jim regarding Wassermann. Carlin had been close to the canoe when he led it away from their campsite in the past, and recognized the man. "He was one of the men that came here before."

"Yes. I recognized the canoe," Jim answered, confirming Carlin's identification. "Something happened to them. There were no signs of the other man, no equipment in the canoe either. This fellow is in shock and can't look after himself."

"It's probably best to let him sleep," Carlin said, "we can take him out with us tomorrow – he may be better by then, and able to tell us what happened. Right now I have something else to do." He looked anxious but happy as he approached the tent where Carol was resting. He looked in and saw her curled up, asleep on her cot. He knelt down beside her and brushed her lips with his, waking her. She smiled and drew him down to kiss him.

"The hunter is home from the hill," she said, turning the well worn phrase to her advantage. "So what's the news ... I mean about the man we found?"

"Never mind him," Carlin replied, "let's talk about us. What do you want to do once we are out of here? You will have enough money to do what you please and the world is your oyster."

"I don't want to be alone again," she said softly, "I'm close to forty and I would like to settle down with a little security. I don't know anything about ..." Carlin recognized the pattern and he interrupted her.

"Would you consider marrying a tired bush pilot with a hell of a lot of money?"

"If I found such a man, would he buy me a big fancy home and my own Ferrari, and staff the estate with a gardener and servants?" She asked, her deep blue eyes twinkling with exhilaration.

"No he would not," Carlin said, "The best he would bring you would be a ring, a three room cabin, excitement, and a hell of a lot of love."

"That is even a better offer," she said hugging him tightly, "and I know where there is a lovely three room cabin on a lake."

"Is that an acceptance of my proposal?" Carlin asked her, smiling broadly.

"Yes," she answered, "if that was a bonafide proposal."

"You know it was Ms. Danse."

"Can we go there tomorrow?" she asked.

"Right after sunrise," he answered,

"Carlin, would you tell me one of your deepest secrets,"

"Which one?" he said with a laugh.

"Tell me why you were so self satisfied after your dive at the upper lake?"

"Okay," he said, trying to suppress a grin, "but you must never tell anyone what I tell you."

"Deal," she said.

"Remember when I told you about the vent that fed the upper lake with spring water?"

"Yes," she replied, "you said the flow was very strong."

"Right, and then I concluded that the water flowing from the vent was not from a spring. I reasoned that it must come from a lake at a considerably higher level, and today I confirmed it. There is a lake about two miles to the north east. It appears to be about fifty feet higher than the vent. The water from it flows underground, and feeds the vent. The gold that we mined here had to come from the highest lake, or from a mother load located somewhere along the underground route. Now I know my theory is correct."

"Okay, but why were you so secretive after your dive?" she asked him.

"Because I saw a carpet of gold Carol," he answered, his eyes glittering brightly. "It comes from the vent and I think it has been that way for a long time. You should have seen it – it was incredible." Once again the normally stoic Carlin was excited and animated.

"I wish I had seen it," she said, teasing him. "But you wanted to go solo." Carol hugged him tightly. "Have you told Jim yet?"

"No," he said seriously, "I will tell him on the way back tomorrow."

When George Wassermann awakened, he felt much better. He was weak, but more lucid, and once again he was very hungry. They gave him more food and drink, and questioned him about what happened. He told them about how he met Harold Cone and how their relationship developed. When he came to the part about acquiring the old lady's cabin for repair work, he faltered.

"Did you do the repairs for her?" Jim asked, studying the man's eyes.

"Yeah we cleaned the place. We cut the grass and fixed some broken windows with plastic. The inside was bad too. Raccoons had done a lot of damage and we cleaned out their nests and all the crap they left around," Wassermann answered. Then he went quiet and became nervous.

"You are bothered by something," Jim said, "something bad happened didn't it?"

"Yeah, I think so," Wassermann said looking away from Jim. "She came out to the cabin once after about six months. She was pissed off at us 'cause the place wasn't fixed like she thought it should be. She said she was coming back in a week and if the place wasn't fixed we would be thrown out. That made Cone really mad." Now Wassermann was in a state of high distress. He couldn't look Jim in the eye.

"What happened then?" Jim asked.

"Cone went out that night and he didn't come back for two days," George Wassermann said, wringing his hands. "When he did get back I asked him where he had been. He just laughed and said he had gone to talk over our agreement with the old lady and she promised not to bother us any more. Cone said he decided to celebrate and he went to Espanola for a few beers. He said he got drunk and spent all his money on hard stuff, and stayed drunk for many hours."

"Did you believe him?" Jim asked the man.

"No," Wassermann said, looking down at his feet, "I think Cone killed her and buried her body – she never came to the cabin again." Jim Peters watched the pulse in the man's neck, and could see his heart rate. He counted the beats in ten seconds – a calculated heart rate of 120!

"Where is Cone now?" Jim asked Wassermann, "Do you know?"

The man began to hyperventilate. His eyes grew wide and he was filled with terror. "He drowned I think," he said, shaking visibly. "There were blood suckers and snakes – they were all over him – even in his eyes! He panicked and then he went under the water in the swamp and he never came up again."

Jim asked him the final question. "Did you try to save him?"

"No, there was nothing I could do. I stayed there for a while, but he didn't come up again. Honest," His eyes filled with tears. "I stayed until the snakes came and I don't remember anything after that – nothing until you found me," he said sobbing. "What are you going to do with me now?"

"We are flying out in the morning," Jim answered, "we will take you to our reserve. If you wish to talk to the police, we will confirm your story as far as we can. They will send divers to find

Cone's body and if there is no evidence of foul play they will not bother you." George Wassermann thought about Jim's words and agreed it was the best way to handle the situation.

They ate a healthy dinner early in the evening, and after preparing a makeshift bed for Wassermann, they sat around the fire and talked about the great "holiday" they had spent here at the lake. There was no reference to mining, gold, or anything that could be construed as work. Jim and Carlin smoked and Jim told them the story of his family totem. By 10:00 P.M. the fire had died down to a bed of coals and they prepared for the night. Jim lit the gas lantern in the tent, while Carlin and Carol took a final walk along the beach. There was no moon, and the night was very dark, holding the promise of frost. The stars twinkled with a brilliance never seen in populated areas, for there was no light pollution at Dawson Lake.

Carol shivered and snuggled closer to Carlin. The air was still and the surface of the lake had become a huge and perfect mirror, making it possible to look down, and see the brightest stars.

"I have never been happier in my life," Carol whispered, "and I am looking forward to going home to Air Ojibwa. She hugged him tighter."Do the Ojibwa have a sign that tells them all is well in the universe?" she asked him.

"I am not sure, but that must mean something," he said, looking up into the heavens. She too looked up, and there, in all its glory, the northern lights were sweeping the sky.

In the silence, they could hear the hiss as the lights danced to and fro. Bands of purple mingled with soft green and pale blue altered to cerise and magenta in a huge celestial ribbon unfolding before them. He kissed her then, and they walked toward the soft light radiating from within the tent.

The day dawned gray and overcast, and a cold wind repeatedly died and then sprang up again. The yellow leaves fell from the birches and poplars of northern Ontario, and at the end of the lake now, the DeHavilland Beaver was clearly visible. It was time to withdraw from Dawson Lake and return to the south, and the three room cabin on the reservation.

Carlin was suddenly filled with an urgency that comes with the late autumn. It was a feeling that there were too many things to do before winter set in, and not enough time to accomplish everything. It was a dull ache pulling at his insides and it came every year at this time. He pushed the canoe into the water, and paddled hard down the lake toward the plane. He untied the mooring ropes and used them to lash the canoe in place along the float struts. In the cockpit, he primed the engine and pressed the start switch. The engine turned over a few times and coughed. He tried again and this time it caught and roared to life. Carlin throttled back and with the engine just above idle, he made his way to the campsite and ran the floats up on the beach. As he climbed down, the aroma of 100 octane aviation fuel and Castrol Aero filled his nostrils. It was a heady aroma and he wanted to be airborne quickly.

Carol and Jim had prepared breakfast. After eating, Carlin returned to the plane, and covered the mining gear with a tarp. They let Wassermann sleep until the concentrate drums and equipment were secure and covered in the back of the plane. Finally, they struck the tent and loaded the remaining camping items.

It was time to go. Jim and Wassermann sat in the rear seat while Carlin and Carol took the pilot and co-pilot positions. Though the Beaver was heavily loaded she was airborne quickly, and Carlin swung her onto a south east heading. He wondered what George Wassermann would think if he knew that much of the load was very high grade concentrate rich in platinum and gold.

From five thousand feet, the forest floor was a riot of colour. The winds had stripped most of the leaves from the deciduous trees and they lay in heaps on the forest floor. Now the dark green of the conifers stood out starkly against the fallen leaf carpet of red and gold. Carlin imagined the sound of the crisp leaves being crushed under foot, and the tangy scent of them as the composting process began. Soon it would be the season to hunt game birds, and he always took two or three ptarmigan or partridge for a single meal at this special time of year. The meal was one of ritual, not one of need. Carlin and all Ojibwa gave thanks each day for all the blessings from the Great Spirit. Somehow, Carlin thought, a plastic wrapped turkey from a supermarket didn't really cut it for a thanksgiving dinner, in honour of Manitou or God the creator. He was very quiet throughout the flight, his mind exploring the rich feelings that accompanied the autumn rains.

It was 1:00 P.M. when the Beaver touched down on the lake where Air Ojibwa was quartered. Carlin was first out of the plane, and made it fast to the dock. He asked Carol and Wassermann to remain in the aeroplane, and he and Jim opened the cabin to air it out.

"Jim, will you take George to the Band office and see that he stays there. I need time to secure the concentrate and the flake and amalgamation gold. So far he has seen nothing and he knows nothing – let's keep it that way."

"Sure – no problem. I will get Johnny Silvertip to look after him until the police have dealt with him," Jim said, "Then I will come right back and help with the off loading."

"That would be very good Jim. I didn't intend to process the concentrate right away – only to bank the gold we have already recovered. When you come back I have some very good news for you," Carlin said with a grin.

"I'll be here," Jim answered. He was very curious about Carlin's promised news. When he and Wassermann had gone, Carlin took Carol to the cabin, and they sat in the miniature bay window that overlooked the lake.

"Carlin," she said laying her head on his shoulder, "will we always live here?" He was surprised at the question and hoped she wasn't dissatisfied. The cabin WAS very compact.

"No, I don't think we will live here forever," he said looking out across the lake's gray brooding waters. "I don't know the mind of The Great Spirit – no one knows the mind of God. We will surely go where He wishes, and do the things He wants us to do. Are you unhappy here?"

"Oh no," Carol answered, "I am VERY happy here – I just don't want it to end. At this very moment I feel safe and protected from everything. I cannot remember a time when I felt so secure." She couldn't see the gentle smile that tugged at the corners of his mouth.

"At this time of year, I always feel very sad," Carlin said,

"Look at the water – it is dark and foreboding like the hearse at a funeral, and I mourn at this time of the year."

"This might be an indelicate question," Carol said, "but are you mourning a lost love?" He was quiet for a minute and a cold fear touched her heart.

"Yes, in a way you might say that." He felt her body stiffen. "I mourn the loss of the summer," he concluded, placing a kiss on her hair. Her fear vanished as smoke is vanquished by a wind, and she relaxed in his arms.

The autumn sky grew darker as the afternoon lengthened, and a brisk, cold wind marched down the lake placing whitecaps on the waves. The cabin took on a definite chill, and Carlin lit a fire in the little field stone fireplace. Soon the cabin was transformed once again, now into a warm refuge where the chill of winter could not reach them.

In the early twilight of late afternoon, Jim Peters hurried to Air Ojibwa. He tapped on the door and Carol opened it to him.

"Ah, it's cozy and warm here," Jim said stepping in, "not like my place." He slipped out of his beautiful buckskin jacket, hanging it on a peg beside the door. "My wigwam is as cold as a well digger's ass," he lied. There will be frost on the walls by morning." Hearing his words Carol became very concerned. Carlin turned away so she couldn't see his face, and silently he was shaking with laughter.

"You live in a tipi?" Carol asked, incredulous.

"No," Jim said, "a wigwam."

"What's the difference?" Carol asked, "aren't they the same thing?"

"Oh no," Jim said, "a wigwam is made from birch bark, and you know how well THAT burns!" Carlin couldn't take it and burst out in a great guffaw.

Carol blushed at having been taken in so completely and swung her hand to slap Jim, but his hands shot out and grabbing her by the waist he held her, struggling, high over his head. Finally, realizing how ridiculous this looked she started to laugh.

"Carol, get down from there this minute," Carlin ordered, "try to be serious for once," he said in mock anger. Jim set her back on her feet and they all laughed at the foolishness.

When they were seated in front of the fireplace, Carlin told Jim about the vent and the carpet of gold. "The lighter stuff is all we have tapped. As the water flow weakens with distance the nuggets don't make it as far as the lake's discharge point. They are lying in a trail along the underwater path, covered with a thin layer of sand. My guess is conservative at a million dollars," he said, "and I'm talking about gold only. With the platinum figured in, it could easily go to three million."

"What are we going to do about it?" Jim asked, the light in his black eyes dancing.

"Nothing," Carlin answered, "we keep an eye on Dawson Lake, and at the first sign of intrusion we will have to secure our leases on the mine."

"Why don't we do that right away?" Carol asked, "Then we would be legally protected and not have to worry about anything."

"Except claim jumpers," Carlin said, "no let's keep it secret."

"As soon as the ice breaks up on the lake we will fly in for a month – three weeks for carpet cleaning and one week for staking claims. Once that is done, I suggest we sell the mine to the highest bidder. I also suggest we put a reserve price of twenty-five million on it."

A pall of silence descended on the room as Jim and Carol digested what Carlin had just proposed. Carol finally broke the silence.

"Do you think we will get that much money for the mine?" Carol asked in wonder.

"It is a certainty," Carlin assured her, "I have a plan," and they celebrated with a bottle of good wine.

When Carol opened her eyes in the morning, Carlin was gone, the cabin was warm and comfortable, and a mantle of frost transformed the outdoors into a sparkling wonderland. The room was filled with the scent of the coffee Carlin made before he left. She wondered where he had gone – there was no note, no indication of when he would return. She poured herself some coffee and sat in the bay window looking across the lake. Somehow, in the glittering frosted world, the lake looked angry, afraid perhaps, of the long winter about to suspend its life with a mantle of ice. Carol thought about how she would deal with the months that lay immediately ahead. Five months would pass before she would see the lake change colour once more – see it

G. WM. GOTRO

change from the blues and greens of the ice to the silver of water at sunrise. How would she fill her time? Would she suffer from cabin fever. Always before, she had spent her winters studying, working, interacting with other people, but now ...?

Her reverie was broken by a tapping at the door. She opened it to find Carlin loaded down with bags and parcels. She took some of them from him and he entered, slipping out of his boots at the door.

"You could have left a poor girl a note," she said, teasing him, "I thought I had been abandoned after my first day at home."

"It is good that you think of it as home already," Carlin said, "I slept in – it was almost 5:30 when I got up to feed the fire. I had an appointment with someone at the Band office."

She was suddenly annoyed by his explanation. How could he have made an appointment with anyone – he hadn't seen anyone but Jim Peters since they arrived yesterday. Rather than dwell on it she asked him. Carlin wasn't offended by her apparent lack of trust. He knew she simply didn't understand – she wasn't Ojibwa – YET.

"When we were rescued, and I came home to the reservation, I went to see Frank Whitefeather. He is an historian of sorts, and he spent a lot of time with the Navajo in the south. They taught him their ways of working with silver, and he was already an Ojibwa silversmith. I commissioned him to do some work for me," Carlin said, taking a small leather bag from a larger parcel. "This is for you." He handed her the pouch.

"Thank you," she said, "What is it?"

He didn't answer, he simply waited for her to undo the drawstring. Opening the pouch she turned it over and an exquisite engagement ring dropped into her hand. The ring was fashioned from 22 carat gold and mounted into it was a 1 carat solitaire diamond. The setting was the most unique design she had ever seen. The band was wide, wide enough to display an intricately carved pattern.

At first glance, the pattern appeared to be a random assortment of lines and curves. A closer examination revealed pictures of the south Ojibwa totems, interconnected around the band and completing the circle. It took her breath away.

"Oh Carlin, it is the most unique and exquisite ring I have ever seen," she said, handing it back to him and extending her hand. He placed the ring on her finger, and she kissed him passionately. "When I opened my eyes and you were gone, I panicked. I thought my dream was over."

"No," he said simply, "your dream is just beginning." He began to put away the items he had brought back to the cabin. "Let's plan the wedding."

By 10:00 A.M. they had finalized their plans. It would be a very small wedding. Jim Peters was to be Carlin's best man, and since Carol's father had passed away years before, she asked Carlin if he had a friend to give her away. Carol contacted her mother and two girlfriends from her university days. Carlin contacted Stuart Fraser, and asked Chief Orren Flagg to give the bride away.

Their wedding day was to be December 1st, and on that day The Great Spirit blessed them with a fine clear morning. Though the temperature was thirty below zero, the bright sun charged the air. The wedding took place in a small church west of Sudbury at 10:00 A.M. When Jim Peters gave Carlin the ring, Carlin smiled as he put it on her finger, and she looked at her hand. The wedding ring was a simple gold band, the same width as the engagement ring, but it too was ornately carved. Around it were the totems of the north Ojibwa, each touching the other to form a perfect circle. Carol remembered his words to her so long ago – "The circle has no beginning nor does it have an end, it is eternal, and unbroken."

They left the church and returned to the reserve. The long house had been prepared in their absence, the people working long hours for more than a week. Orren Flagg invited the guests into the long house for a simple reception, his manner so dignified and yet so humble, told them of the privilege offered. Within the long house the decorations were breathtaking. It was festooned in ribbons and painted masks. Quilts and blankets filled the room with colour, and in the centre, the fire pit glowed with great burning logs. When they entered, a drummer began a complex beat and then it grew silent. Chief Orren Flagg, now dressed in the traditional Ojibwa costume welcomed the guests in Ojibwa and in English, then turned his words to the matter at hand.

"When I was a young man – a long time ago, I heard all the

stories of our people from the beginning of time. One story told of a people who fell into dispute with the Mediwewin. They came to believe the dispute could never be resolved, and they left their home here in the south and taking all their worldly possessions, traveled to a place that would come to be called Crystal Lake. After many generations, The Great Spirit prepared a Messenger to go to them. He told the Messenger to tell them, they should return to the south and their brothers, for the secrets of the north must remain secrets for a long time yet. When the Messenger saw how tired the old people were, and he saw how restless the young people were, he chose to spare the elders." In the background the drum highlighted Orren Flagg's words.

"It would be improper to chastise the elders in the presence of the young, and it would be improper to speak to the young in secret. Thus it was that the Messenger spoke to them in two tongues at the same time. To the elders, he spoke in the tongue of Ke-Noushay the pike, but they did not understand him. To the children he spoke in the tongue of the bear and they heard and understood." Orren Flagg lifted his arms in a gesture of supplication.

"The Messenger told the young people to go south and resolve the differences with the Mediwewin," the chief said, "he told them that the future of the Ojibwa would worsen for a long time, and then a new son of the Ojibwa would bring us a new beginning." The chief raised his hands to the heavens and continued... "The Great Spirit brought Carlin and Jim Peters together as brothers. By an agreement of the families on the day Carlin McKenzie was born, Jonathan Peters and his wife Tisha became surrogate mother and father to the boy. Together Jim Peters and Carlin have begun to fulfill the promise of a new beginning. They have halted the suicides of our youth and they will build our hospital." Orren Flagg put his hand out to Carol, and she took it, moving to his side. It seemed as though he was her father and she drew strength from him. The chief concluded his address.

"Now Carol has taken Carlin as her husband, and no doubt she will chronicle the true history of our people, for it was Carol that suffered much to learn about the Crystal Lake people. Welcome them to our community as man and wife – welcome them as

Ojibwa in the Ojibwa tradition." The drums started then, and some of the women sang a song of friendship.

Carol's mother called her aside, concerned for her future. "Carol, the old Chief seems to think you will be living here with the Indians. It would be best if you told him now that you will be living within the white society."

"Mother, we haven't talked in depth about anything in years. My husband is a white Ojibwa. My place is at his side. You just heard the Chief accept me into the band. We have a lovely home here on the reserve, and I am happy with my life." Carol looked into her mother's eyes, searching for acceptance, and found only doubt.

"How can you, a trained archaeologist, settle down with a man you hardly know on a poverty stricken Indian reserve?" Carlin, standing behind the woman, overheard the comment. He approached Carol's mother with a faint smile.

"I guess I should be calling you mother," he said, "but it is important to point out a few thing you seem to have overlooked. First, I know Carol better than you do." The woman bridled and furious outrage was in her eyes. "I cared for her for a year in the wilderness." Carlin continued, then he went silent for a few moments, looking deep into her eyes. "By the end of January my wife will be worth a minimum of eight and a half million dollars in her own right, and I can't imagine her as poverty stricken. The wealth of our people lies in their spirituality and now for the first time they are about to experience financial security." He looked down at the Gucci loafers on his feet – then – "Please excuse me for a moment. I will return and listen to your concerns and try to address them." The woman was outraged, and she looked at him in disgust as he walked away. Ten minutes later Carlin returned to the long house. He was no longer dressed in the dark gray suit, white shirt and conservative tie, but in Levis and buckskin shirt with moccasins on his feet. Around his forehead he wore the beaded black leather headband, given to him by his surrogate Ojibwa mother, Tisha Peters. He approached Mrs. Danse.

"Would you mind coming outside with me Mrs. Danse, I have something you should see." They walked through the woods in silence, to Air Ojibwa and Carlin opened the cabin door for her.

G. Wm. Gotro

"Please," he said with a sweep of his arm, indicating that she should enter. Inside the cabin, she removed her boots and parka.

"This is my home," Carlin said simply. "Carol seems to love it here – how do you feel about that?"

She evaded the question. "Why did you change from a suit to this on your wedding day?" she asked, indicating his jeans and buckskin shirt. "You are not an Indian," she concluded with a touch of sarcasm. Then as an after thought, "And on what grounds can you possibly see my daughter as a millionaire – it seems you live in a dream world Mr. McKenzie."

"Ma'am, I am the adopted son of an Ojibwa family, and a member of this band. Only my colour prevents me from being Anishinawbe. These are my people – they accept me as one of their own, and I accept them. Carol would be hard pressed to turn away from them – she owed her life to Jim Peters and repaid him by saving his life in a crisis. This is no dream world Mrs. Danse, it is the real world, where one lives through hunger and horror, to abundance and happiness. Now, having said that, would you like a cup of hot tea or coffee while we discuss the pros and cons of Ojibwa life?" He placed his hands on her frail shoulders and beamed the Carlin smile of understanding at her.

She was quiet and introspective for a brief time before answering him, then to his surprise, "Yes Mr. McKenzie that would be most pleasant. Thank you."

"Carlin," he said, "my name is simply – Carlin – by choice I use only one. I could never decide whether I was a McKenzie or a Peters or perhaps McKenzie-Peters." He laughed and within minutes, he brought her a tray containing a sterling silver tea pot, cream pitcher, and sugar bowl. There were two bone china cups and saucers. "I think I would like to join you," he said, setting the tray down in the bay window, "come and sit here – it's the best view in the house."

She smiled at him at last, and in a comfortable silence they drank a delicious tea, faintly flavoured with mint. Finally she looked at him again, this time with a grudging respect. "Would you answer a question from your new mother-in-law?" she asked.

"Of course," he said quickly. "I will certainly try."

"Would your birth mother be happier if you retained the

McKenzie name or Peters name?" She had instinctively done the right thing by the Ojibwa rules – she didn't tell him to retain one or the other.

"She would have been happy if I retained my birth name," he said, "and so it shall be."

"Good!" she replied with a lovely smile, "Now, I think we had best be getting back to the big house."

"Long house," he corrected her with a gentle laugh, "it is the meeting place for everyone and it has a spiritual connotation too. You could call it"Ki-Gi-Tong" which means the talking place."

They walked back through the snow in silence, but before they entered the long house, she stopped. "Carlin, I've learned a lot today. I am still uncertain about Carol's future, but I am confident that you will take good care of her – thank you. Oh, and I won't call you Mr. McKenzie if you promise to refrain from calling me Mrs. Danse. My name is Aida."

"We have a deal Aida, and I think I'll like you a lot."

When they entered, Carol was in the midst of a group of Ojibwa women. Aida Danse spoke first to Chief Orren Flagg.

She apologized for her earlier comments, and thanked the Ojibwa for taking care of her daughter. She then searched out Jim Peters.

"Mr. Peters, Carlin has told me about you saving my daughter's life. I want to express my gratitude to you." A deep rumbling laugh came from him, and he placed his hands on her shoulders.

"I didn't save her life," Jim said shaking his head, "but she certainly saved mine. The scars on my face were the result of a fight with an angry black bear. He was winning, and toppled me over backward. He was moving in for the kill when Carol stepped between the bear and me, and shot him in the head." He took a piece of maple sugar and offered one to Mrs. Danse. "We are very happy that Miss Danse has become Mrs. Carlin McKenzie, and we are proud that she is associated with the band. Please Mrs. Danse, be aware that you too, will always be welcome here, and treated with respect."

When the ceremonies were over, Orren Flagg insisted that Aida Danse spend the night with his family. She did so, and she remembered the event fondly, for the rest of her life. Jim Peters

G. WM. GOTRO

bade everyone farewell about 9:00 P.M. then he and his family went home.

Carlin and Carol returned to the cabin before 11:00 and stoked the fireplace with fresh logs. Then, sitting together in the bay window they looked out across the lake. A full moon bathed the snow with white light, the wind blew the surface powder in snakelike trails, and just before midnight they watched a big male wolf, silhouetted against the moon, howling for his mate.

"I'm glad I have my mate with me," Carlin said, and taking her hand he led her to the big bed and they consummated their marriage and their love for one another.

9

MULTIPLYING BY A MILLION

When the concentrate had been leached of its gold, and the platinum had been recovered and refined, Carlin, Carol, and Jim estimated the value of their gold and platinum reserve to be in excess of $350,000. Early in March, after some serious discussion they registered a company named Northern Assets Limited. The company placed its precious metal resources in a bank vault and when the ice left Dawson Lake they flew in for what was expected to be the last time.

Their purpose was to mine the 'Carpet of Gold' – the upper lake floor from the vent, to the mouth of the lake's outlet. They used a suction dredge whose pump was driven by a small gasoline engine. Carol operated the surface equipment and collected the concentrate while Carlin operated the underwater suction tube. Jim Peters staked claims from the beach to the upper lake, and from there, across the valleys that led to the feeder lake for the system, two and a half miles away.

Carlin badly misjudged the time it would take to dredge the carpet corridor. He was sure he could do it in two or three days, but the concentrate had been falling in the corridor for years. At the end of the third week, he was still removing very high grade concentrate, from deep down, and finally gave up from shear exhaustion and a lack of air for the scuba tank. In the end, they would fly out four loads of concentrate. To reduce the transportation time, they ran the amalgam barrel every day, reducing the concentrate to gold and other precious metals.

By late April they had returned to the reservation, and the leases were registered with Energy, Mines, and Resources. They processed the remaining concentrates near Ojibwa Air throughout the month, The gold was placed in Northern Assets Limited's vault, and the platinum was shipped away for recovery and refining. The rich carpet at the underwater vent proved to be a bonanza. In thirty nine days they accumulated $370,000 in gold alone. When the platinum was returned to them by Brinks armoured car, its value came to a staggering $485,000. Northern Assets Ltd. was worth better than $1,250,000 and it was time to start doing business.

They spent eight weeks studying everything from the value of mining shares to the sale of mining companies. They talked with stock brokers and investment companies, never telling them exactly what they had. At Carol's suggestion they bought a top quality computer and bought time on the Internet. Young Jim Sampson was very good with computers and was able to secure details on the best mining transactions in the world. All of the collected data from the net, and from their inquiries was collated and printed out in four identical dossiers. Then the data was stored in an encrypted file accessible by the three partners when all three entered their own part of the code. As the eighth week drew to a close they had formulated a plan that was almost foolproof.

Carlin leaked a news report to a newspaper dedicated to mining in northern Ontario, and a week later it made the headlines. "DISASTER SURVIVORS STRIKE IT RICH". The story went on to say that one of the principle owners of Northern Assets Ltd. suggested they would be selling the mine in the near future. Two days later they allowed a bank employee to leak the value of their precious metals assets.

Hungry investors, playboys, and the very greedy tried to buy stock, only to find the company was privately owned, and not being offered on the stock exchange. Stock promoters smelled big money, and hunted Carlin down, urging him to go public – urging him to go for a ten million share offering. When he turned them down, they publicly stated that the whole thing was probably a hoax to raise money with moose pasture mining stock. The brokers ploy backfired. The little guys backed away from their quick money dream and they were replaced by large corporations who had investment money, and still Northern Assets Ltd. refused to go public.

Carlin had anticipated the reaction of the financial community and was prepared. He hired an auditor from a very prestigious corporation to examine the books of the recently registered Northern Assets Ltd. Carlin took the man to the bank vault and showed him boxes of gold and platinum. He followed up with the assay results and shipping documents for the platinum, and told the auditor he wanted a high class financial brochure produced. The brochure was to stress the fact that the company held a fortune in precious metals, that it owned one of the richest gold mines on the continent and that the company would be sold at private auction within ninety days.

Two weeks later, the brochures were sent to one hundred of the top mining companies in Canada and the United States of America. Brochures were also sent to the major foreign mining companies around the world. The first response came from Japan, requesting more information regarding reserve bids. Northern Assets replied by cable, informing the Japanese that a reserve of twenty-five million was in place. All bids would have to be greater than that. Finally, the auction date was set for July 8th. at 10:00 A.M. in Toronto.

Carlin, Carol, and Jim took seats near the back of the room. They had insisted on remaining incognito, and thus they were treated as potential buyers and given a dossier of information by the auctioneer's staff. By 9:45 most of the bidders had arrived with lawyers and accountants. There was standing room only for the press and TV personnel. The auctioneer arrived at 9:58.

"Ladies and gentlemen we will shortly open the bidding on the Sun Gold Mine. This fabulous property yielded in excess of one million dollars to the operator/owners in less than six months of hand mining. Documents verifying the yield are in the possession of the firm of A.R. Donaldson Accountants and Auditors. Before we begin the bidding we will take thirty minutes to answer any final questions you may have. Questions anyone?"

A tall gaunt man raised his hand and got slowly to his feet. He was dressed very casually in white shirt and tie and a sleeveless cardigan. He wore dark gray chino trousers, and stood with his right hand in the trouser pocket. He appeared to be the epitome of a very relaxed individual. He raised his left hand to his face, the index finger touching his forehead in an unconscious parody of Peter Falk as Lieutenant Columbo before speaking.

"Errrr, aaah, the original brochure doesn't give us much technical detail sir. Now we have been given a new dossier of information and no time to study it. Might I suggest that it would be appropriate to give us thirty minutes to read and digest the contents of the document. After all, we are talking about twenty five million dollars here." He sat down awaiting an answer.

Jim Peters glanced at Carlin, and seeing an imperceptible nod of the head, got to his feet. "The gentleman is right, he said, nodding to the tall man,"we do need a little more time to study the new information."

"Very well," the auctioneer agreed, "we will adjourn until ten thirty, when the half hour question period will begin."

Everyone filed from the room. Carlin suggested that Jim and Carol should go separate ways and do a little talking and a lot of listening. It wasn't an easy suggestion to follow. The tall man had effectively thrown the fox into the chicken house, and almost everyone was busy reading their dossiers and had little time for small talk. The half hour passed too quickly and everyone gathered in the auction room again.

"What did you find out?" Carlin asked Carol as she sat down beside him.

"The tall man is from Interland Mines & Resources, and he is the C.E.O. – pretty casual for such an exalted position eh," she answered in an undertone.

Carlin turned to Jim, but he had no need to ask the question. "The Japanese think the resource is overpriced. They are going to walk as soon as the bidding begins," Jim said softly.

The auctioneer waited until everyone was seated. "Are there any questions from the floor?" A dozen hands were raised. Most of the questions were mundane and easy to answer. Only two were loaded.

"My name is Ken Werther from Excelsior Properties. Are diamond drilling results available?" The question came from a rotund little man whose hairless head shone like a beacon.

"No, all of the technical details are in the dossier."

The second important question came from David Crawford, C.E.O. of High North Minerals. It sounded very foolish when he voiced it, but it clearly set his interest in the project. "Can financial, and other arrangements be made to look the property over before closing a deal?" Carlin had anticipated such a request and addressed it. The auctioneer looked to him for permission to answer. Once more only the auctioneer noticed the slight tilt of the head that said okay.

"Yes, but only after the bidding ends," the auctioneer answered. A murmur of surprise rippled through the crowd. "Anyone wishing to do due diligence at the site, may do so by submitting a cheque in the amount of two hundred thousand dollars with his bid. The bidder will be flown to the mine site and accompanied throughout his inspection. On completion of the due diligence visit, the bidder will be flown back to Sudbury, Ontario. The sum already paid will be deducted from the purchase price payable by the purchaser – all others will forfeit the deposit. If the highest bidder chooses to drop out he forfeits his deposit, and the second highest bidder becomes the successful bidder."

A murmur rippled through the crowd and half a dozen intense conversations broke out between the potential buyers. The deal makers were working at top speed to circumvent the rules that had been laid down. Instantly, merger deals were being discussed between many company representatives, but Carlin's ground work was solid. The deal makers were out of time – the sale would be concluded within two hours at the most.

At 11:00 A.M. the auctioneer held off the start of bidding – the potential purchasers present, were in turmoil. When the big wall clock in the room reached 11:30 Carlin nodded to Jim Peters. Jim went to the auctioneer and spoke to him briefly. The auctioneer banged his gavel for attention and the room grew quiet.

"Ladies and gentlemen, I now proclaim the bidding open, with a reserve bid of twenty-five million dollars." Carlin was holding his breath as potential buyers scanned their brochures for what seemed to be the thousandth time. The tall man from Interland Mines & Resources made the first offer at twenty-five million.

"Twenty-six." The call came from the Japanese consortium.

"They think it's a good day to go fishing," Jim pronounced.

"Twenty-eight." This bid from Excelsior Properties.

"Do I hear twenty-nine? Anyone at twenty-nine?"

"Thirty-two." The bid was from Interland Mines & Resources

"Any advance on thirty-two?" The question was met with silence, 'for the last time – any advance on thirty-two? The auctioneer paused for almost a full minute. "I have thirty-two – going once – going twice ...

"Thirty-five." It was from Excelsior Properties again. The C.E.O. from Excelsior meant to end it by jumping up by three million.

"Forty," the tall man from Interland said, and the room became very quiet.

Carol heard the whispers behind her. There were four people in the Japanese contingent. Three Caucasians and one Japanese.

Two were talking in English, the third was speaking to the Japanese in his own language. The Japanese executive uttered a few guttural words and got to his feet. Then followed by his cortege of employees he left the room. in a state of high anger. He now knew that SunGold was a bargain and he had been limited to thirty million by his superiors.

"I have forty-million," the auctioneer called out, "is there any advance on forty?" This time there was no answer. "Forty million – going once," he paused for an unusually long time. "Forty million ladies and gentlemen – going once, going twice," a brief pause, "Sun Gold Mine, sold to Interland Mines & Resources for forty million dollars. Congratulations Mr. Brooks! I also have an offer of thirty-five million from Excelsior Properties. Final transactions must be executed within thirty calendar days. Thank you for your presence here today."

Carlin, Jim, and Carol approached Interland's C.E.O. "Congratulations Mr. Brooks," Carlin said affably, shaking the man's hand. You will triple your money within a year – I'm certain of it."

"Thank you," Brooks said with a smile, "I sure hope you are right." He paused in reflection for a moment, then, "I noticed that you didn't make a bid," he said.

"No," Carlin replied, "we weren't here to buy – we were the sellers." He flashed Brooks the Carlin grin. "This is my wife Carol, my brother Jim, and I am Carlin McKenzie."

"Well it certainly is a pleasure to meet this trio," Al Brooks said extending his hand to Carol first. "Mrs. McKenzie I hope you realize that you are far too attractive to be a miner."

He shook hands with Jim. "Is she really a miner?" he asked.

"Nah," Jim said teasing her, "she is just the camp cook."

"Actually, I'm the camp cook," Carlin said laughing, "Carol is an archaeologist – retired so to speak."

Brooks enjoyed the banter. He looked at his watch. "Tell you what," he suggested, "I blew forty million dollars this morning and I have seventy-five dollars left. C'mon I'll buy us lunch."

"Where?" Jim asked, "I am really fussy about who prepares my pemmican."

"I have a standing reservation at the restaurant at the top of the CN Tower, I hear the buffalo pancakes are good there," Al Brooks quipped. "Let's go!"

They enjoyed each other's company and had a fantastic lunch in a light, free and easy atmosphere. During the meal Carol glanced down from her window seat, and three hundred feet below, a Cessna from the Island Airport swept past the tower.

"Oh look Carlin," she said pointing to the top of the little plane, "it is just like your old Cessna, and he couldn't get very far off the water either." Al Brooks didn't catch the innuendo, but Jim Peters couldn't stop laughing.

"She is referring to a little accident I had with a Cessna 172 a few years ago," Carlin said by way of explanation for their host. "We crashed on Crystal Lake in the northern part of the province. It was while trying to get back to civilization that we found the site of what is now SunGold Mine.

"I remember that incident," Al Brooks said, "you folks were given up for dead, and somehow you survived the winter in the wilderness. Was it a mining exploration trip?"

"No," Carol replied, "it was an archaeological expedition that went bad. We should have gone in a month earlier – but we lived through it and it turned out to be a blessing for all of us. I didn't get any of the artifacts I wanted, but I got Carlin and Jim, a few million dollars, and lunch in the CN Tower restaurant."

It was past 3:00 P.M. when they parted company with Al Brooks and made their way to the dock where the Beaver was moored. On the flight back to the reserve, they experienced an entire range of emotions. They were frightened that something would go wrong at the last minute and the dream would fall apart. They experienced intense elation – they were worth forty million dollars plus their precious metals reserve of more than one and a quarter million. They were grateful that a disastrous archaeological expedition resulted in them becoming multi-millionaires, and sad that the excitement of mining their own gold was over.

The trepidation and responsibility of the money was awesome. They were about to fund the building of a hospital and a sanitation system of major proportions, and were unsure of where to begin. Carlin was very quiet as he flew the Beaver over southern Ontario. He loved to fly over the province on a bright summer day, to watch the panorama of the land unfold, to see whitecaps marching down the length of a lake, and he was thrilled by the very immensity of the land. He wondered what Jim was thinking and feeling, and he looked back at his partner. Jim's face was serious, but he smiled and nodded – he too was thinking of his responsibilities.

"What are you thinking about Carol?" Carlin asked softly.

"Oh I was just trying to assess my feelings about being a millionaire, and somehow it doesn't seem real. I can't imagine all that money. When I think about losing you or Jim – that is real, and I would trade all the money to get you back." Her eyes were clouded and very serious. "Right now, with or without the money, my life is perfect. Without you, the money means nothing Carlin."

He reached across and squeezed her knee. "My gut turns to jelly when I think about life without you now," he said, "I never knew how cold and empty life was in the past." For the rest of the flight back to the reservation, all of their dialogue was internal.

Seven weeks passed before their attorneys contacted them with the news, that the business transactions between Interland Mines & Resources and Northern Assets had concluded. The lawyers were in possession of forty million dollars for deposit to Northern's account. The trio were jubilant – they had pulled it off –

what began as a tragedy had become a fairy tale! Their attorneys added that the C.E.O. of Interland requested that Carlin call him at his earliest convenience. Two days later, Carlin placed the call.

The tall gaunt C.E.O. of Interland Mines & Resources answered his own phone. "Good morning, Brooks speaking." It was abrupt, but cordial and straight to the point.

"Mr. Brooks, Carlin from Northern Assets. My attorney advised me that you wished to speak with me."

"Yes Mr. McKenzie – I appreciate your calling me back so promptly. I have a lot of questions about SunGold Mine. I believe you can provide me with the answers. Could we arrange a meeting?" Brooks asked.

"Of course I will meet with you Mr. Brooks, but please understand that I know little or nothing about geology or mining. That being said, where and when would you like to meet?"

"Since I am asking the favour," Brooks said graciously, "I will be happy to come to you – tell me when and where." There was a broad hint of joviality in Brooks words. Carlin decided to test the man's loquacious limits.

"I live at the east end of a small lake eighty miles from Sudbury. It is known locally as Little Spirit Lake. If you have access to a float plane, I will meet you here – if not I will pick you up on a lake of your choice. Wednesday morning would be fine." There was silence at the other end of the telephone line for a few seconds. Carlin waited for Brooks' alternate suggestion.

"I will be landing between 10:00 and 10:30 A.M. Mr. McKenzie. You put the coffee on, and I will take care of the bagels and brandy," Al Brooks said decisively, and the joviality was back in his voice. "Fair enough?"

"More than fair," Carlin said, "Tell your pilot I will moor your plane at Air Ojibwa's dock."

Two days later, at 10:15 A.M. an old Noordyne Norseman made a sharp sideslip and its floats touched the water in a gentle caress. The plane looked as though it had just come out of the factory. It taxied up to the dock and Carlin caught the wing strut drawing the beautiful old aeroplane gently to the canvas rub strips of the dock. Carlin made it fast to the mooring rings. The door opened and Al Brooks swung down from the cockpit. He shook

Carlin's offered hand. His handshake was strong and spoke of sincerity. Carlin's respect for the man skyrocketed.

Here was an executive from a company that just spent forty million dollars for a mine, chauffeuring himself around northern Ontario in an ancient aeroplane, for a business meeting.

It was almost instantaneous – there was a mutual admiration society founded between the two men. Brooks turned back to the Norseman and withdrew a large paper bag and handed it to Carlin.

"I hope you make good coffee Carlin – there is nothing more insipid in this world than bad coffee." Carlin glanced into the bag. It contained a dozen fat bagels, a pound of dairy butter, and a bottle of fine Napoleon brandy.

"The coffee is ready Mr. Brooks," Carlin said, leading the way toward the cabin. The door opened, and Carol stepped out in a swim suit, smiled and nodded briefly, then ran across the dock to plunge into the cold water of Little Spirit Lake.

"Wow – what a beautiful woman!" Al Brooks exclaimed, glancing back over his shoulder.

"Yes, I am the luckiest man in the world," Carlin said, laughing, "she will join us in a few minutes." They entered the little cabin and Carlin gestured to Al Brooks to sit in the bay window seat while he poured coffee. A refreshing cool breeze came in through the open windows stealing the precious scent, of cedar logs and drying spearmint hanging from the rafters. Carlin brought a silver tray to the bay window. On it were three identical pale, blue-gray mugs, a silver coffee pot, sugar and cream. Two of the mugs were filled with steaming coffee.

"Mr. McKenzie," Al Brooks said, "I have a proposition for you." He fixed his coffee with sugar and laced it with brandy.

"Do you take yours the same way?" he asked. Carlin nodded in the affirmative, and Brooks prepared Carlin's coffee as well. "Would you consider flying back to SunGold and walking over the property with me. I need to know what you found and what you would do with the property now." He sipped the coffee and examined the mug carefully, making mental notes about questions to ask later. "Your input will save me from making a great many mistakes, and wasting a lot of money – what do you say?"

"Of course I will help in any way possible," Carlin replied, "but there will be conditions."

"What kind of conditions?" Al Brooks asked, cautiously.

"I will ask my Ojibwa brother to come with me, and of course Carol will accompany us too."

"I don't see any problem with that," Brooks said, "but may I ask why?"

"They are my family and my partners," Carlin replied, "we make all our decisions jointly and insitu."

The door opened and Carol entered, crossing the room to their bedroom. Moments later she reappeared dressed in Levis, moccasins, a T-shirt and a richly beaded doeskin vest. Around her forehead she wore a buckskin head band, decorated with the beaded pattern of circles separated by blocks of four vertical lines.

"Good morning," she said, crossing to the bay window, "Welcome to our home Mr. Brooks, it is nice to see you again." Al Brooks stood and offered his hand.

"It's a pleasure to be here Carol, may I pour you coffee?"

"Yes, she said,"and how are things at Interland Mines & Resources?"

"Just fine, but I need your help to get this thing going."

Carlin was busy toasting bagels and the scent of them was tantalizing. "I am certain we can assist you, but if you will excuse me for a moment Mr. Brooks, I should help Carlin with whatever he is immolating in the kitchen. He is a great cook outdoors but ..."

"By all means Carol," he said, "but please call me Al."

"Agreed," she said, and smiling she left him and joined Carlin. "He's nice," she said, kissing Carlin's cheek, "go in and keep him company while I prepare some late breakfast for everyone."

"Thanks," Carlin said with a grin, and kissing the back of her neck, he made her shiver.

While they enjoyed a hearty breakfast of poached eggs, thick slices of bacon, toasted bagels, and good coffee from freshly ground beans, Al Brooks divulged his real purpose in being there.

"If Interland had the financial reserves, we would buy all the crown land in the north," he said seriously, "Not to rape it or to turn it into a great cottage country estate, but to preserve as much of it as possible. We would naturally mine the resources, but in a controlled way. Interland would also try to settle land claims with the First Nations, but unfortunately we are not financially able to do those things." His eyes became clouded as he thought about the future. "We are running close to the financial edge and that is why I need your help. You can save us a great deal of money by cutting down our exploration costs, and that brings me to the big question."

"Fire away," Carlin said, we will help you any way we can."

"How soon could we go back in." Al Brooks was very anxious.

"Are you ready to go back to Dawson Lake Carol?" Carlin asked.

"Sure," she replied, her eyes dancing with the anticipation of a new adventure. "We need one day to provision though."

"I'll call Jim right now," Carlin said, hoping his big Ojibwa friend was not too involved with the community for one last thrust into Dawson Lake. Francine answered the phone.

Francine had come to live with the Peters family six months before. She had come to the band from Fort William when her eighty year old mother passed away. Fran lived with her sister and brother-in-law who resided on the Little Spirit Lake reserve, but Jimmy Wapitee was a drunk who frequently abused his wife. The day he came home in a rage, after a three day bender, he put his wife in hospital, Francine cooled his rage with a baseball bat to the forehead. Her sister died from Jimmy's beating and Jimmy was sent to prison. Jonathan Peters welcomed the poor girl to his home, where she became a happy and welcome addition to the Peters family.

"Jim isn't home Carlin. He may be on his way to Air Ojibwa though. He said he wanted to see you today." Carlin thanked her and returned to his guest.

"Okay Al, I'm sure Jim will make time for this project. As Carol said, we will need a day to provision, so ..."

"There is no need for you to provision Carlin, Interland will take care of that. Let us be the outfitters for a change and you be the client," the man from Interland said, happy that the project was a go. "We will pick you up here Friday morning if you agree. Interland's Grumman Goose will be on the water by 10:00 A.M."

"Okay – okay," Carlin said laughing, and raising his hands in surrender. "You are one gung-ho executive Mr. Brooks!"

Later, after a brief farewell, Carlin watched as the man from Interland taxied the Norseman out to the far end of the lake. He turned into the wind and opened the throttle. The almost empty aeroplane was up on the step in a few hundred yards, and Brooks held her down to gain more airspeed. The Norseman flew directly toward them, passing over them at two hundred feet or so, and Carlin knew the man was both a careful and competent pilot.

"Who was that?" Jim asked, having arrived silently, only moments earlier.

"That was the Man Who Bought SunGold," Carlin said, his eyes dancing. "He wants us to go in to Dawson Lake with him – he needs our help."

"How long?" Jim's question was couched in concern.

"Not more than a week," Carlin answered, "Are you concerned about the time?"

"Yes. I've been talking with the engineering people about the sanitation system, and they are suggesting some very expensive changes to the design. They want to double the capacity. At the rate the young people are leaving the reservation I can foresee a system that will never reach capacity." Jim's hands were thrust deep into the pockets of his jeans and his brow was furrowed.

"How much will the changes cost?" Carlin asked.

"The original system proposed, was to cost $3,100,000. The proposed changes will almost double that figure," Jim said, his voice low, and filled with angry disappointment. "I think I should stay here and get this project back on track."

"Yes, I agree with you Jim, but I too, have an obligation. Interland didn't balk at putting up forty million dollars for SunGold. It stretched their financial resources to the limit. Brooks, the C.E.O. has asked for our help to reduce his exploration costs. I think we have a moral obligation to assist him."

"Then let it be so," Jim said with finality. "You must do what you can for them, and I must stay to wrestle with the sanitation system decisions – the system must be completed before winter sets in." The big man carried a look of one defeated in a competition.

"Jim, you are deeply troubled and I don't think it is because you cannot make a decision on the sanitation system. What is it you are not telling me brother?" Carlin asked gently.

"Remember the time you treated Mary Whitebird's little boy when he was bitten by the rattler?" Jim asked in a shaky voice.

"Yes – yes, I remember."

"He died last night," Jim said bitterly, "It was typhoid fever Carlin. They left it too long – they didn't know."

Bile rose in Carlin's throat. He remembered the child on the brink of death, remembered Mary Whitebird willing her child to live, remembered the child's father in shock and his subsequent rejection of alcohol. Their world had been shattered completely – Mary was too old now to risk another pregnancy. Carlin's throat constricted with sorrow, and he found it difficult to speak. "I will stay here and help with the situation. Carol will you call Interland and tell Brooks we cannot oblige him until later?"

"No," Jim said, "I can deal with the engineers, and there is nothing you can do for the boy. You are free to go. I will be very happy when you return to the reserve. I will do as much as I can handle and the Great Spirit will do the rest." Carlin looked into Jim's eyes and there he saw a determination he had never seen before. The engineering company was in for one hell of a time.

One final change of plans took place early Friday morning. Carol brought Mary Whitebird and her husband to the cabin. It was a clever ploy to try to raise them from their sorrow by asking them to stay with her while Carlin was gone. When she told him her plan he was delighted. He knew Carol could ease the pain of their loss.

The Grumman landed on Little Spirit Lake at the appointed time, Carlin kissed Carol goodbye, and took his place in the right hand seat. The flight over northern Ontario was uneventful and they landed on Dawson Lake two hours after their departure from the Air Ojibwa dock. Carlin lead Al Brooks to the original campsite while the two crewmen secured the Grumman on the beach. By two P.M. two tents and a cooking shelter were erected, and they had a lunch of Spam sandwiches and coffee.

Al Brooks gave the crewmen the task of unloading the mining equipment, then at Carlin's suggestion, he and Brooks climbed the hill to the upper pool.

"We began mining at the wrong end," Carlin said, "we were so excited at recovering a few nuggets and a little flake gold, that we never considered where it originated. We picked a lot of moss from the lower creek banks and burned it. Then we panned the ashes and found several grams of flake gold. It wasn't until a long time later that we began recovering concentrate from the lower lake."

"From the lower lake?"

"Yes – where the creek enters the lake there is good concentrate, but now I want you to look at the surface of the pool very carefully," Carlin said, a faint smile on his face. Al Brooks scanned the upper pool from side to side and from end to end to no avail.

"What am I looking for?" he asked in resignation. Carlin pointed to the spot where the vent was located.

"Notice that spot over there where the water seems to be unruffled by the breeze."

At first Al Brooks couldn't identify the area, then suddenly it became apparent to him. "Yes," he said, "I see it now – what is it?"

"It is high pressure water entering the pond from the lake bottom twenty feet below. It is what I call the vent, and it is this little lake's source of water..."

"Ah, so the lake is fed from an underground spring!" Brooks said grasping the implication.

"I thought so too," Carlin answered, "but on a more sober reflection I decided there was far too much pressure from below to originate from a spring." He got to his feet and clambered to the top of an outcropping of boulders. "Come up here Al," he motioned with his hand, "Come up here and it will all come clear." Brooks climbed the rocks and stood beside him. Carlin turned through almost ninety degrees pointing with his arm and hand. "Look through the trees on the skyline – see the glitter of water?" They were not quite high enough and Al Brooks was about to give up when he noticed the faint but definite clue.

"Yes, now I see it but ..."

"It is a lake, two and a half miles from here, and it is between fifty and one hundred feet higher than we are. The vent is fed from that body of water via an underground tunnel. The gold originates somewhere between that lake and the vent right here," Carlin said, pointing back to the vent. Al Brooks was silent, thinking about Carlin's last words and the implication.

G. WM. GOTRO

"Thank you Carlin. You just saved me about ten million dollars in exploration costs. Now I know why there was a twenty-five million reserve on the sale." They climbed down and Carlin led the way back to Dawson Lake. On the beach he stopped. "Is something wrong?" Al Brooks asked, looking intently at his guide.

"No, nothing wrong," Carlin replied, "I found this place quite by accident," he said, drawing lines in the sand with the toe of his boot. "But there was a funny feeling here ... it was like a promise ... and then it came true!"

"Well when you get that feeling again," Brooks said laughing, "how about letting me in on it BEFORE it costs me forty millions."

Carlin laughed heartily at the comment. "I'll keep it in mind," he said, but he didn't tell Al Brooks that there was a new feeling of excitement growing in the centre of his being. He believed that another important event in his life would take place in the near future. Carlin was unaware, however, that a single case of typhoid fever on the reserve, was rapidly growing into an epidemic. Conversely he was painfully aware that he was needed at Air Ojibwa on the reserve.

The disk of the setting sun was precariously balanced on the tips of the northern forest's spruce trees, and soon it would set the sky aflame as it settled below the horizon. The light breeze that ruffled the surface of Dawson Lake had divested itself of the sun's warmth and now carried a distinct chill. Carlin shivered and found comfort in the warmth of his jacket.

"Al, I don't think I can give you much more help here, and I am needed at home ..."

"Yes, I know there are problems there. I will fly you back tomorrow morning," Brooks said, understanding the feelings of his new friend.

10

BACTERIUM SALMONELLA TYPHI

Jim Peters was furious when Mary Whitebird's boy died, but when four year old Anita Winter died the following day, he placed a dozen angry phone calls. Two of them would rock the government and the media. The first call was to the federal government, telling them that their lack of involvement in the health of the Ojibwa community had cost two lives, and the possibility of a typhoid epidemic was very real. He also told Ottawa that the roads through the Reservation were now closed and blockaded. Ottawa replied that a health officer and a team of disease specialists were on the way.

The second call was to the media and within the hour, the situation was a prime news topic. Television crews arrived within two hours and did an interview with Jim Peters, Mary Whitebird, the parents of Anita Winter, and Chief Orren Flagg. The TV reporter was a woman and she wanted to talk to Jim Peters first, but he deferred her to Chief Flagg.

"Chief Flagg, we understand that a child from your reserve has died from typhoid fever – how has this affected you and your people?"

"Two children have died from typhoid in the last twenty-four hours," Orren Flagg answered. "We mourn them and are trying to comfort their parents. I am frightened for the safety of our people."

"The Medical Officer of Health says the disease probably originated in the drinking water supply," the woman said. "How would you respond to that?"

"Look around you. Every second or third resident has an outhouse. Others use old and failing septic systems. Is it not obvious how the water is contaminated?" A bitter undertone tainted Orren Flagg's voice.

"Has the health officer confirmed the source of the disease?" the reporter asked. Again the provocation.

"The health officer hasn't been on this reserve in years – how would he know where the disease originates?" The chief turned away from the interviewer and spoke a few words in Ojibwa. He turned back to the camera. "We asked for help a long time ago and we were rewarded with promises. Now we want you to see something." Mary Whitebird carried her dead child to the reporter. "The promises didn't prevent this death," Orren Flagg said.

The camera operator shot footage of the little corpse with the full belief that it would never be aired, and the reporter covered her nose and mouth with a handkerchief. Jim Peters stepped into the breach.

"We are in the throes of building a new sanitation system with our own resources," he said, "but it may be too late. We asked the government for financial assistance to help us build a hospital – they refused. I wonder if they will allow us the right to use ampicillin or chloramphenicol to stop the impending deaths." He withdrew a worn and tattered leather work glove from his back pocket, and threw it at the feet of the TV reporter. "The gauntlet is down right now and the fight is on." Then Jim Peters turned his back on the camera and walked away.

Chief Orren Flagg approached the reporter again. "You, miss, and your colleague," he said, pointing to the cameraman, "have much power. Why not use it to stop what will surely be an epidemic instead of using it to provide light entertainment."

"Go away now," said Mary Whitebird, "go away before you too are infected with typhus."

The Health Officer arrived an hour later with a team of doctors and nurses. They remained on the reserve for three days giving injections of vaccine prepared from killed typhoid bacilli. The day following the TV program which tastelessly showed the corpse of the Whitebird's little boy as part of the interview, the federal government quietly responded by beginning construction of a first class water treatment plant. The project took four months to complete. Water from a new pump house on Little Spirit Lake, was routed to the treatment plant, and from there to each and every house on the reserve. The entire project was completed without any fanfare, the government not wishing to draw adverse publicity.

When Carlin returned home he found Sam and Mary Whitebird staying with Carol at Air Ojibwa. All three had been given short term immunity from the fever by taking the injection of killed typhoid bacilli. Sam and Mary were happy to see him home and returned to their own dwelling to continue the grieving process.

The day after Carlin's return, Jim called on him, filling in the details of the epidemic and the government's response. A total of six people had succumbed to the disease, the Whitebird boy, Anita Winter, two other children, and two adults. There hadn't been any other deaths in more than a week, but four adults were in hospital isolation wards recovering from the fever.

"Some good comes from every tragedy," Jim said, "The federal government is funding the entire water system project, but the price in lives is still much too high."

"Well, now that I have fulfilled my obligation to Interland Mines & Resources, we can get on with the construction of the sanitation system," Carlin said. The project would cost them $4.2 million, and it would become operational five days before Christmas – their Yuletide gift to the small, south Ojibwa reservation.

Early in January they approved the plans for the hospital, and after an expenditure of five and a half million dollars it would open the following September. It was staffed by an elderly surgeon who came out of retirement to take the post, and two young Ojibwa doctors. The nursing staff was comprised of eight graduate nurses, four of them Ojibwa. The hospital provided thirty-one jobs of a non medical nature for the people of the reserve. Once the hospital was up and running there would never be another tragedy like the typhoid epidemic that had taken six lives in the small community.

By the end of March, both Carlin and Jim Peters were suffering from near exhaustion. They often argued and snapped at each other, and didn't really understand what was wrong. Orren Flagg was the first to bring it to their attention. He called them together formally in the sweat lodge.

"Jim – Carlin, my heart is heavy. You have changed the lives of our people for the better. Where they would have suffered sickness and death, you have given them a fine hospital and hope. You have given them the dignity of a proper sewage disposal system and cleanliness. You have built schools where there were none and, you have provided centres for the young people to gather, and thus you have diminished the spectre of suicide."

"All of these things bring happiness to the children, their parents, and to me. The heaviness in my heart is for you. You are tired and worn, and you argue and fight each other as enemies rather than brothers. As your elder – your chief, I ask you to rest and recover. There will be no more projects for one year – that is the law!"

The two younger men looked at each other and nodded in assent. Carlin got to his feet and opened his arms, and Jim Peters embraced him.

"What our elder has spoken is true. The time has come for us to rest and to let The Great Spirit come into our hearts," Jim said softly, "We have become obsessed with our grand plan, and forgotten how to enjoy life – we were better on the trail."

"Thank you Orren," Carlin said, "the people were right when they chose you to lead them," He held his hands out to the old man. "You are a great chief not because you are old, but because you are wise. Jim Peters and I have heard you, and we will follow the path you have marked for us."

An early spring break-up left Little Spirit free of ice by April fifth, and a brisk spring wind set the whitecaps to marching down the lake. Carlin was tired. He recollected how they had been relentless in the pursuit of a finished hospital, a finished sanitation system, and the hiring of the personnel to operate everything faultlessly. They had undertaken the general clean-up of areas of the reserve that had been left to the effects of entropy. Now it was time to rest.

Carol had scolded him about the sixteen hour days without rest. He wasn't getting any younger either – it was time for a change and she decided to trigger the old Carlin back to life.

"I've been thinking," Carol said, looking out the window, "and

I have reached the conclusion that I'm not very happy here any more." Her casually spoken statement hit Carlin like a lightening bolt.

"I thought you were very happy here – this is serious Carol – what is wrong?" Carlin asked, his concern showing in his eyes. He walked over and put his arms around her. "Let's talk it out before it becomes a BIG problem."

Her real purpose in telling him she was no longer happy, was not to have him change her life, but to change his. He needed a respite – he needed to be away from Air Ojibwa, and the cares and concerns of the reserve for a while. "Oh it isn't that I'm unhappy with you or our life here," she said, "It is a feeling that I wasted my education in archaeology. I never finished anything and yet my life keeps on marching toward its inevitable end, doesn't it?"

"What have you left undone?" Carlin asked.

"I would really like to finish what I started out to do when we met," she said, laying her head on his chest. "I would REALLY like to go back to Crystal Lake and finish the project I started so long ago." He gently pushed her away and walked to the bay window. He said nothing for a long time – she went to the kitchen, and dropped two slices of bread into the toaster.

"Okay Carol," he said turning to face her. "If that is what it takes to make you happy, we will go tomorrow. How long will it take for you to finish your research up there?"

She came to him then and hugging him she opened her heart. "It will take one day longer than the time for you to become fully rested and restored," she said, "Every day I see you becoming more and more exhausted and it is breaking my heart."

"We don't have to wait until tomorrow," he said, holding her at arms length and looking deep into her eyes. "We still have a couple of million dollars left – why don't we go to Europe or Australia for a few months."

"Because the airlines won't let you fly a 747, and you would go nuts if they kept you out of the left hand seat," she answered. "Look at the lake Carlin." A strong spring wind was blowing straight down the lake, and the Beaver heaved and rolled at the mooring. "With a wind like that, we can start the takeoff run from the dock, and have the Beaver airborne before we cross the centre

G. Wm. Gotro

of the lake," she said. He laughed and hugged her tightly.

"Let's do it," Carlin replied with enthusiasm. He glanced at his watch. It was 8:15, and he was certain Jim would be up. "Would you like Jim to come along?"

"Yes of course," Carol answered, "we would both miss him if he wasn't there."

Carlin called Jim Peters to invite him along, but Jim declined, saying he was committed to organizing the July 1st Pow Wow. Jim told them Stuart Fraser would fly him in to Crystal Lake in three weeks. Carlin listened until Jim was finished and then asked him if the Pow Wow had a project number, and if Orren Flagg sanctioned his involvement. "No," Jim answered, "no, I forgot my promise. You are right Carlin, my involvement would offend Orren Flagg. If you can hold off until noon I will be there."

11

To Name a Village

The Beaver was loaded by mid-morning, but they waited for Jim until noon. It was five minutes before the hour and Carlin had just finished lashing the canoe to the float struts. Francine and Jim Peters, appeared in the clearing at the edge of the woods. Carol and Carlin hurried over to greet them. It was very clear that Jim was not a happy man, and it had something to do with the woman.

Francine was a pretty girl twenty-nine years old, but unlike her peers she had gray eyes. She was very proud of her Ojibwa heritage and refused to dress in manufactured clothes. Fran used every scrap of deer or moose hide she could get, and she had learned the techniques of bleaching the skins until they were a very light beige in colour and soft and pliable as chamois. She made all her own clothes by hand, and her only concession to the modern world was to use manufactured needles. She was the proud owner of a rich wardrobe of clothes. On several occasions young men from the reserve bought her gifts of manufactured modern garments, but she politely refused to accept them, or the advances of a potential suitor.

"Carlin, will you take me with you this time?" she asked directly. "Yes – of course you can come Fran," he said, looking carefully at Jim.

"The woman thinks I am unable to take care of myself," Jim said, his eyes blazing. "if you come on this trip, you stay the hell away from me," he said directing his words to her.

"Well, now that we are all in agreement," Carlin said

sarcastically, "let's load your gear into the plane before dark." He winked at Carol who was not sure this was such a good idea.

They lifted off Little Spirit Lake and turned north-northwest. Carlin was comfortable with Jim – he knew now that Jim was in love with Francine Talbot.

Carol's observations were not quite so profound. She was quiet for a time, thinking about why the gentle Jim Peters was so disgusted with the bright and pretty Francine. Carol examined the thought that Jim was just a natural born loner and didn't need anyone. Then she remembered that he almost stayed behind to organize the Pow Wow – he was NOT a loner – he was a quiet lover of people. As the Beaver droned over the wilderness of northern Ontario she came to the conclusion that Carlin was right again. Jim and Francine were in love – they just didn't know it yet.

"Carlin, I wasn't unhappy at Air Ojibwa, she confessed,"I guess I used it as a ploy to get you away from the place because I knew you needed to rest."

"Ah, now the truth comes out," he said, with a touch of laughter in his voice. Then he became very serious. "Since you were so honest with me, I feel obliged to be honest with you."

An alarm bell rang in her mind. "What is it Carlin – what are you trying to tell me?"

"Our last financial wasn't very good," he said, his brow wrinkled. "When you think you have forty million dollars it's easy to be magnanimous. We spent money like water building the sanitation system and the hospital."

"Then there was all the equipment – dozers and backhoes, trucks and jackhammers." He adjusted the trim tabs and throttled back slightly. "You keep deducting sums from the original total, but the fact is we never really had forty million."

"What do you mean Carlin, we sold SunGold for forty million," Carol said.

"Tax," Carlin answered, "taxes took a huge bite out of the money. The truth is that we have a little more than two million dollars left." Carol was quiet for a long time, and Carlin prompted her. "What are you thinking?" he asked softly, expecting the worst.

"Well," she said with a laugh, "for a guy who hadn't had a square meal for a week before I chartered his aeroplane ..." Carlin started to laugh too.

"Yeah, but two million is almost broke! What I still haven't told you, is what I was going to do before you coerced me into flying you to Crystal Lake."

She studied him, trying to figure what he was about to say.

He looked very serious. "Well the truth is, I was about to suggest we take some time, and fly up to Crystal Lake for old times sake." The mild tension that had come between them in recent weeks, vanished as down before a wind. "There IS one other thing," he said, "I have this funny feeling that something great is about to happen." Carlin didn't tell her they had two million EACH, and that didn't count their bullion. He checked the map and turned onto the final heading for their destination. During their extensive time together Carol had always respected his skill as a pilot and never distracted him during a takeoff or a landing.

A few miles beyond the nose of the plane, lay the blue exclamation mark – Crystal Lake. She tensed. "Don't forget the third sentinel," she whispered, but her words didn't go unheard.

As they approached Crystal Lake Carlin was remembering the crash of the Cessna. He wasn't afraid, but he was somewhat more than cautious, and circled the lake at a low level looking for deadheads or other dangerous conditions. The lake was calm and its surface reflected the sunlight like a mirror, a condition some pilots dread, due to its propensity to create depth perception errors. Aware of the danger, Carlin's approach was slightly nose high, settling down gently, feeling for the aft tips of the floats to touch the water. The landing was text book perfect. He taxied to the beach and cut power before the float tips touched the soft white sand. Within a few minutes they had unloaded their equipment and Jim was busy setting up their shelter.

Carol appreciated Francine's help to fix a late lunch. When it ended, she and Carlin went for a walk along the lake shore. Carlin was quiet, but she knew there was something amusing going on inside him. Carol studied his face for a moment, and her eyes grew misty ... "I hope they will love each other as much as I love you Carlin," she said, and continued the walk.

The sun rolled off the tree tops, and fell below the horizon. and though the western sky blazed briefly with red, gold and purple, deep twilight enveloped them rapidly. Only the wavering light from their campfire held the darkness at bay. Carlin filled his pipe with kinnikinnick and sitting cross legged in front of the fire he and Jim smoked in silent contentment. During the late afternoon, Fran had collected some sweet grass, and now passing it over the coals of the fire it began to smoke, filling the air with its sweet pungent odour.

Carol looked out from the tent. Carlin's eyes were closed and he was cleansing his soul in the smoke. She knew he was truly a white Ojibwa living between the past, participating in an ancient spiritual rite, and in the present, a millionaire, wilderness camping. Francine's sweetgrass bundle was burning low, and she tossed it on the fire. A last puff of aromatic smoke enveloped them. Bright orange sparks spiralled into the air, dying in the darkness as though carrying a prayer to the Almighty.

Jim tapped the ashes from his pipe. "What did you have in mind for tomorrow?" he asked Carlin.

Carlin stood up and stretched. "I would like to go to the old village," he said, "maybe the old ones were right about Crystal Lake and it is an evil place." He looked up at the heavens seeking Polaris. "while we were here there was trouble. – the ice on the wings, the crash, the injuries, the wolverine that damned near killed us. Then there was the spotter plane that never saw us, and the rescue plane that landed when we were gone for food – Crystal Lake is not a good place Jim."

Jim Peters followed Carlin's thoughts. All the tools of survival came from the village. Most of the game came from there, the clay came from the river banks at the village. Most of the wild rice and bush coffee roots came from there. it was a giving place, and his people lived there for a hundred years. "You're right," Jim said, "Crystal Lake is a bad place, but the old village was fine."

Carol wondered if Carlin was going to the old village for her sake, and fervently hoped that was not the case. She had finished with the Archaeological Institute and was uncertain that the University Of Toronto would be interested in her paper. Carol was content just being with Carlin.

The morning dawned crisp and sunny and they were on the trail before 7:00 a.m. Fran followed Jim who led the procession. She had heard all the legends about the village. The O-Mush-Kas-Ug, The People Of The Swamp had lived not far from the village, and traded with the villagers. It seemed odd to Fran that the history of the O-Mush-Kas-Ug was well documented, but only legends existed about the demise of the villagers. She wanted to see for herself, exactly what they left behind. Fran knew that the joy, the pain, fear and contentment of the ancients, left an imprint where they had lived yet few could feel or see it. Francine was one of the few – she could read the village and no one knew of her gift.

They arrived at the village site two hours later. Jim naturally went to the site of his grandfather's home, while Carlin and Carol perused the entire area looking for the best possible dig location. Francine however, stood at the nucleus of what had been a thriving community, slowly turning this way and that, a human antenna, drawing in a plethora of information from the past. As she scanned the area from her vantage point she was filled with emotions that registered on her face. Carlin was the first to notice it. Concerned, he approached her, asking if she was okay. She didn't seem to understand his concern and assured him that she was just fine. She pointed to an overgrown pile of rubble, and her face broke into a radiant smile.

"The family that lived there," she said, "in 1849 – the woman was pregnant – she gave birth to twins!"

"How can you possibly know that?" Carlin asked.

"Can't you feel it in the air Carlin? The feeling is strong. Both babies are crying," she paused, listening. "They are crying on opposite sides of the room."

Carlin thought about her words later in the day, at first thinking her revelations were unjustified with no basis in fact. After lunch Carlin said he wanted to spend some quiet time at the river. Carol, Jim and Francine had plans too, and went about their individual pursuits.

Sitting on the quiet river bank, watching the detritus of winter sweeping past in the turbid water, Carlin wondered about feelings. He remembered the day long ago, when he took his first deer with a bow. He had never seriously tracked an animal though he had often gone hunting – but that day he HAD to make a kill. They were hungry and Jim's blistered and infected feet prevented him from providing food for them. Carlin remembered his prayer to the Great Spirit, asking Him for the hunting skills he needed. After the prayer, Carlin had tuned each of his senses, listening more intently, looking at everything with much more observant eyes. He sniffed the air trying to detect the scent of deer, and he touched the tracks he found with much more sensitive fingers, and it had happened. Though he couldn't see it, he had FELT the deer's presence, and he had made the impossible kill.

Carlin concluded that he, and everyone else had senses that were rarely ever used to their limits. Perhaps Francine was using here inner feeling senses to their limit – perhaps she could know exactly what happened at the village a hundred years in the past. A voice within, told him to withhold his criticism, and to accept the gift Francine had been given.

Carol had been working hard, marking out dig areas and working them carefully. She tagged each artifact, photographed it, wrote a thorough description of it, then stored it in an appropriate container, and she was bored to death. She looked up from her notes, to find Fran studying her.

There was a sudden bond between the two women. Each sensed in the other, a sadness, an unfulfilled need.

"Hi Fran," Carol said, closing her notebook, "how have you passed your morning so far?"

"Oh, I have just been exploring the old ruins, making mental notes about what really happened here." She lowered her eyes and blushed. "I know that is what you are doing too," she said, "your purpose is to find material things in the ruins – it must be exciting for you." She came closer and kneeling down beside Carol, she sat back on her heels. "I am finding things in the ruins too, but they cannot be seen – they are just feelings."

"You DO feel deeply about this place don't you? Did you have an ancestor who lived here?" she asked the younger woman.

"No, my people were of tribal mixed blood. My grandmother was a Mohawk. I lived on a reserve outside Montreal for three years. I have no ancestral connection to this place – the feelings I speak of, are the feelings of those who lived here long ago."

"How can you feel what those who have gone before you felt?" Carol asked incredulous.

"If the scent of roses was very strong near you, could you see it?" The question was rhetorical and didn't require an answer. Francine continued, "and rose petals pressed in a book, permeate the pages with their scent long after they are gone. Then one day, someone opens the book and inhales the sweet scent and identifies it as that of roses. It's like that with feelings – a part of them stays behind after the people are gone. I sense the feelings, just as you would identify the roses."

The analogy made Carol see the young woman in a different light. There was far more depth of character there than she previously suspected. Then something strange happened – Carol perceived a strong feeling of sadness from Francine. "With a gift like yours, why are you so sad?" she asked, "It is to do with Jim, isn't it?"

Once more Fran lowered her head and her eyes and blushed deeply. "Yes. I see you have discovered feelings too. Do I look so sad?"

"No," Carol replied with a little laugh, "It's just feelings." She put her arm around Fran's shoulders. "Want to tell me about YOUR feelings?"

"Well, you are right," Fran answered, hopelessness in her voice, "I guess I have loved him from the first time I saw him. Unfortunately he doesn't respond no matter what I do. For some reason his reticent manner just makes me love him more." She shrugged her shoulders in helplessness. "I don't know what to do."

"I know enough about the Ojibwa to never tell anyone what to do, so I'll put it in other words. If I wanted Jim, and he treated me like that, I would reverse the roles. No matter what he said or asked of me, I would ignore him until he loved me! It works both ways Fran." Carol smiled at her and Fran's face looked as though it was lighted from within. She stood and hugged Carol.

"Thank you Carol," she said, "I was too frightened of losing him to do that. You have given me the gift of understanding" Francine was about to leave, then remembered – "Oh I almost forgot why I came to you," she said with a brighter smile. "You will find some really fine artifacts in that house over there."

She pointed to a very low mound, overgrown with small trees and gorse. "The man who lived there long ago was a shaman." And when Carol looked back from the mound, she was gone.

Carol remembered every site that Jim had identified when they made their first foray into the ruins of the village. He made no mention of the low mound, but marked out all the other dwelling sites from memory. Had he hidden something for religious reasons or did he not know of the shaman? Carol decided to ask him when the opportunity arose.

When supper ended, Jim told Francine he wanted to talk with her, on a private matter. They walked toward the river. Carlin and Carol were happy to be alone, for she wanted to tell him about Francine's deep feelings for Jim, Carlin wanted to tell her about his quiet time through the morning.

Jim and Fran walked along the river, in silence. She stopped suddenly, and looked him in the eye. "Well Mr. Peters," she began, "what have I done wrong now – say what you have to say so I can get back to my friends." Her cold words took him by surprise, battering him like a winter storm. This wasn't the Francine he knew – this was a harridan of the first order. He had brought her here to tell her that he was in love with her, and she had exploded like a fireball.

"What the hell is the matter with you?" he asked, "Have you got a bee up your backside or are you always obstinate – and nasty." He was taking it far worse than she expected and the result she got was not what she wanted.

"No – I am NOT nasty by nature and you know it, but it seems that being aggressive is the only way I can get your attention." The scowl on his face was like a dark thunder cloud about to unleash a lightning bolt, but she would ride out this storm. "What do you want to say to me?" She asked bluntly.

With the dark glower still dominating his features he stepped closer to her. Her heart pounded in her breast, and she feared he could hear it beating. "I brought you here to tell you that I am in love with you, and I want you to love me." His words hit her like a slap. Dammit – she had done it all wrong again! She had to recover somehow and she whispered an internal prayer to The Great Spirit for guidance.

"I do love you," she blurted, "I have loved you since the first day I saw you but ..." Taking her frail shoulders in his big hands, he drew her close and kissed her tenderly. Her heart soared to the stars, and without another word, they expressed their love for one another in a thousand ways.

Carol told Carlin about the low mound that had been the house of the shaman. They decided to ask Jim if he remembered it when he returned. They considered it a delicate subject to be handled tactfully. They knew the developing relationship between Francine and Jim was fragile and didn't want to place it in jeopardy. When the couple returned to the campsite, they were as happy as children at a birthday party, and both Carlin and Carol were delighted that Jim and Francine had finally found one another.

Jim Peters had no knowledge of the house that belonged to the shaman – in fact he didn't know this small band of Ojibwa had ever had a shaman in their community. The only person who might have the answer was Orren Flagg, and he had never been to the village. Jim thought Orren might remember conversations from long ago, that mentioned a shaman at the village.

He was anxious to see what the site would yield, and helped Carol with the dig. Francine was right, the mound was comprised of the foundations and rotting logs, that had once been a dwelling.

As the dig progressed, the site began to yield a rich booty of artifacts. They found bones in an almost decomposed leather pouch of the type that would be worn around the neck. It wasn't until they found the collection of rattles, that they were convinced. The long deceased resident had indeed been a shaman. On the third day of the dig Carol was to become famous for the second time in her life – first as the woman survivor of the crash, and now as the finder of the mask.

There were several masks in a cedar box. The box had been built with flat cedar boards pegged together with wood dowels, and dating would later show that it was constructed between 1750 and 1775. Curiously the box was crafted without the use of steel cutting tools. The lid was fastened with strap hinges similar to those used in a modern door, but the hinge portions were made from a hardened leather and the hinge pin was of bone. Within the box were five masks. Two were fashioned from wood and they appeared to represent autumn and winter. Two were made from

G. WM. GOTRO

leather, and they represented spring and summer. The fifth became known as THE MASK, for it was fashioned from clay and it very accurately depicted man. In fact it was a casting made from a mould taken from a human face, and the mask reposed on a human skull.

They had been at the village site for more than a month and their supplies were running out. Carlin was concerned about the safety of the Beaver, and Carol wanted desperately to deliver the artifacts and her notes to the University of Toronto. Carlin suggested that they return to the reservation, but Jim was happy just to be in the wilderness with Francine.

It was decided that Carlin and Carol would return to the reserve, and take care of the artifact transfer. They would then re-stock the food stores and return to Jim and Francine within a week or ten days. Carlin left Jim with a high powered transceiver and fresh batteries, to insure that he could call for help in an emergency. Carol and Carlin parted company with Jim and Francine on May 17th, and flew back to the reservation and Air Ojibwa.

The radio proved to be more than an emergency device. On the tenth day Francine used it to tell Carol she and Jim had decided to get married as soon as possible. She asked if Carol could make arrangements to have them picked up the following day. Carol agreed, and told Carlin Jim had something important to tell him – important enough to keep it off the airwaves.

Carlin was almost certain that it had to do with a possible wedding but he played a very stern role. "I sure hope it is important," he said, "It's a two and a half hour trip each way."

"C'mon Carlin you know you love to be in the air," Carol said, "We WILL be going back in the morning – right?"

"Yeah we can go in the morning," he teased.

The following day he was up before dawn, checking the Beaver out, impatient to be flying again. He got Carol out of bed as soon as it was light, and they had breakfast. Before she knew what was happening he bundled her into the plane and they were airborne just minutes after sunrise. He landed at Crystal Lake at 9:00 am. He unloaded the cargo which included another twenty gallons of fuel for their storage dump. Then taking as many items as they could carry they set off on the hike to the old village. They met Jim and Fran just beyond the half way point and stopped to rest.

"Carol tells me you have some important news. What's happening Jim?" Carlin asked.

"I asked Francine to marry me," Jim said with a big grin.

"And she turned you down flat because you are such a miserable bugger," Carlin said, laughing.

"No, it's worse than that – she accepted my proposal," Jim said, and he radiated the happiness that filled him.

"When," Carlin asked.

"When we get back to the reservation," Jim said seriously, "but we aren't in a hurry." He winked at Carlin.

"Like hell we aren't," Carol and Francine chorused in unison.

There was a true holiday atmosphere in the camp that night, and they decided to stay for a few more days. In the following days every waking hour was filled with enjoyment. It was simple things – hiking, swimming, fishing, and playing cards. They dined on the very best foods and each night they toasted the fantastic days with fine wine.

They adopted a philosophy that was unique – the more remote they got from civilization, the more pristine the meal and its preparation. The night before they left the old village, Carlin cooked a roast of venison, spiced with garlic, rosemary and onion. It was served with a fine red wine, fresh baked bread, and chilled caviar from a 100 pound sturgeon taken from the river that morning. The mashed potatoes were topped with a thick gravy flavoured with a touch of oregano and tarragon.

When the main meal ended, from the solar powered freezer Carlin served a Haagen Das vanilla ice-cream topped with a generous portion of Irish Cream liquor. When it was finished, he and Jim packed their pipes with Erinmore Flake and smoked in silence. The stars blazed in the clean air above them, and the four were for a moment, filled with reverence.

Knowing this was their last night at the village of the Old Ones, Jim closed the magnificent evening in his own way. He stood at the edge of the fire and with the little pipe held in both hands, he raised it to the heavens.

G. WM. GOTRO

"Mighty Manitou," he said softly, "hear the prayer of your Ojibwa child. I thank you for giving me my white Ojibwa brother. You have brought us through adversity and never faltered. You have rewarded us with riches beyond comprehension, and you have given us Carol and Francine to love and be loved, to cherish and be cherished. Though we do not know what the future holds, we are not afraid. Mighty Manitou hear our prayer of thanksgiving."

He sat down once more before the fire. Carol and Carlin sat with heads bowed, thinking of the words Jim had spoken, and how he had expressed their precise and innermost feelings. Francine looked up to the heavens – "Look," she whispered, "He has answered you."

They turned their eyes to the stars and for a few brief moments a band of shimmering light whispered across the night sky, in a rare spring Aurora. It began in the north west and faded out in the south east. "He is showing us the way," she said, and they all knew the truth of her words.

The following morning, they packed their gear and trekked out to Crystal Lake. The Beaver was loaded within the hour.

Before the sun began its swing across the sky, the lake rang with the sound of the big radial engine accelerating the aeroplane across the water.

Though the terrain below them was a chaotic jumble of glittering water and barren rock, of languid rivers and dense forest, Carlin navigated by instinct. An oddly shaped little lake here, and a long narrow patch of bed rock there, were the tools of his trade. His most precious instruments were his watch, and the airspeed indicator, and now he knew that within twenty minutes he would see the Vermillion River through the patchy cloud cover.

Carlin considered the events that were about to take place. Jim and Francine would soon be married and they would need a place to live. He was certain they would want to live on the reserve, and that meant building them a house. They would have to hurry – once the frosts of autumn settled, the ground would be too hard to dig, and footings would be a problem. Carlin resolved to talk with Jim tomorrow, and get something started.

Still deep in thought, he lost track of time and was surprised to see the Vermillion River bridge below the aeroplane's nose. He turned on a heading for Little Spirit Lake and minutes later he set up his landing pattern. He chastised himself for a light bounce on landing, and resolved to do circuits for an hour tomorrow.

Sam Whitebird and a couple of kids were at the dock to meet the plane. They helped Carol and Jim secure the Beaver to the mooring rings, while Carlin went through the shut down procedure.

"Hi Sam, how have things been while we were gone?" Jim asked.

"Most things are going well," Sam answered, his eyes downcast. He was quiet for a few moments.

"Orren Flagg isn't very well. Doctor James had him transferred to the Sudbury General. Stuart Frazer flew him there. Mary phoned this morning and he is in stable condition."

"What was it – a heart attack?" Jim asked.

"Yes. The doctors are doing an angiogram today. They say said he might come home in a couple of days." Sam was in deep distress.

Carol opened the cabin and helped with the unloading of the plane. When everyone had gone, she asked Carlin a tough question. "Who will become the band chief if Orren dies?"

"I don't know. I suppose the elders will elect a new chief – my guess is Jim. He has done a great deal for the people. He is trusted and is very responsible," Carlin said, lighting his pipe.

"What about you?" Carol asked.

"Oh, I think Jim will be a great chief," Carlin replied.

"No," Carol said, "what about you for band chief?" Her question jolted him. "What if the elders choose you?"

"That will never happen – most people see me as a white man. The elders would take that into consideration and I would be probably be eliminated as a candidate."

Late in the day, Jim and Francine returned to Air Ojibwa, looking quite happy. Jim had called the hospital in Sudbury, and found that Orren's angiogram was okay. Orren would be released the following morning. Both Carlin and Jim thanked the Great Spirit for sparing Orren Flagg – neither of them wanted the job of band chief.

Carol and Francine prepared a late supper and they talked the evening away. They had told Jim's family about the wedding and everyone began to make plans. The couple stayed at Air Ojibwa that night, and in the morning Jim and Carlin flew to Sudbury to bring the chief home. On the flight to Sudbury, Jim told Carlin more about his plans.

"We set the wedding date for two weeks from now," he said with excitement in his voice, "and we have chosen a place for our honeymoon."

"You going to tell me?" Carlin said, teasing Jim.

"Can't avoid it – you're the only one I would trust to fly us there."

"And just where is 'there'," Carlin asked as he made a course correction.

"Francine and I want to go back to the old village – we have things we want to do there."

"What kind of things?" Carlin asked trying to sound disinterested.

"I want to build a home there. Carlin, we want to raise a family in the old village. You were right when you said Crystal Lake was a bad place and the old village was a giving place. Fran says it feels right and I agree with her. For the first time in my life I find myself questioning the old legends. Something went terribly wrong in the past and now that wrong must be corrected. Fran and I feel the task is ours – given to us by The Great Spirit."

Carlin thought about Jim's words for a long time before he answered. He had no doubt that Jim was very serious about his perceived task, but how could he correct something he didn't understand? How could he find the truth when no one was left alive to tell the story? He, Carlin, was Ojibwa enough not to tell Jim what he should do. The correct protocol was to give Jim other choices. "Perhaps Orren will appoint you to band chief," Carlin said, as though it was just speculation.

"Or appoint you," Jim answered, effectively blocking Carlin's suggestion.

"He cannot do that," Carlin replied, "I am not of the Anishinawbe." Carlin was setting up his landing on Ramsey Lake.

When Jim and Carlin arrived at the Sudbury General Hospital, Orren Flagg was pacing in the lobby. He was fed up with hospital procedures and hospital food. He considered it unhealthy, for there was little fibre content, and in taste, the strawberries were almost indistinguishable from the corn.

"The people here have been very good to me, they have done everything necessary for my continued health. Now please Cloud Walker – take me home!"

Jim and Carlin were relieved that Orren was well and in a feisty state of mind. There was no need to search for a new band chief. Preparing for take off, Carlin seated Orren Flagg in the right hand seat. Throughout the flight he asked the old man to help with the flying. He showed him how the controls worked and let him feel the thrill of a shallow dive, a tight turn, and banking right and left.

When Carlin landed, twenty or more people were at Air Ojibwa to greet their beloved chief. All were concerned over his health and his state of mind. When the Beaver was moored Carlin helped the old man down to the dock. The people began to applaud when they saw the look on Orren Flagg's face. He was beaming with pride and excitement, and briefly he turned to hug Carlin and Jim. When he faced his people again he raised his hand for quiet.

"My friends," the chief said, "this day I have been given a great honour, for today I have become a cloud walker too! For a few precious moments I have flown the great eagle. He turned to look at the Beaver in wonderment, for HE had made it dive and climb, tilt and turn. Then laughing, Orren Flagg teased Carlin and Jim. "These two," he said gesturing to them, "have asked me to give up my position as band chief so I would be free to fly for Air Ojibwa. But fortunately for Carlin I declined his generous offer." Everyone roared with laughter and for days, the joke went around the reservation.

Francine and Jim pledged their wedding vows to one another, exactly two weeks from the day they arrived back at the reserve. The wedding was a grand affair – both bride and groom dressed in original Ojibwa garments. The ceremony was conducted in two parts. Jim and Francine were married by a Jesuit priest and there followed an Ojibwa marriage ceremony. The celebration went on for two days, and the day after it ended, Jim Peters called on

Carlin.

"Can I count on your help tomorrow?" Jim asked, "There will be a mountain of stuff to fly up to the village."

"Carlin's smile said it all."You know damned well you can count on me," he said, walking out to the plane with a large heavy bag. What are we doing tomorrow?"

"A three ton truck is delivering a load of building materials to the dock at the reserve. Sam Whitebird and some young fellows will bring the materials here by boat, so we can load it into the Beaver," Jim replied as he rubbed his hands together in excitement.

"What kind of materials are we talking about?" Carlin asked.

"Four bags of cement, a roll of wire mesh, tools, and insulation – oh, and some other stuff."

"What kind of other stuff?" Carlin said, pretending to be deeply concerned.

"Um – ahh, well a nine by twelve aluminum garden shed kit," Jim replied, looking sheepish.

"You don't need a De Havilland Beaver, you need a Lockheed Starlifter," Carlin said teasing him. "And there is something else to consider Mr. Peters – you are not staying there on your own!"

Early the following morning, Carlin taxied the aeroplane to the reservation dock, before the truck arrived with Jim's building supplies. He reasoned that the time to move the supplies by boat to Air Ojibwa could be better used at the destination. Jim had overlooked the fact that the freight would have to be hauled by hand from Crystal Lake to the old village. As they loaded the plane, Carlin tallied the weight of the materials. They ran out of room before they reached maximum weight, so Carlin substituted Sam Whitebird for some of the insulation.

The heavily loaded plane's takeoff run was considerably longer than normal. It was noon when he landed at Crystal Lake.

They unloaded the plane, secured it, and began the long job of transporting the building supplies to the old village site. They managed to make two full trips over the five mile trail, and moved all the cargo to the village. The three men sat down exhausted. It was 8:00 pm and the sun was dipping below the trees to the west. Carlin didn't want to make a night landing on Little Spirit Lake, and delayed his return until morning. Sam Whitebird and Carlin cut boughs and made sleeping pads around a fire pit, while Jim fished the river for supper.

When Jim returned he was carrying three large lumps of clay. Each contained a cleaned pickerel or bass. The clay coated fish were placed in the coals of the fire and an hour later dinner was ready. When the clay was broken open, the steaming white fish was exposed and the skin and bones remained with the clay. After eating, the men lay down to sleep – they had trekked fifteen miles since landing at noon.

Carlin flew the trip twice more before all the materials for Jim's dream, were delivered to the old Village. Now, sitting on a small concrete pad, was the nine by twelve aluminum building. It had been modified by the addition of insulation and two large plexiglass windows. It would serve well as a comfortable dwelling until the log house was completed.

Toward the middle of July, Carol and Francine joined them at the old site, and the construction of the cabin progressed rapidly. The women worked at chinking the log walls as the men raised the rafters into place. Using a small Alaska mill they cut their own lumber for the roof and later they split cedar shakes in the old way. By the end of August the house was secure against the weather, and not a moment too soon. On September second, Francine happily announced that she was pregnant.

By mid September, Jim and Fran had moved into their new home, and Carlin and Carol occupied the little aluminum building. The nights were growing cold now, and there was a hint of colour change in the broad leafed trees. The mornings and evenings were chilly.

"We will have to leave soon," Carlin said softly, as he and Carol settled into the sleeping bag for the night.

"Yes, I know," Carol answered, "I have been dreading this day for quite some time. You know they don't want to return to the south don't you?"

"Yes," he said, staring at the ceiling, his hands behind his head. "I will try to talk to Jim tomorrow, but I am sure he will give me an argument. He wants the child to be born here, and she insists on it. There are some difficult days ahead I think."

G. Wm. Gotro

Carol tossed and turned throughout the night, and Carlin was awakened several times. Just after 5:00 am. Carlin arose and put coffee on to brew. He walked outdoors to check the weather for the day. To his surprise, he saw Jim sitting on a log at the water's edge. Carlin sauntered over to his friend's side.

"The weather is changing isn't it?" he said, taking his pipe from his pocket. Jim nodded his head in the affirmative. "We will have to fly out soon," Carlin continued, "I'd hate like hell to be trapped here for the winter."

"We did it once before," Jim answered in a dull monotone. "It would be easy now – we have living quarters and equipment."

"I know how much you and Fran want to stay," Carlin replied, "It could be very dangerous since this is her first child. Medical help is far away if it is needed."

"I have been dreading this conversation for weeks," Jim replied. "I know I'm going to get an argument from Fran."

Carlin sat down beside Jim and started to laugh, "Those were the exact words Carol said last night." He scanned the sky, assessing the clouds. "There is a good side to this though – we do have an aeroplane and a hell of a good bank account. Once the lakes are frozen we can come in on skis for the rest of the winter."

"I have already made my decision Carlin, you don't have to convince me. We are going back with you but I still have to convince Fran that she isn't invulnerable."

Jim talked with Fran at breakfast, telling her about Carlin's suggestion they fly out within a day or two. She countered by saying she wanted to have the baby here in the village.

"Look Fran, can you be sure there will be no complications? The firstborn child is often a problem baby. There is a chance that I could lose you and the baby, and I am unwilling to take that chance." She could see the concern in his eyes – the fear of losing her and the baby. Francine loved him too much to let him go on hurting.

"Jim, I can't tell you how much it means to me to have the baby here, but I am hurting you, and that isn't fair. Let me hold onto my dream for another few days – please," she said.

"Okay," Jim replied, "I'm sure Carlin will understand – I will talk to him after breakfast." He drew his pipe from his pocket and felt for his tobacco. Then he remembered he had finished the last of it the previous evening. Fran watched his frustrated actions as he put the pipe back in his pocket.

She went to the sleeping area and returned with a coffee tin, handing it to him. "Here," she said, "I made this up for you when we returned from our first trip here. There just wasn't a right time to give it to you." She watched as he removed the plastic lid from the tin. It was half filled with rubbed kinnikinnick, and there were three other items in the tin. The first was a fresh tin of Erinmore Flake, the second was an unopened pouch of Sail tobacco, and the third was a small box of matches sealed in a plastic bag. There was a strong religious connotation to the gift of tobacco in the Ojibwa culture.

"Thank you Fran," Jim said softly, "That was very thoughtful." He mixed a little of each tobacco and filled his pipe, then lighting it, he let the smoke rise to the Great Spirit. "Thank you Manitou – thank you for this woman and her gift."

Two weeks later, they closed the buildings and returned to the Reserve. A runner from the band office was at the Air Ojibwa dock to meet them. With him was Doctor James. The young man from the band office handed Carlin a bundle of mail, and told Carol that one of the letters was for her. He said someone from Toronto had called for her several times. Unable to reach her they requested that she contact them immediately on her return. The runner gave her a number and a name.

Tisha Peters had asked the doctor to meet the plane. Tisha was aware that Fran was pregnant before Fran knew it herself. Doctor James ordered Fran to be at the hospital in the morning for a full medical check.

When they had all left Air Ojibwa, hand in hand, Carlin and Carol walked to their little log cabin and made a pot of tea. Sitting at the table, Carol opened the mail addressed to her. Three letters were of some importance. The first was from her mother, who asked if she could visit for a few days. Carol was delighted and made a mental note to ask Carlin if he would pick her up to save Mrs. Danse some travelling time.

The second letter was from the local archaeological institute. Carol couldn't imagine why either the director, Borland, or for that matter Mrs. Stapp was writing to her. In part, the letter read:

Dear Mrs. McKenzie:

It is with more than a little trepidation I am writing this letter. Some weeks ago, I was going through the Institutes employee documents. When I came across your file, I was astounded at the shoddy way you seem to have been treated as a professional. You must have had a great love for your career in archaeology to have remained as long as you did.

David Borland was replaced ten months ago, as was his confederate Mrs. Eva Stapp. I will not go into the reasons for their dismissal, but be assured they were cogent. There has been a lot of house cleaning here since their departure, and the Institute is a far more professional place to work now. With that in mind, I would like to make the following suggestions.

I humbly request that you contact me to discuss the possibility, of you playing a major role here at the Institute.

I am aware of some of the work you have done since your resignation, and would like to help you explore new fields in archaeology. Please contact me – it would be to our mutual advantage to talk.

Sincerely yours,
Ralph Borthwicke
Director and CEO.

Carol was astounded. Borthwicke had really done his homework. He had traced her even to her married name, he had cleaned house at the Institute. He was offering her some sort of association, and she was vindicated at last. Carol was filled with happiness and her heart soared. She wanted to tell Carlin, but he was in the water alongside the dock, fixing a damaged rudder on one of the floats. Carol examined the final letter instead.

The return address gave her no inkling of what could be inside. Who was 'TIME AND SCIENCE OF MAN FOUNDATION'? She would have discarded the letter as junk mail had it not been double registered. Orren Flagg had signed for it. She opened the envelope and was shocked at the content of the letter.

Ms. Carol Danse:

The artifacts you sent to the university were forwarded to us for analysis and evaluation. When we first examined the mask, we believed it to be a hoax. However, carbon dating revealed that the mask was made four hundred and twenty-five thousand years ago. The skull is from the same time period. Computer models suggest, that the mask was in fact made on the skull itself. Our computer programmers provided a face for the skull. The resulting construct matches the mask itself in ninety eight percent of the details.

As an archaeologist, you know that the features in the mask are the more delicate features of modern man, and a long way from pre-historic. We are unable to comprehend how this was accomplished and wish to meet with you at the earliest possible opportunity. Please contact me at ....."

Carol was astonished. She dropped the letter on the table and ran to Carlin. He looked up, to see her running toward him.

"What's wrong?" he asked, hoisting himself up on the dock.

"Carlin something very strange is happening – come into the house and see for yourself." She was trembling. He followed her into the house and first he read the letter from the Institute.

"They want you back," Carlin said, "They want you back as a director! That is just great ..."

She handed him the second letter. Carlin read it rapidly, then he read it again – more carefully the second time. "These guys want you too. I wonder if there is some collusion going on," he speculated. "If what he is saying is true, you have the most valuable archaeological artifact in history. It would be worth millions, and it would change many things we know about past!" He paced the room, thinking. "In fact, if it is true, it changes everything. What are you going to do?"

Carol telephoned the people in Toronto, and Dana Banes, the writer of the letter suggested he come to meet her in Sudbury. Carol agreed. He was to arrive two days hence. She then phoned the Institute, identified herself, and asked to speak with Ralph Borthwicke. The secretary put her through immediately.

"Mrs. McKenzie, how very good of you to call. Did you enjoy your vacation?"

G. WM. GOTRO

"I wasn't on vacation," Carol answered, "But I did enjoy my time away and I am glad to be home. You wanted to talk." She made it a cool statement rather than a question.

"I thought we might get together," he suggested. Do you think we could meet in Sudbury in the immediate future?"

"Yes, that is a possibility but improbable. I would be much more comfortable talking with you in my own home Mr. Borthwicke."

"Ahh, I see," he said, "It was thoughtless of me to suggest you make the long trip after just arriving home. I could come to you if you give me directions. I think this is very important to both of us."

Carol took the lead. "If you are at the main dock at Ramsey Lake tomorrow at 10:00 a.m. my husband will pick you up," she said with a hint of finality.

There was a long silent pause, then ... "Yes. That will be just fine Mrs. McKenzie. I will be there. How will I know your husband?" he asked.

"Oh you won't miss Carlin," she said, winking at her husband, "He's the only white Ojibwa bush pilot around."

At 9:50 the following morning, Carlin landed the Beaver and taxied to the dock. He secured the plane to a pair of mooring rings and stood waiting in the shade under the wing. He was dressed in Levis, a buckskin jacket and he wore the beaded black sweat band around his head. On his hip was a knife with a honed nine inch blade, and on his feet were richly beaded black moccasins. One of the local Airway bush pilots approached him, accompanied by a dapper little man in a business suit.

"Hey Carlin," he called, "how much longer are you going to fly that clapped out old Beaver – A guy with your kind of money should be flying a new turbo."

"If I bought a new turbo, I would have to take flying lessons and I wouldn't be a millionaire very long," Carlin replied with an engaging smile. He turned to the businessman. "Ralph Borthwicke?"

"Yes, and you are Mr. McKenzie I believe." The little man seemed very genuine and affable. "Mrs.McKenzie said you wouldn't be hard to recognize and she was right." Carlin laughed and helped Borthwicke board the Beaver. He checked his passenger's seat harness and fired up the engine. Forty minutes after leaving Sudbury they landed on Little Spirit Lake. The flight had been through some turbulent air. Ralph Borthwicke had never flown in a single engine light plane, and was tense throughout the flight. Standing on the dock he was unsteady on his feet, and his colour was transformed from ruddy to putty. Carlin felt sorry for the little man – he rather liked him, but he found it difficult to suppress a smile at his state.

"Come along Mr. Borthwicke, Mrs. McKenzie will have the water on for tea. She will probably suggest a Camomile blend. It will settle your stomach and ease your tension," Carlin said leading the way to the cabin. Carol liked Borthwicke right from the start, and it quickly became a mutual admiration society of two. In less than two hours she had a position with the Institute once again. This time, things were different. She was a salaried free agent, whose only obligation was to keep the Institute advised on new finds. In addition she was expected to initiate and plan a new expedition to expand the knowledge base on North American Indian Culture.

Borthwicke was to draw up a memorandum of agreement, setting out the key points of their discussion. She would receive it by registered mail, for her signature. When the negotiations ended, Carlin said he would refuel the Beaver and then he could take Mr. Borthwicke back to Sudbury. Borthwicke politely refused his offer. "I must admit, I am not very comfortable in a small aeroplane," he said, snapping his briefcase shut. "Perhaps I could get a taxi or a bus," he suggested. "That may present a problem,"Carlin said, "Let me call the band office. It is possible someone there will have a better solution." He knew it would take longer to get a taxi to the Reserve than to fly the man to the city. The young man at the band office answered on the second ring. A minute or so later Carlin returned to the living room. "Mr. Borthwicke, It will take an hour and a half to get a taxi here and the next bus is at 11:10 tomorrow morning. One of our friends, Sam Whitebird, wants to go to the city too. He will take you back with him. He is waiting at the band office.

Carol took him to the office and introduced him to Sam. When she returned to Air Ojibwa it was obvious that Carlin was amused

G. WM. GOTRO

about something. "What's so funny Carlin?" She asked, "Did you scare that lovely little man on the trip out here?"

"No," Carlin said breaking into a full belly laugh, "he was just afraid of small planes."

"Well that's not funny," she said, "you're being really insensitive."

"Not true," Carlin replied, "you have to drive with Sam Whitebird to understand. He drives like Mario Andretti with a death wish."

The following morning, Carlin flew her to Sudbury to meet with Dana Banes. The Time and Science of Man Foundation had chosen their man well. Banes was deceitful, conceited, consummately ruthless, and very handsome. Banes paced the room, rarely taking his eyes from the glass wall that overlooked the courtyard of the hotel.

As each automobile stopped under the portico at the entrance to the building, he stopped pacing momentarily to examine the arriving persons. He had created a mental picture of Mrs. Carol McKenzie, and he was unaware that he had invested it with the traits of an exploitable woman. He envisioned her as a rotund little business woman carrying an over sized briefcase. She would, he imagined, be wearing flat heeled shoes and be very snippy and overbearing. Banes paid little attention to the sveldt blonde in the fitted navy slacks, black stiletto pumps, and white buckskin jacket. He made a brief mental note to look her up after his meeting with the potentially boring archaeologist.

The telephone rang. Banes answered with a clipped, "Yes, what is it?"

"Mr. Banes, Mrs. Carol McKenzie requests that you join her in the coffee shop," the desk clerk said with a professional air.

"Thanks," Banes snapped, and slipping into his sports jacket he picked up a leather portfolio and left the room. This is all wrong, he thought, whoever she was, she should be coming to him. He would have to sort her out very quickly. He entered the almost empty coffee shop and scanned the tables from the doorway. From behind, a man took his elbow in a firm grip.

"Banes?" he said with a disarmingly confident smile, "Mrs. Carol McKenzie is waiting for you – come and meet her."

"And who the hell are you?" Banes asked, failing to shake off the hand gripping his elbow.

"I'm McKenzie," Carlin said with a hard grin, and he steered the playboy to Carol's table.

Banes whole strategy had just collapsed into a pile of splinters, and he sat down uncertain what to say next. He had a mission to accomplish and he was failing badly – he summoned up an abundance of false charm.

"Mrs. McKenzie, I am delighted to meet you at last," he said effusively, offering her his hand. She effectively negated his handshake with a slight nod of her head, indicating cautious acceptance. Banes face flushed as he withdrew his hand. She was wise to him – he would have to tread very carefully with this one. The conversation between Dana Banes and Carol developed slowly. She didn't like the man, didn't trust him in the least. After ten minutes of one sided verbal fencing he revealed his purpose.

"Mrs. McKenzie, the fact of the matter is – we want to do some very 'in depth' research on the mask, but it may be damaged in the process," he lied, "I don't want you to suffer any loss by our procedures." He didn't realize he was rubbing the fingers of his right hand with the thumb of his left, an action he unconsciously used to relieve tension in a stressful situation.

The motion didn't go undetected – Carol had correctly assessed the Time and Science of Man Foundation as a scam but she said nothing, forcing Banes to continue.

"The most equitable and satisfactory way to handle this would be for our foundation to buy the artifact from you," he said. This was it – time for the sting. He was certain he had her when he saw the faint smile cross her otherwise inscrutable, but beautiful features. He mistakenly concluded that the smile was a warming to the prospect of money for junk. "I have been authorized to make you a very generous offer so we can continue with our research," he lied again.

Her enigmatic smile broadened slightly, "Yes?" she said. It was more question than acceptance. He had been directed to offer no less than $100,000 for the artifact but decided to horse trade and keep the difference.

"How does twenty-five thousand sound to you?" he asked, watching her reaction carefully. Now her smile became rapturous and it was accompanied by a throaty chuckle. "I see that our offer pleases you," he said smiling, and withdrawing a contract agreement from the leather portfolio. "Shall we sign the contract?"

"No," she said, "I have made more than that in interest from my investments since we talked on the telephone." She stood up, looking down at Banes. "You simply confirmed what I already suspected – your foundation is fraudulent, and the university had no right to release the mask to you. When your letter came, I notified the Ontario Provincial Police and they recovered our property this morning." Carlin steered her toward the exit. She turned to Banes once more. "How very fortunate you are Banes," she said to his back, you are so pitiful I can't bring myself to press charges – perhaps the foundation will deal with you." And Dana Banes knew he had just been out gunned. Within a week the mask was placed in the hands of Ralph Borthwicke for safe keeping and study.

The general status of life on the reservation was quite high now, and though Carlin had a steady flow of charter flights after the lakes were frozen over, he and Carol spent long happy hours carving and sculpting. Late in February Francine Peters gave birth to Jesse, a beautiful baby girl, and by mid March Francine and Jim were anxiously awaiting spring break up so they could return to their northern wilderness home.

After an observation flight to Crystal Lake Carlin installed the floats on the Beaver and pushed her back into the water. Three days later Fran and Carol, Carlin and Jim flew back to the high north, and they brought with them the newest resident of what they now called 'Giiwedin'. The word was a term for the place of the North Wind.

Jim spent most of his time building furniture and making the new log house a home. Within ten days of his return, it sported a new field stone fireplace. He dug a well and hit good water at fifteen feet. He lined the well with stone and installed a pump. Carol helped Fran with the baby, and together they did all the things that make a comfortable home. Often Carlin was restless, and if Jim was working on a 'one man job' Carlin made forays to every point of the compass. For some inexplicable reason he was drawn ever northward. He had been flying extra fuel in at every opportunity, and now he had a reserve of four hundred and fifty gallons, and full tanks.

Carlin considered a flight to Hudson's Bay, then rejected the idea. It required meticulous planning, better maps, and aviation weather data. The anxiety dogged him and he wanted respite from Giiwedin. He wanted to fly north for a while and asked Carol to come with him.

They left the following morning, climbing to seven hundred feet in clear skies. Ten minutes passed, and Carlin throttled the P&W Wasp engine back to idle, descending to three hundred feet. He circled a star shaped lake several times, then landed. With Carol's help he managed to moor the plane and get the canoe in the water. The shoreline was rough and the water was crystal clear.

"This is a beautiful lake Carlin, the water is very cold. I don't think a swim would be comfortable," Carol said, dangling her hand in the water.

"It is spring fed," Carlin explained, "the water is clear, and without tannin. This lake is perpetually cleansing itself. I think it empties over there," he said. pointing to a northwest bay. "Let's go see." They slipped the canoe into the water.

As they entered the wide mouth of the bay they could hear the gurgle of the water as it spilled into a wide creek. They landed the canoe at a long sloping rock, and drew it high on the bank. There was almost no muskeg in the vicinity of the lake. Large conifers dominated the forest and walking there, was like being in a well tended park. The land rose gently away from the lake. Suddenly Carlin stopped. "Look," he said, pointing.

A hundred yards ahead, crumbling with the ravages of time, there lay the remains of a tiny log cabin. It had been well built, with a peaked roof, but now one wall had collapsed. The remaining half of the roof, lay almost horizontal, still covering the cabin's interior. The door stood open, hanging by one hinge. and something told Carlin to keep Carol back until he had looked inside. "Stay here," he said, "there may be a bear or some other animal in there." She stopped dead in her tracks, a mild fear pervading her being.

       G. WM. GOTRO

Carlin slipped the Colt Python from his holster as he moved toward the dilapidated cabin. He peered into the gloom of the interior and stopped. The skeleton of a man, sat at a rotting table within. Shreds of rotted clothing still hung from the bones. The man was seated and bent at the waist, his arms outstretched and his head resting on the table.

Inches away from the boney hands lay a rusted unfired pistol, the hammer cocked, and six live rounds remained in the cylinder. A mouldy leather pouch lay on the table. Carlin touched it and it crumbled into dust. Within the mould, lay eight crystals. Quartz is often found with gold. He guessed the man had found a rich vein and something killed him before he could mine it. Carlin pocketed the crystals, and then called Carol.

Before she entered, he warned her about the skeleton. Carlin wanted her opinion on the era when the man might have lived. Rather than examining the skeleton, Carol concentrated on the artifacts within the building. Most of them were from the late eighteen hundreds. Beneath the dust, lay the remnants of a rotted eagle feather. Only the heaviest part of the quill remained in tact. It had been shaved to a pen point. Over the bunk, on a shelf thick with the dust and detritus of the years, Carlin discovered an explanation. In an oiled silk wrap, a mildewed diary bound in leather, revealed the man, his purpose, and his life. The flyleaf and first few pages were indecipherable leaving no clue to his identity. Carlin turned to the last written page in the middle of the book. It read – *I know not the date now, but I opine it is the year of our Lord 1894. The month must be September, for the leaves have turned to gold – the only gold I have found in this God forsaken place. The nights grow colder now, and I am plagued by fever and the cough. The sputum is veined with my blood and I have not the strength to search for food. Last night I was visited again by my sweet Elspeth and she bade me come to her. Our life lines have run out, for neither she nor I have kith nor kin to carry the blood line. I will pray to the Lord this night to take me mercifully to paradise or hell, whatever my eternal destiny will be. I think no other man will ever journey to this remote place, nor will my mortal remains be ever found, neither do I care. if I am alive tomorrow ..."* It ended there and Carlin closed the book.

"He was going to commit suicide," he said, "but he couldn't take his own life. How sad there was no one to mourn him."

They dug a shallow grave beneath a towering pine tree, and buried the remains of the man from the past. Carlin fashioned a cairn of rocks to mark the grave. From the rotting cabin they took the artifacts that survived the ravages of time. They would refurbish them, donate them to some small museum, and in so doing, give meaning to the final days of the deceased man from the past. Carlin would keep the diary to study every nuance for a clue to the location of the quartz.

They wandered through the unusual terrain until late afternoon, then returned to the Beaver. Carol cooked a fine dinner and it was almost 10:00 P.M. when the deep red of the sunset was transformed into gray twilight. An air mattress and double sleeping bag in the cargo bay of the plane served them as a bedroom. They lay awake for a long time, holding each other and talking before sleep came to them. The gentle rocking of the moored plane fostered a deep satisfying slumber.

Three days passed before Carlin found the obscure signs in the woods. The blaze marks were little more than the faintest scars on the old trees, but slowly the findings led him to the site. A small creek ran through a clearing. The man needed water if he had panned for gold, and the creek was his source. On the far side of the clearing Carlin noticed another anomaly. The indistinct outline of a saucer shaped depression. At its centre the vegetation was stunted, suggesting that perhaps, standing water may have hindered growth for many years. While Carol searched the creek for signs of gold, Carlin removed the overburden and detritus of the years to no avail. He walked to the creek where she was working. "How are you doing?" he asked, helping her to her feet. "I can't find anything that proves he was working here."

"The creek certainly isn't named Bonanza," she quipped, "there isn't a trace of gold – nor is there black sand. It's just a creek Carlin – just a creek."

"I must read the diary again," he said, "It is hard to follow. In some places it seems to be very disjointed."

"It is almost a hundred years since he wrote the last page," she said grasping his arm. "Remember – he was dying of tuberculosis and probably wasn't thinking very clearly in the days before death came to him." Carlin was scrutinizing the saucer shaped depression.

"No," he said, "It is me who isn't thinking too clearly."

He took her arm. "Come on," he said, "leave the tools here. We will be back tomorrow," and he led her back to their campsite.

After the evening meal, they sat close to the fire and Carlin leafed through the diary again. In two places, pages were stuck together. The first pair yielded little helpful information, but the second provided the proof he needed – *"if gold is here it may be deep underground." I have this day, begun to clear a large area of the detritus covering the sub surface of the land. I am provoked by the certainty that the crystals will lead me to a vein of gold. There IS gold in this country – for have I not seen it adorning the arms and ankles of the Indians? I pray the good Lord will care for me long enough to find the precious stuff and return to civilization...*

In the centre of the saucer, the damp soil fostered the growth of a jack pine after the man's death. It had grown for fifty years before the frosts of winter split its trunk for twenty feet. The tree died and rotted to a mound of compost through the years leaving a slight rise in the centre of the depression. Now, Carlin knew exactly where to apply his excavation efforts.

A day after they began the dig they encountered a different type of overburden. It was there that Carlin discovered a tiny crystal no bigger than a pea. He studied it for a minute or two, searching his memory for something. He carefully wrapped the crystal in his handkerchief and put it in his pocket. There was a tightness in his chest and his spirits soared. Carol, busy working fifteen feet away, had her back turned to him and had not seen the discovery. He called to her. "Carol, stop digging. We have to put all the earth and compost back."

"What?" she answered astounded, "You mean we did all this work for nothing and you've changed your mind." She threw the shovel down. "Carlin you can be the most aggravating ..."

"I found what I was looking for – this is the place." He began replacing the overburden, composted material, leaves and grass. She knew he would say nothing nor would he be dissuaded until this event in his life ended – it was the way of the Ojibwa.

Quietly she helped him complete the camouflage process. They went back to the plane and to her surprise he slipped the moorings and prepared the Beaver for flight.

"Where are we going now?" she asked.

"Home," he said, "home to Little Spirit Lake." He lashed the canoe to the float struts and helped Carol into the right hand seat. "We will stop at Giiwedin and tell Jim and Fran what we found – then we go home." He started the engine and taxied down the longest arm of the lake, then turned into the breeze for take-off. The flight was short and they landed ten minutes later.

Jim and Francine were fascinated by the story of the skeleton and the diary. Fran wanted to go there to use her unusual ability to detect the residual feelings of the past. Carlin promised to take them there before autumn. The following morning Carlin and Carol returned to Little Spirit Lake and rested for a day before going to Toronto where they would contact an expatriate Israeli businessman. They met him for breakfast and questioned him about his business while they dined. Satisfied that he was genuine, they visited his establishment later in the morning.

Jeff Rothman examined the tiny crystal with an eye loupe. "It is a beautiful specimen," he said smiling, "it should cut out at a little over one carat. I won't ask you where it came from – that would be an indelicate question."

"Someday I will tell you Jeff, but for now, I have a second crystal for you to assess," Carlin said, removing one of the large crystals from a soft leather pouch. He handed the stone to Jeff.

The man's expression was one of pure astonishment, and he looked into Carlin's eyes. "this has to be a bad joke," he said handling the stone as it were the Holy Grail. He peered at it for a long time, turning it this way and that. "It IS real," he said, "This stone is worth a fortune! If it is cut with care, it could break the record of The Star of Africa at 530 carats."

Carlin made arrangements to have the three largest crystals cut into gemstones, and paid Jeff with a brilliant stone of 70 carats. The deal was concluded as all diamond deals are – with honour and a firm handshake. Before the month's end, Carlin registered claims to the area where the diamond find occurred. The first of the three crystals was cut, yielding four diamonds with a total value of

$130,000. One other event marked this period of Carlin's life. It promised to be a blessed one – Carol announced she was pregnant.

Carlin had a backlog of three flights to be made for the people on the Reservation. Having cleared those tasks from his agenda, he soon grew restless. He thought about Carol's condition, and how it would affect their travels. Thus it was, when he landed on Crystal Lake, he was prepared for the five mile hike to Giiwedin. He unloaded a six wheeled ATV. Carol rode beside him as he made his way over the well worn trail to 'The Village of the North Wind'. Jim met him part way, and laughed when he realized their life had instantly become much easier. His joy escalated when Carlin told him he had bought two of the little machines, but he could only bring them in one at a time.

That evening, as the sun set at Giiwedin, and Fran's baby was in her bed, the four adults sat round a small fire. The men filled their pipes, and in the stillness of the evening, gave thanks to the Great spirit for the blessings He had bestowed upon them.

The wild cry of a loon shattered the twilight stillness, and set their hearts to vibrating.

"He has answered us again," Fran said, in a voice barely above a whisper. "Why do you think He has given us so much and others so little?"

"No one has ever been able to answer that question since the beginning of time," Jim replied. "When we try to do the tasks He has given us, He provides the means."

"I am very happy here," Fran said, snuggling closer to Jim. "Would you be happy living here Carol?" she asked.

Carol gave the question a lot of thought before she answered. "I could live here and be very happy," she replied, stirring the fire with a stick. Tiny orange sparks climbed high into the night before dying out. "But I DO have commitments back there," she continued. "When and where Carlin is happy, so I shall be."

"It is the mask, isn't it?" Francine said, "you want to solve the mystery of the mask."

"Yes. If it is true that the mask is four hundred and twenty-five thousand years old, it violates everything we believe about anthropology. The only other explanation is much more controversial – the skull would by necessity, be from another world," Carol answered staring into the fire. My greatest fear is that I may never know the truth about the skull and mask."

"If I could tell you the absolute truth would you believe me?" Francine asked suddenly. She made a firm eye contact and held it.

"Yes, I would believe you unless there was clear and substantial evidence that you were wrong," Carol answered, holding the eye contact. "And if I could furnish the proof that you were wrong, could YOU believe ME?"

"Yes," Fran replied, smiling amiably, "we have an understanding then – so let's get busy. You already know that I am a shaman, and I have the power to explore the faint residue of feelings from the past – feelings of others long gone." Carol nodded in assent and Fran continued. "When I touched THE MASK, it was almost magical – I knew it came from the other world! Remember the story of the old village and the Messenger sent by the Great Spirit. The mask was from his face. It is holy and you must never let it go. The Ojibwa will ask you to give it back to them.

"Are you saying the face was that of an angel?" Carol asked incredulous. "The last angels I remember hearing about were biblical – three or four thousand years ago perhaps but certainly not four hundred and twenty-five thousand years ago!

Carlin placed his hand on Carol's arm. "Maybe angels are with us now," he said, "maybe we just don't recognize them."

Carol turned to Jim. "Will the Ojibwa take the mask from me?"

"No," he replied, but I think they will ask you to give it to the people. It was given to the people a long time ago, and in truth, it is theirs." He smiled at her in understanding. "They will not take it from you until all your research is completed. They will want to know all about the mask too."

They had reached consensus and Carol was satisfied with the potential arrangement.

Carlin told Jim about the diamond find and as always, included Jim and Fran in his good fortune. Ten days later, they returned to the Reservation.

Carol contacted Ralph Borthwicke shortly after her return. The Archaeological Institute had done a new carbon dating and were amazed to find that the mask was indeed four hundred and twenty-five thousand years old. They could not explain the glaring incongruity of the modern day facial features in a pre-historic artifact, and it would be years before the truth became known. Carol suggested that Borthwicke come with them to Giiwedin as part of a discovery project. Once again the theme was to ascertain the nature of the death of the village. The little man hated flying, but he amazed her when he accepted the offer. He felt it would do him a great deal of good to be away from the Institute, and once more to be on a dig.

There were other surprises at the reserve. Sam and Mary Whitebird adopted a little girl and wanted to go to Giiwedin to be with Jim and Francine. They too, wanted to build a home in the Village of the North Wind. Two other families were also considering the prospects of Giiwedin and returning to the old way of life.

Carol gave birth to a fine baby boy five days before Christmas and she was attended by Francine Peters. Crowded though it was, in the cabin at Little Spirit Lake, they celebrated the birth of Christ, the birth of Robert McKenzie, and the Yuletide season. On Christmas day, the Air Ojibwa cabin was bursting at the seams, for within its limited confines were – Jim and Francine Peters and their baby, Carlin, Carol, and Robert McKenzie, Chief Orren Flagg, Sam and Mary Whitebird and their new daughter, and a surprise arrival. Just after 2:00 p.m. A ski equipped Norseman landed and taxied to the Air Ojibwa dock.

The door opened and Al Brooks helped Aida Danse from the plane. Carol was glad to see her mother. but couldn't understand why she was with Al Brooks of Interland Mines. Carlin was happy to see Al Brooks again – he was a decent and honest businessman.

"Merry Christmas Al," Carlin said, shaking his hand warmly, "and just where did you find such a lovely companion?" Brooks laughed, and steered Carlin to the scant privacy of the bay window."

"Ahh well the secret is out," Al said with a grin, "I fell in love with her when we were studying at university. I knew she married a guy called Danse, and wrote her out of my life. It wasn't until we bought SunGold, and I met you and Carol that the name Danse came up again. I wondered if Carol was related to Aida so I finally found the courage to call her. As you know she was widowed a long time ago – we agreed to meet for dinner one evening and the rest is history."

"Well why don't you marry her and I can call you dad," Carlin said laughing. Someone tapped his shoulder, and turning he looked into the incredibly happy eyes of Aida Danse.

"Meet your new, soon to be, mother-in-law, Mrs. Aida Brooks!"

Carlin hugged them both. "Does Carol know yet?" he asked.

"Yes," Aida said, she has known for a long time now – she wanted it to be a Christmas surprise for you."

Carlin told them about the growth of Giiwedin, – the Village of the North Wind, and how Jim and Fran had built a home there. He also told them about Sam and Mary Whitebird going there.

"Surely you and Carol are not thinking about going ..." Aida began to say.

"Of course we are," Carlin said. "When Giiwedin is established as the newest town in the north, we will have completed what the Old Ones tried so hard to do."

Al Brooks protested, "Are you not subjecting yourselves to a great deal of hardship?"

"Only for a short time," Carlin said with a twinkle in his eyes. "Less than half a mile from the village site there is a waterfall of twenty feet in the river. I have already let the contract for a miniature power station with a capacity of ten thousand kilowatts, upgradable to fifty thousand. The price is less than two million dollars."

"Wow – you really AREN'T fooling are you?" Brooks said, stunned again by the dynamic character of this man.

"No," Carlin said, "we are not fooling, but we ARE about to create a small Shangri-la in the north. For another $750,000 we can tap and pump thousands of cubic feet of bio-gas from nearby bogs. We will limit the population by allowing a maximum of fifty homes in the development. That will give Giiwedin an ample and inexhaustible supply of power and fuel."

"You are making me jealous," Al Brooks said, "Can Aida and I come for long extended stays?"

"It is quite possible you could be involved Al. I have been

thinking about you for a while and suddenly you show up. It is more than coincidence – it is the will of the Great Spirit."

"How could I possibly involved in a project like Giiwedin – I am a mining engineer," Al Brooks replied wistfully. Carlin's enthusiasm had fired the man's imagination, and he was excited by the prospects of Shangri-la.

"We are not going back to Giiwedin until the spring breakup. Fly in with us. Your Grumman Goose will haul a hell of a lot more freight than the Beaver," Carlin said.

"You're on," Al Brooks said, "Call me the day before you want to leave and I will be here."

Later, in the longhouse, a formal Christmas dinner was served. Everyone helped and enjoyed the friendship and happiness of the Yuletide season, and Orren Flagg made Aida the guest of honour.

The winter months at Little Spirit Lake passed quickly for Carol and Carlin. They watched the development of the baby and experiencing mild anxiety, for he was not a robust baby. Carlin kept saying that what he lacked in baby fat, he made up for with energy. A dozen times a day, the baby threw his toys over the side of his crib. When Carol picked them up and gave them back to him, he threw them out again. When Carlin carved him a little wooden wolf, the baby played with it for hours.

By April third, the ice was gone from Little Spirit Lake. Carlin and Jim Peters converted the Beaver to floats and at 7:00 a.m. the following morning, took off for Crystal Lake. In the high north, the weather for the three weeks previous, had been unseasonably mild. Strong winds had prevailed and Crystal Lake was free of ice, allowing a safe landing. The ATV (All Terrain Vehicle) was at Giiwedin and they walked to the village. No one had been there, for the only signs of life were deer and bear tracks.

After a light meal, Jim made them a pot of coffee, and filled a thermos for the return trip. They had accomplished what they set out to do – find out if Crystal Lake was open. They refuelled and returned to the reservation just before dark.

Carlin made a phone call to Al Brooks, and on the Monday of the following week they began hauling freight to Giiwedin. Jim and Sam Whitebird remained at the village and with the ATV they moved the freight from Crystal Lake to Giiwedin. The Grumman

Goose and the Beaver often made two round trips per day. In the evenings at Little Spirit Lake, tired but fulfilled Al Brooks and Carlin relaxed with a pipe of Erinmore tobacco, and a glass of Glenlivet malt whisky. Al Brooks was having the time of his life – it was as if he was a young man again, working in the field.

By mid June the turbine was operating at Giiwedin, they had reliable electrical power, and the Whitebird's cabin was liveable. All hands turned to the task of building a home for Carlin and Carol. Seven weeks after laying the foundations the shell was completed and weather tight. The three houses were built in the same manner as those of the original Ojibwa who first settled at Giiwedin, with the exception of the windows and the roofs. Windows were double glazed, and the cedar shake roofs were insulated. Each house was set high on the river bank overlooking the water on the north side, and the old village site to the south. Perhaps it was the passion of the new residents, combined with one hundred and fifty years of history, that gave the village a feeling of steadfast permanence.

The power plant installation crew, and the team working on the bio-gas system, all wanted to stay – wanted to be part of the wilderness experiment.

On July first, Al Brooks married Aida Danse in a small quiet ceremony, and a week later, they paid the village a visit. Carol was delighted with her mother's choice of husband, for she had always liked Al. For the duration of their visit Aida preempted her grandson completely, Samantha Whitebird, Mary's adopted twelve year old daughter followed Aida's example and claimed Francine Peters baby Jesse. At loose ends for the first time in months Carol and Fran had time for things other than children.

"I envy you Carol," Fran said wistfully, "Your archaeology gives you a noble purpose in life. I wish I had something to work toward." She sat on the river bank studying her hands.

"That's an easy wish to fulfill Fran – why don't you work with me," Carol replied after a few introspective moments.

"What could I do to help – I am not an archaeologist," Fran replied with a cynical little laugh.

"And I can't detect the feelings of a people that existed a hundred and fifty years ago," Carol countered. She put her arm around Fran's shoulder. "I have decided to write a book about the Ojibwa who founded the first village here. I want to capture the atmosphere of that era, but it can only be speculation with a few artifacts thrown in. Pretty dull stuff. With your talent and gifts we could collaborate on a best seller!"

"Will it work?" Fran asked, her black eyes sparkling.

"I know it will work – will you do it?"

"Oh YES Carol, that would be wonderful." Her eyes were brimming and she was truly happy.

"Well, c'mon partner – let's get started. We have a year of work ahead of us!" Carol said, and they walked back to the village to tell Carlin and Jim.

Al Brooks and Aida had taken over the aluminum building previously used by Carlin and Carol. They dubbed it their summer cottage. Al had grown quiet and detached in the last few days, and Aida asked him if there was something wrong.

"No," he responded, "but I am not looking forward to going back. I love it here. The excitement of seeing a new village growing in the wilderness – the challenge of doing the impossible quickens my blood. For the last month I have really been ALIVE!" He leaned against the window frame looking wistfully out across the river. "I don't like the thoughts of retirement and mouldering away in some Toronto mansion. Attending and giving dinner parties is not my idea of happiness." She crossed the room and put her arms around him.

"Tell me exactly what you want Al – what would make you happy?" She searched his eyes trying to find the truth.

"I would be very happy if I could stay here and be part of this project, but I doubt you would want that." She stepped back from him and started to laugh.

"I have four reasons to stay here. My daughter is here, my grandson is here, my son-in-law is here, and finally you want to be here. How many reasons do you have Al?"

She had answered his question with a rhetorical question of her own. They decided to live a new life in Giiwedin, the Village of the North Wind.

The unrestrained activity in the village appeared to be bedlam, but it was highly organized. Two more men from the reservation arrived in Giiwedin to help with the building. They would work to complete the house for Al Brooks and Aida, then return to the reserve for the winter. In the springtime, like the big Canada geese, they would fly north again, and with the help of the others at Giiwedin they would establish their own homes there.

Al and Aida moved into their new log house the first week in October. It was devoid of interior partitions and furniture, but there was a whole winter to work on indoor projects and they were blissfully happy in the village. Eleven people, including the children were sworn to care for each other and enjoy the coming months of winter. Jim built a wigwam to shelter some equipment and the ATVs, and they built a root house into the hillside. Within its confines the temperature would never rise above 55 degrees nor drop below 40. It allowed the storage of vegetables year round, and it was animal proof.

The days were growing short when Carlin and Al made their last flight south before the freeze-up. They landed just before twilight, and in the morning, loaded the Grumman with supplies. After paying their respects to the folks on the reservation, they returned to Giiwedin for the first winter. As the Grumman approached Crystal Lake, Carlin asked Al to give him control. He turned onto a north north-west heading, overflying the village.

"Where are we going?" Al asked, carefully surveying the landscape below, and checking the instruments.

"I just want to look at another lake about twenty miles from here," Carlin replied, "remember the headings Al, you will probably want to visit it in the future."

Carlin had descended to less than a thousand feet and in the middle distance he pointed out the blue water of what he had named Star Lake. "That's the one there. Remember it, because it isn't on any of the maps." He passed over the collapsed prospector's cabin at 150 feet, but Al didn't see it. Satisfied that the diamond pipe was still undisturbed, Carlin climbed back to a thousand feet and set up his approach to Crystal Lake, then turned control and the landing back to Al Brooks.

The two ATVs were there to meet them and Jim and Sam Whitebird helped them unload the cargo. Later that afternoon Carlin brought a big unmarked carton into the house and set in the corner. Carol smiled – Carlin had brought them into the computer age!

When all the supplies had been distributed Carlin asked Jim, Sam, and Al to join them for a final outdoor meal at sundown.

They built a huge bonfire and prepared an autumn dinner. It was time to reminisce a bit, and look into the future. This particular evening was a special time, and each of them did a little soul searching. The stars overhead glittered like diamonds and frost was in the air. The loons called to each other in the deep twilight, and Carlin, Carol and Jim remembered one specific night like this. It was the night before the crash so many years ago. They were lucky to be alive and they were grateful. Once again Jim offered his pipe of tobacco to the Great Spirit. He had dressed in buckskins and a beaded band of leather was around his forehead. He was the epitome of the Proud Ojibwa from the past.

"Mighty Manitou – accept our gift of tobacco." He raised the pipe in offering. "You have blessed us with the gifts of each other, and You have spared our lives in times of adversity. You have led us to this place and we accept the challenge of rebuilding the dream of our forefathers."

"We have named it the Village of the North Wind because the north wind is clean and pure. So shall it be at Giiwedin. The Anishinawbe and the white nations will learn to be brothers by the example of Giiwedin. Bless us and bless this place Mighty Manitou – this is our prayer."

Unseen, a meteorite flashed across the heavens and everyone was in total accord with Jim Peters words. The hour grew late and one by one they said goodnight and returned to their houses. The women left first, for it was uncomfortably cold as the fire died. The last to leave were Carlin, Jim, and Al Brooks. Before they could disperse, Carlin asked Al if he could find his way to Star Lake again.

"Remember when you told me if I ever got that funny feeling that something good was about to happen – I should tell you BEFORE it cost you forty million dollars?" Carlin asked with a wide grin.

"Yes, I do, and you are going to tell me there is gold at Star Lake," Al said, his eyes twinkling.

"No, there is no gold at Star Lake," Carlin countered, "but before we turn in, I have a surprise for you and Jim."

Jim knew what was coming and responded. He spread his arms wide and took Al's hand, then reached for Carlin's, forming a circle. "We are all part of the unbroken circle," he said, "and each of us depends on the other to keep the circle whole. We need you to help us make Giiwedin successful – welcome to the circle."

"Thank you," Al Brooks said, "but what can I do to make the Village of the North Wind grow and prosper?"

"That's an easy question to answer," Carlin replied. "You are going to finance it!"

"Finance it," Al said. "Carlin, I am not a poor man but my resources are limited. How do you expect me to finance the building of a town?"

"By teaching the men in the village to mine," Carlin replied.

"You want me to hire them to work at Dawson Lake!" He paused, thinking about rearranging the operations at SunGold. "We could do it," he said cautiously, "but it will take time."

"No Al," Carlin said gently, seeing the man was taking the whole thing far too seriously. "Here," he said, "this may help you to understand." Carlin held out two small leather pouches, offering one to Jim and the other to Al Brooks. They opened the pouches and emptied the contents into their hands. In the dying firelight the two huge diamonds flashed and sparkled in the orange afterglow.

Al looked carefully at the crystal. "My God, it's diamond! Carlin, this stone is worth a fortune." Jim was grinning and hefting one of equal size.

"They are no damned good," he said with a straight face, "They are too big for jewellery. If they were bigger they might be of some use as bookends." Al looked at Jim in total amazement until he realized Jim was only kidding.

"You'll get used to him after a while, but it isn't easy," Carlin said putting his arm around Jim's shoulder, then "Good night gentlemen."

"Carlin don't leave me hanging until morning," Al said, "Are you telling me you have a diamond mine?"

"Nah," Carlin said with a grin, "It's just a big depression about a hundred feet in diameter. It could be worth a hundred million or more. I thought we could use it to help people with no hope. I'll take you over there in the morning – then we can decide what we want to do after Giiwedin is established. It should be fun."

In His place in the heavens the Great Spirit smiled on them. He knew that the hearts of His children were clean and good. And the people of Giiwedin knew that The Great Spirit had truly blessed the Village of the North Wind.

THE END

Beyond Survival is the first of a series of six books by Gerry Gotro. The characters from North Wind demand true justice in each of the following stories. Watch for:

Justice For Freddie
North Wind Enigma
The Lazarus Incident
The Eleventh Commandment
Aurora

These Books are also available on unabridged audio tape sets from:
Books In Motion
9922 E. Montgomery, Suite 31
Spokane, Washington
99206
1-800-752-3199

ISBN 1-55212-279-4

9 781552 122792

G. WM. GOTRO